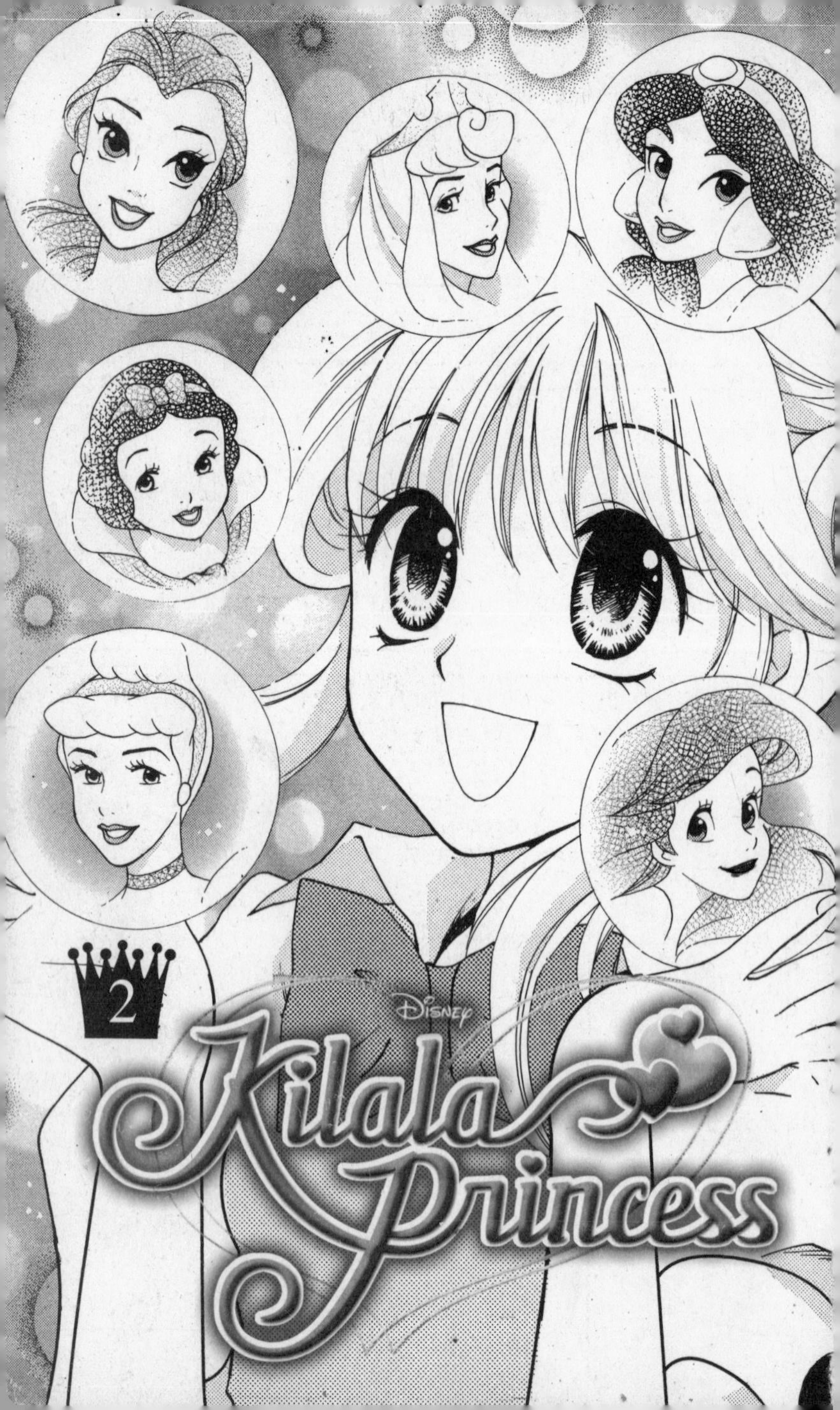
2
Disney
Kilala Princess

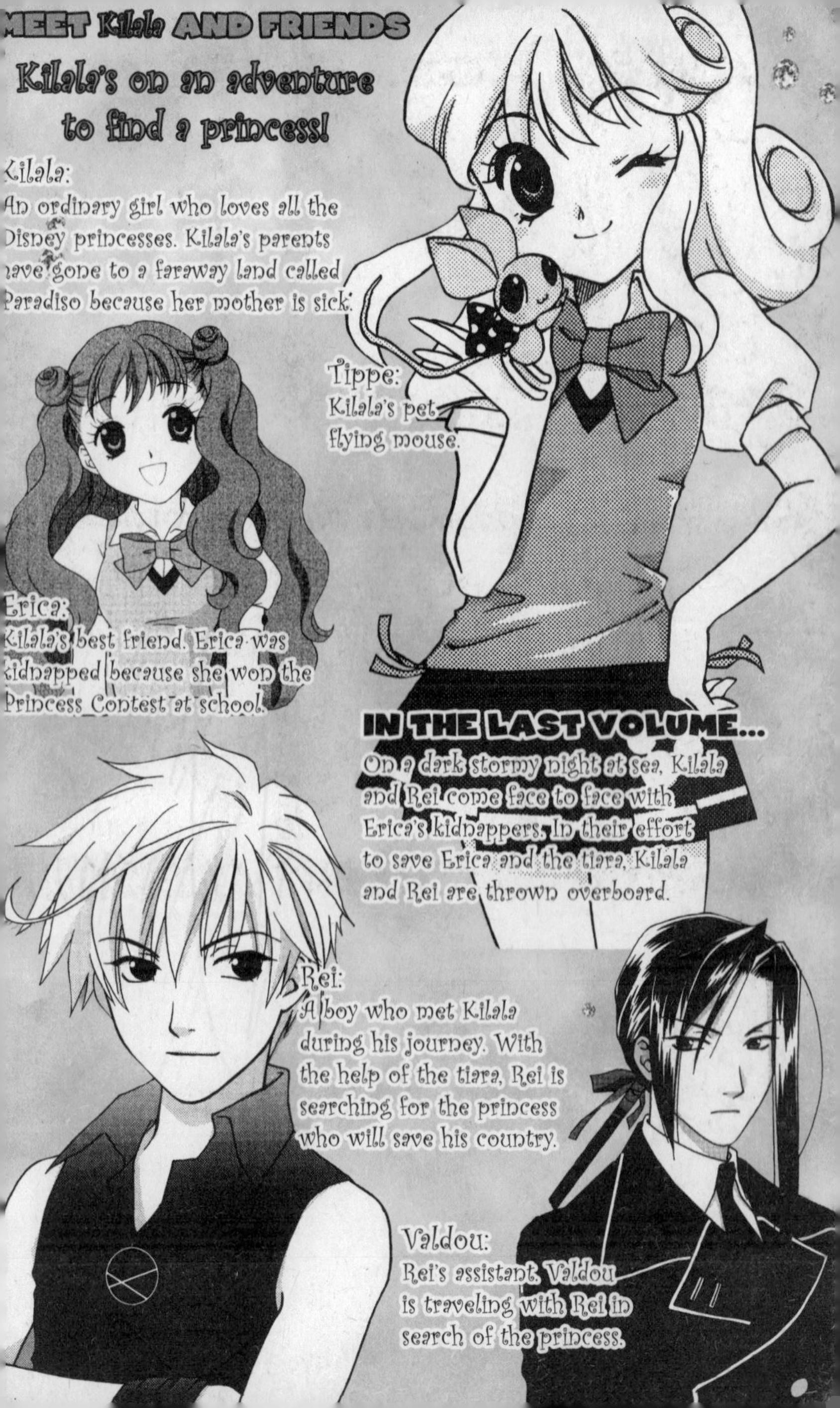

MEET Kilala AND FRIENDS

Kilala's on an adventure to find a princess!

Kilala:
An ordinary girl who loves all the Disney princesses. Kilala's parents have gone to a faraway land called Paradiso because her mother is sick.

Tippe:
Kilala's pet flying mouse.

Erica:
Kilala's best friend. Erica was kidnapped because she won the Princess Contest at school.

IN THE LAST VOLUME...

On a dark stormy night at sea, Kilala and Rei come face to face with Erica's kidnappers. In their effort to save Erica and the tiara, Kilala and Rei are thrown overboard.

Rei:
A boy who met Kilala during his journey. With the help of the tiara, Rei is searching for the princess who will save his country.

Valdou:
Rei's assistant. Valdou is traveling with Rei in search of the princess.

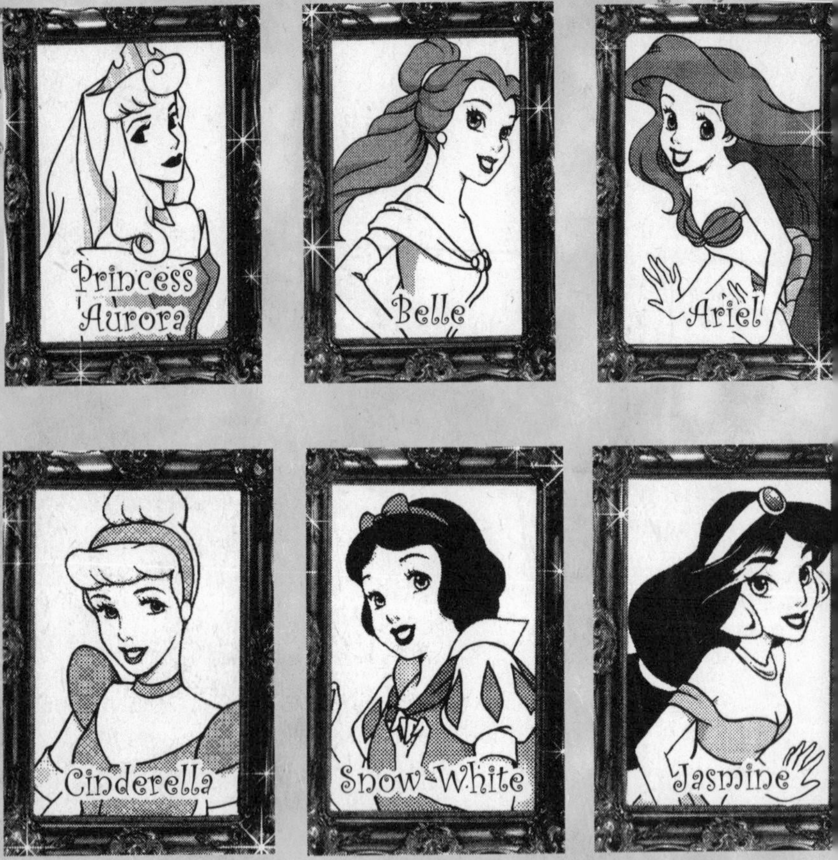
Ariel
Belle
Princess Aurora
Jasmine
Snow White
Cinderella

MEET

The Disney Princesses

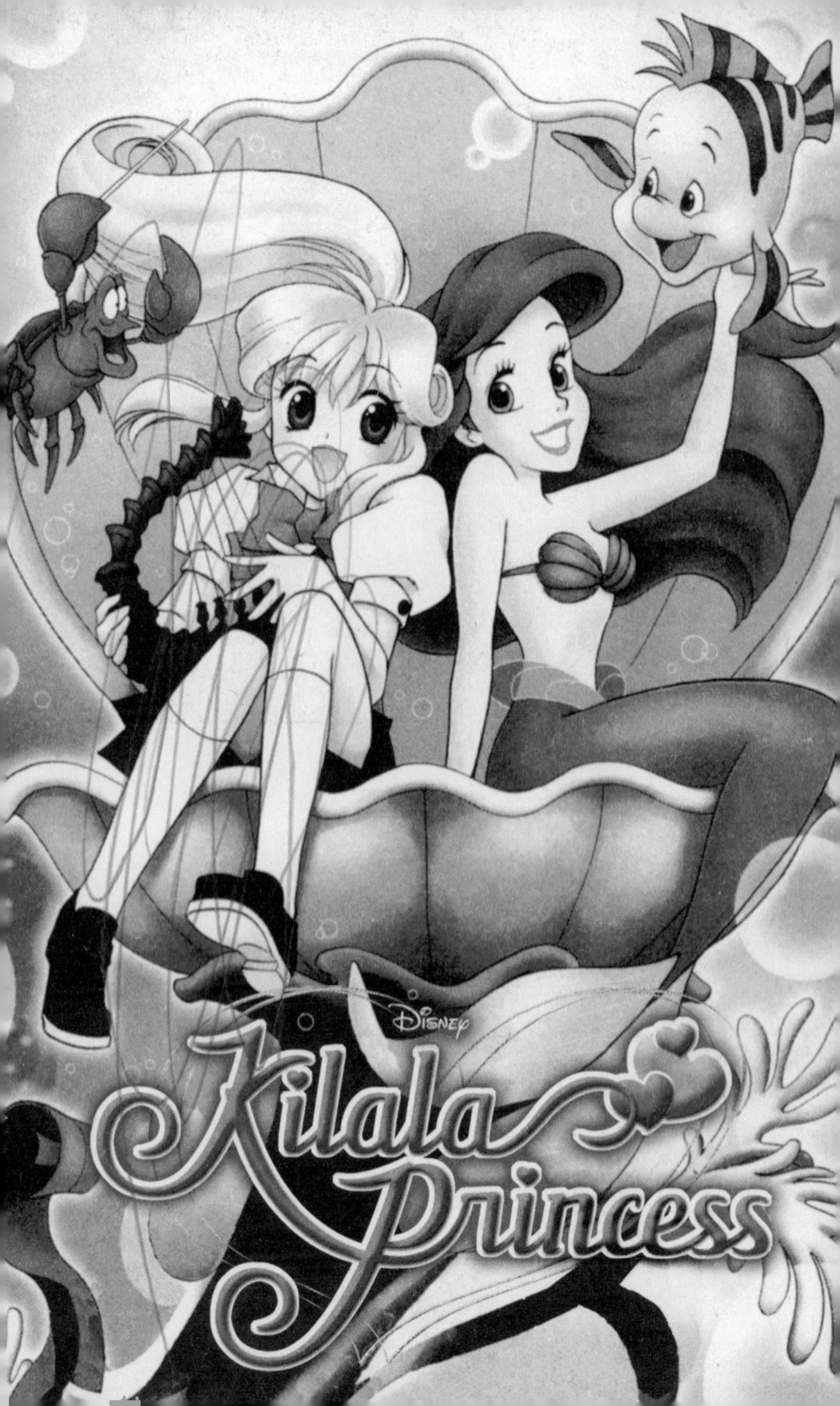
Disney
Kilala Princess

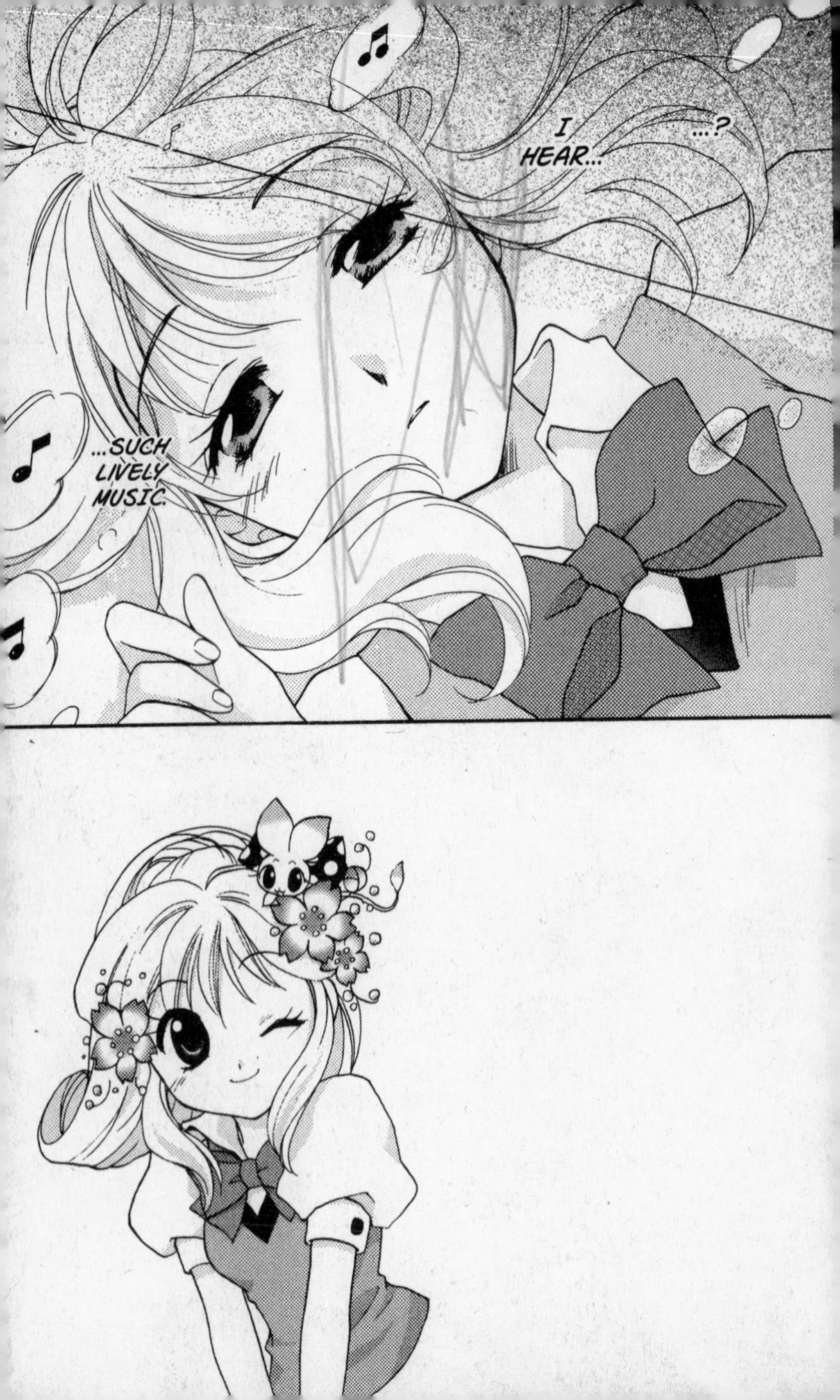
...?
I HEAR...
...SUCH LIVELY MUSIC.

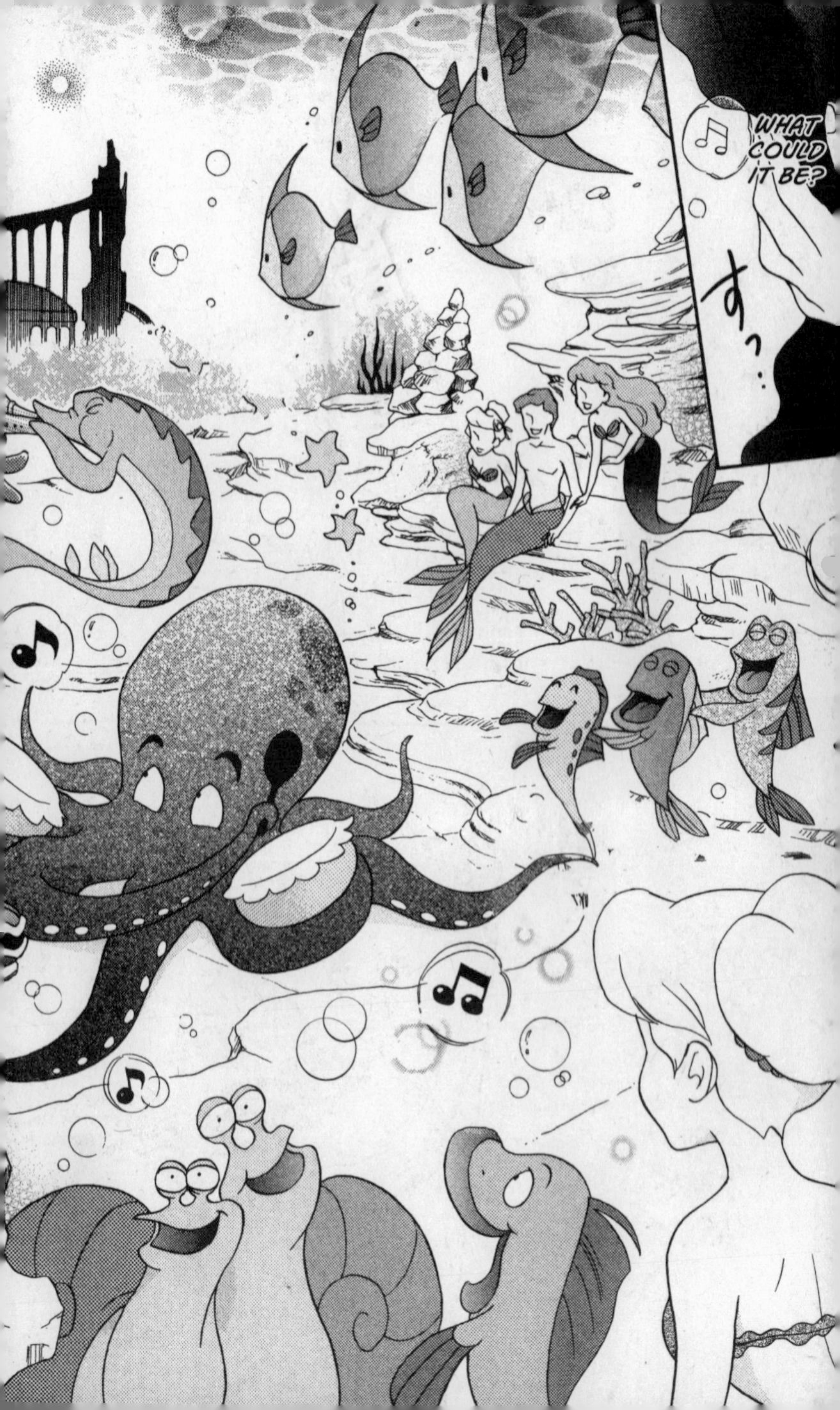
WHAT COULD IT BE?
すっ…

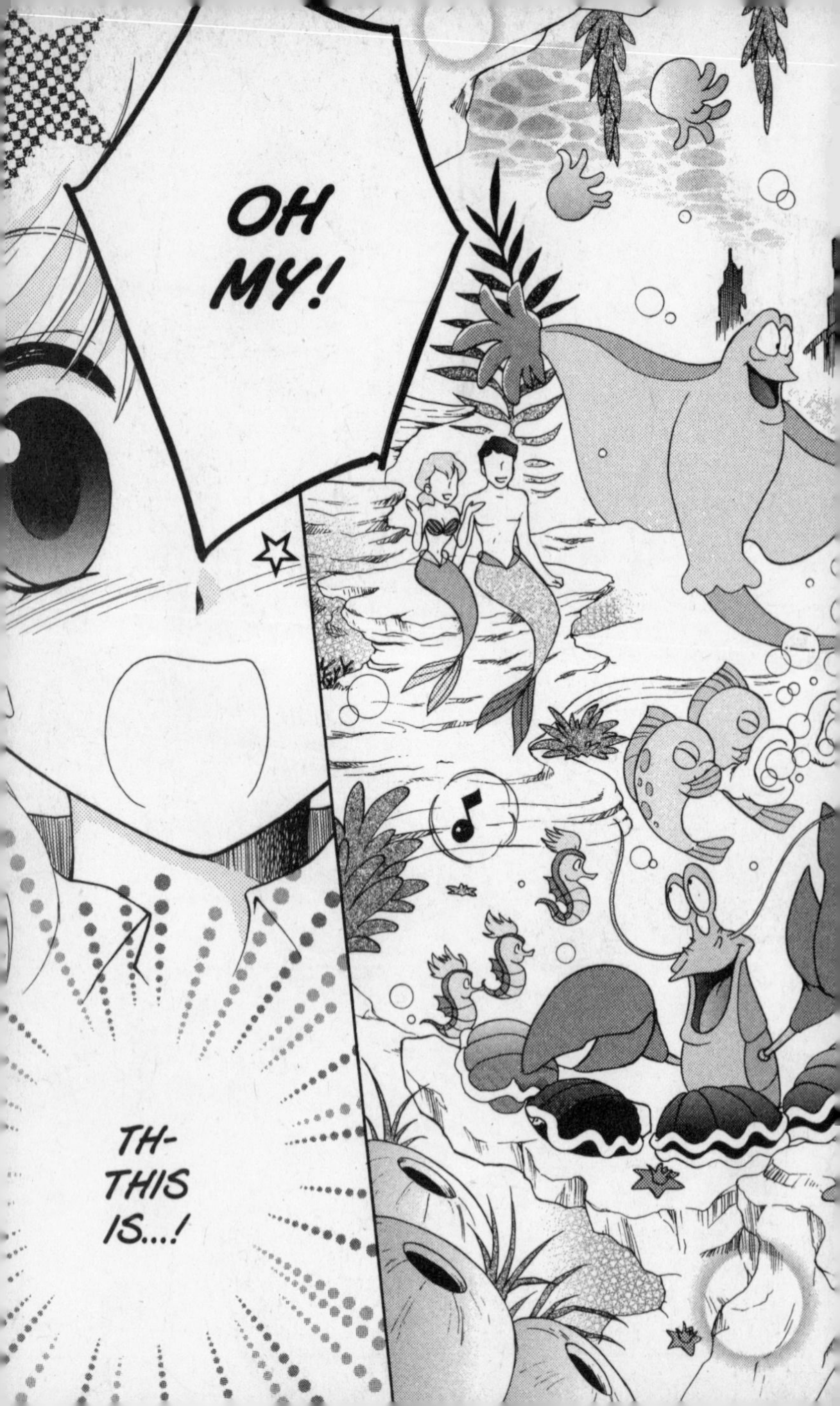
OH MY!
TH- THIS IS...!

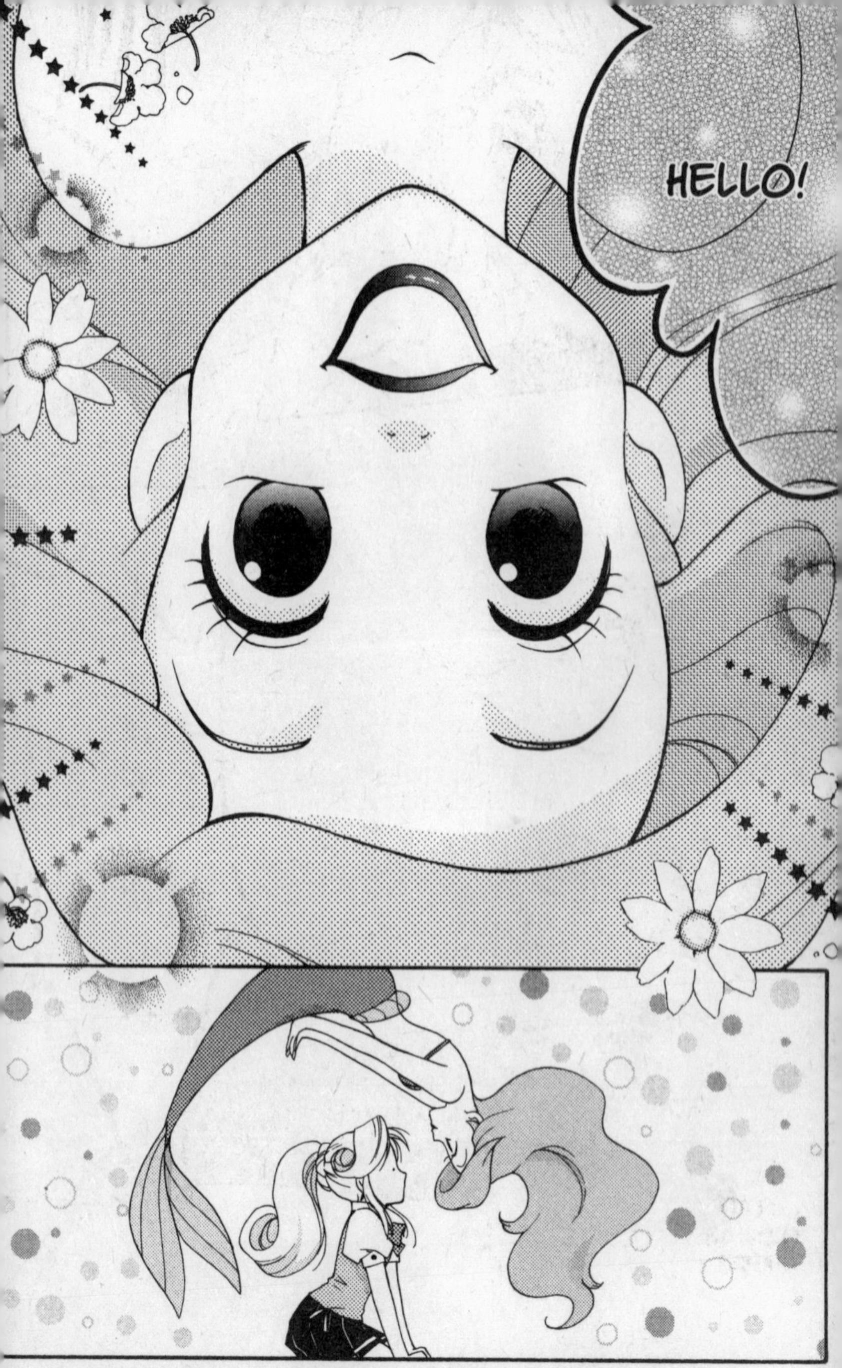
HELLO!

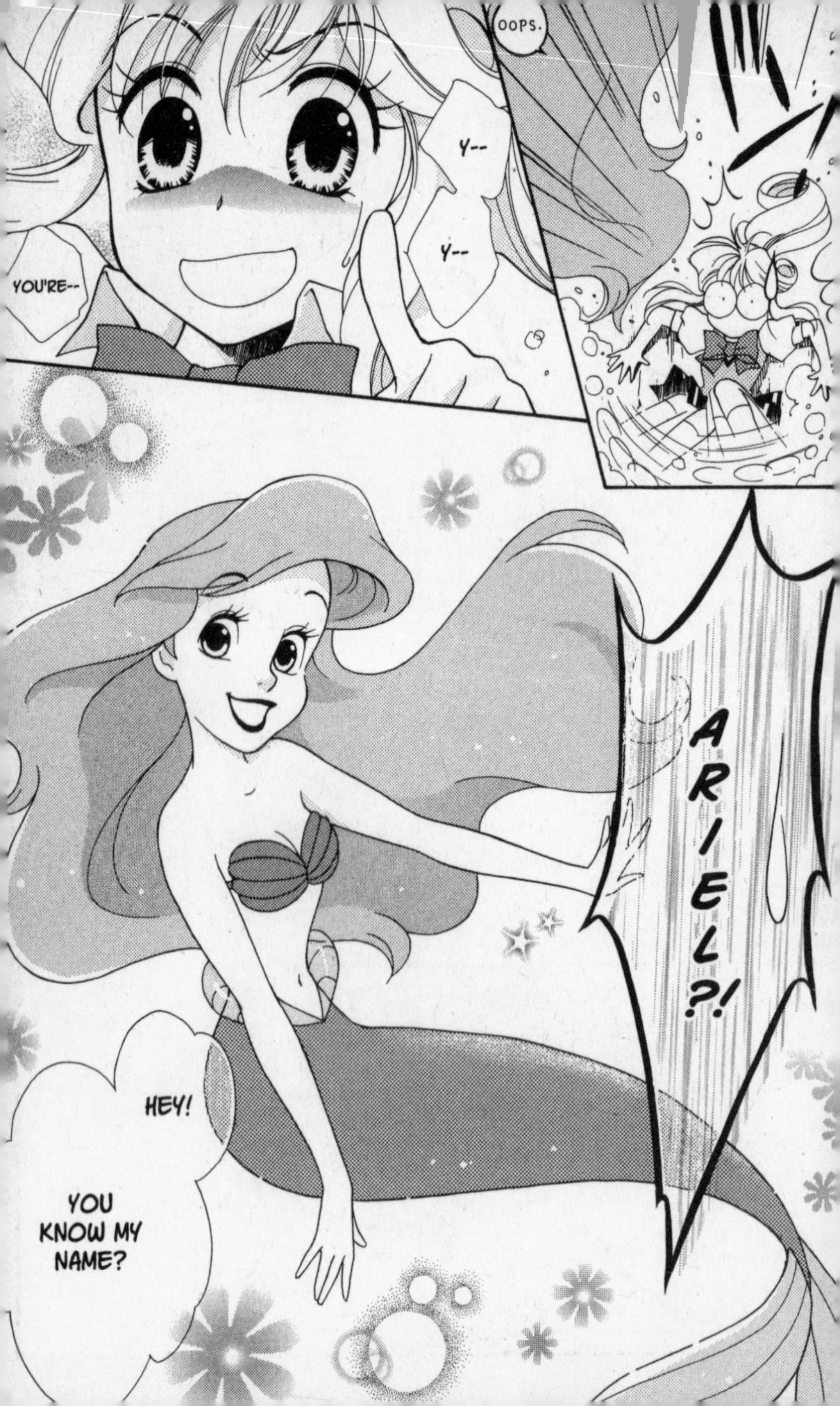
OOPS.
Y--
Y--
YOU'RE--
ARIEL?!
HEY!
YOU KNOW MY NAME?

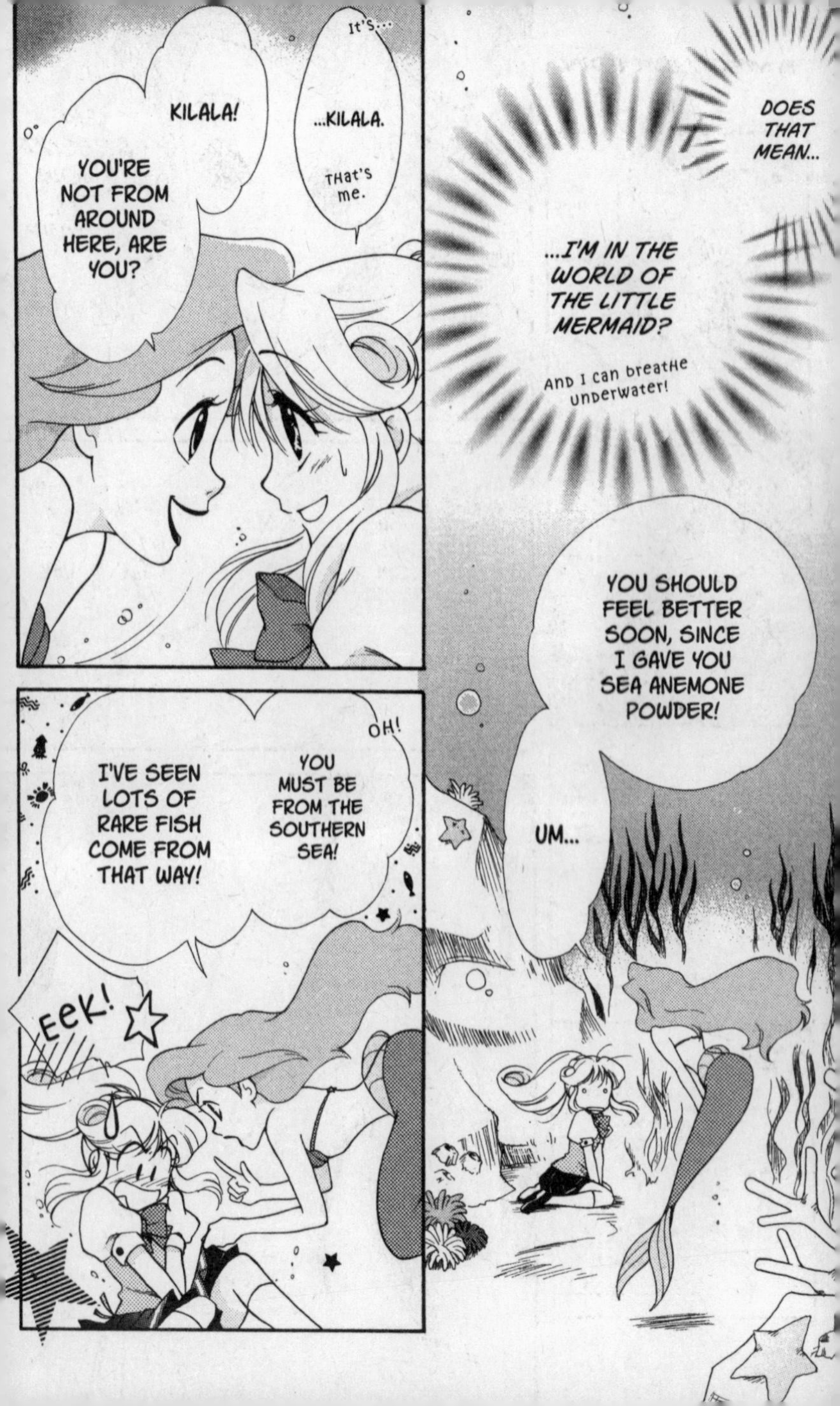
DOES THAT MEAN...
...I'M IN THE WORLD OF THE LITTLE MERMAID?
And I can breathe underwater!
YOU SHOULD FEEL BETTER SOON, SINCE I GAVE YOU SEA ANEMONE POWDER!
UM...
It's... ...KILALA. That's me.
KILALA! YOU'RE NOT FROM AROUND HERE, ARE YOU?
OH! YOU MUST BE FROM THE SOUTHERN SEA!
I'VE SEEN LOTS OF RARE FISH COME FROM THAT WAY!
Eek!

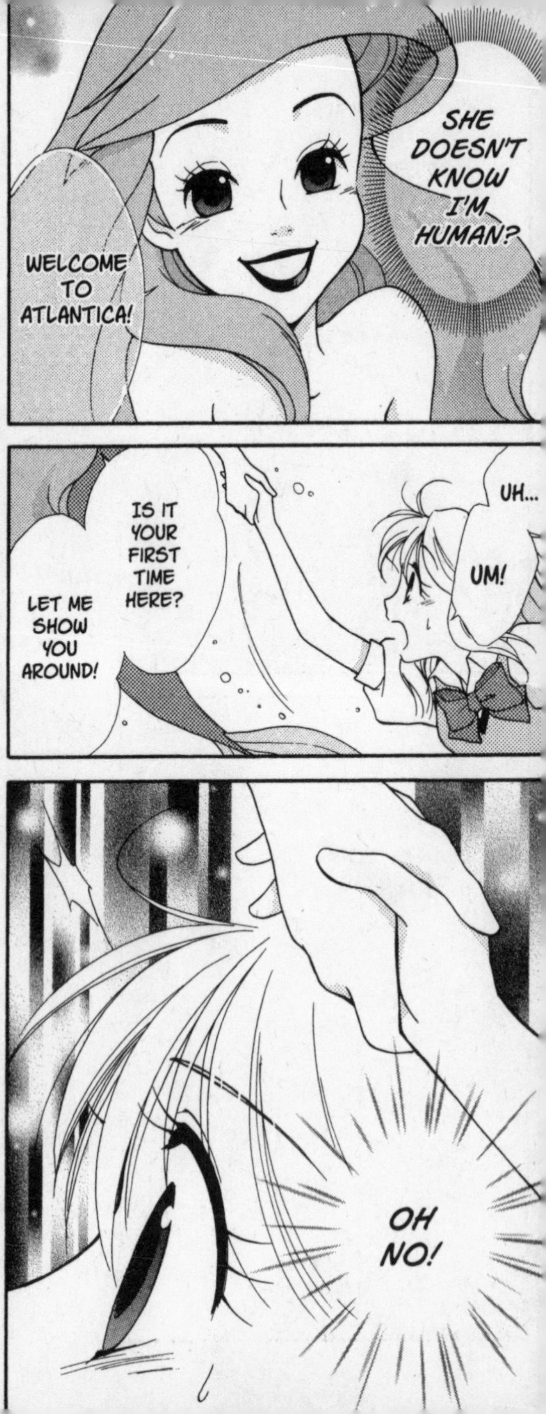
SHE DOESN'T KNOW I'M HUMAN?
WELCOME TO ATLANTICA!
UH...
UM!
IS IT YOUR FIRST TIME HERE?
LET ME SHOW YOU AROUND!
OH NO!

A WORD FROM TIPPE

1

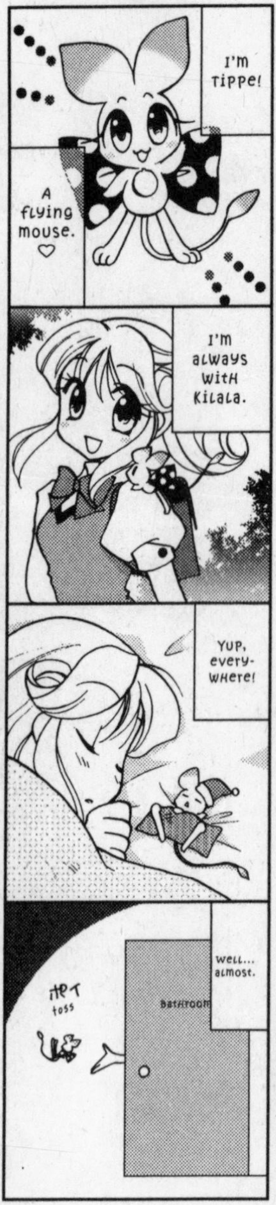
I'm Tippe!
A flying mouse. ♡
I'm always with Kilala.
Yup, every-where!
well... almost.
toss
BATHROOM

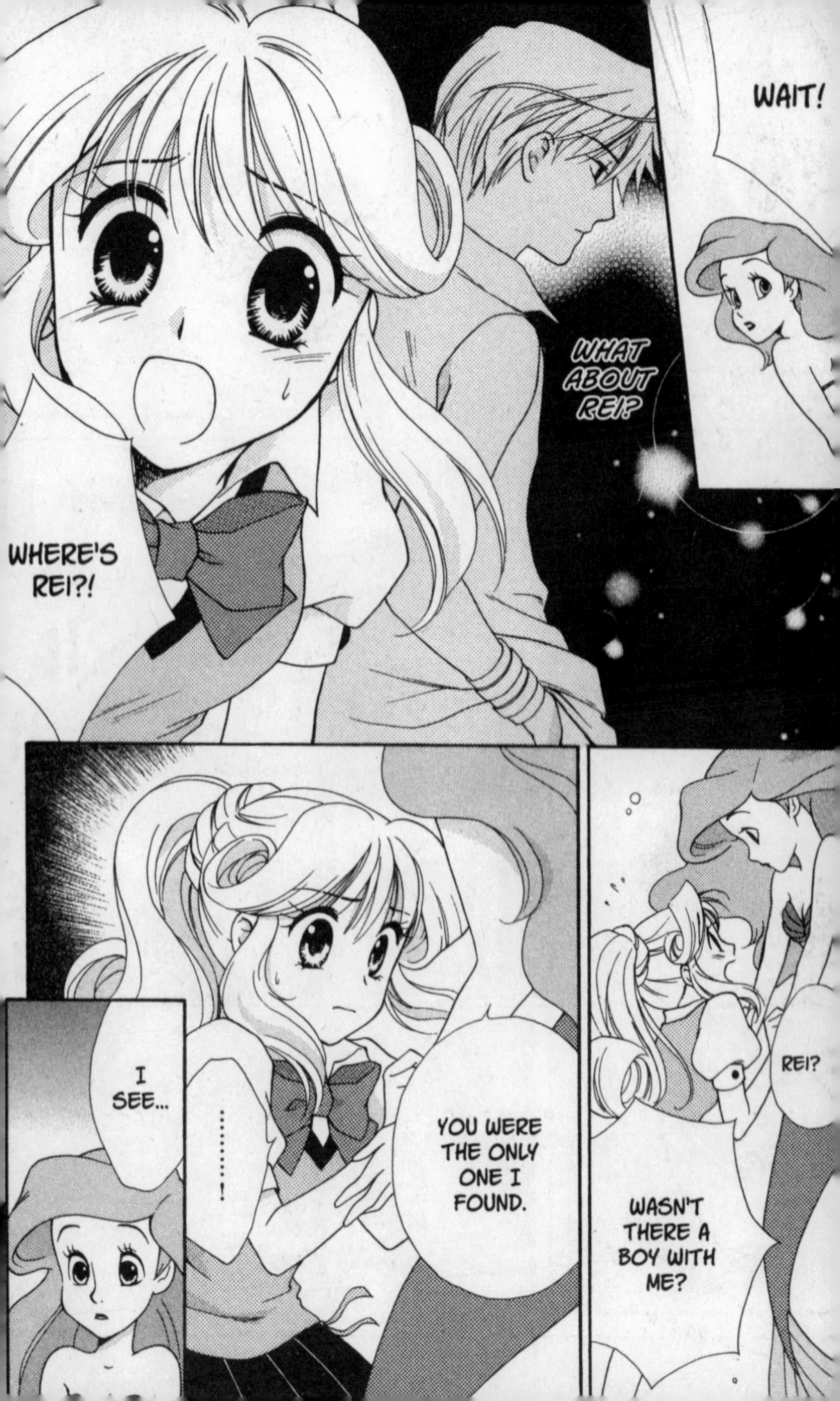
WAIT!
WHAT ABOUT REI!?
WHERE'S REI?!
REI?
WASN'T THERE A BOY WITH ME?
YOU WERE THE ONLY ONE I FOUND.
......!
I SEE...

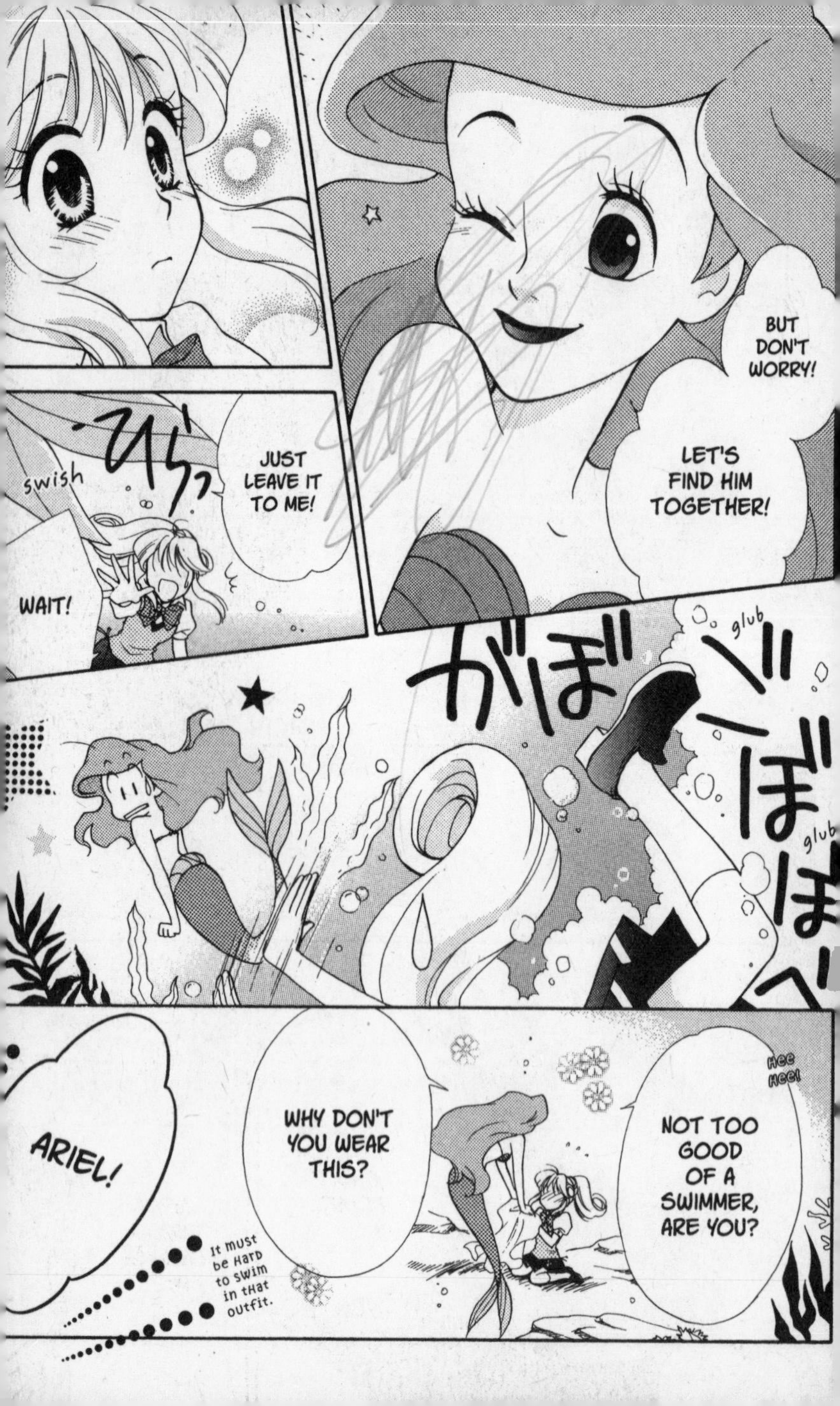
BUT DON'T WORRY!
LET'S FIND HIM TOGETHER!
ひらっ
swish
JUST LEAVE IT TO ME!
WAIT!
がぼ
glub
glub
Hee Hee!
NOT TOO GOOD OF A SWIMMER, ARE YOU?
WHY DON'T YOU WEAR THIS?
ARIEL!
It must be hard to swim in that outfit.

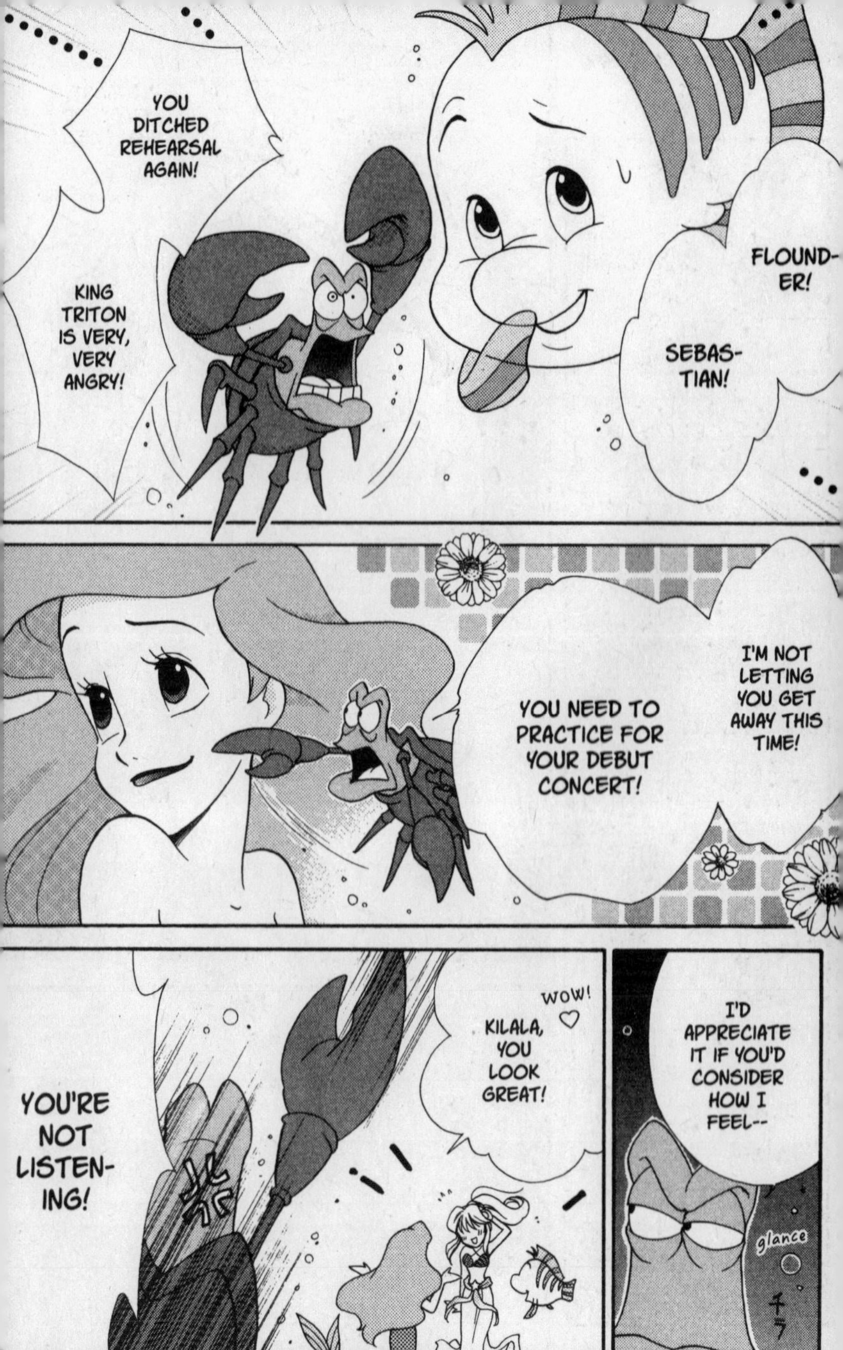
FLOUNDER!
SEBASTIAN!
YOU DITCHED REHEARSAL AGAIN!
KING TRITON IS VERY, VERY ANGRY!
I'M NOT LETTING YOU GET AWAY THIS TIME!
YOU NEED TO PRACTICE FOR YOUR DEBUT CONCERT!
I'D APPRECIATE IT IF YOU'D CONSIDER HOW I FEEL--
glance
チラ
WOW! ♡
KILALA, YOU LOOK GREAT!
YOU'RE NOT LISTENING!

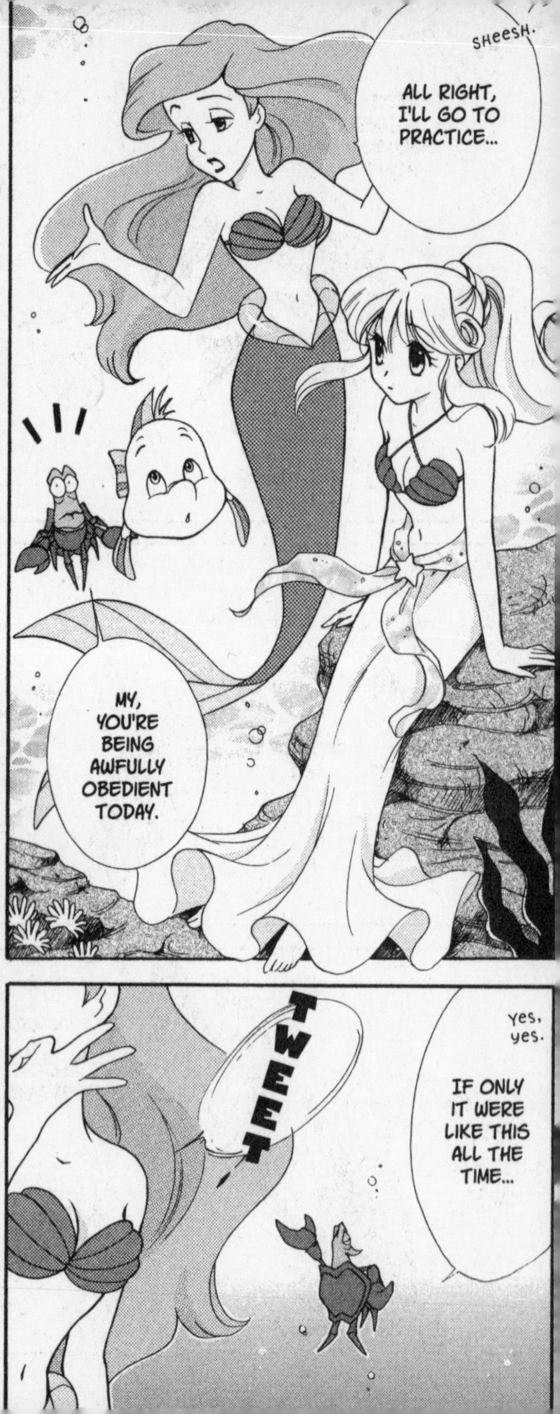
SHEESH.
ALL RIGHT, I'LL GO TO PRACTICE...
MY, YOU'RE BEING AWFULLY OBEDIENT TODAY.
Yes, yes.
IF ONLY IT WERE LIKE THIS ALL THE TIME...
TWEET

A WORD FROM TIPPE

2

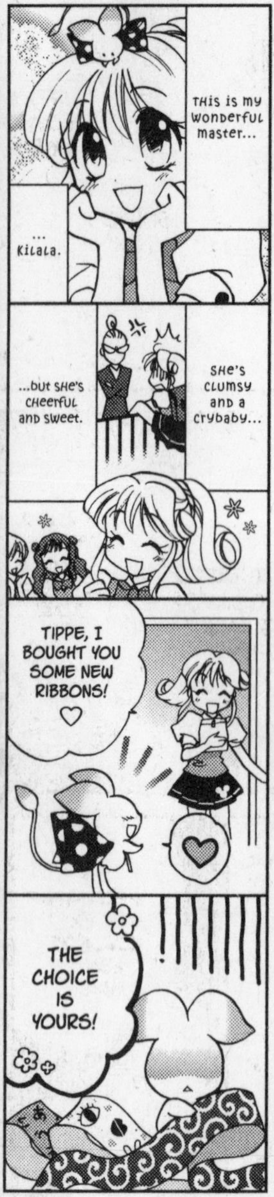
This is my wonderful master...
...Kilala.
She's clumsy and a crybaby...
...but she's cheerful and sweet.
TIPPE, I BOUGHT YOU SOME NEW RIBBONS! ♡
THE CHOICE IS YOURS!

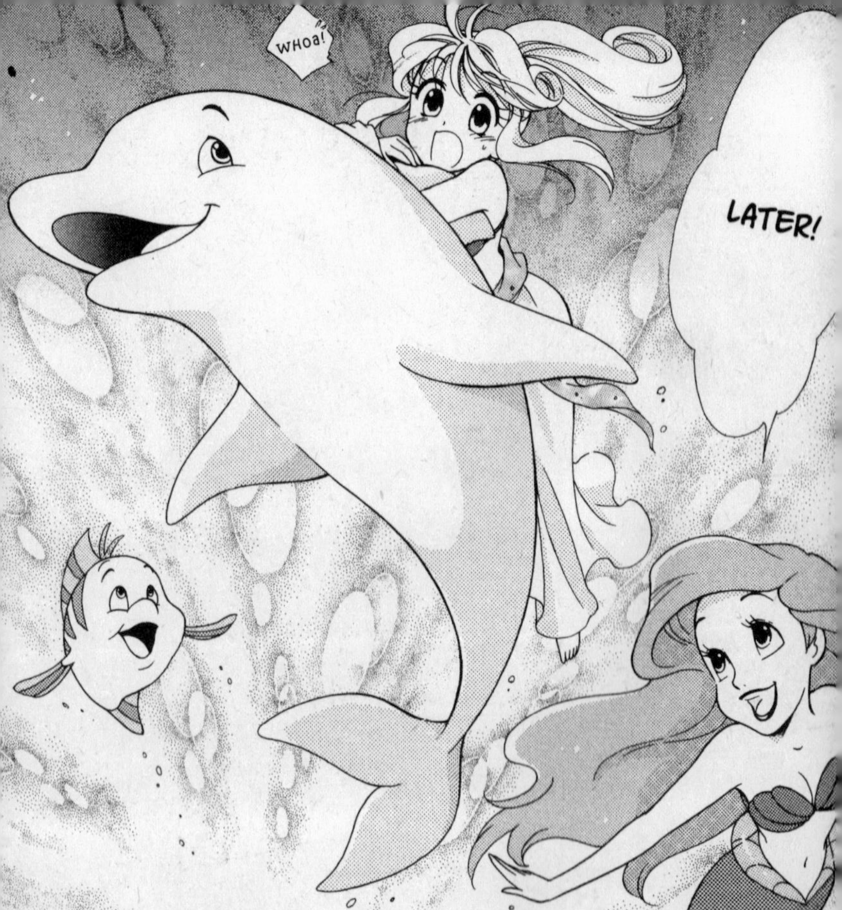
LATER!
WHOA!
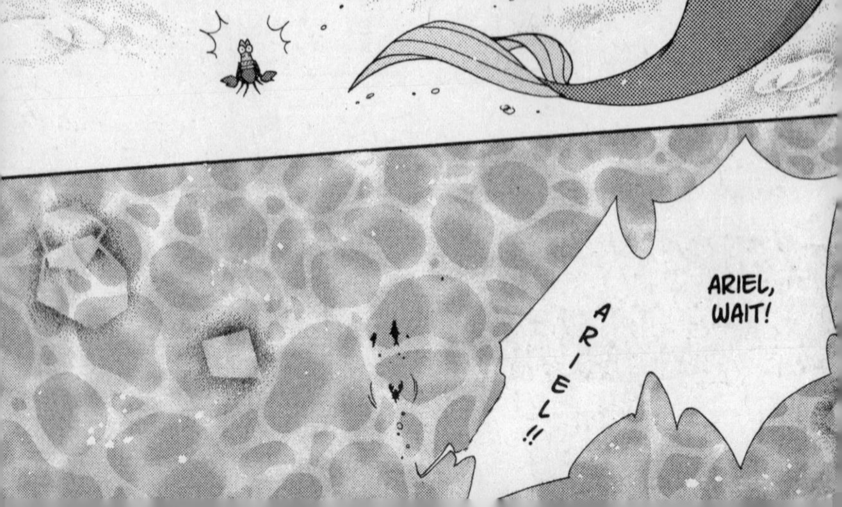
ARIEL, WAIT!
ARIEL!!

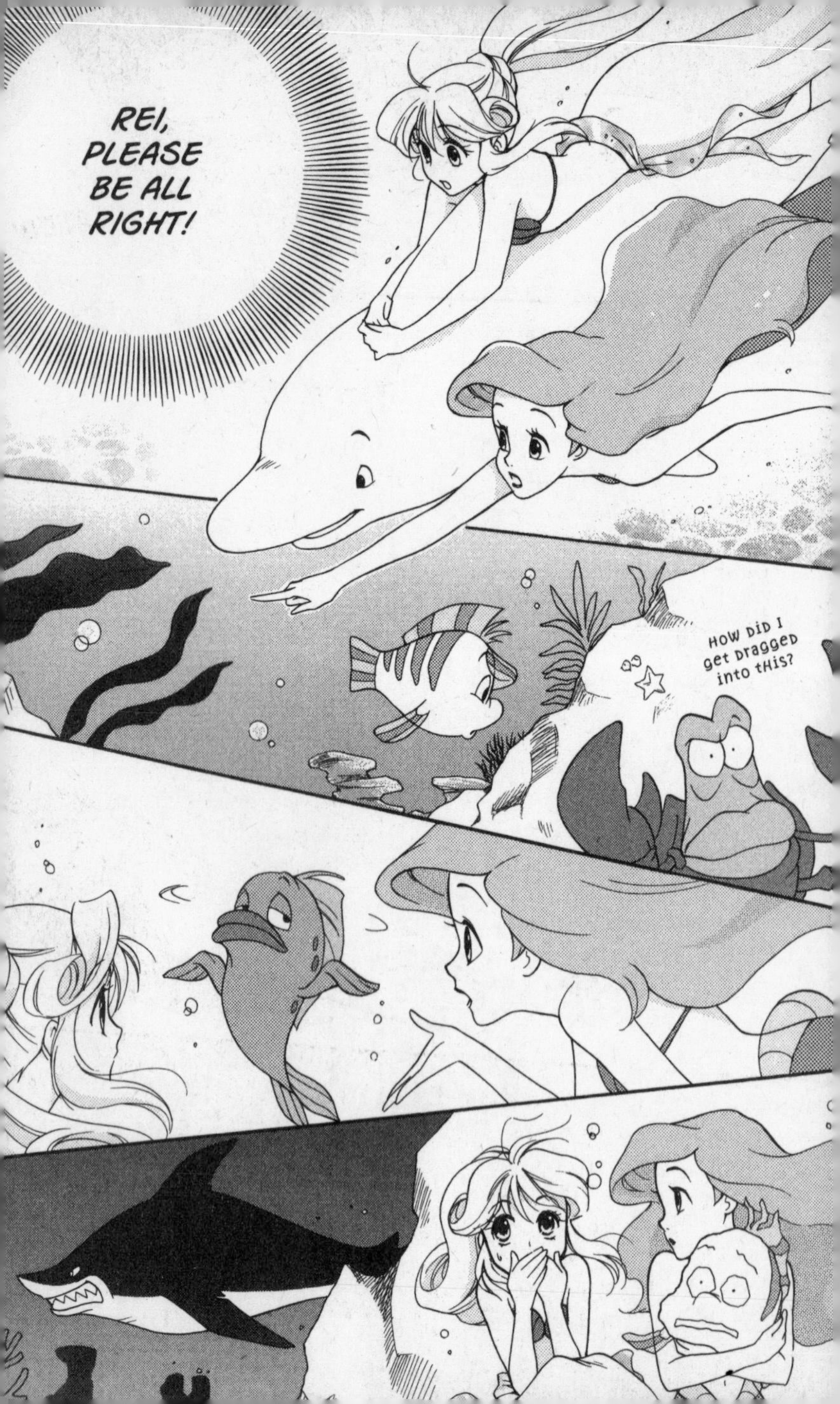
REI, PLEASE BE ALL RIGHT!
HOW DID I get DRAGGED into tHIS?

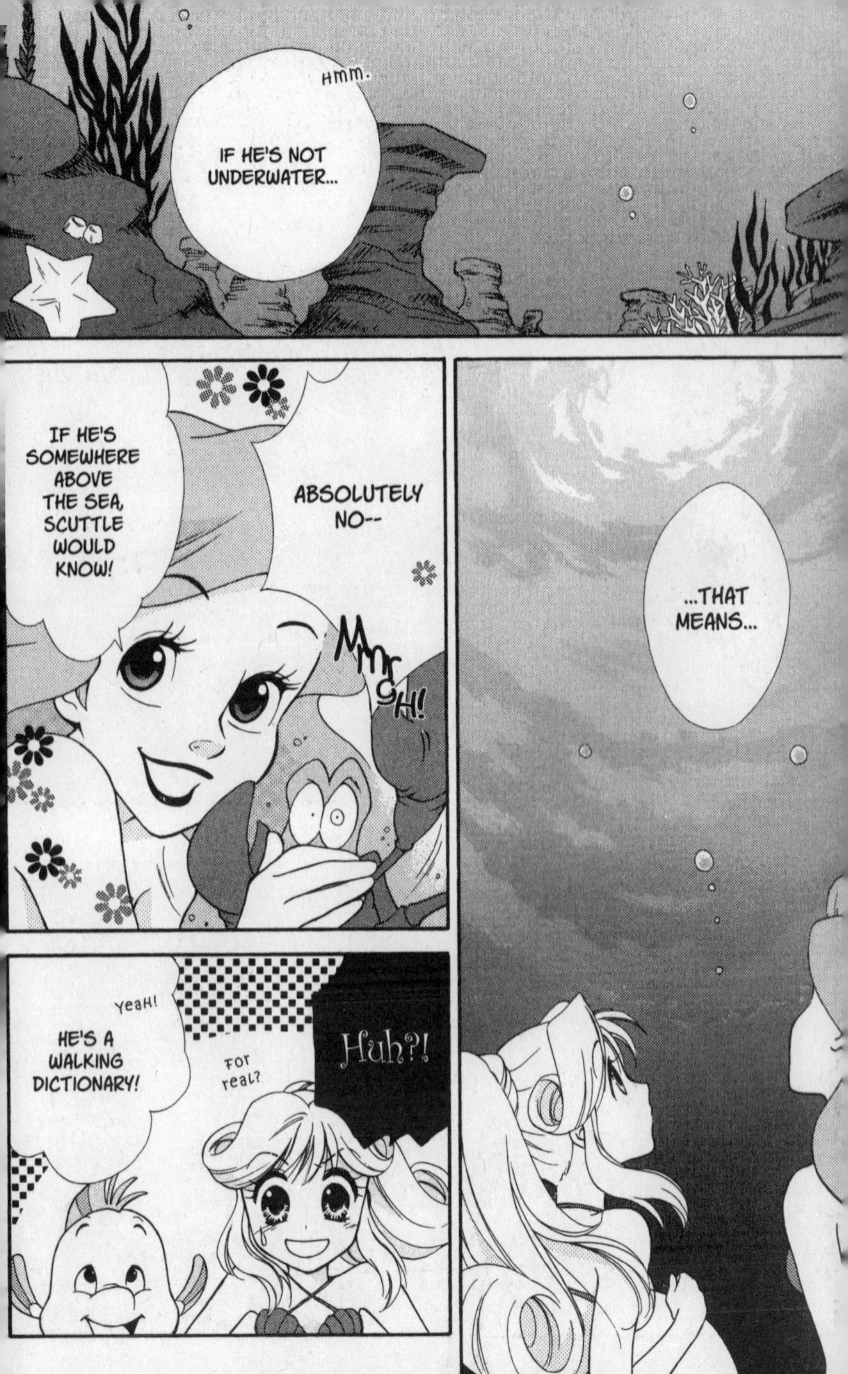
Hmm.
IF HE'S NOT UNDERWATER...
...THAT MEANS...
IF HE'S SOMEWHERE ABOVE THE SEA, SCUTTLE WOULD KNOW!
ABSOLUTELY NO--
MMRGH!
Huh?!
For real?
Yeah!
HE'S A WALKING DICTIONARY!

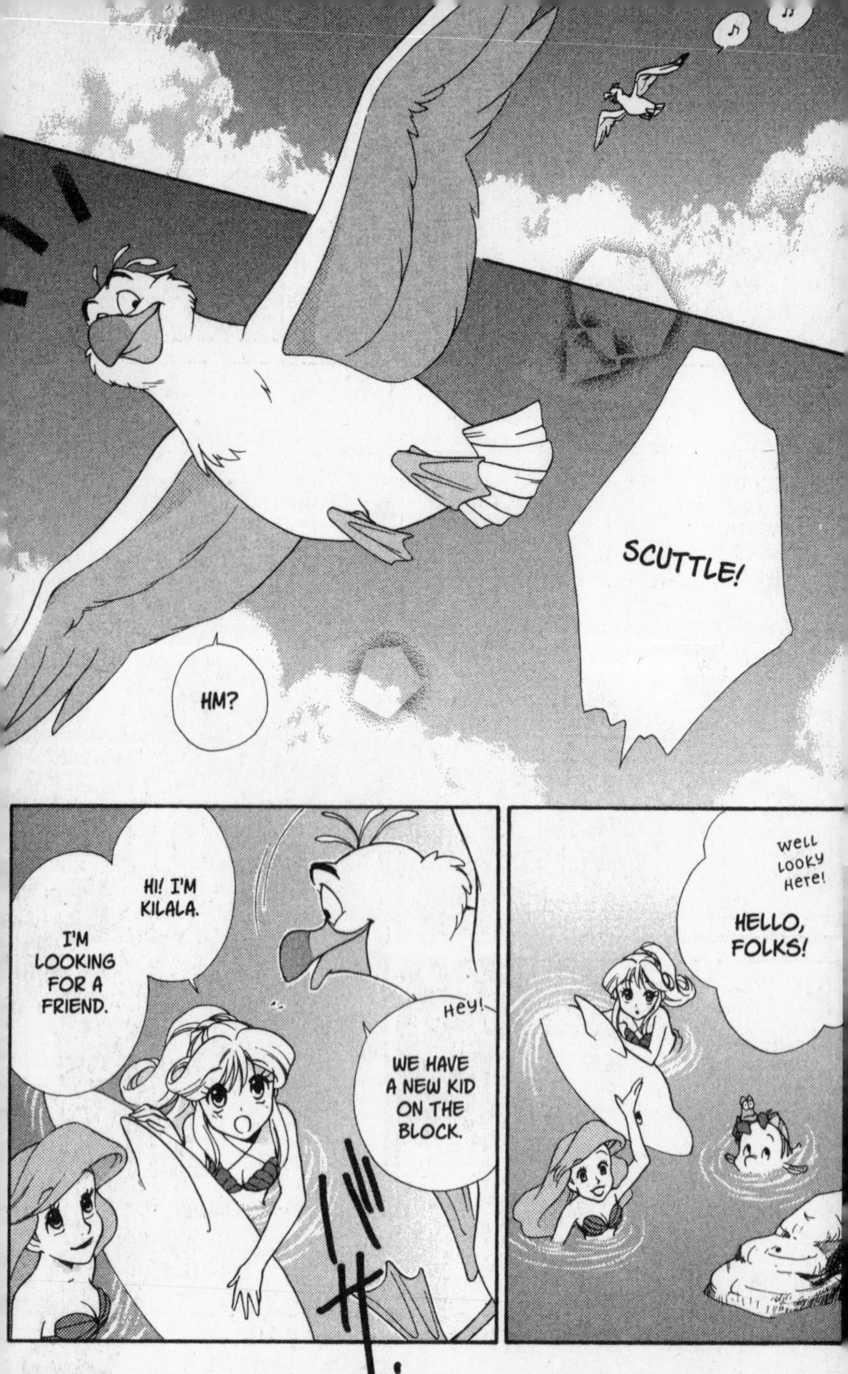

SCUTTLE!
HM?
well looky here!
HELLO, FOLKS!
Hey!
WE HAVE A NEW KID ON THE BLOCK.
HI! I'M KILALA.
I'M LOOKING FOR A FRIEND.

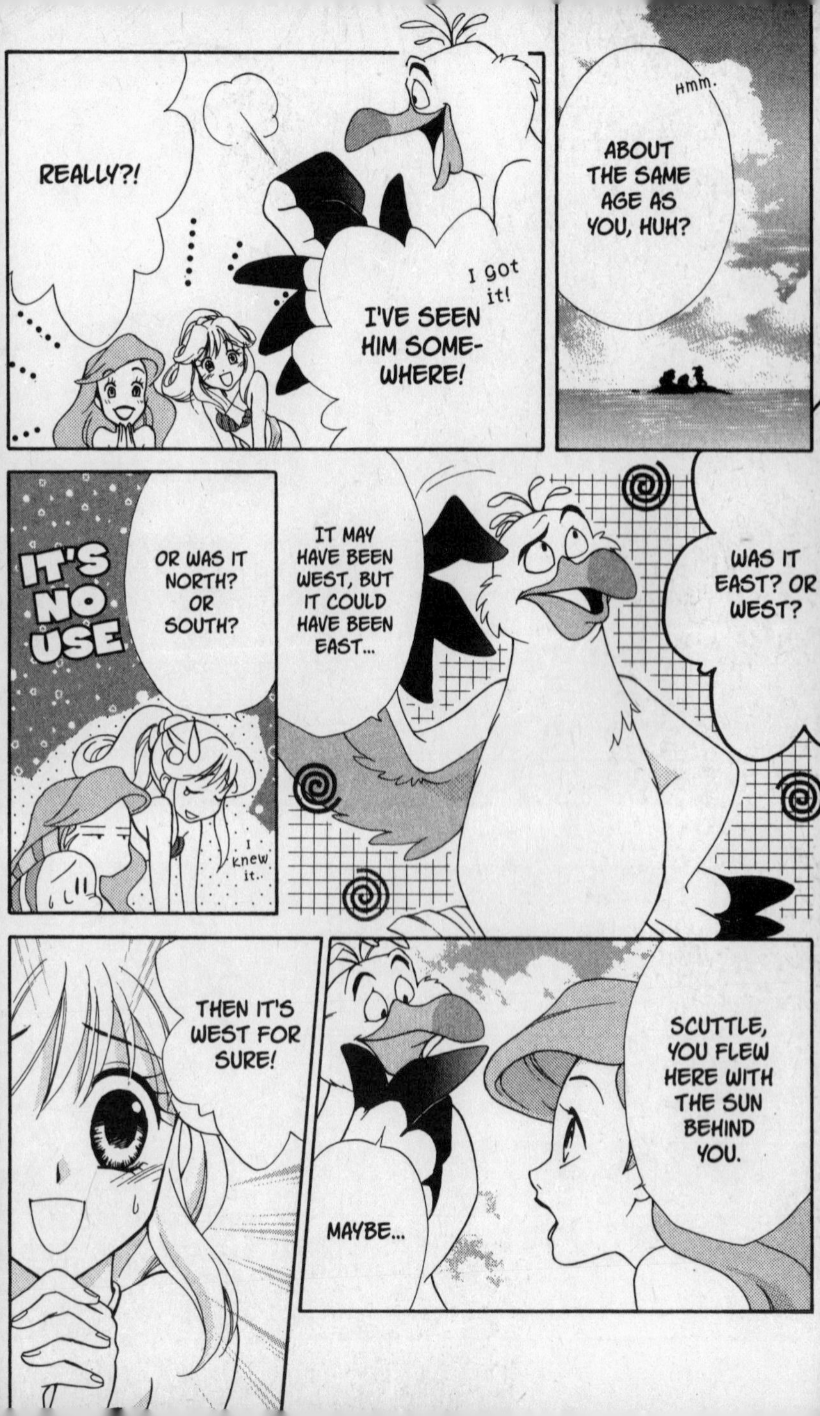
Hmm.
ABOUT THE SAME AGE AS YOU, HUH?
I got it!
I'VE SEEN HIM SOME-WHERE!
REALLY?!
WAS IT EAST? OR WEST?
IT MAY HAVE BEEN WEST, BUT IT COULD HAVE BEEN EAST...
OR WAS IT NORTH? OR SOUTH?
IT'S NO USE
I knew it..
SCUTTLE, YOU FLEW HERE WITH THE SUN BEHIND YOU.
MAYBE...
THEN IT'S WEST FOR SURE!

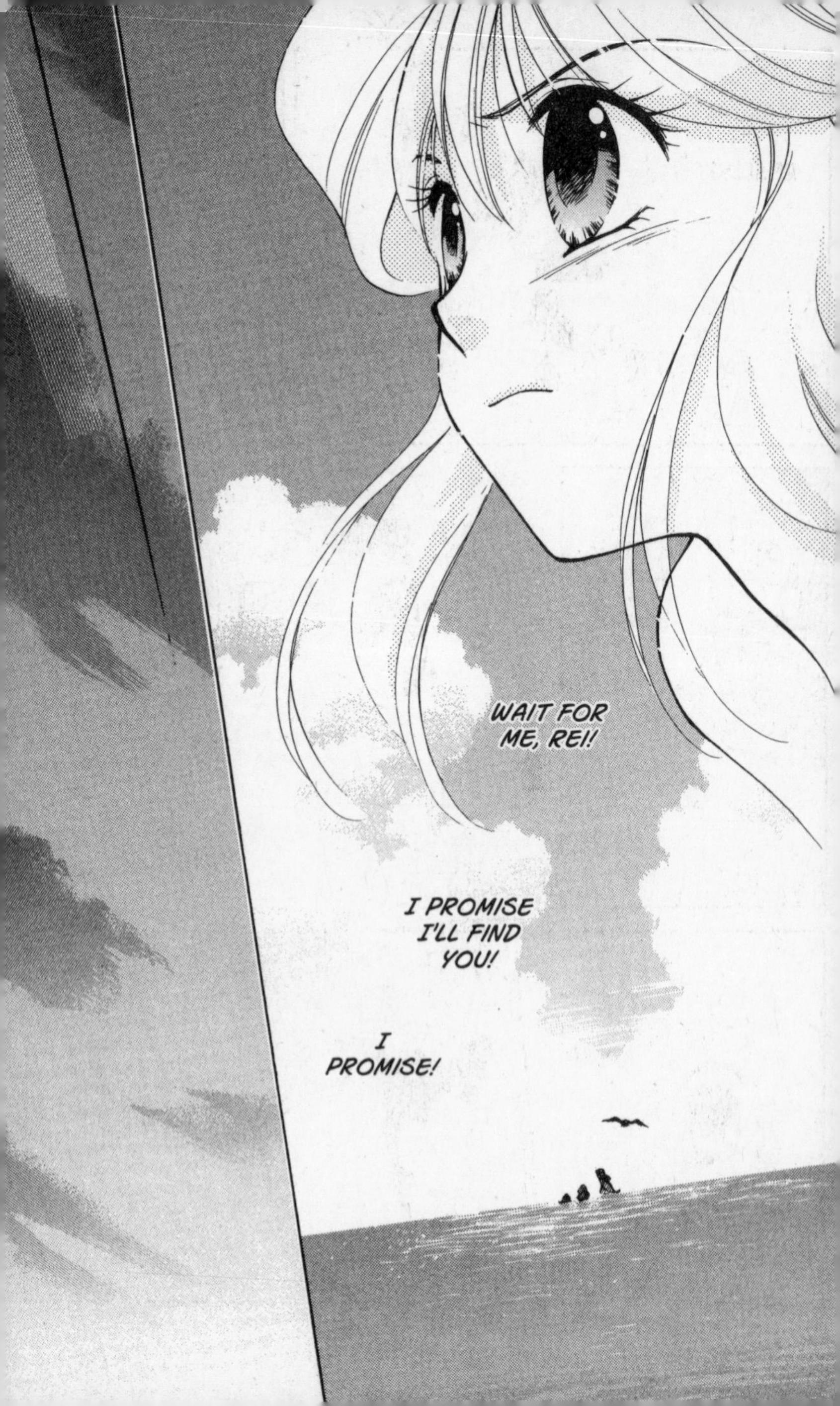
WAIT FOR ME, REI!
I PROMISE I'LL FIND YOU!
I PROMISE!

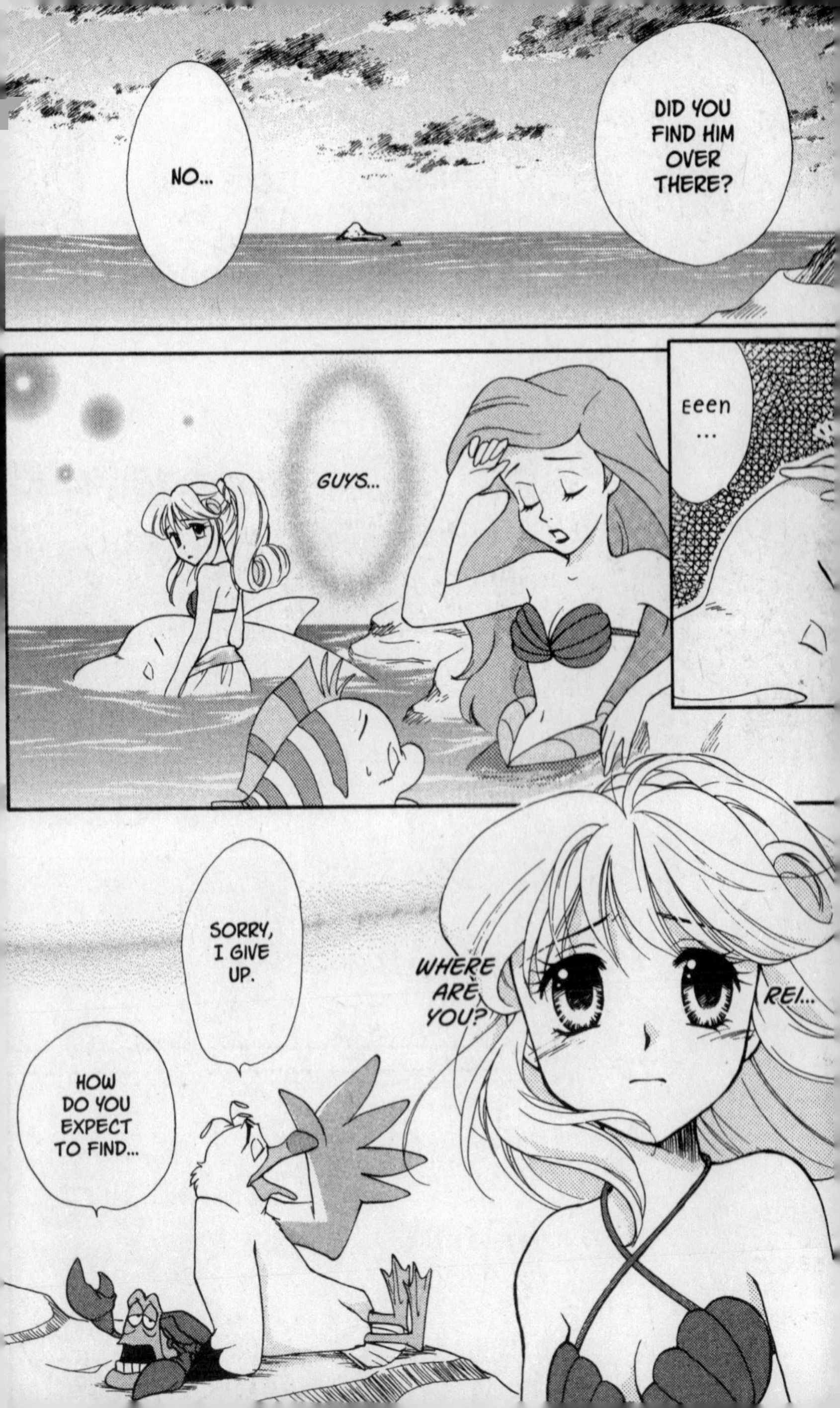
DID YOU FIND HIM OVER THERE?
NO...
Eeen ...
GUYS...
REI...
WHERE ARE YOU?
SORRY, I GIVE UP.
HOW DO YOU EXPECT TO FIND...

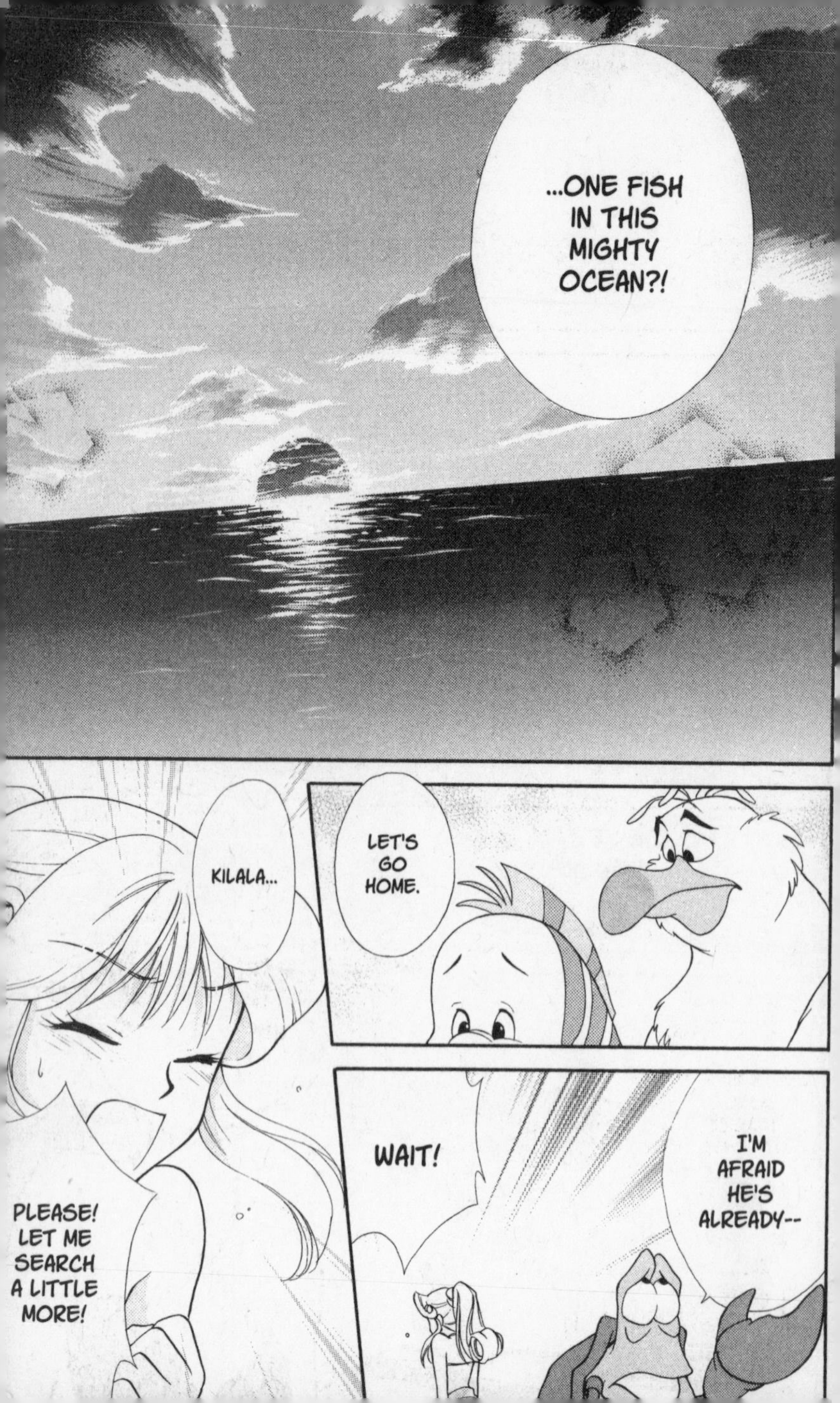

...ONE FISH IN THIS MIGHTY OCEAN?!
LET'S GO HOME.
I'M AFRAID HE'S ALREADY--
WAIT!
KILALA...
PLEASE! LET ME SEARCH A LITTLE MORE!

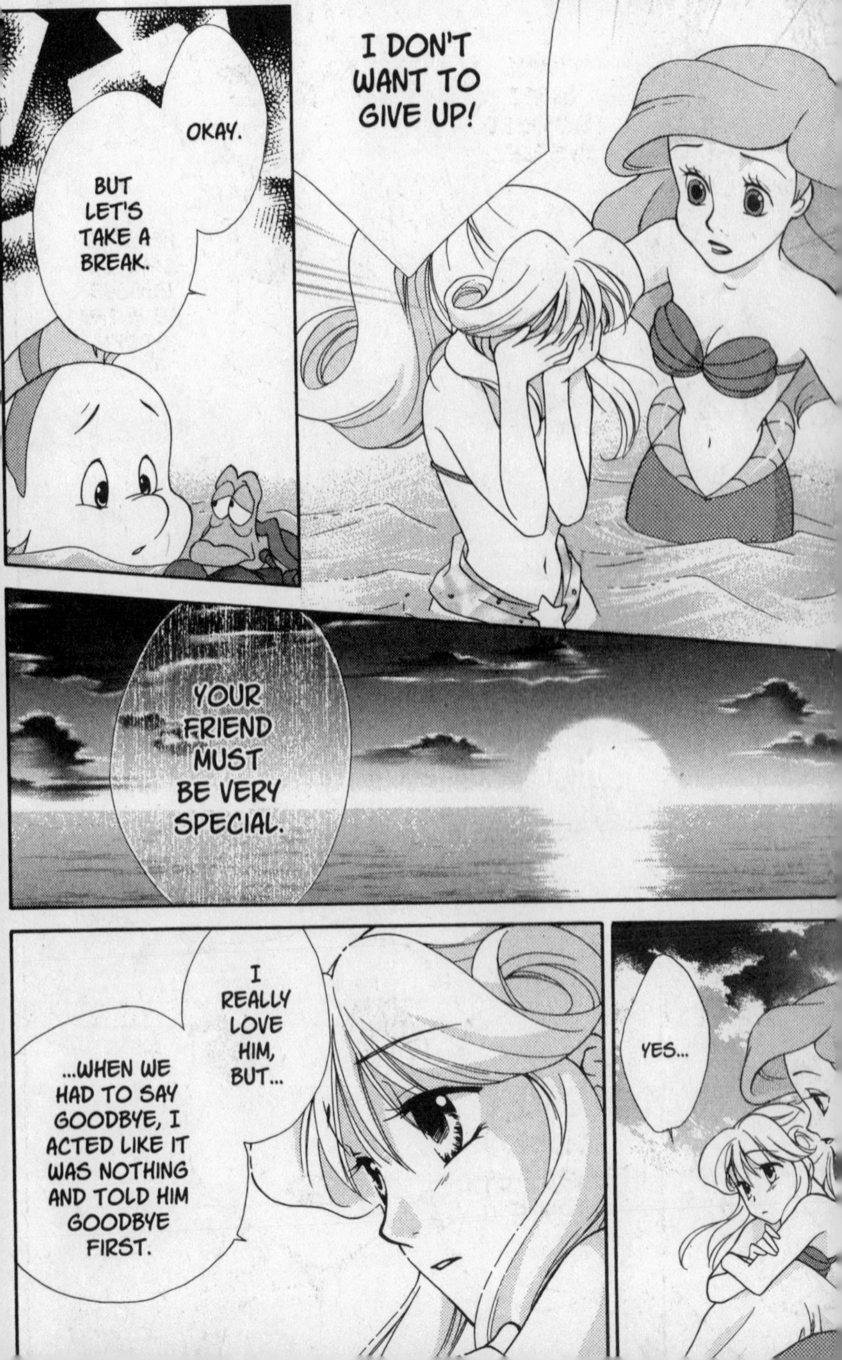
I DON'T WANT TO GIVE UP!
OKAY.
BUT LET'S TAKE A BREAK.
YOUR FRIEND MUST BE VERY SPECIAL.
YES...
I REALLY LOVE HIM, BUT...
...WHEN WE HAD TO SAY GOODBYE, I ACTED LIKE IT WAS NOTHING AND TOLD HIM GOODBYE FIRST.

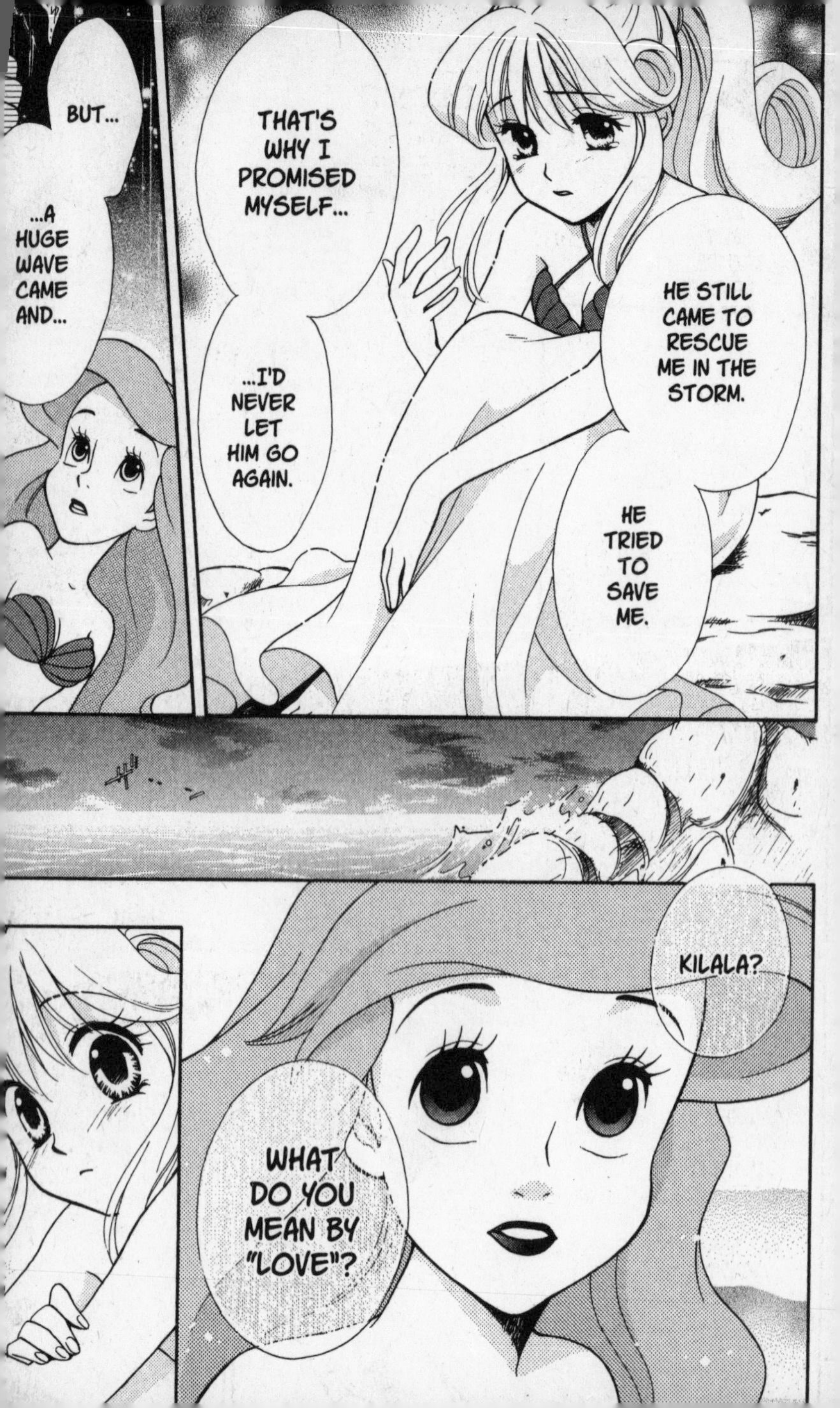
HE STILL CAME TO RESCUE ME IN THE STORM.
HE TRIED TO SAVE ME.
THAT'S WHY I PROMISED MYSELF...
...I'D NEVER LET HIM GO AGAIN.
BUT...
...A HUGE WAVE CAME AND...
KILALA?
WHAT DO YOU MEAN BY "LOVE"?

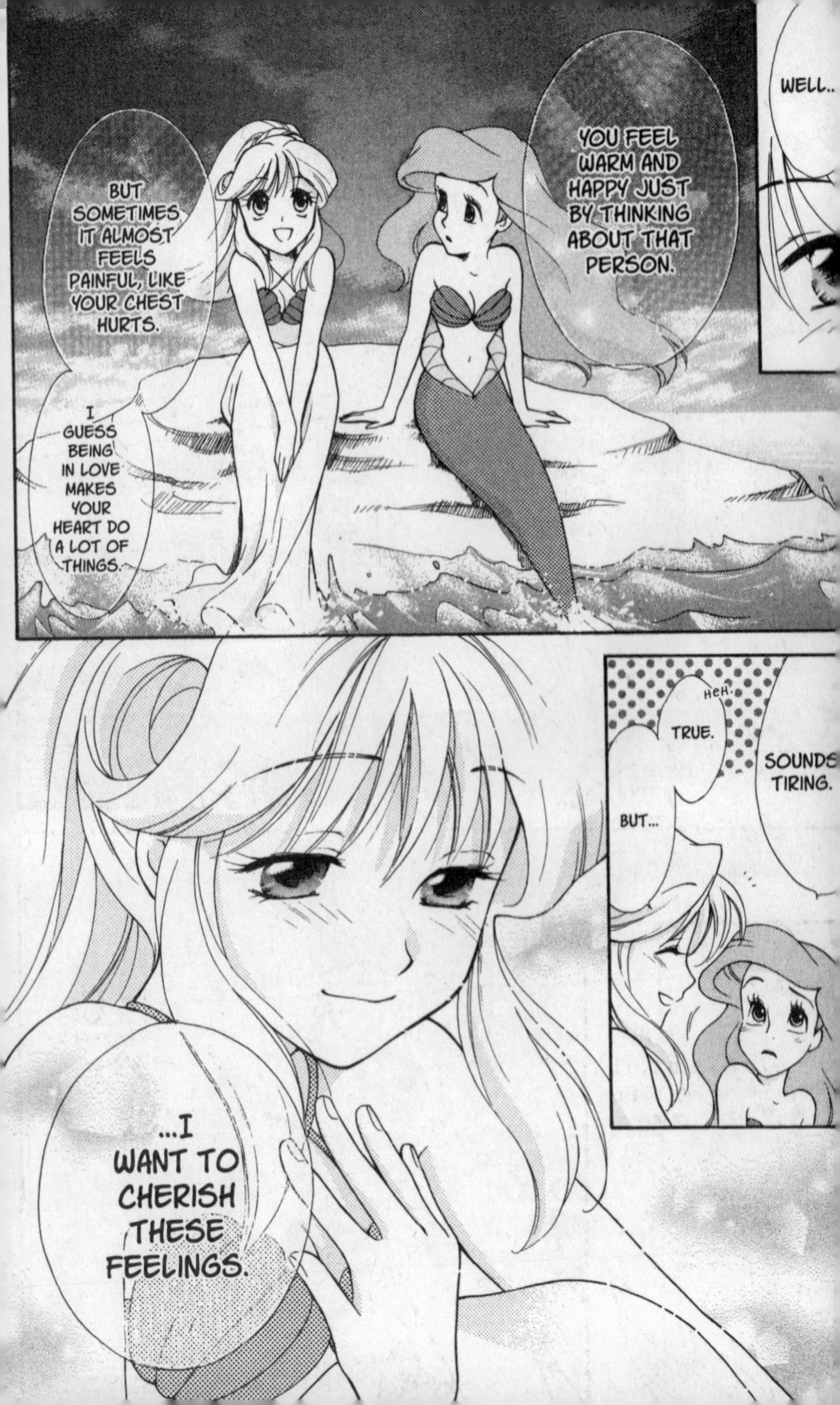
WELL..
YOU FEEL WARM AND HAPPY JUST BY THINKING ABOUT THAT PERSON.
BUT SOMETIMES IT ALMOST FEELS PAINFUL, LIKE YOUR CHEST HURTS.
I GUESS BEING IN LOVE MAKES YOUR HEART DO A LOT OF THINGS.
SOUNDS TIRING.
HEH.
TRUE.
BUT...
...I WANT TO CHERISH THESE FEELINGS.

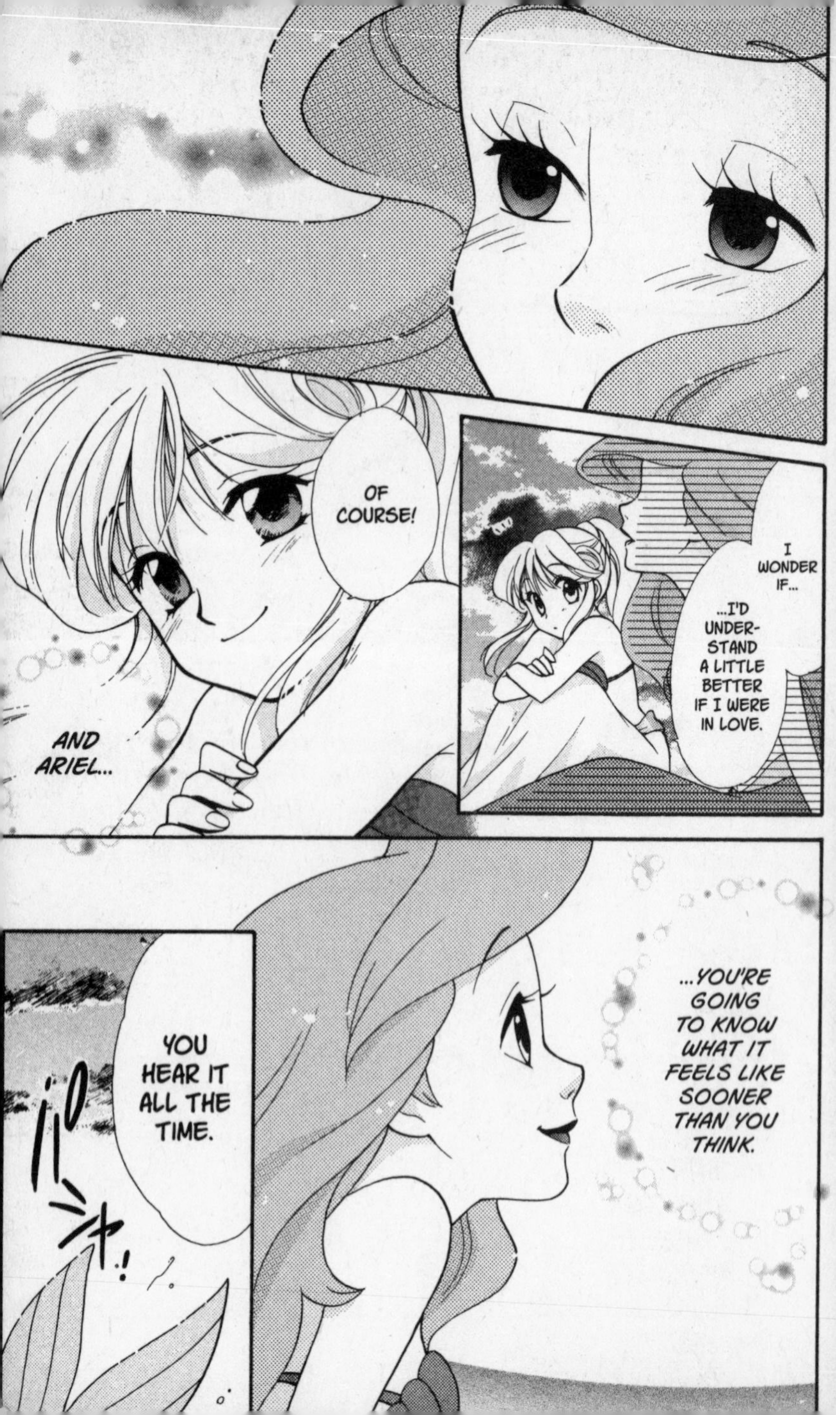
I WONDER IF...
...I'D UNDERSTAND A LITTLE BETTER IF I WERE IN LOVE.
OF COURSE!
AND ARIEL...
...YOU'RE GOING TO KNOW WHAT IT FEELS LIKE SOONER THAN YOU THINK.
YOU HEAR IT ALL THE TIME.
パシャ!

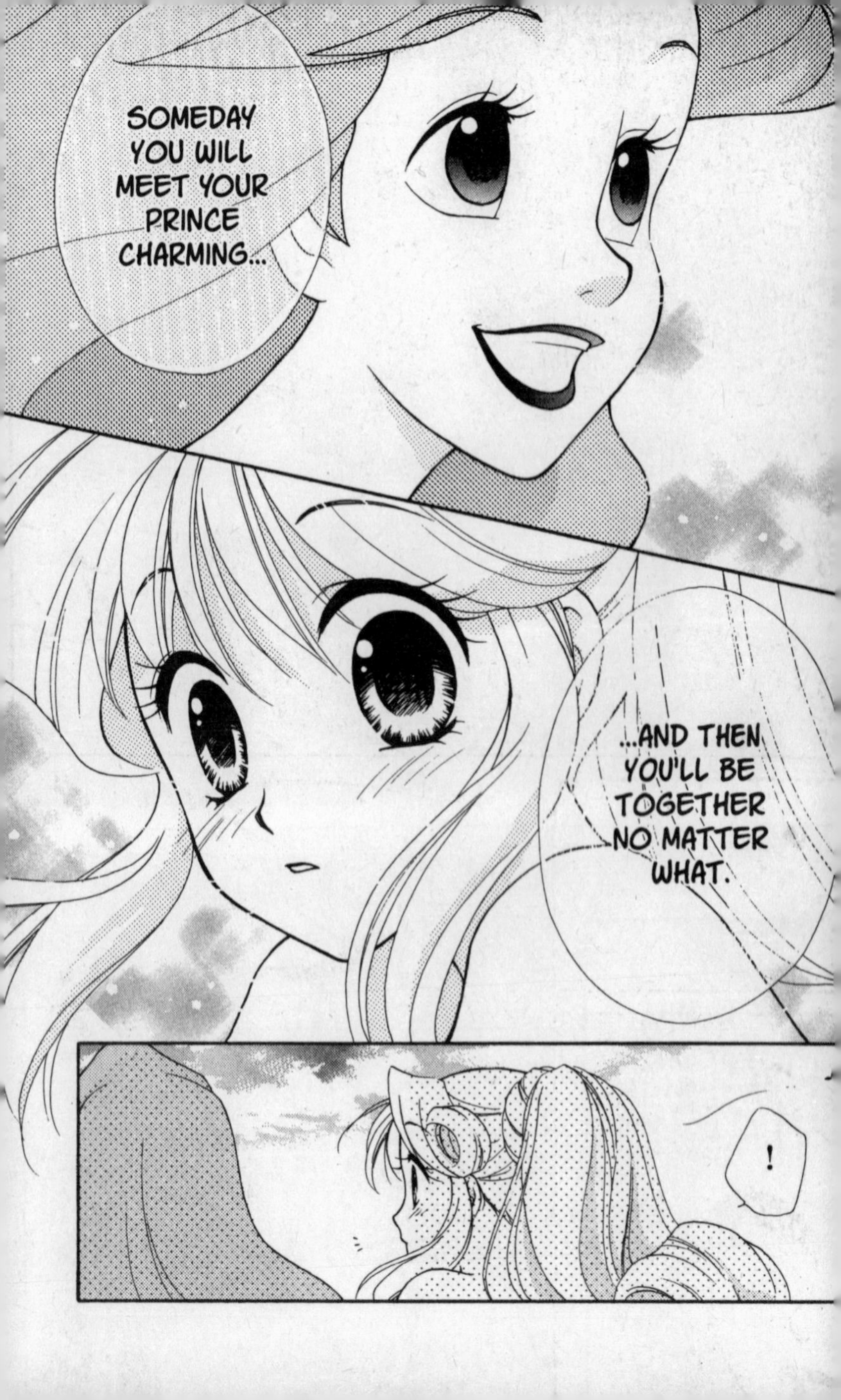
SOMEDAY YOU WILL MEET YOUR PRINCE CHARMING...
...AND THEN YOU'LL BE TOGETHER NO MATTER WHAT.
!

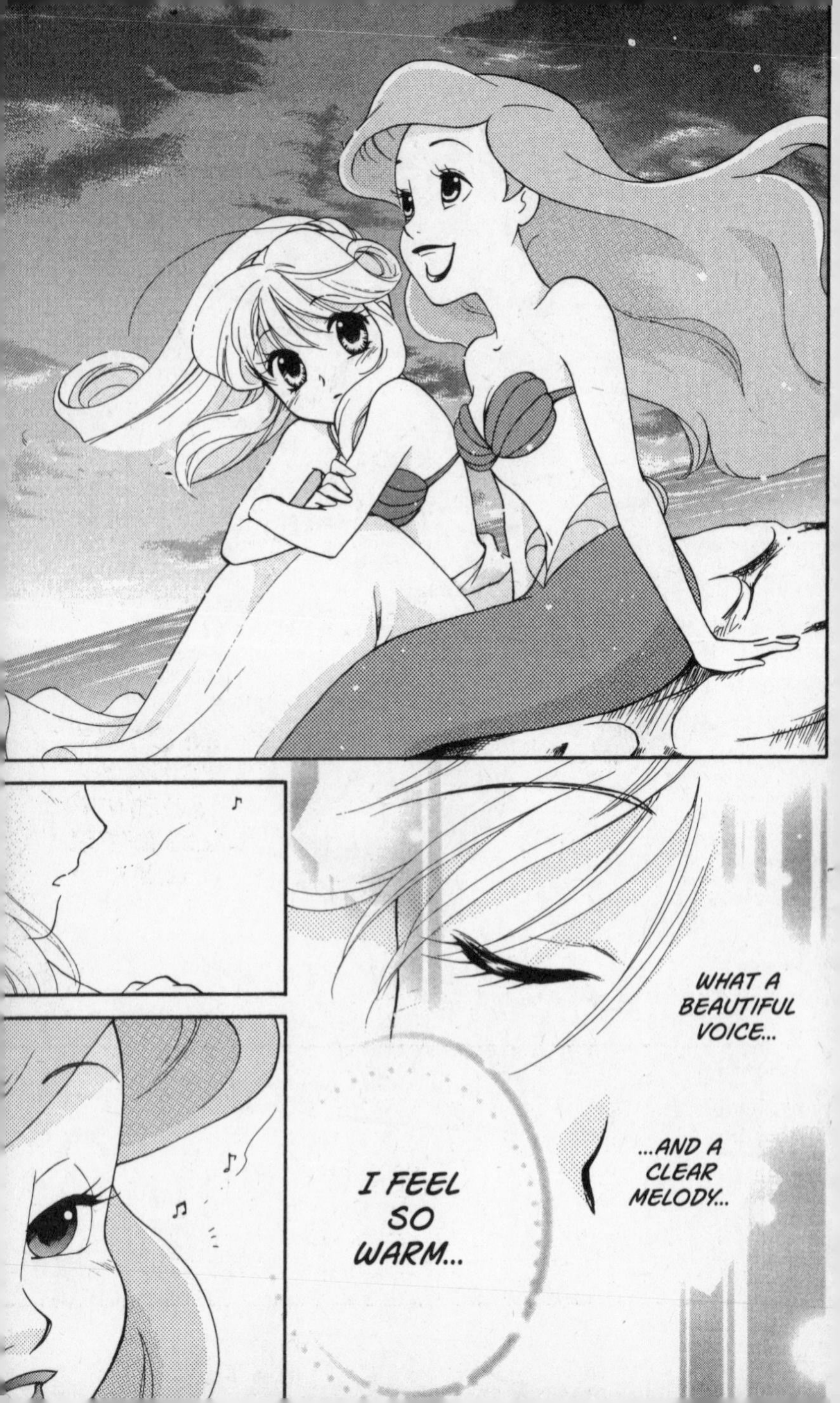
WHAT A BEAUTIFUL VOICE...
...AND A CLEAR MELODY...
I FEEL SO WARM...

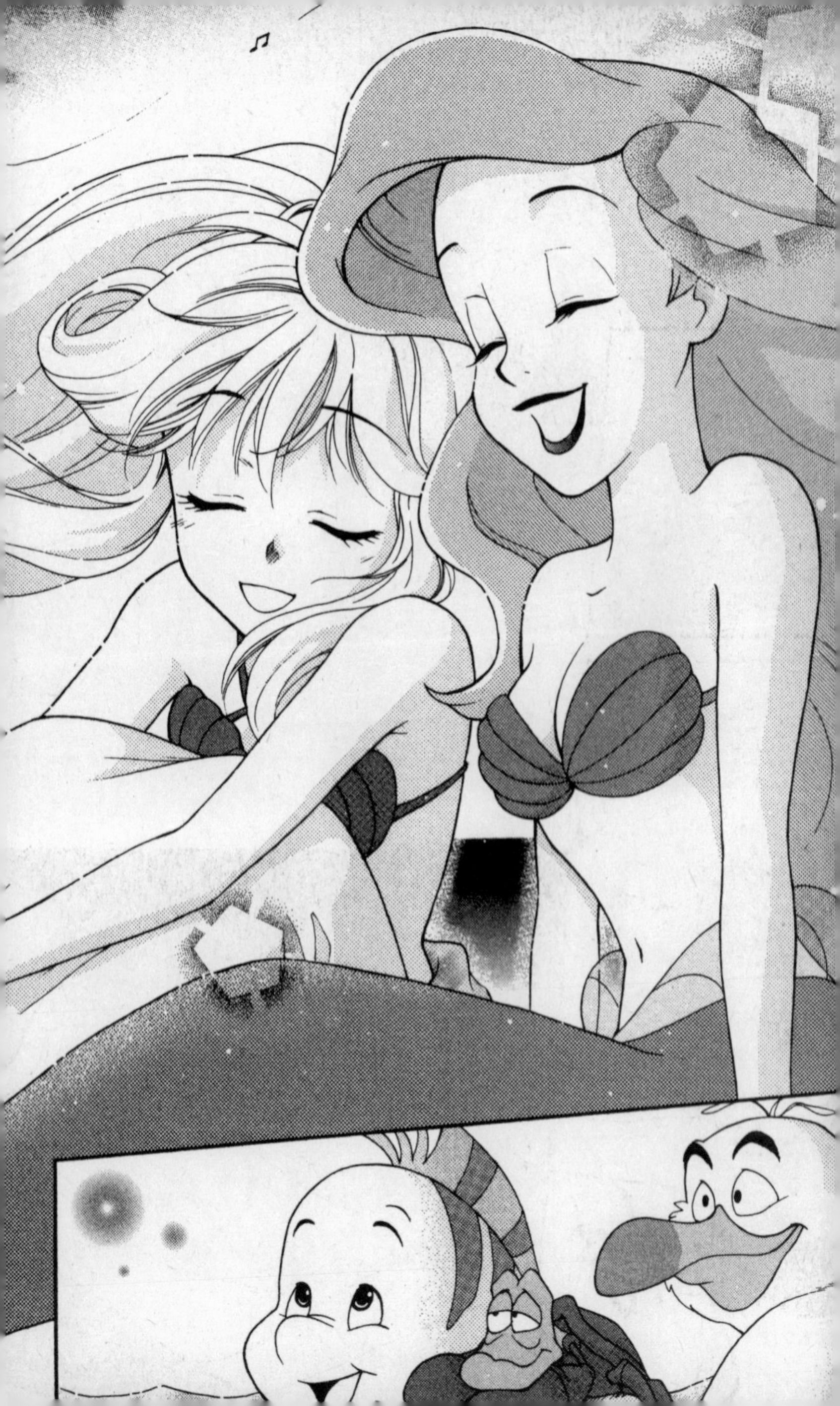

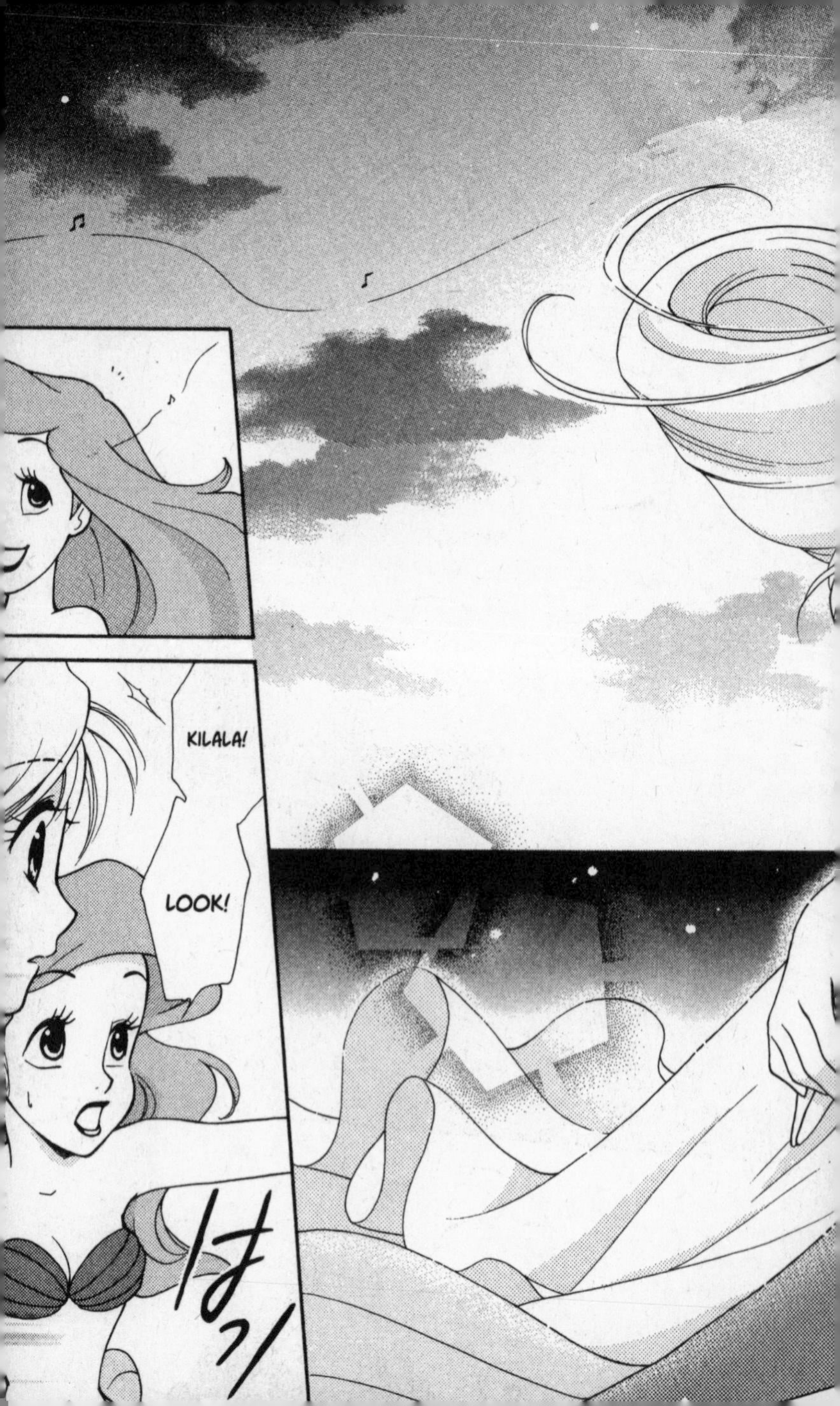
KILALA!
LOOK!
はっ

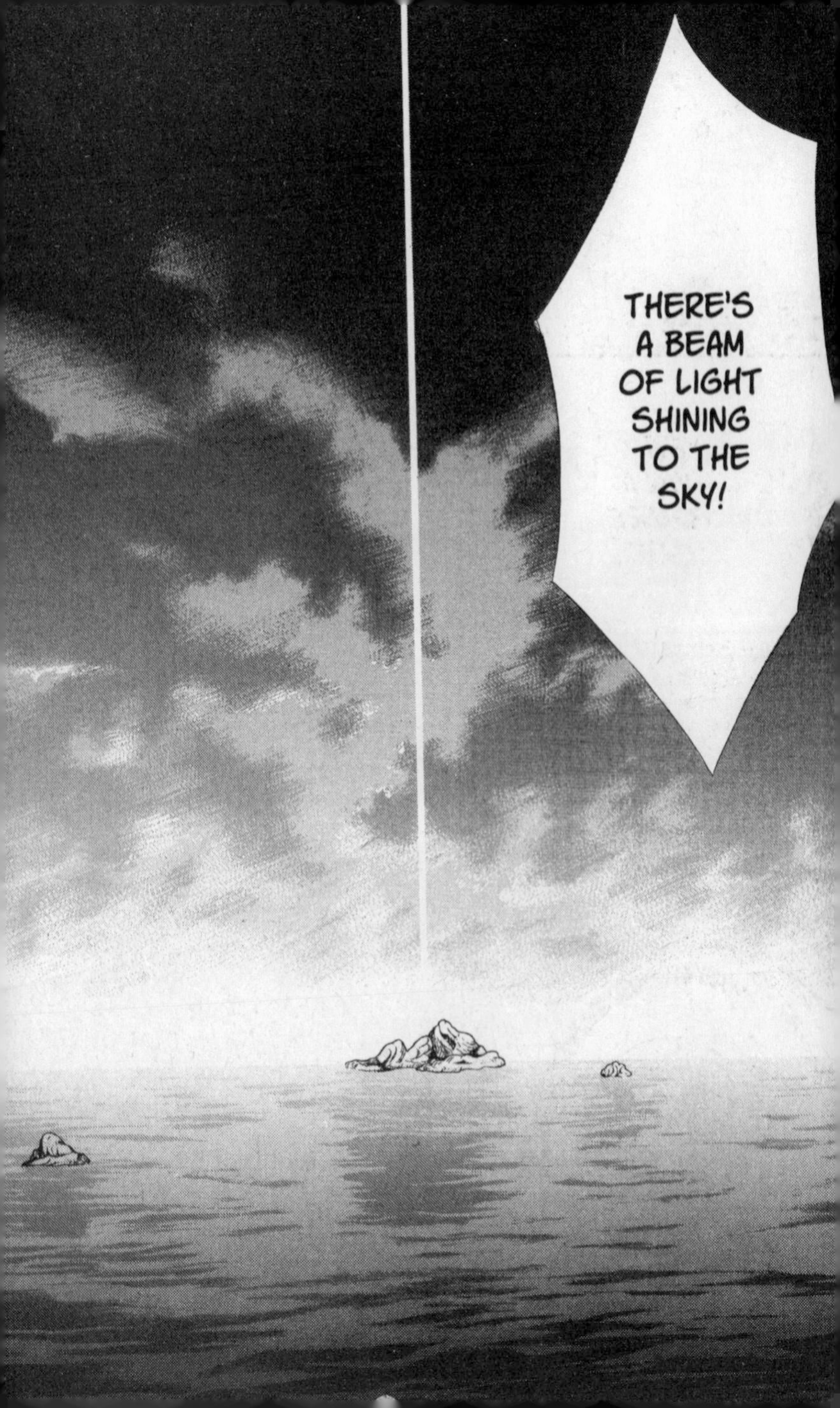
THERE'S A BEAM OF LIGHT SHINING TO THE SKY!

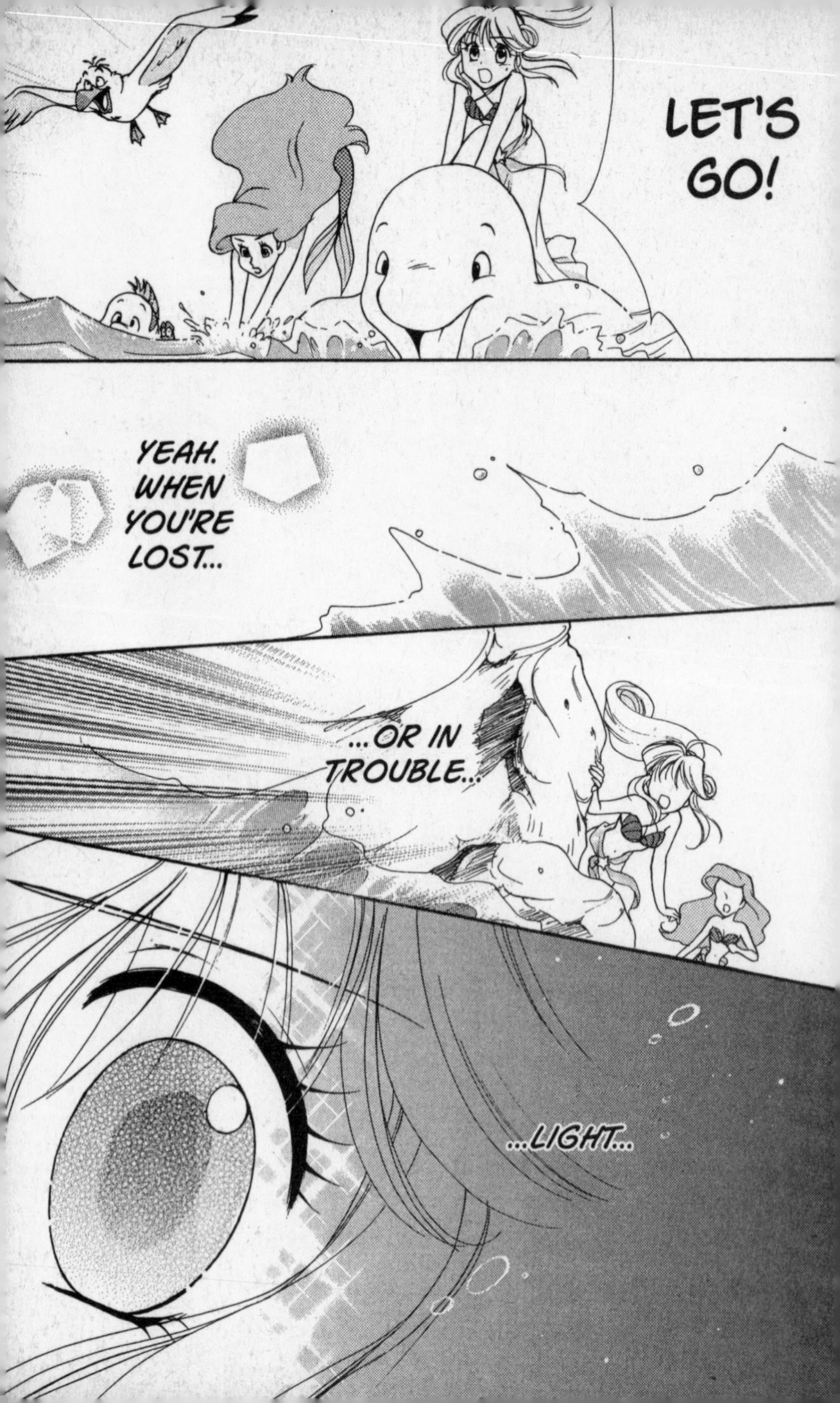
LET'S GO!
YEAH. WHEN YOU'RE LOST...
...OR IN TROUBLE...
...LIGHT...

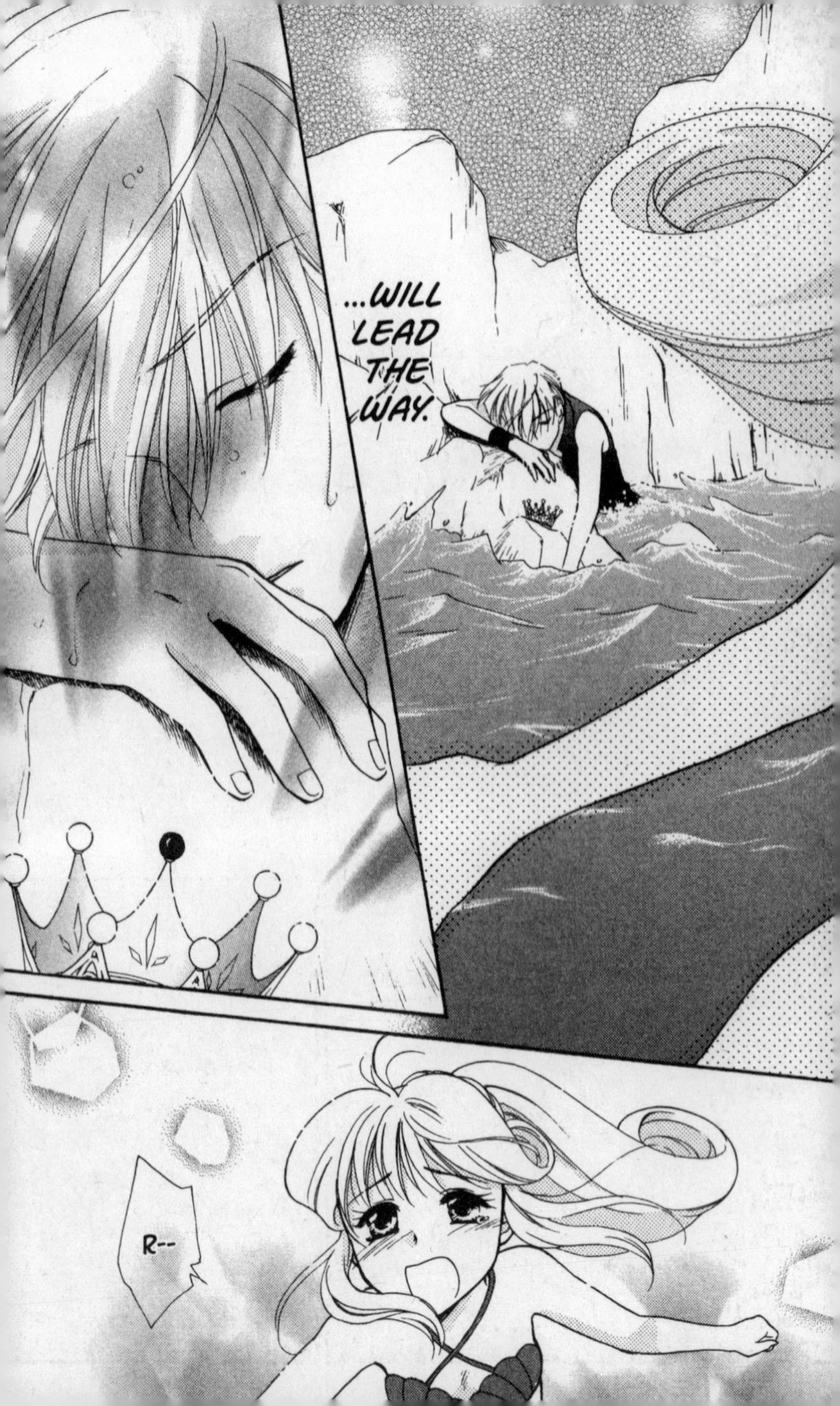
...WILL LEAD THE WAY.
R--

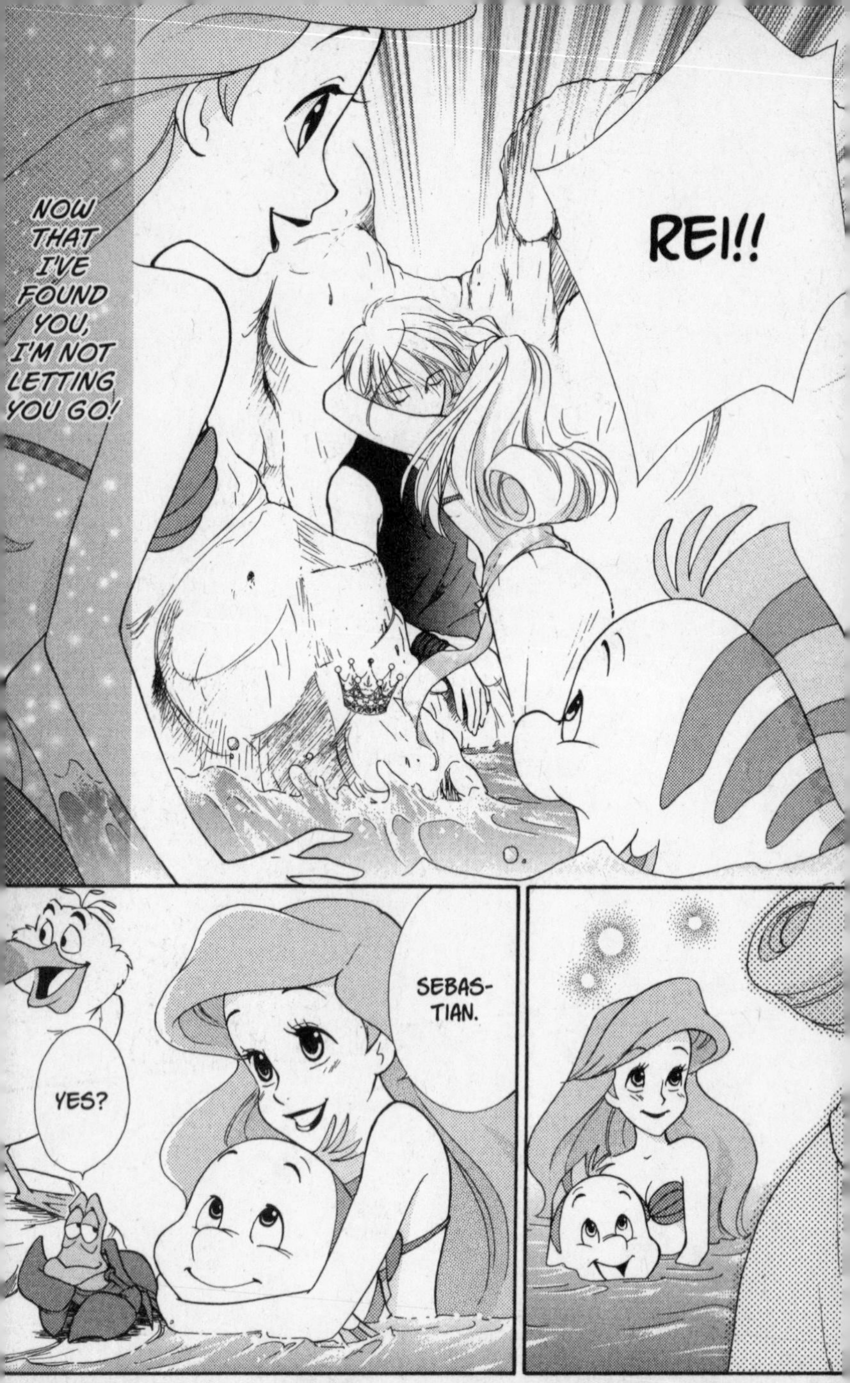
REI!!
NOW THAT I'VE FOUND YOU, I'M NOT LETTING YOU GO!
SEBAS-TIAN.
YES?

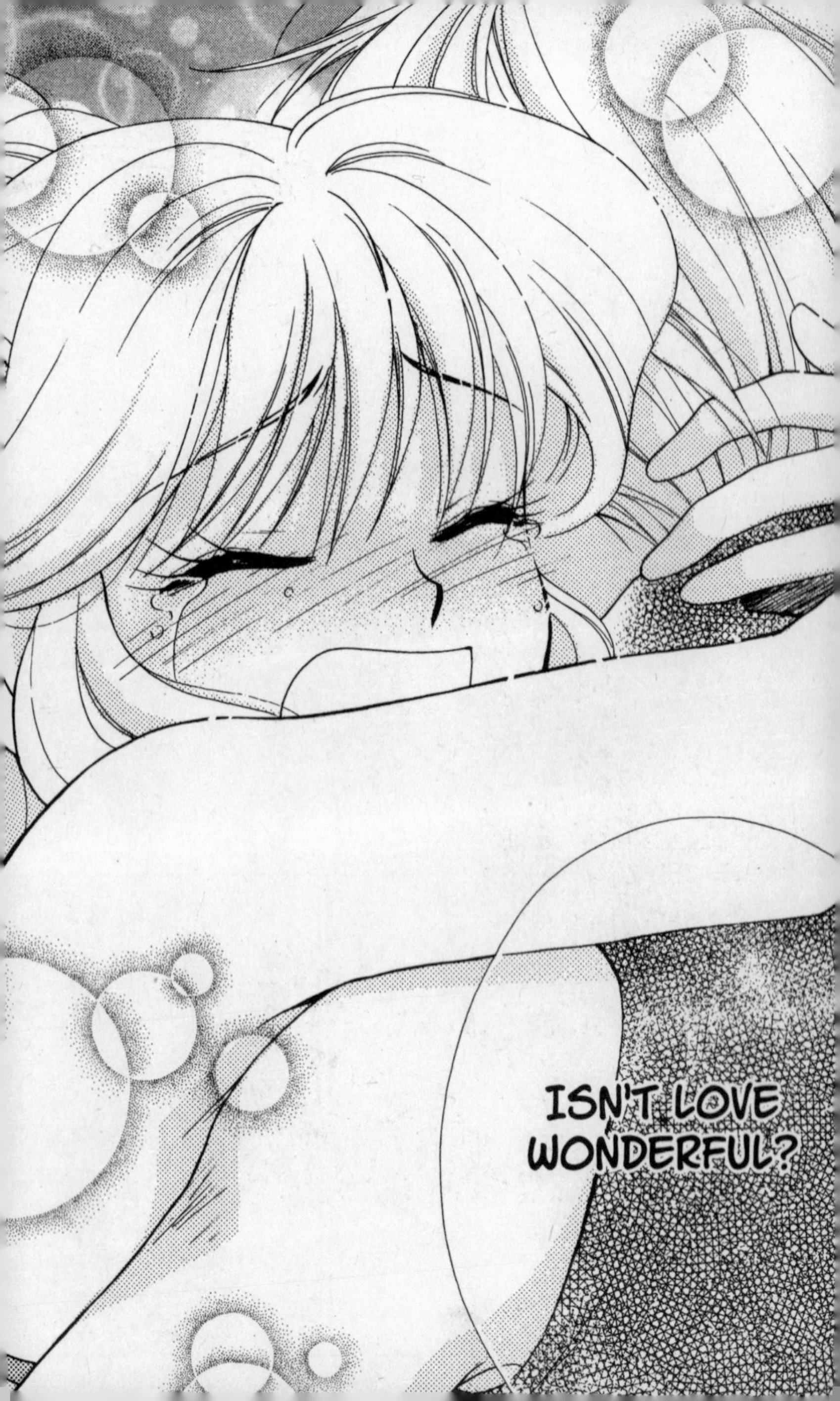
ISN'T LOVE WONDERFUL?

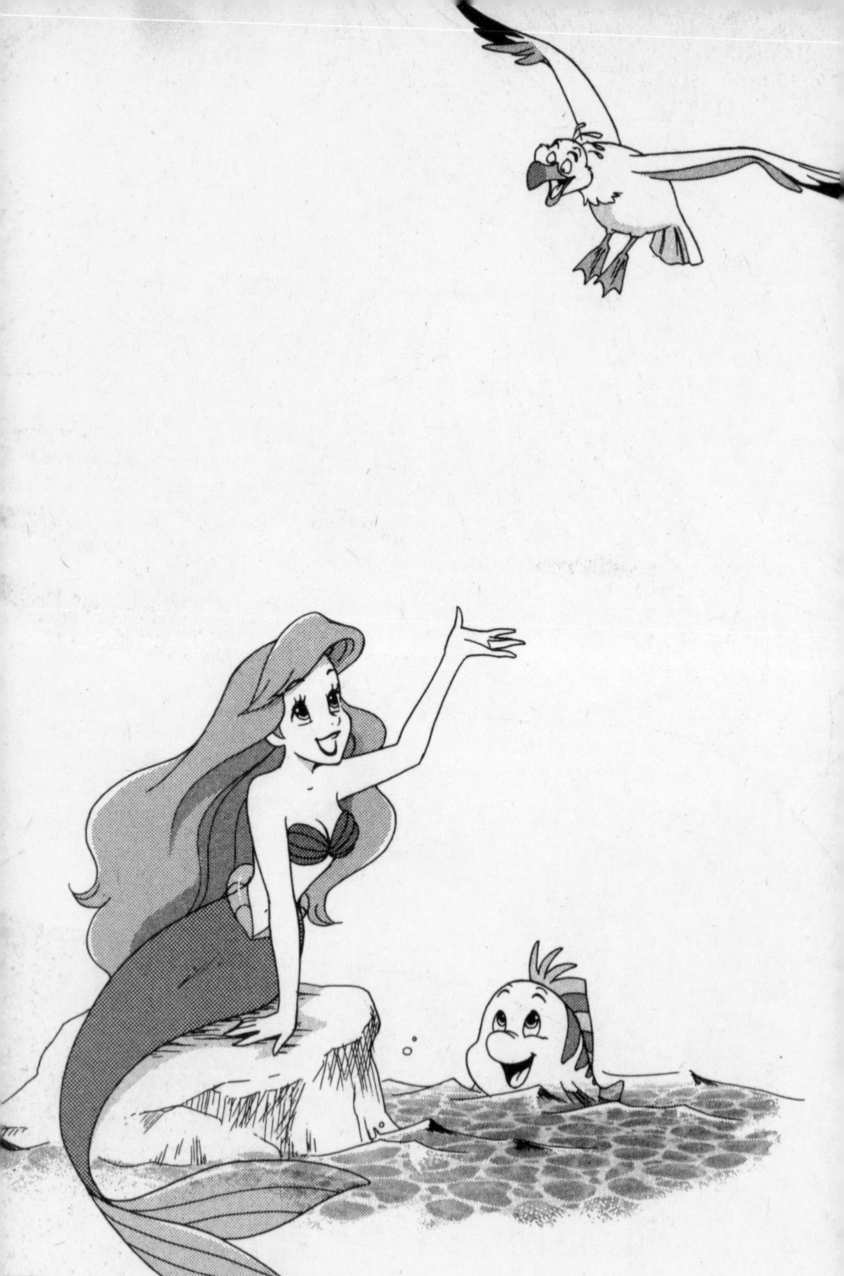

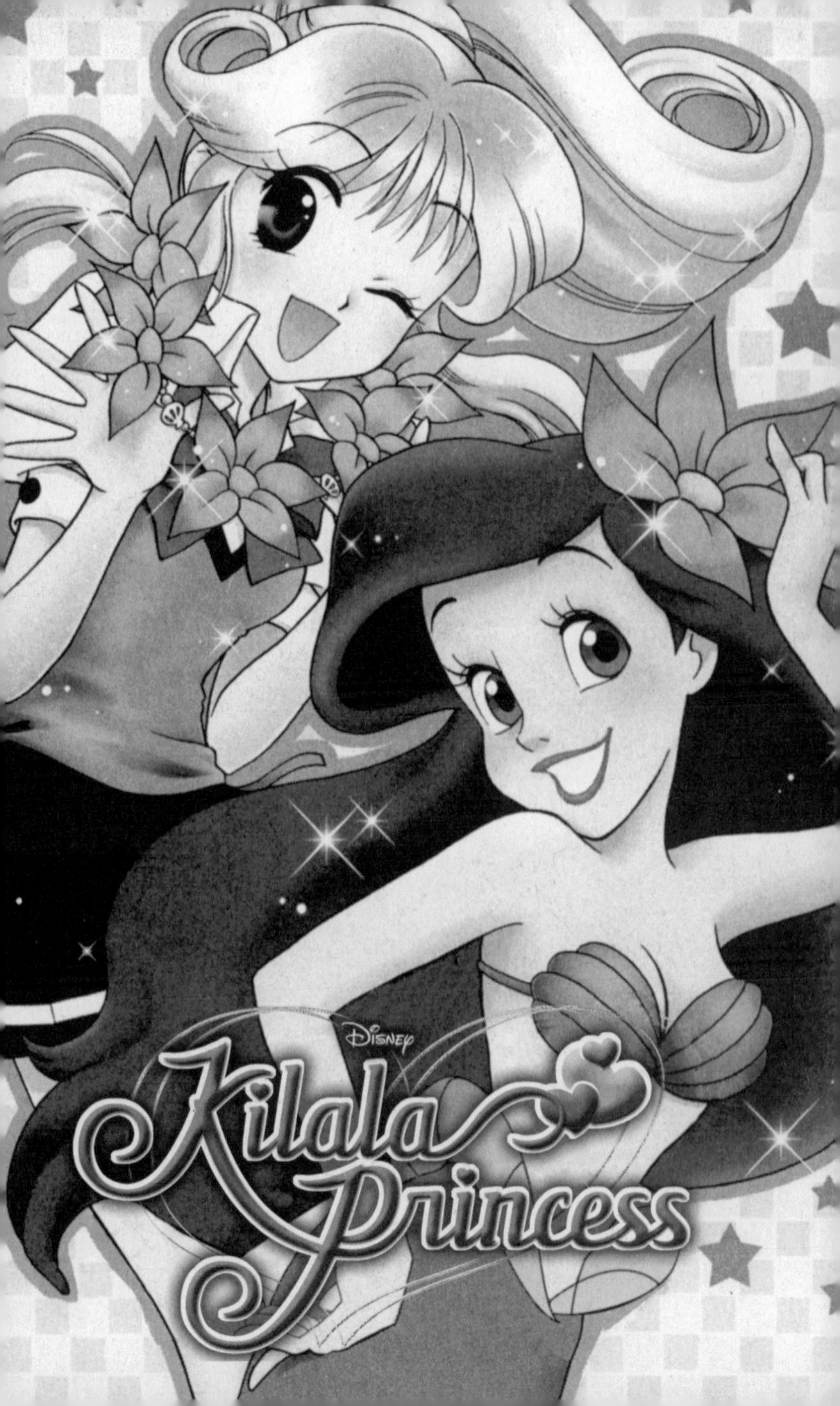
Disney
Kilala Princess

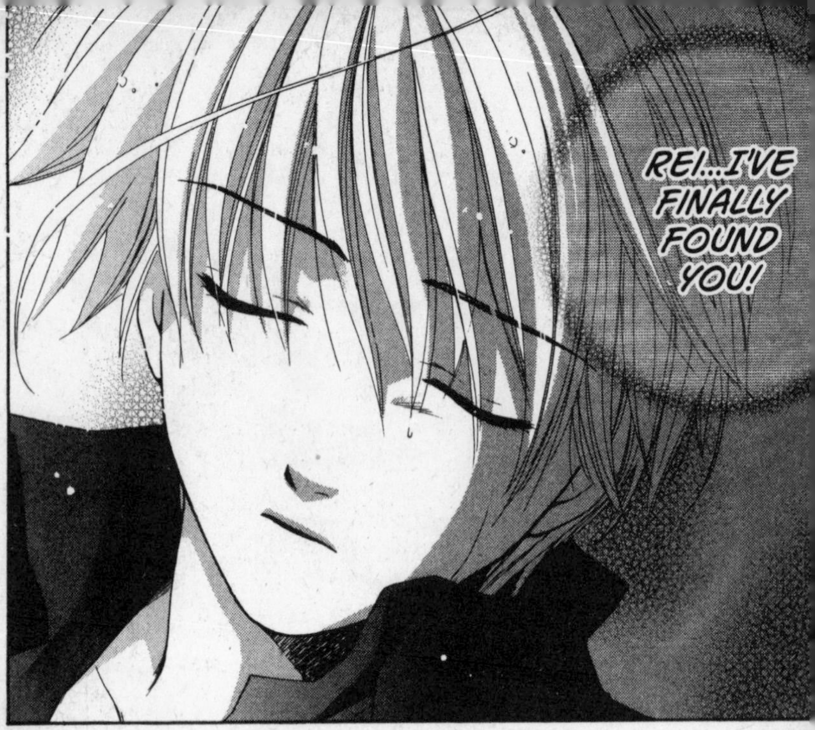
REI...I'VE FINALLY FOUND YOU!

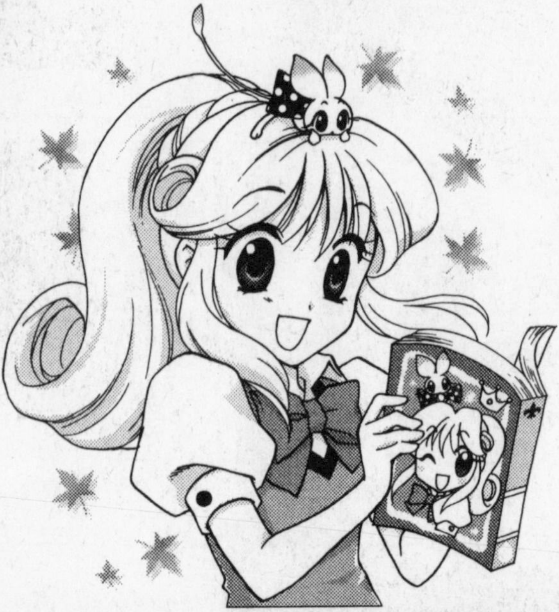

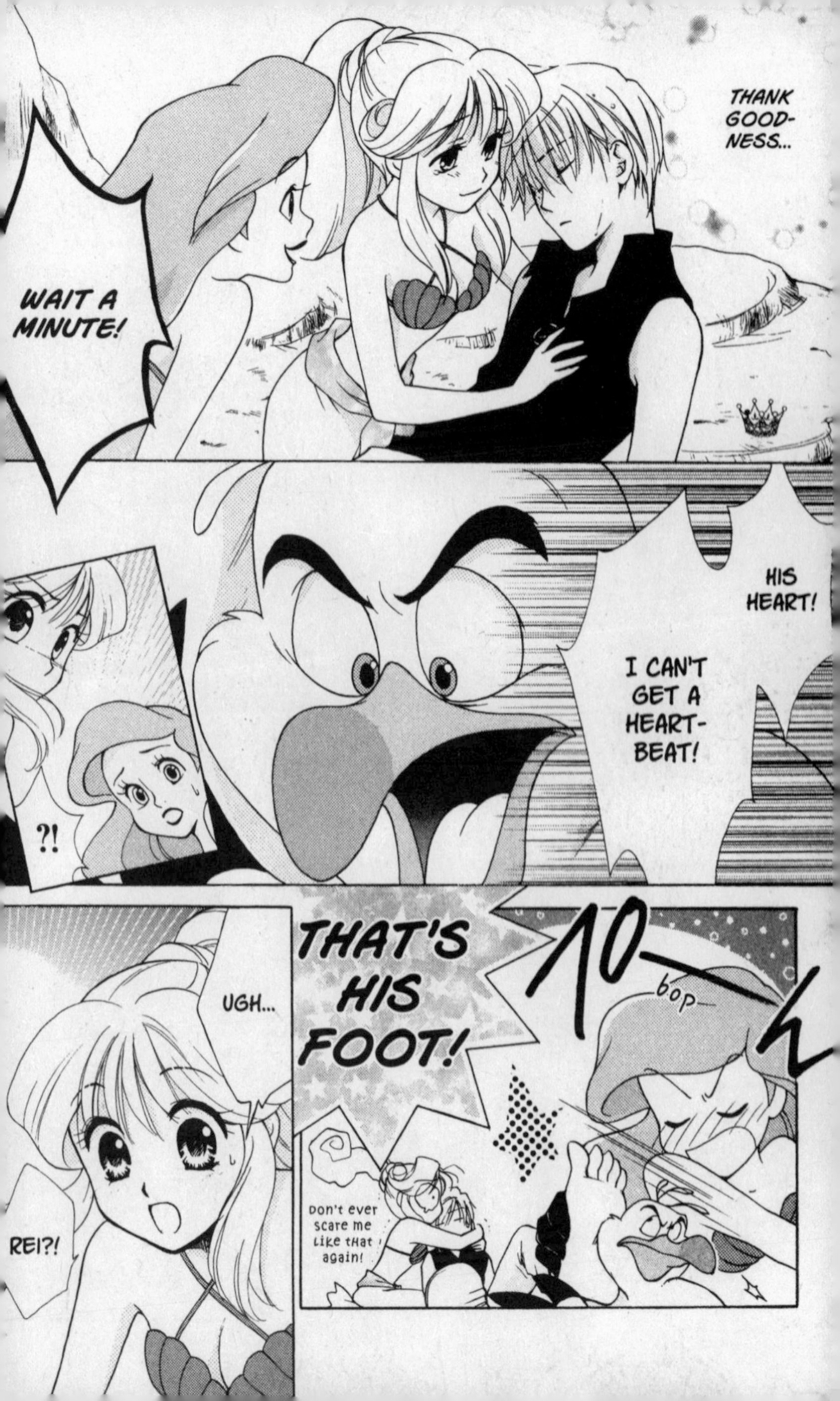
THANK GOODNESS...
WAIT A MINUTE!
HIS HEART!
I CAN'T GET A HEARTBEAT!
?!
THAT'S HIS FOOT!
bop
Don't ever scare me like that again!
UGH...
REI?!

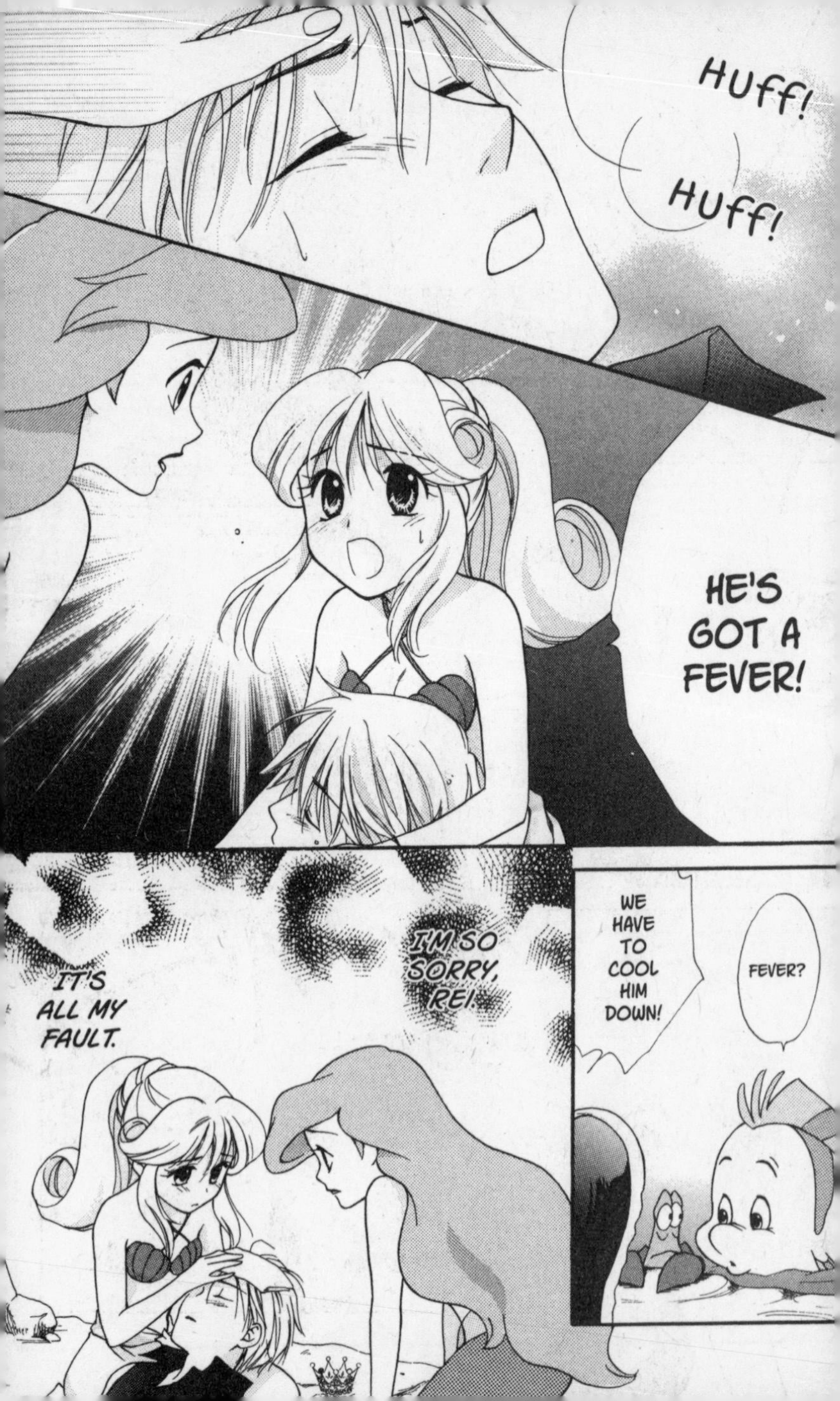
HUFF!
HUFF!
HE'S GOT A FEVER!
FEVER?
WE HAVE TO COOL HIM DOWN!
I'M SO SORRY, REI.
IT'S ALL MY FAULT.

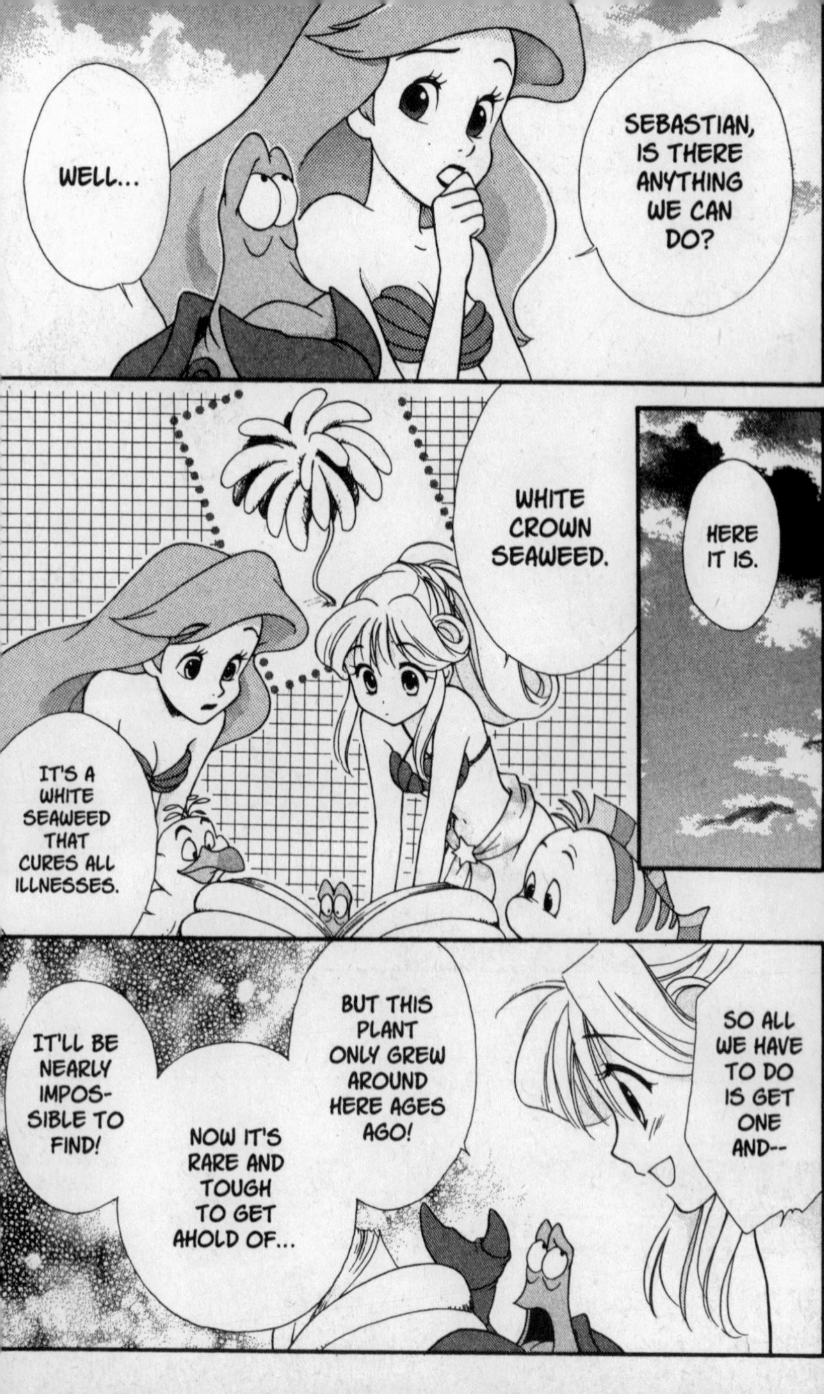
SEBASTIAN, IS THERE ANYTHING WE CAN DO?
WELL...
HERE IT IS.
WHITE CROWN SEAWEED.
IT'S A WHITE SEAWEED THAT CURES ALL ILLNESSES.
SO ALL WE HAVE TO DO IS GET ONE AND--
BUT THIS PLANT ONLY GREW AROUND HERE AGES AGO!
NOW IT'S RARE AND TOUGH TO GET AHOLD OF...
IT'LL BE NEARLY IMPOS-SIBLE TO FIND!

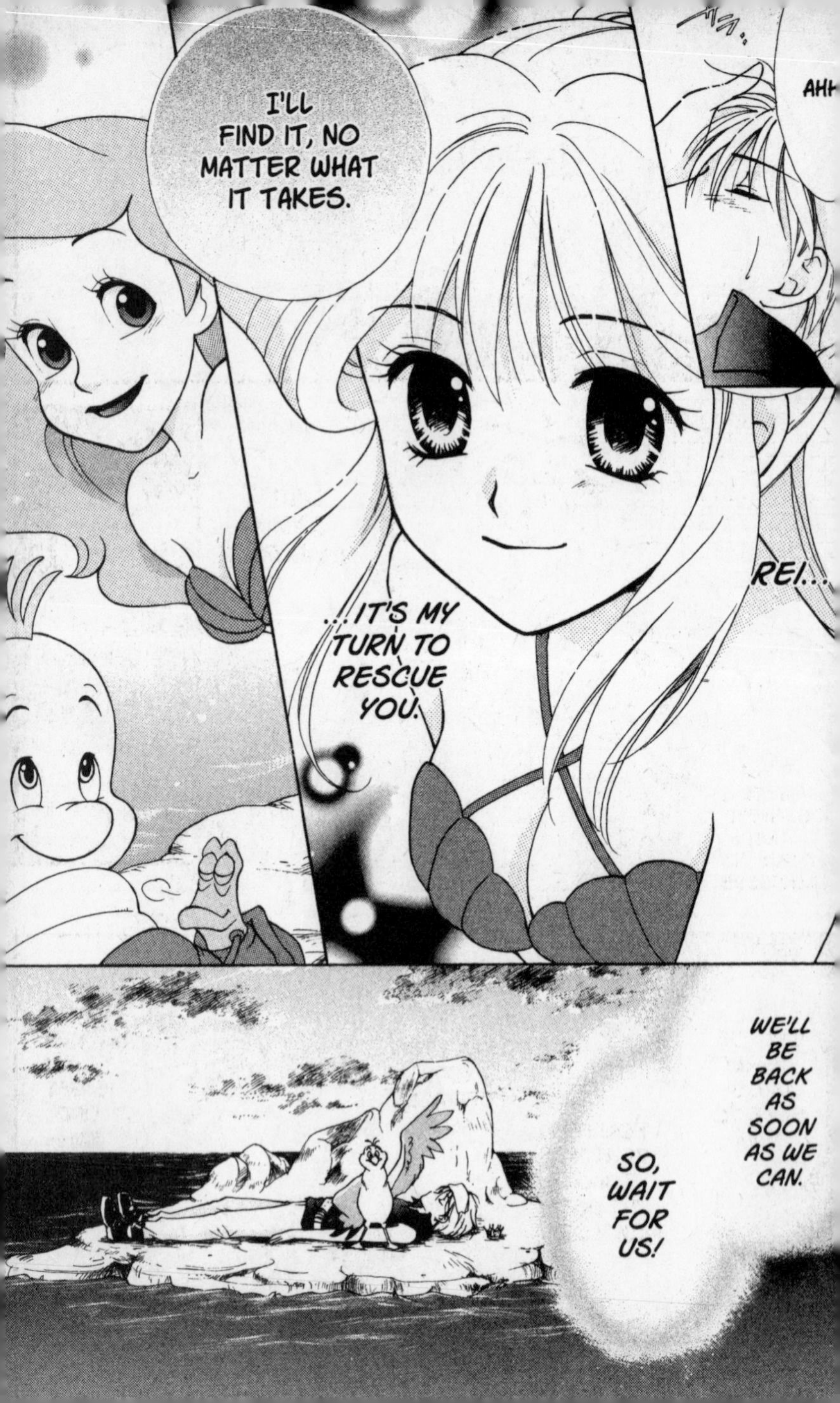
AHH
REI...
...IT'S MY TURN TO RESCUE YOU.
I'LL FIND IT, NO MATTER WHAT IT TAKES.
WE'LL BE BACK AS SOON AS WE CAN.
SO, WAIT FOR US!

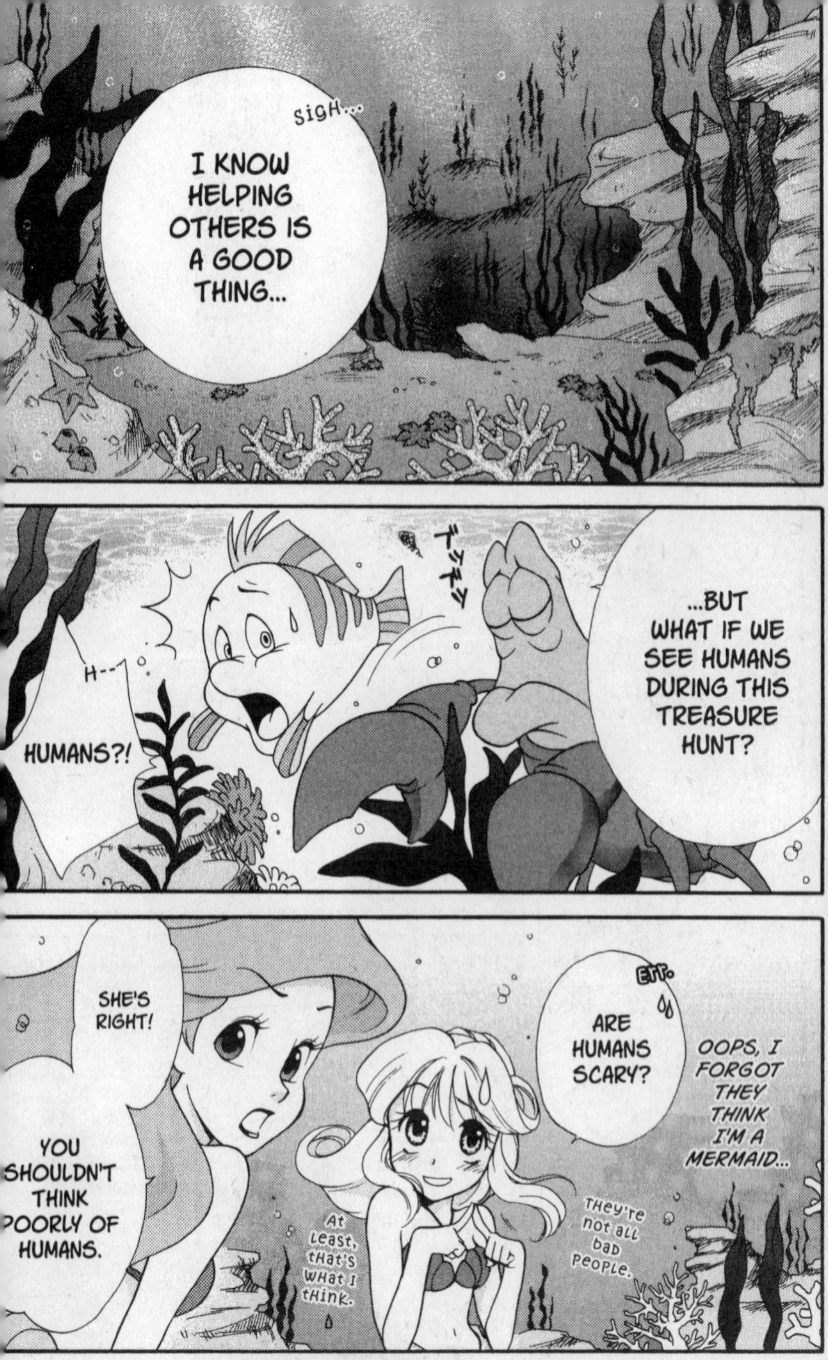
SIGH...
I KNOW HELPING OTHERS IS A GOOD THING...
...BUT WHAT IF WE SEE HUMANS DURING THIS TREASURE HUNT?
H--
HUMANS?!
Err.
ARE HUMANS SCARY?
OOPS, I FORGOT THEY THINK I'M A MERMAID...
They're not all bad people.
At least, that's what I think.
SHE'S RIGHT!
YOU SHOULDN'T THINK POORLY OF HUMANS.

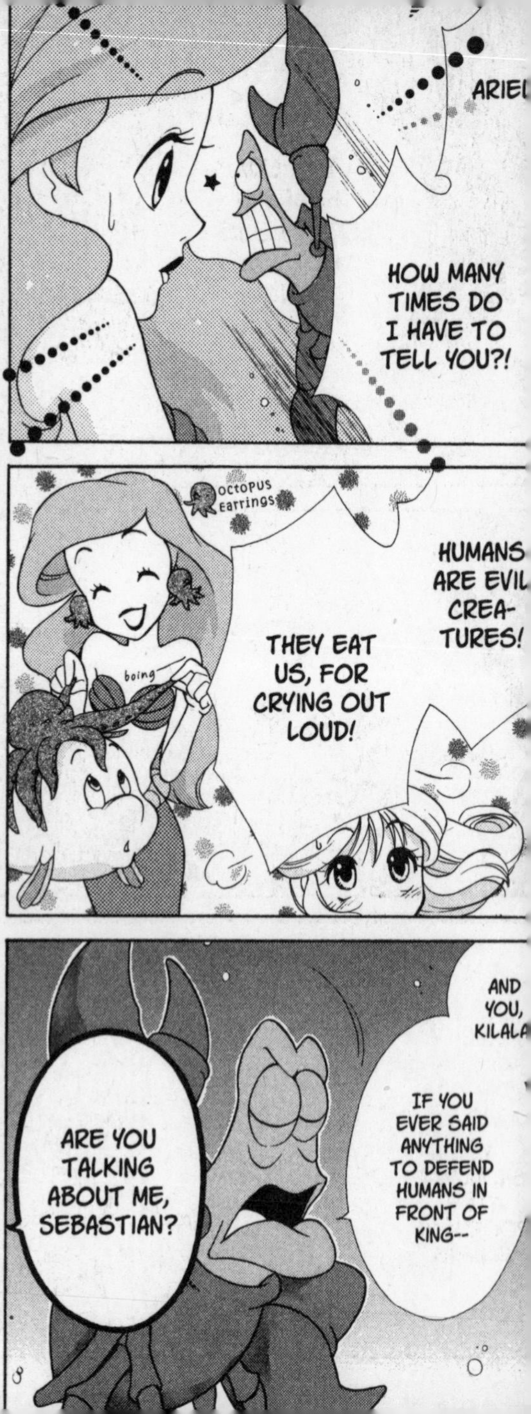
ARIEL
HOW MANY TIMES DO I HAVE TO TELL YOU?!
HUMANS ARE EVIL CREATURES!
THEY EAT US, FOR CRYING OUT LOUD!
Octopus Earrings
boing
AND YOU, KILALA
IF YOU EVER SAID ANYTHING TO DEFEND HUMANS IN FRONT OF KING--
ARE YOU TALKING ABOUT ME, SEBASTIAN?

A WORD FROM TIPPE

3

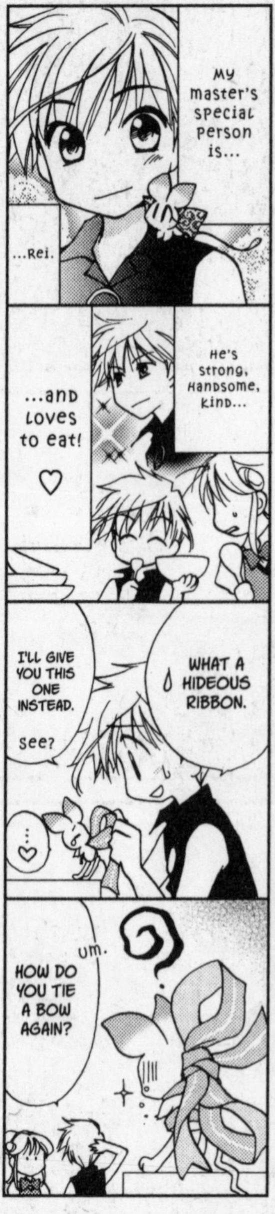
My master's special person is...
...Rei.
He's strong, handsome, kind...
...and loves to eat! ♡
WHAT A HIDEOUS RIBBON.
I'LL GIVE YOU THIS ONE INSTEAD.
see?
... ♡
um.
HOW DO YOU TIE A BOW AGAIN?

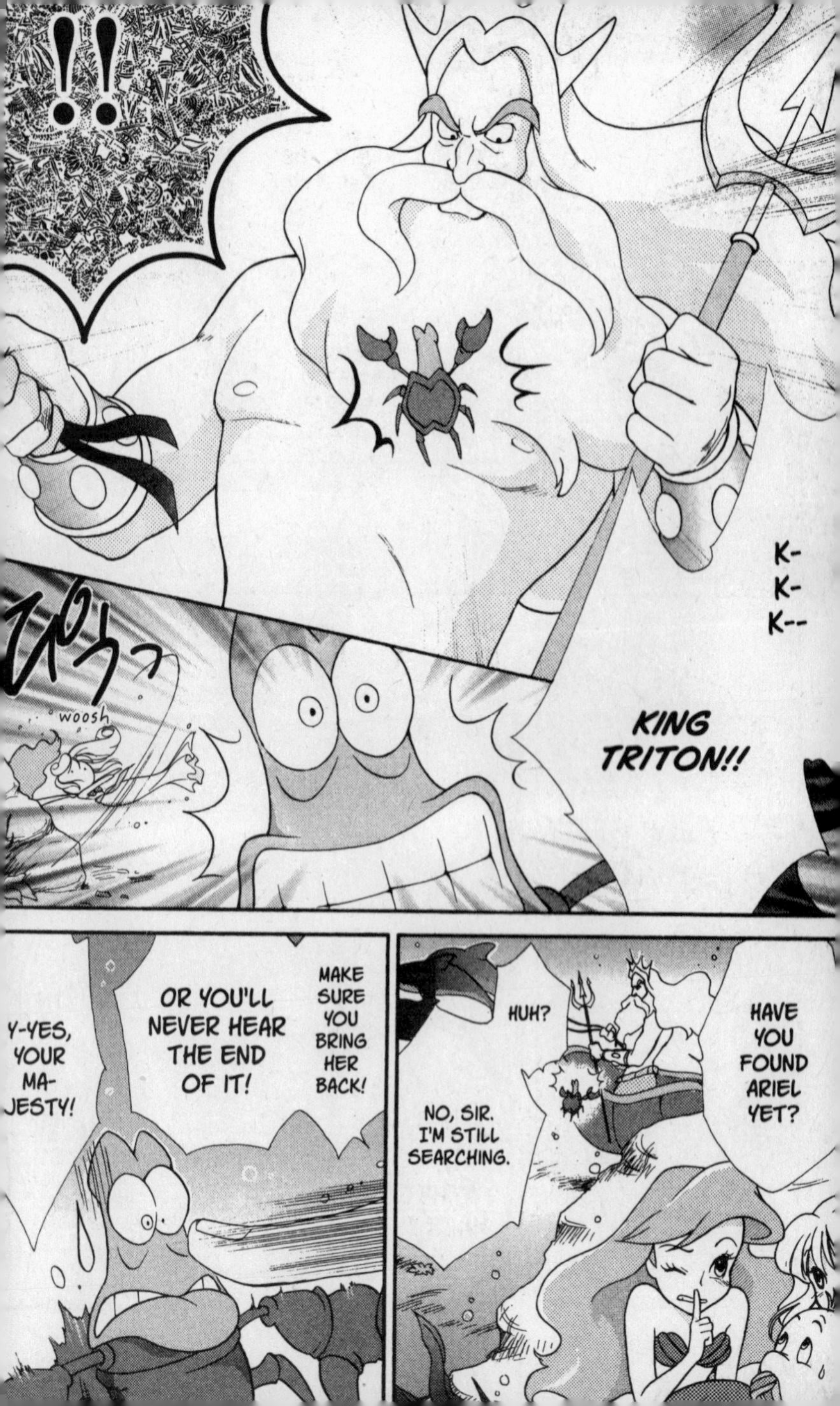
!!
K-
K-
K--
KING TRITON!!
woosh
HAVE YOU FOUND ARIEL YET?
HUH?
NO, SIR. I'M STILL SEARCHING.
MAKE SURE YOU BRING HER BACK!
OR YOU'LL NEVER HEAR THE END OF IT!
Y-YES, YOUR MA-JESTY!

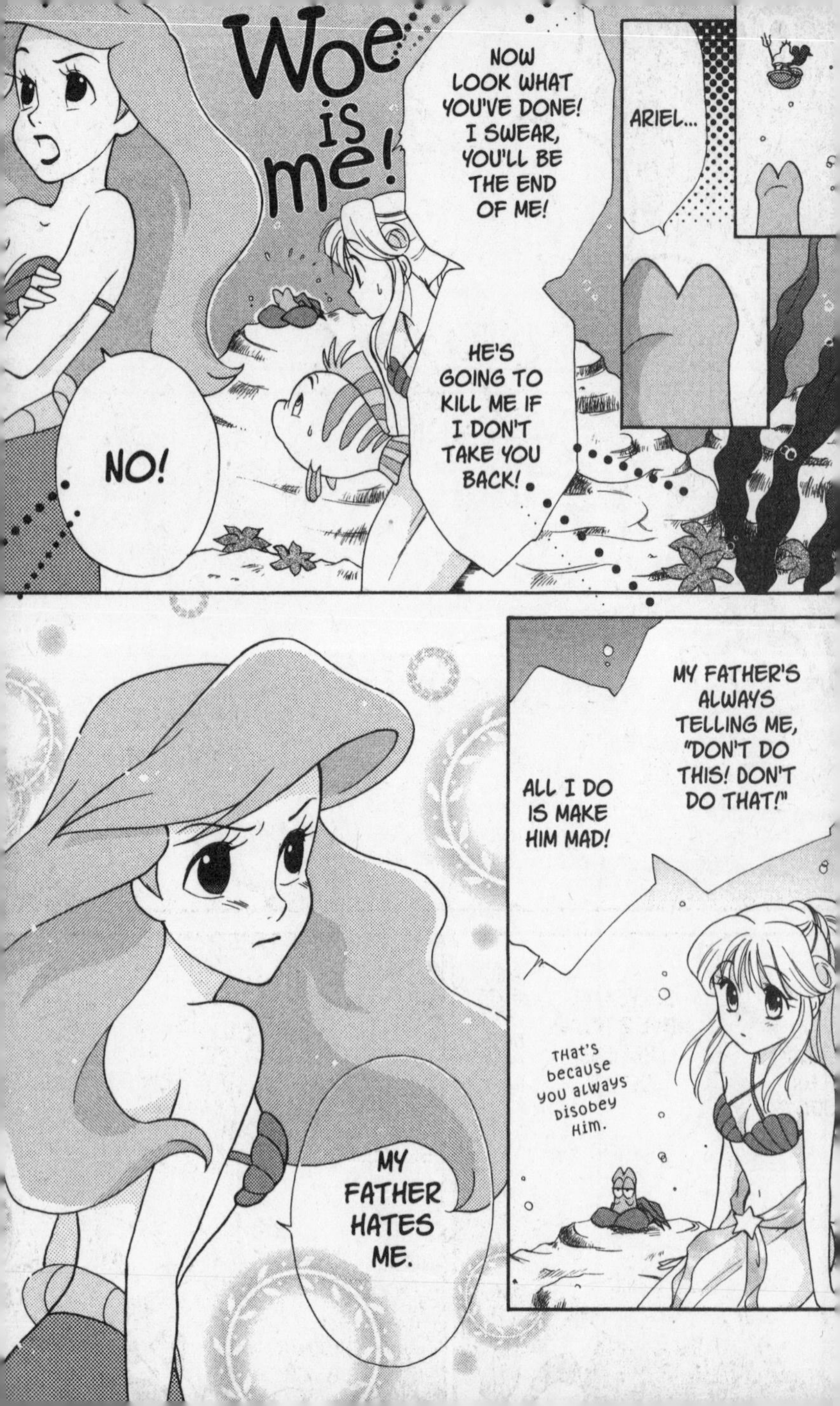
ARIEL...
NOW LOOK WHAT YOU'VE DONE! I SWEAR, YOU'LL BE THE END OF ME!
Woe is me!
HE'S GOING TO KILL ME IF I DON'T TAKE YOU BACK!
NO!
MY FATHER'S ALWAYS TELLING ME, "DON'T DO THIS! DON'T DO THAT!"
ALL I DO IS MAKE HIM MAD!
That's because you always disobey him.
MY FATHER HATES ME.

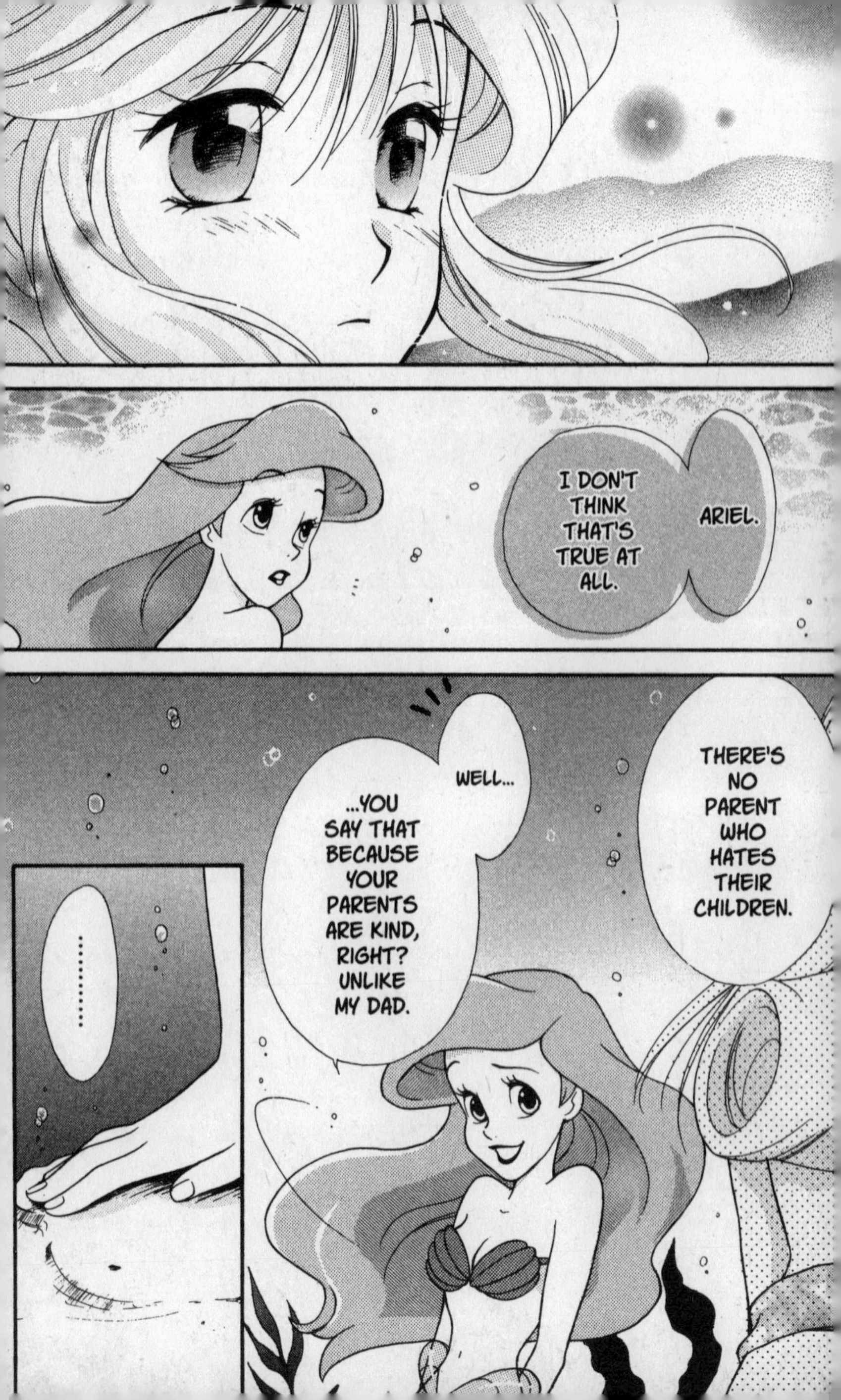
ARIEL.
I DON'T THINK THAT'S TRUE AT ALL.
THERE'S NO PARENT WHO HATES THEIR CHILDREN.
WELL...
...YOU SAY THAT BECAUSE YOUR PARENTS ARE KIND, RIGHT? UNLIKE MY DAD.
....

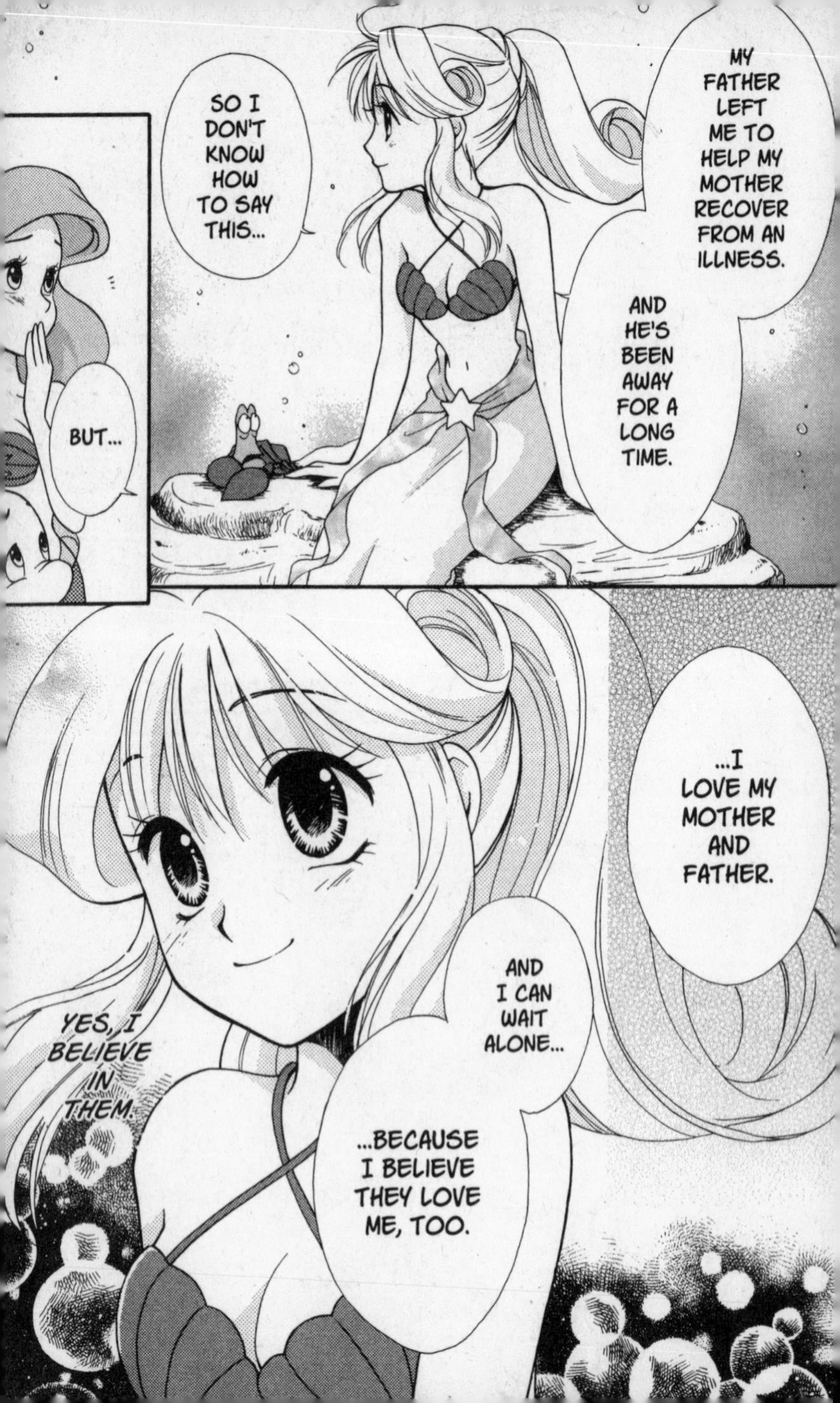

MY FATHER LEFT ME TO HELP MY MOTHER RECOVER FROM AN ILLNESS.
AND HE'S BEEN AWAY FOR A LONG TIME.
SO I DON'T KNOW HOW TO SAY THIS...
BUT...
...I LOVE MY MOTHER AND FATHER.
AND I CAN WAIT ALONE...
...BECAUSE I BELIEVE THEY LOVE ME, TOO.
YES, I BELIEVE IN THEM.

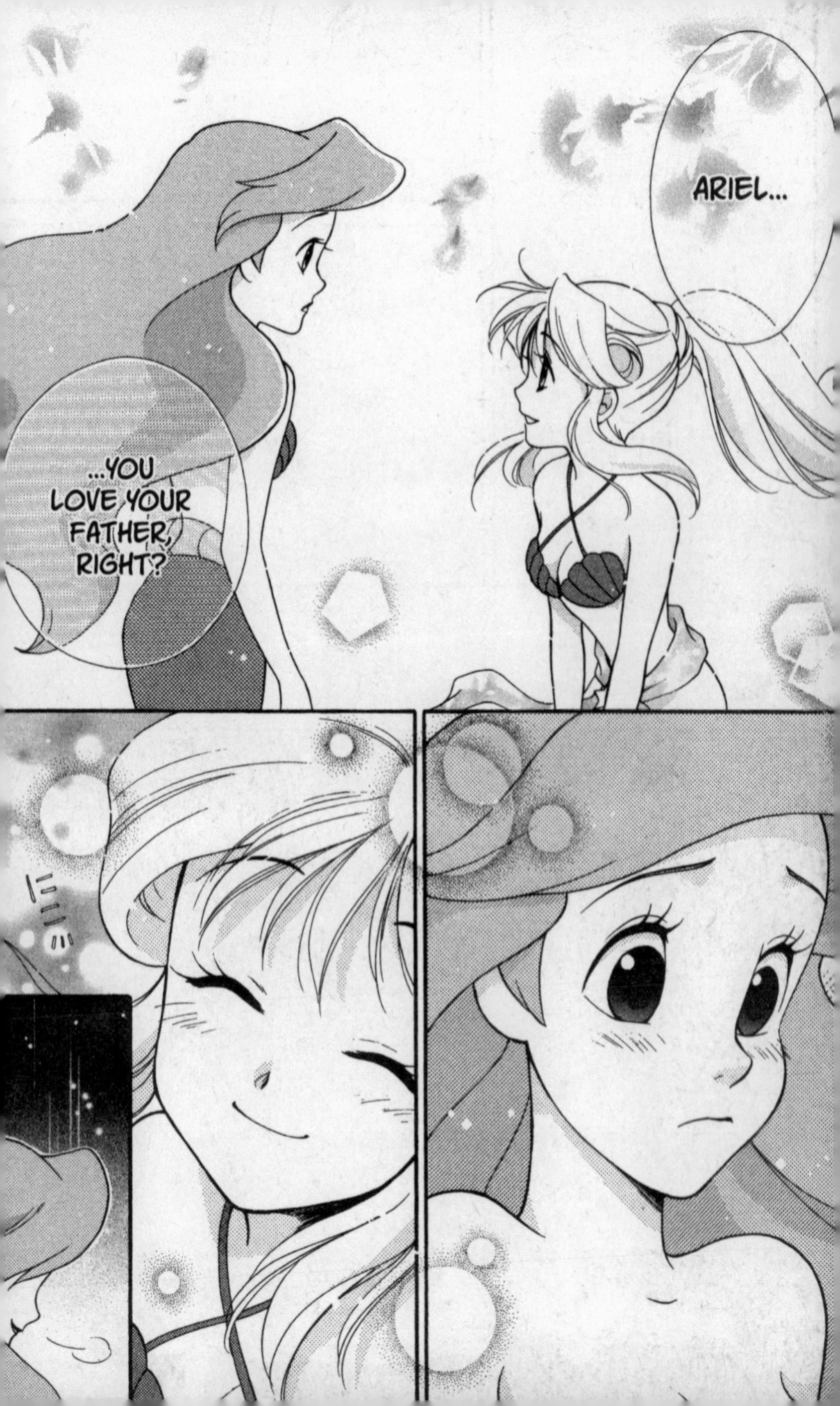
ARIEL...
...YOU LOVE YOUR FATHER, RIGHT?

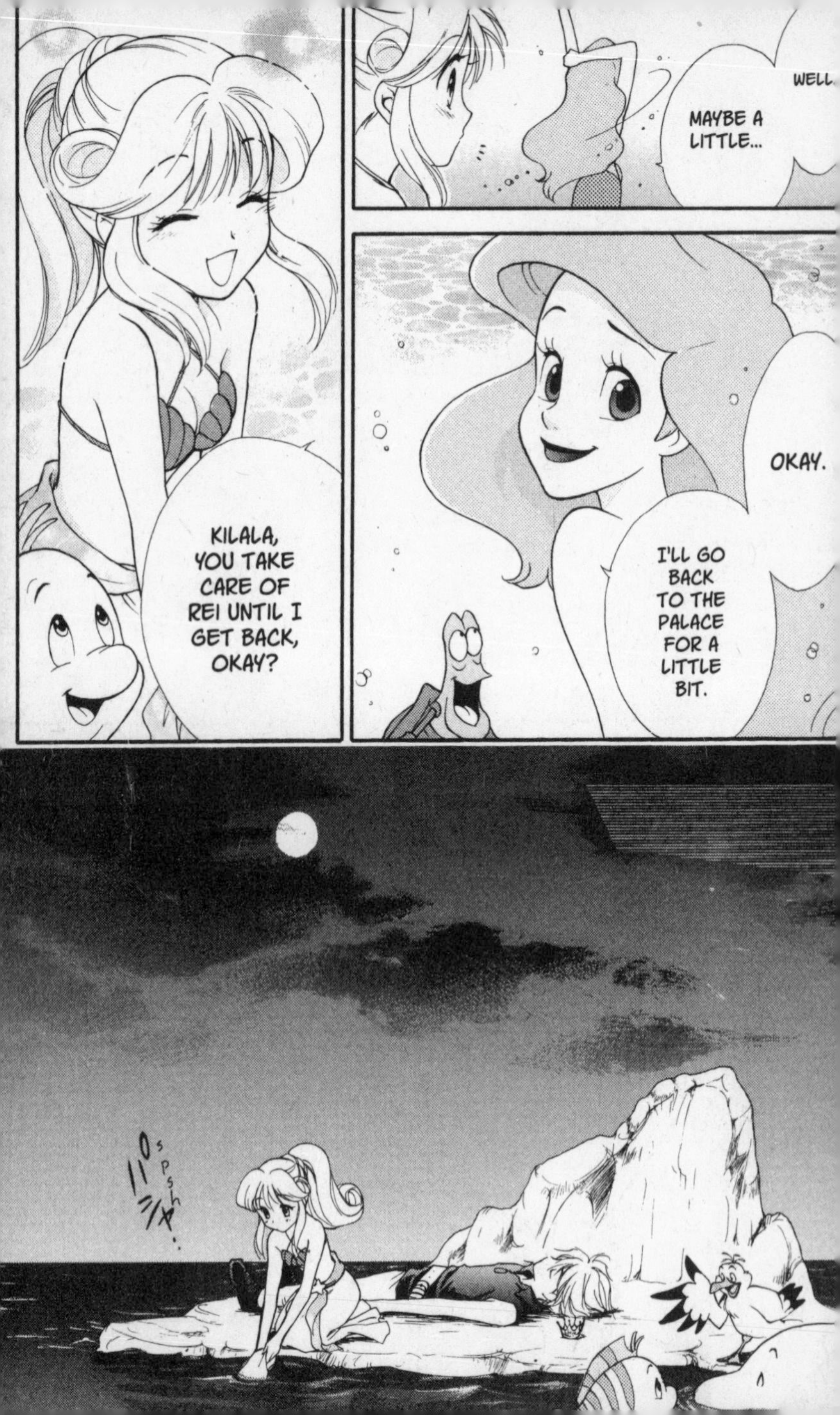
WELL. MAYBE A LITTLE...
OKAY.
I'LL GO BACK TO THE PALACE FOR A LITTLE BIT.
KILALA, YOU TAKE CARE OF REI UNTIL I GET BACK, OKAY?
SPSH

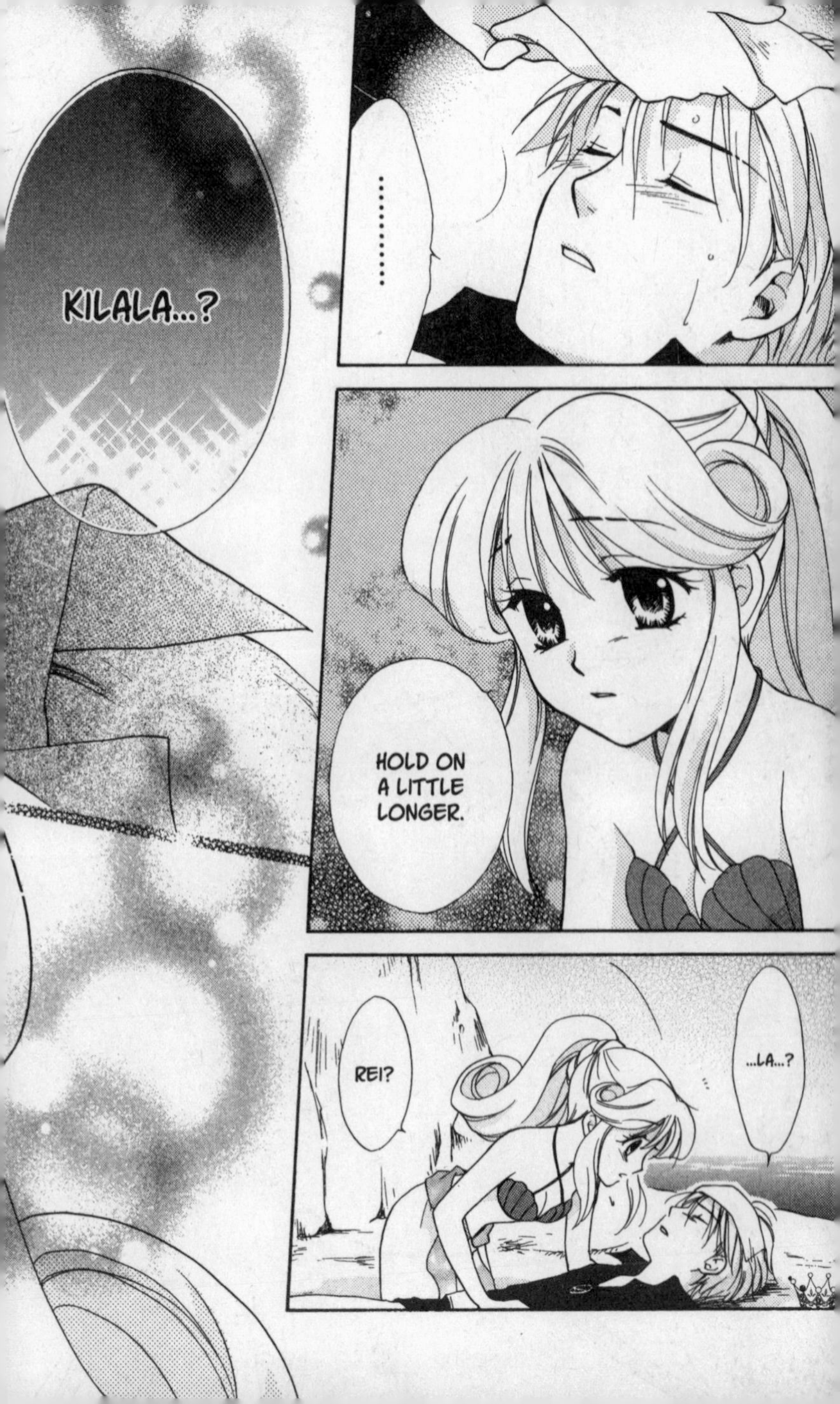
……
HOLD ON A LITTLE LONGER.
...LA...?
REI?
KILALA...?

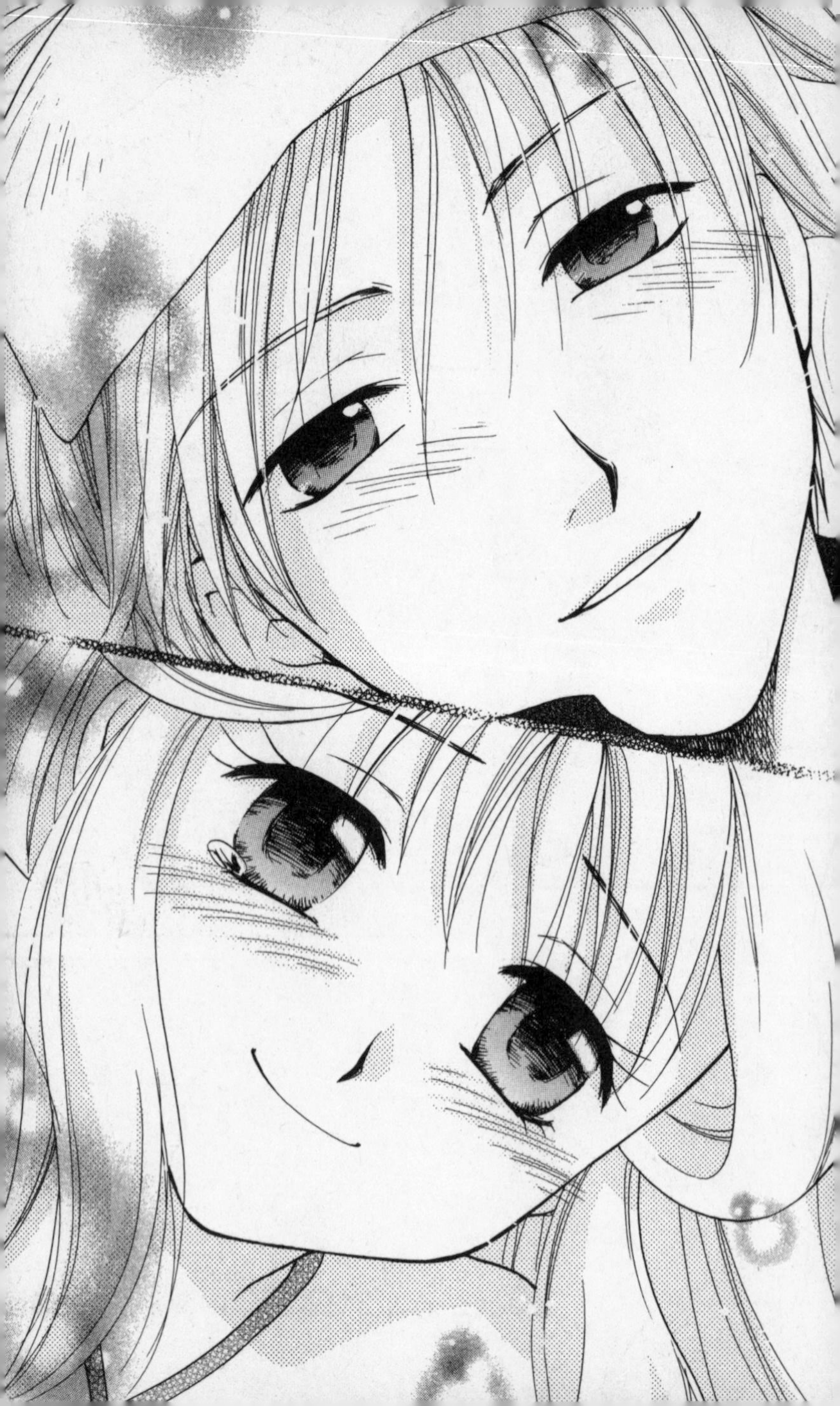

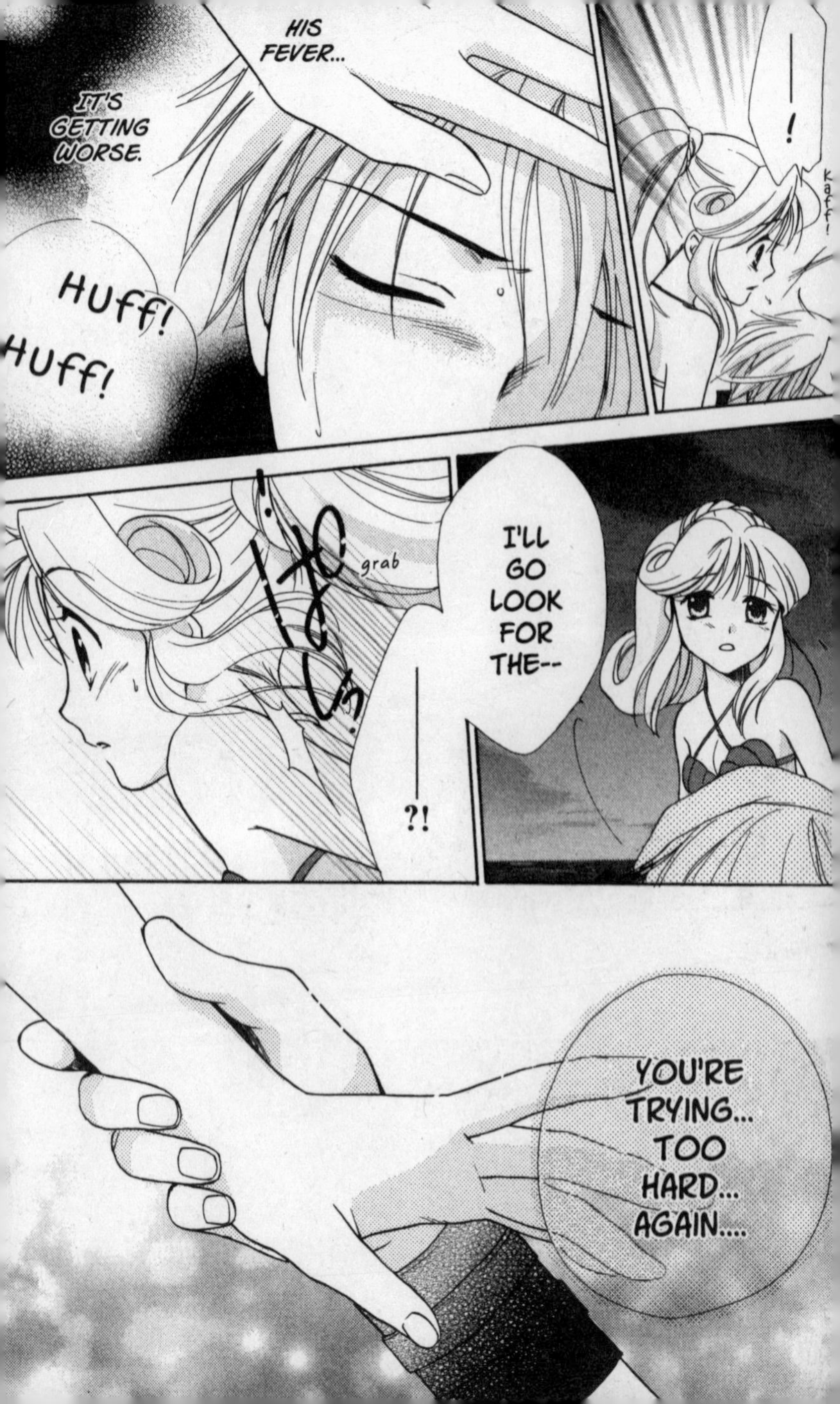
!
kaff!
HIS FEVER...
IT'S GETTING WORSE.
HUFF! HUFF!
I'LL GO LOOK FOR THE--
grab
—?!
YOU'RE TRYING... TOO HARD... AGAIN....

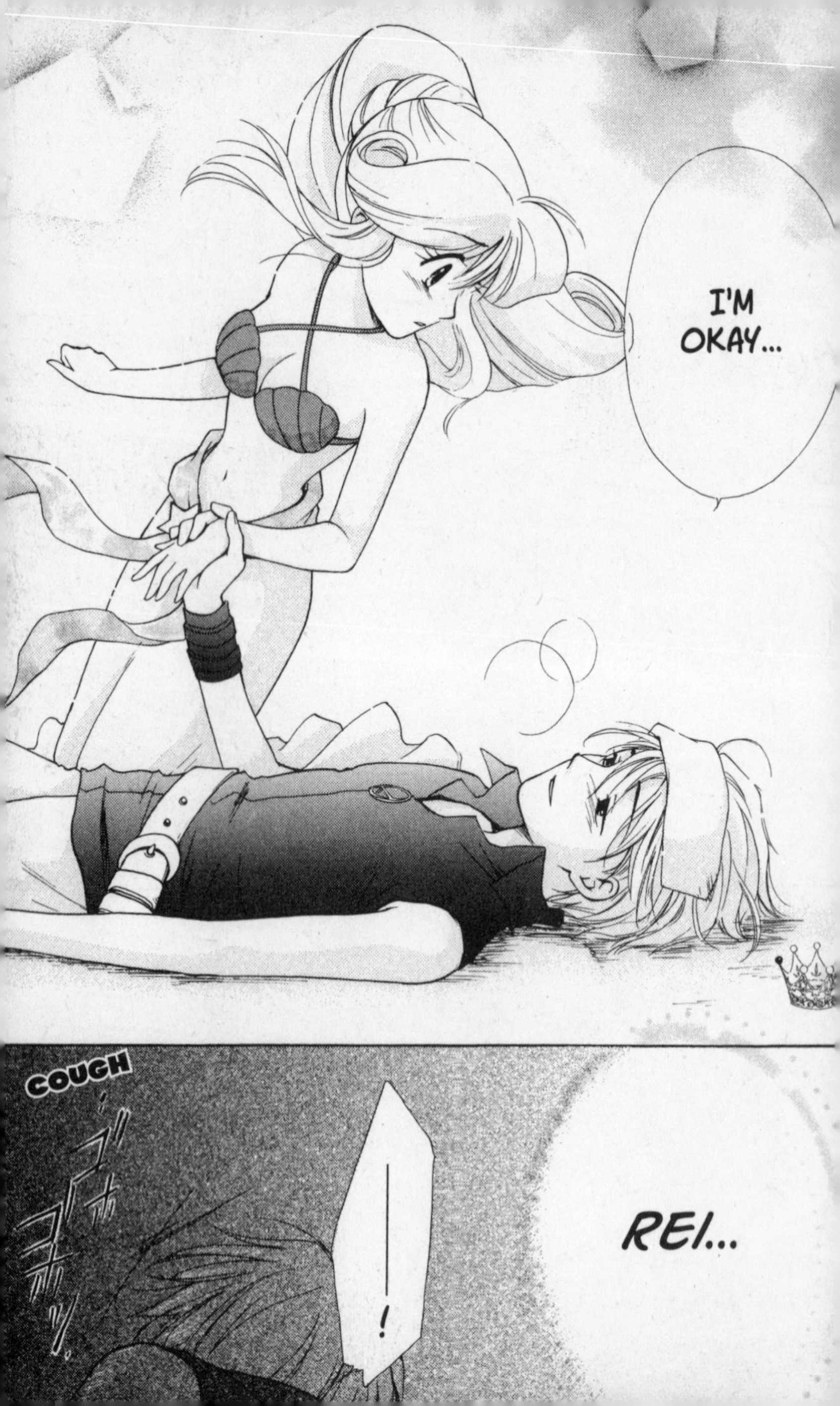
I'M OKAY...
REI...
—!
COUGH

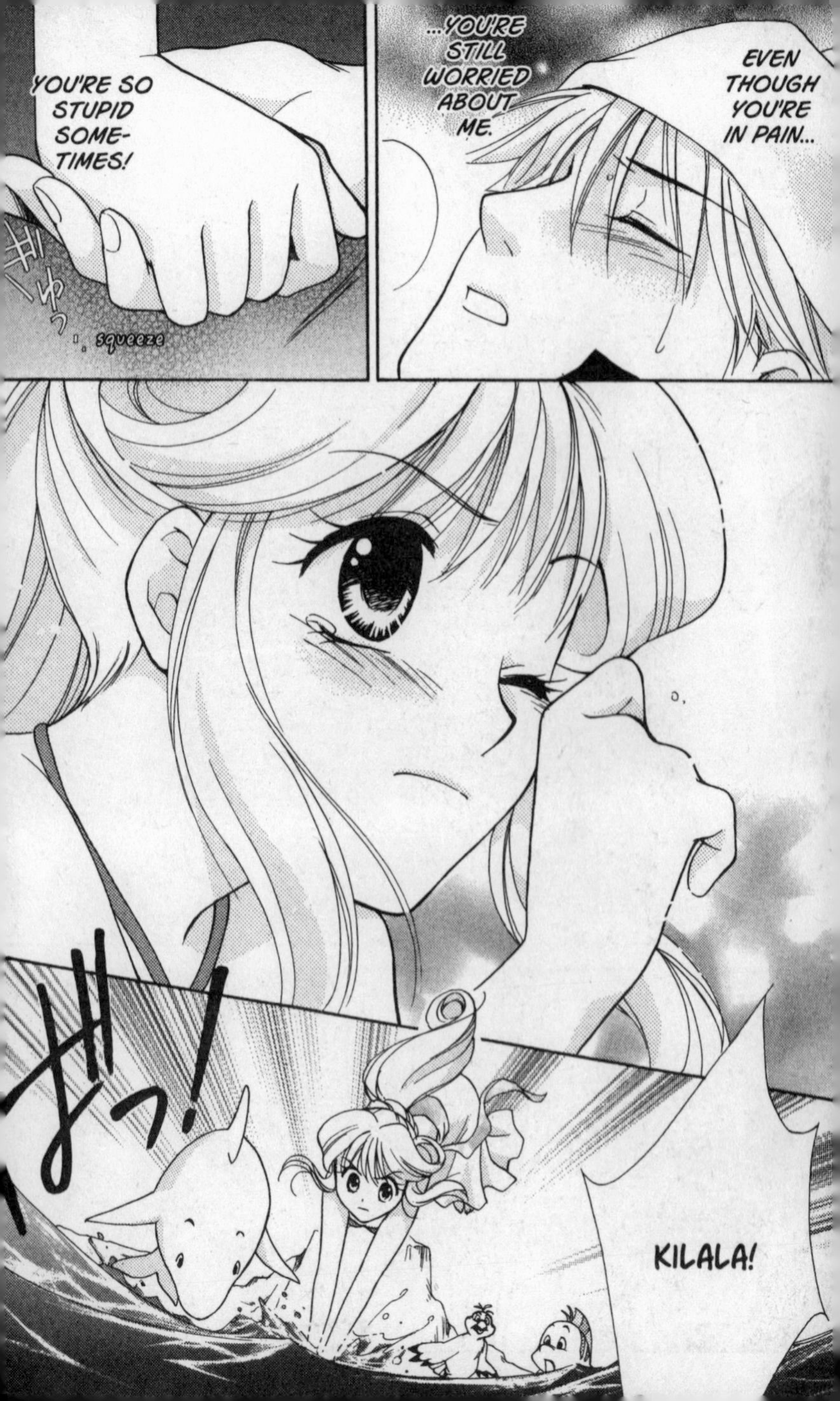
EVEN THOUGH YOU'RE IN PAIN...
...YOU'RE STILL WORRIED ABOUT ME.
YOU'RE SO STUPID SOME-TIMES!
squeeze
KILALA!

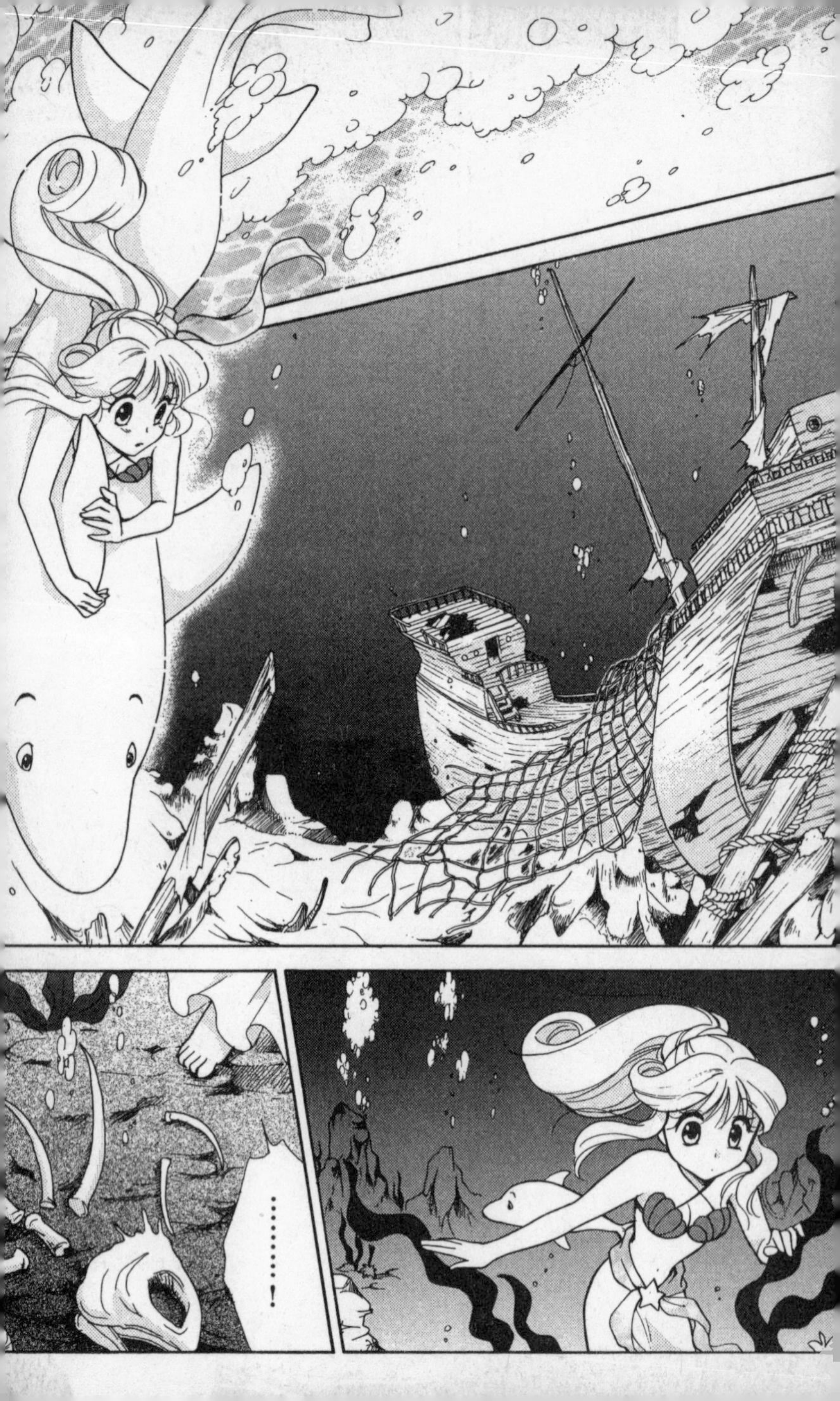
……!

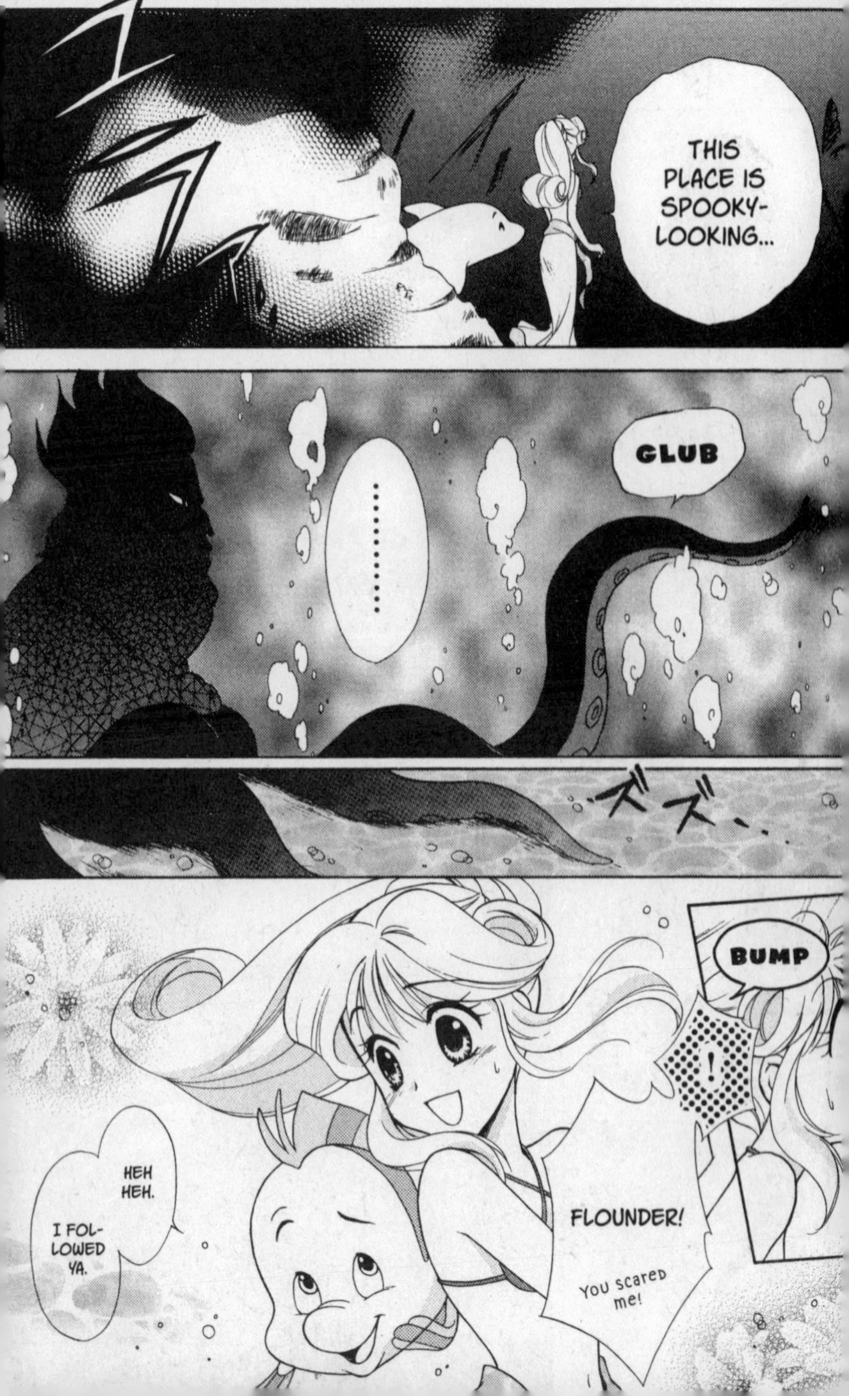
THIS PLACE IS SPOOKY-LOOKING...
GLUB
......
ズズ…
BUMP
!
FLOUNDER!
You scared me!
HEH HEH.
I FOL-LOWED YA.

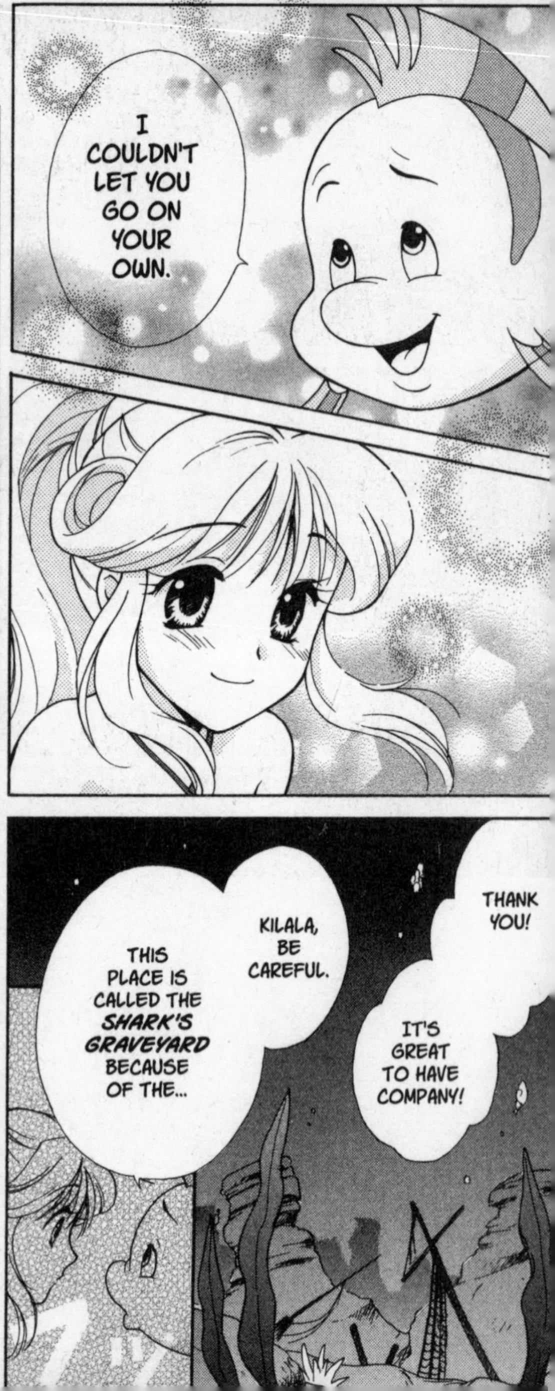
I COULDN'T LET YOU GO ON YOUR OWN.
THANK YOU!
IT'S GREAT TO HAVE COMPANY!
KILALA, BE CAREFUL.
THIS PLACE IS CALLED THE *SHARK'S GRAVEYARD* BECAUSE OF THE...

A WORD FROM TIPPE 4

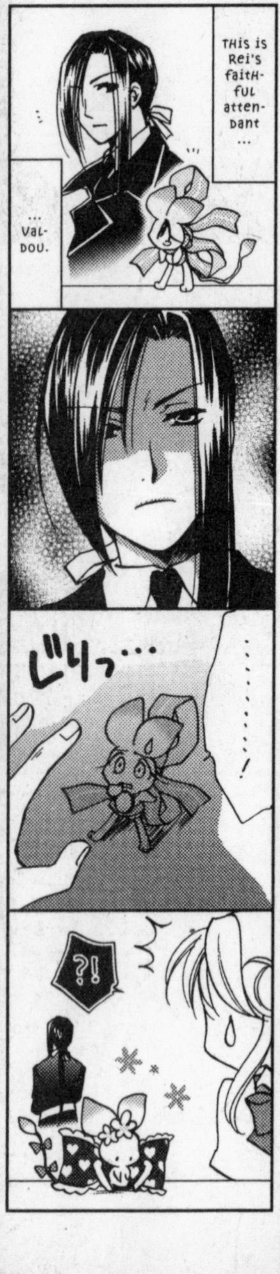
This is Rei's faith-ful atten-dant...
... Val-dou.
...
じりっ…
.........!
?!

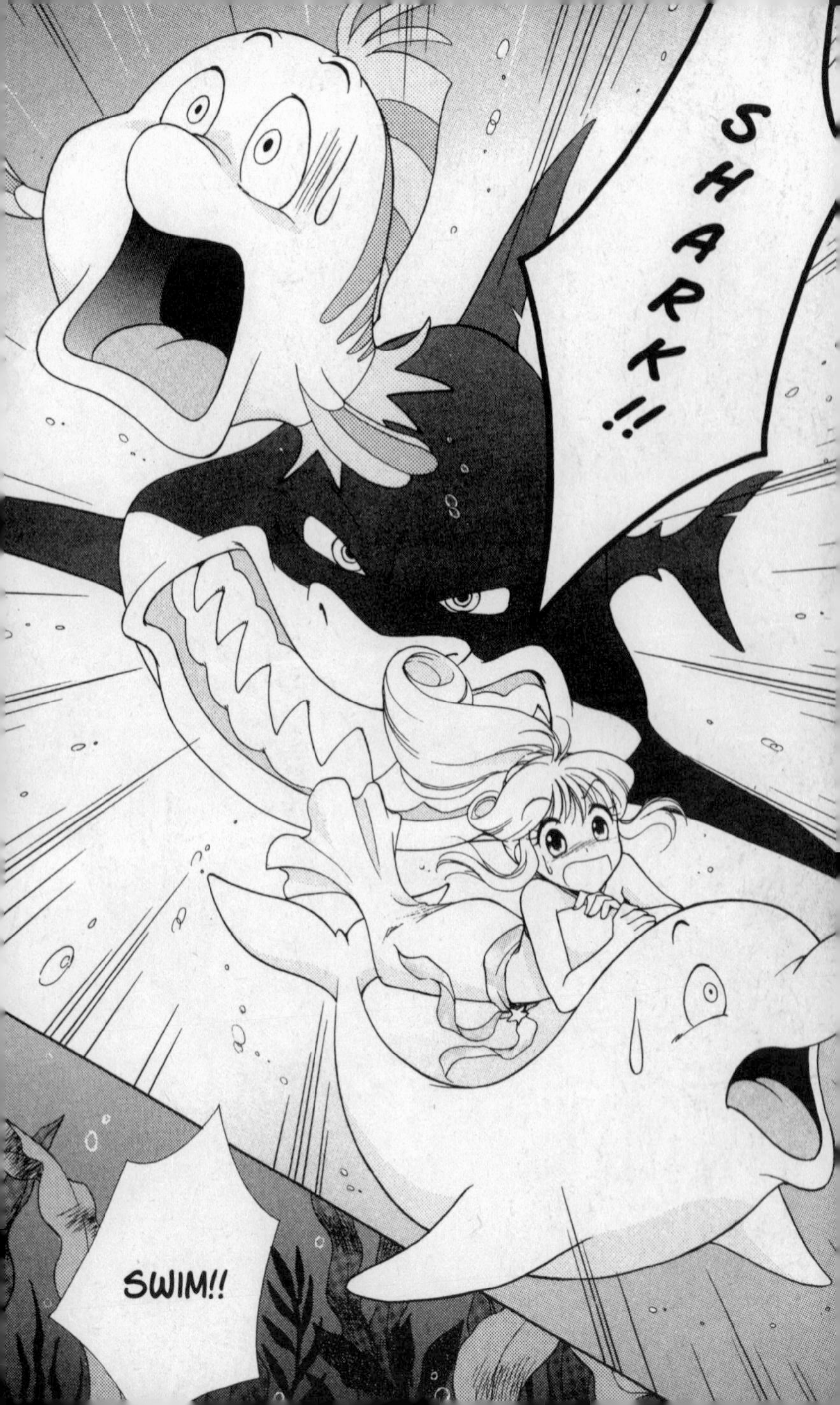
SHARK!!
SWIM!!

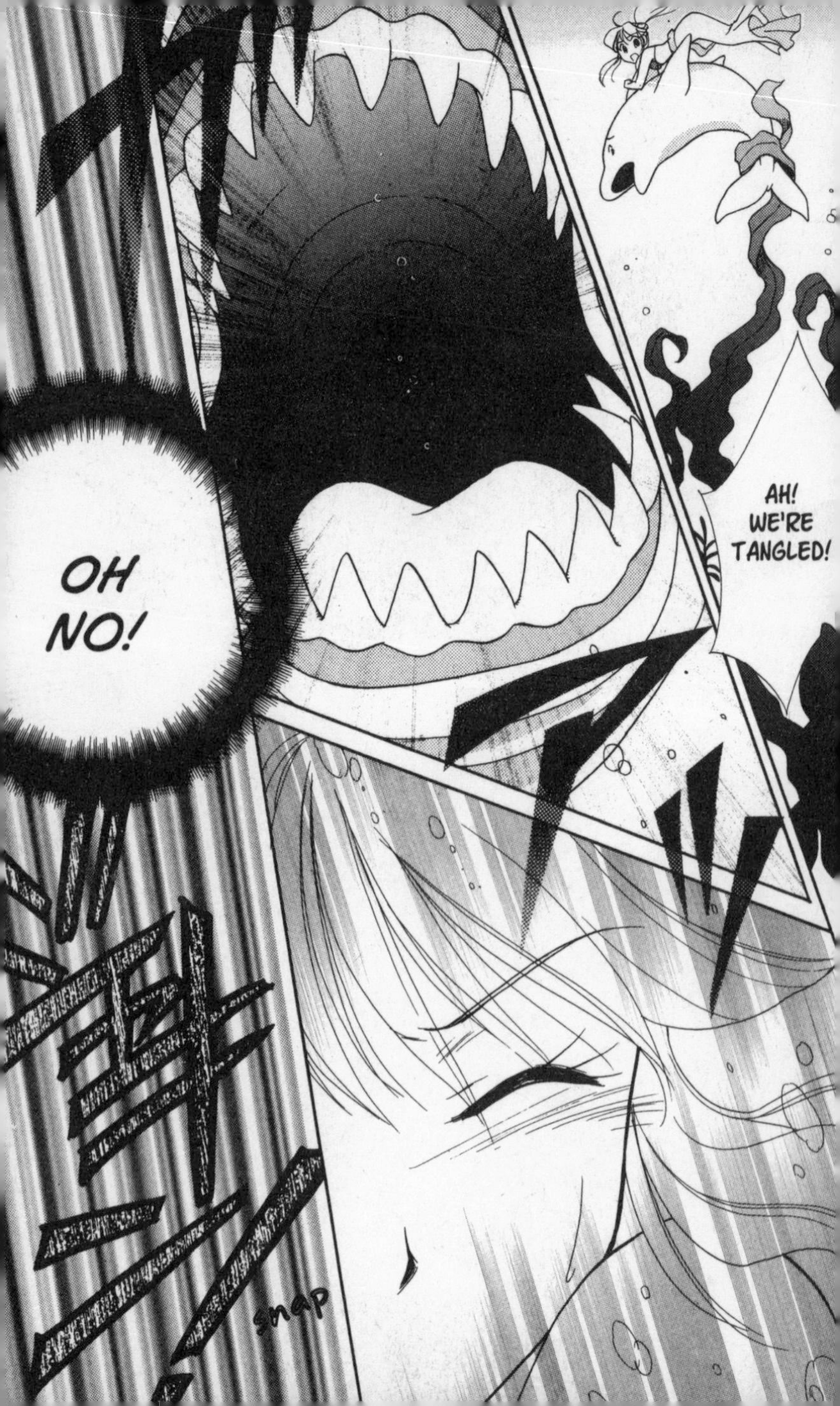
AH! WE'RE TANGLED!
OH NO!
snap

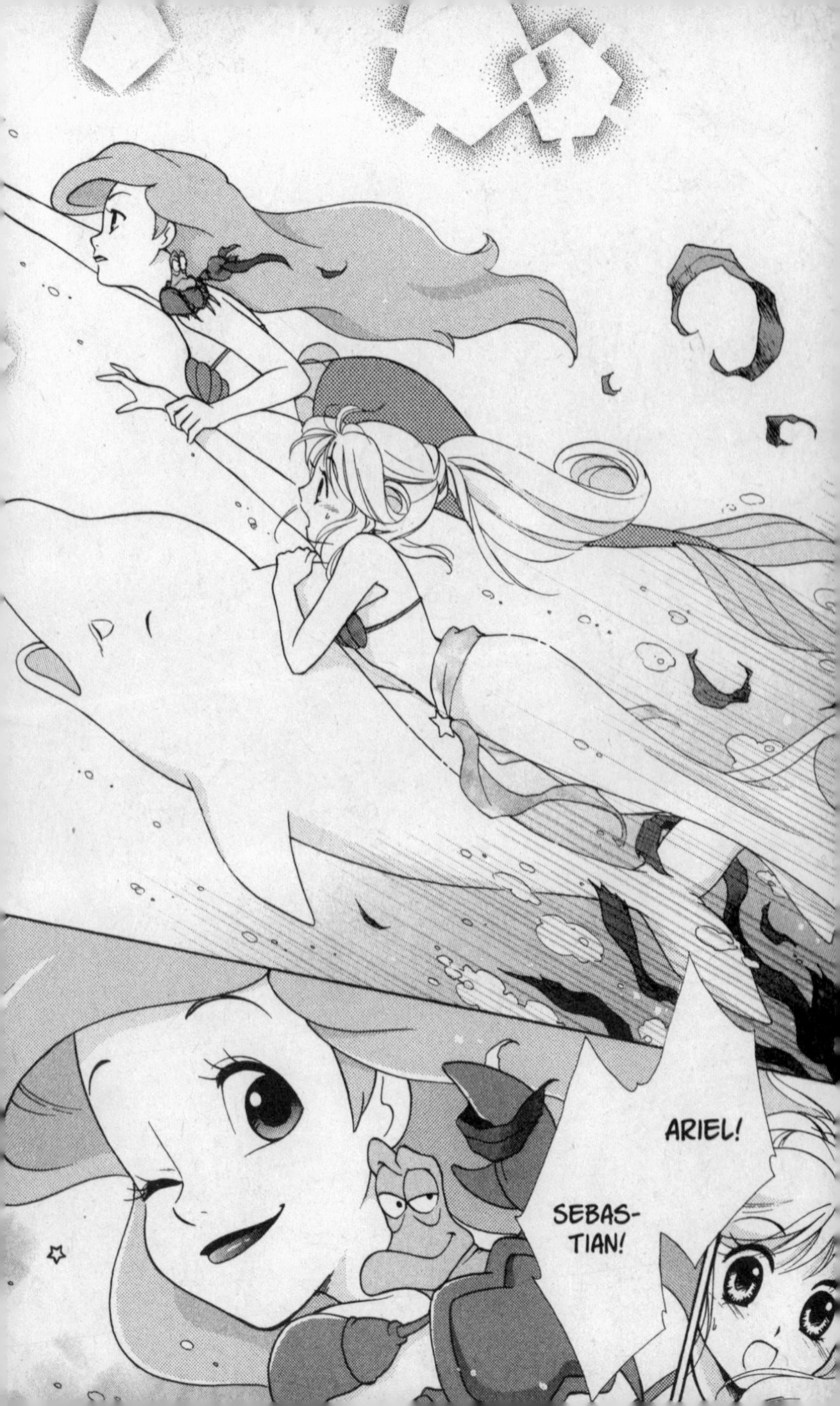
ARIEL!
SEBAS-TIAN!

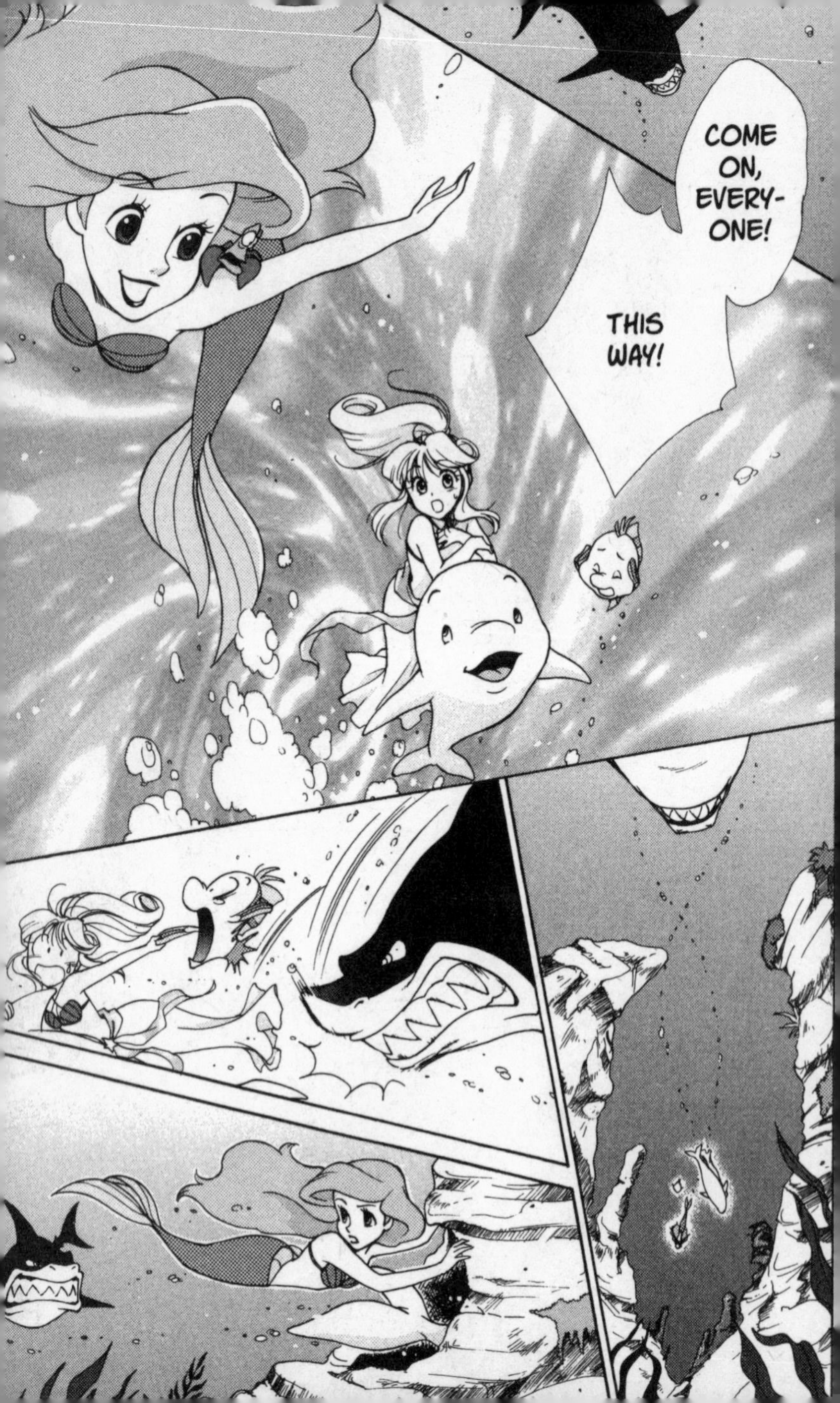
COME ON, EVERY-ONE!
THIS WAY!

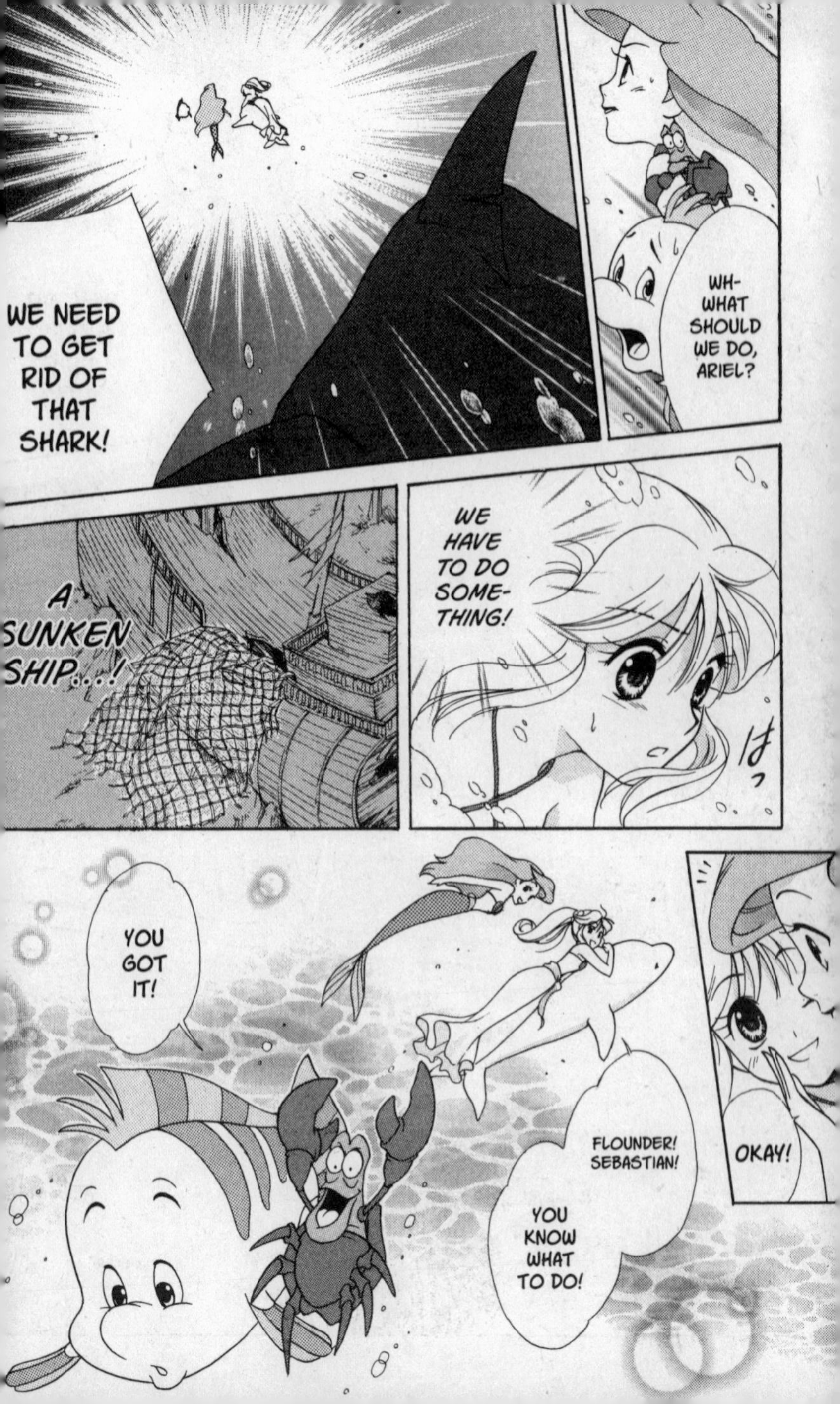
WH-WHAT SHOULD WE DO, ARIEL?
WE NEED TO GET RID OF THAT SHARK!
WE HAVE TO DO SOME-THING!
はっ
A SUNKEN SHIP...!
OKAY!
FLOUNDER! SEBASTIAN!
YOU KNOW WHAT TO DO!
YOU GOT IT!

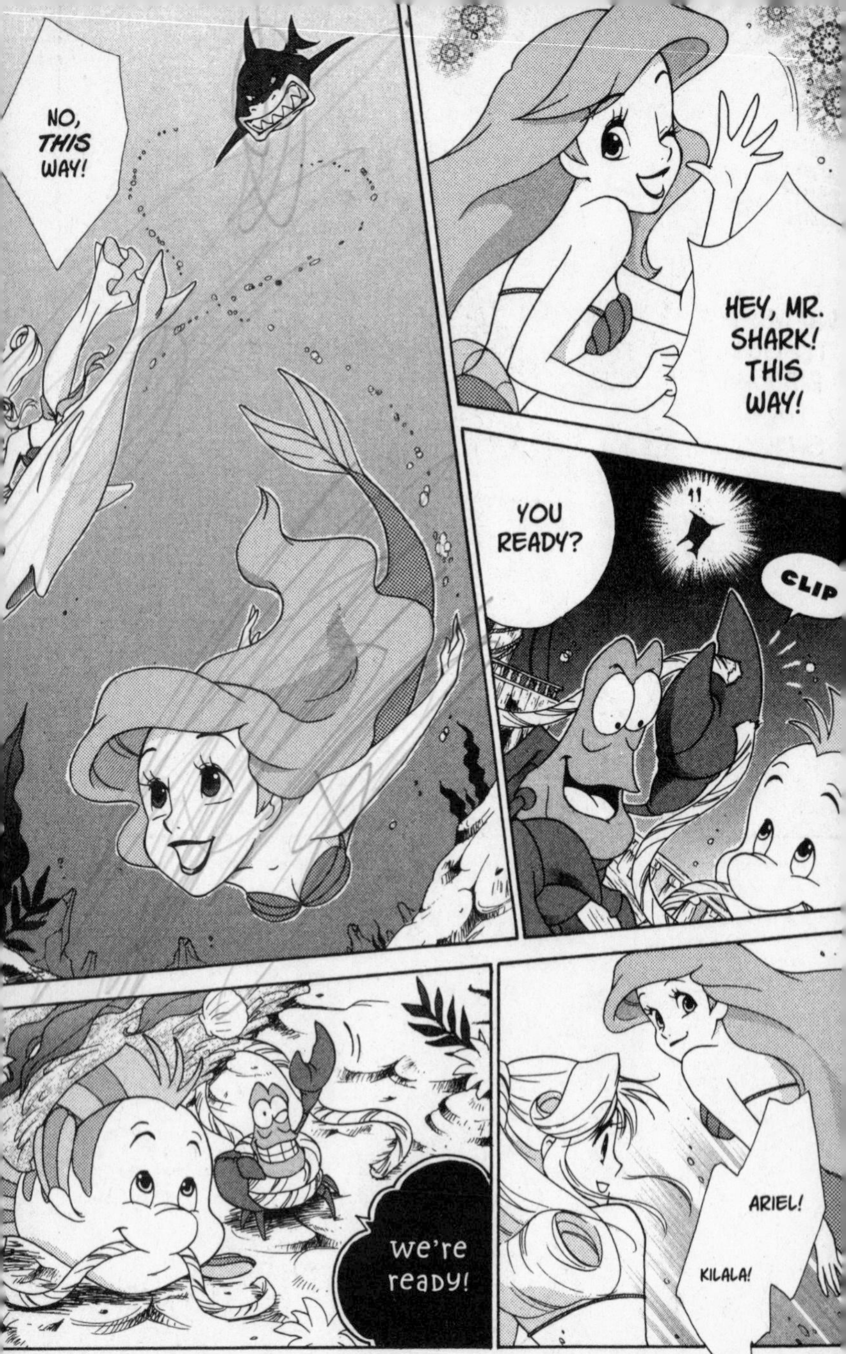

HEY, MR. SHARK! THIS WAY!
YOU READY?
CLIP
NO, THIS WAY!
ARIEL!
KILALA!
we're ready!

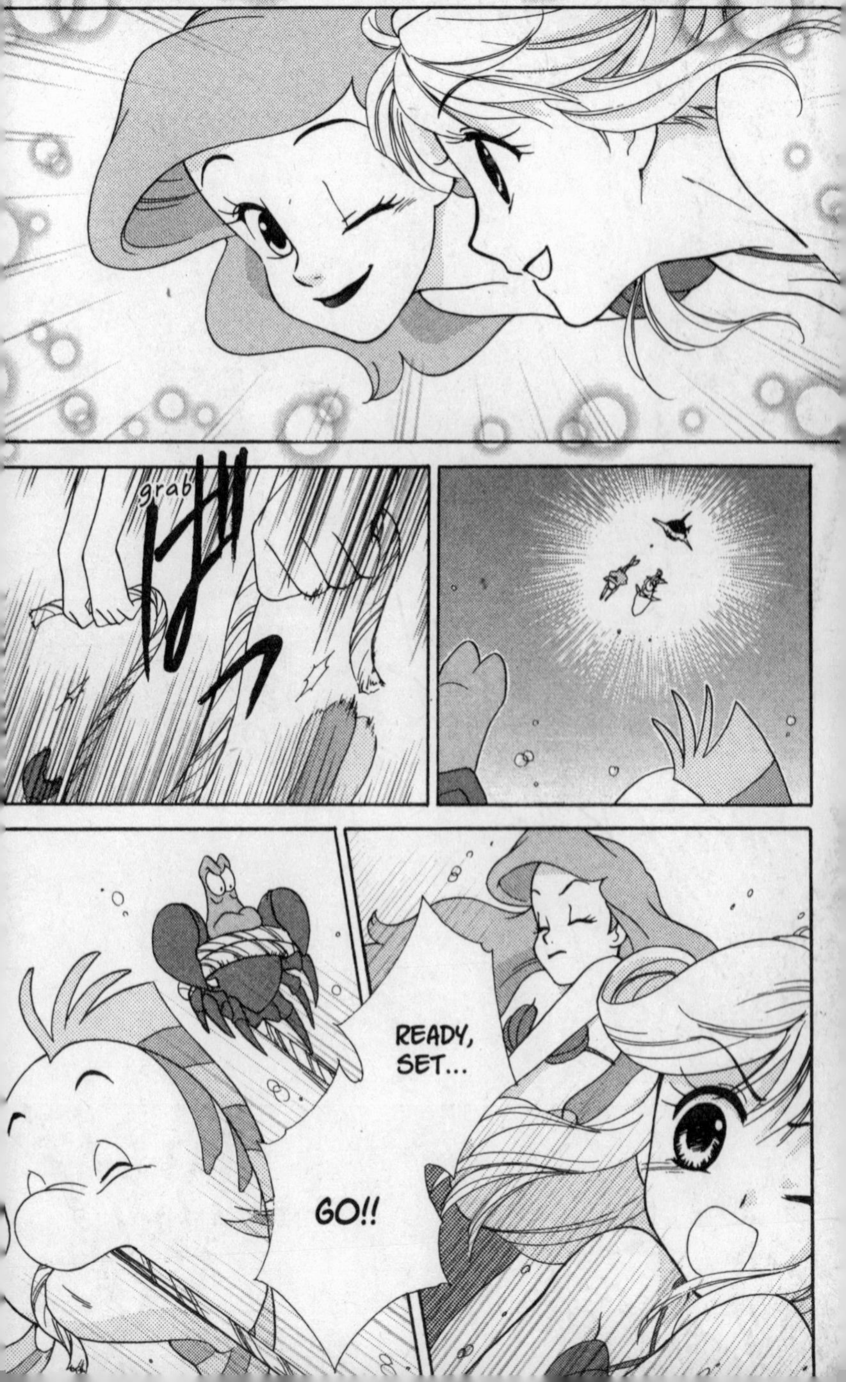
grab
READY, SET...
GO!!

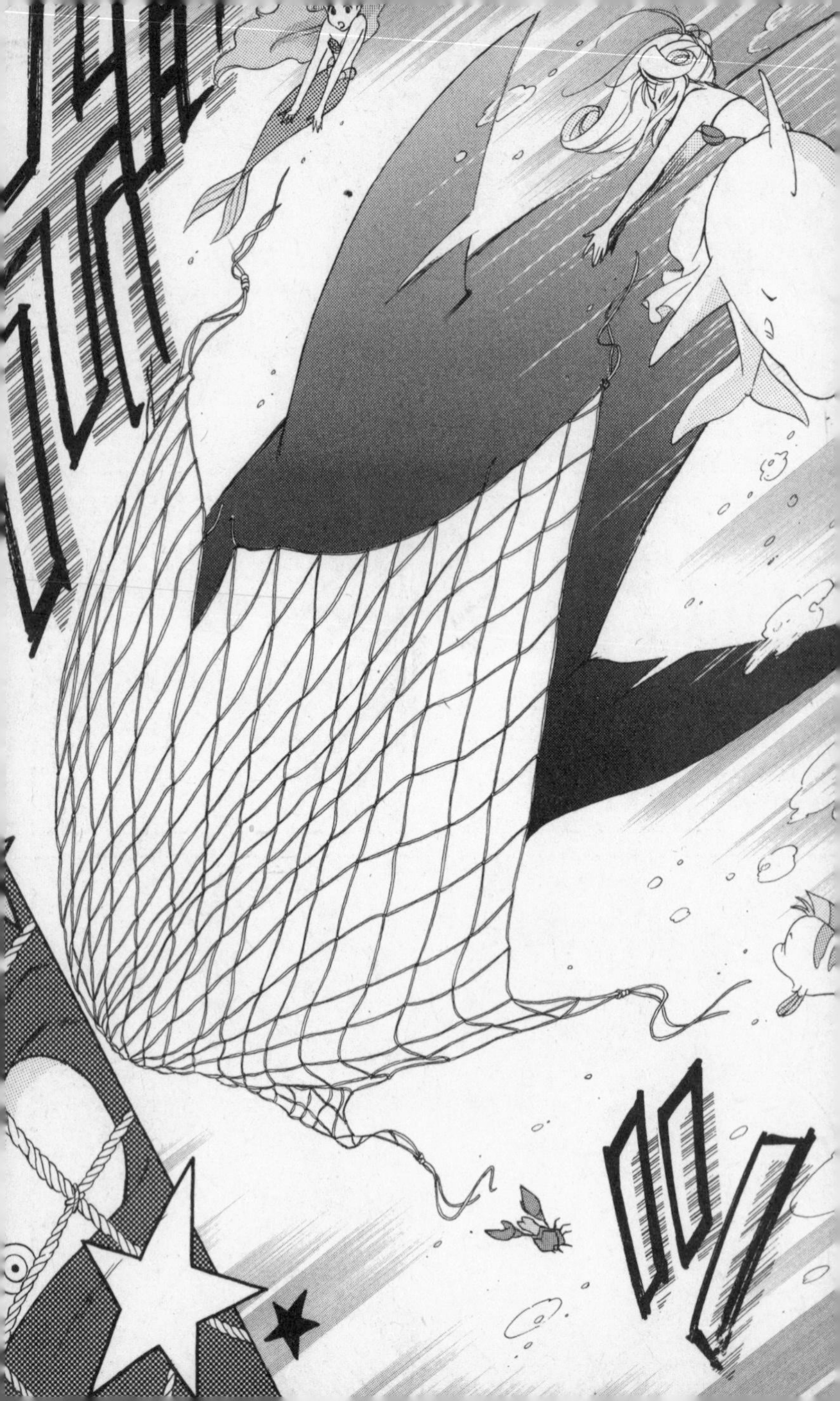

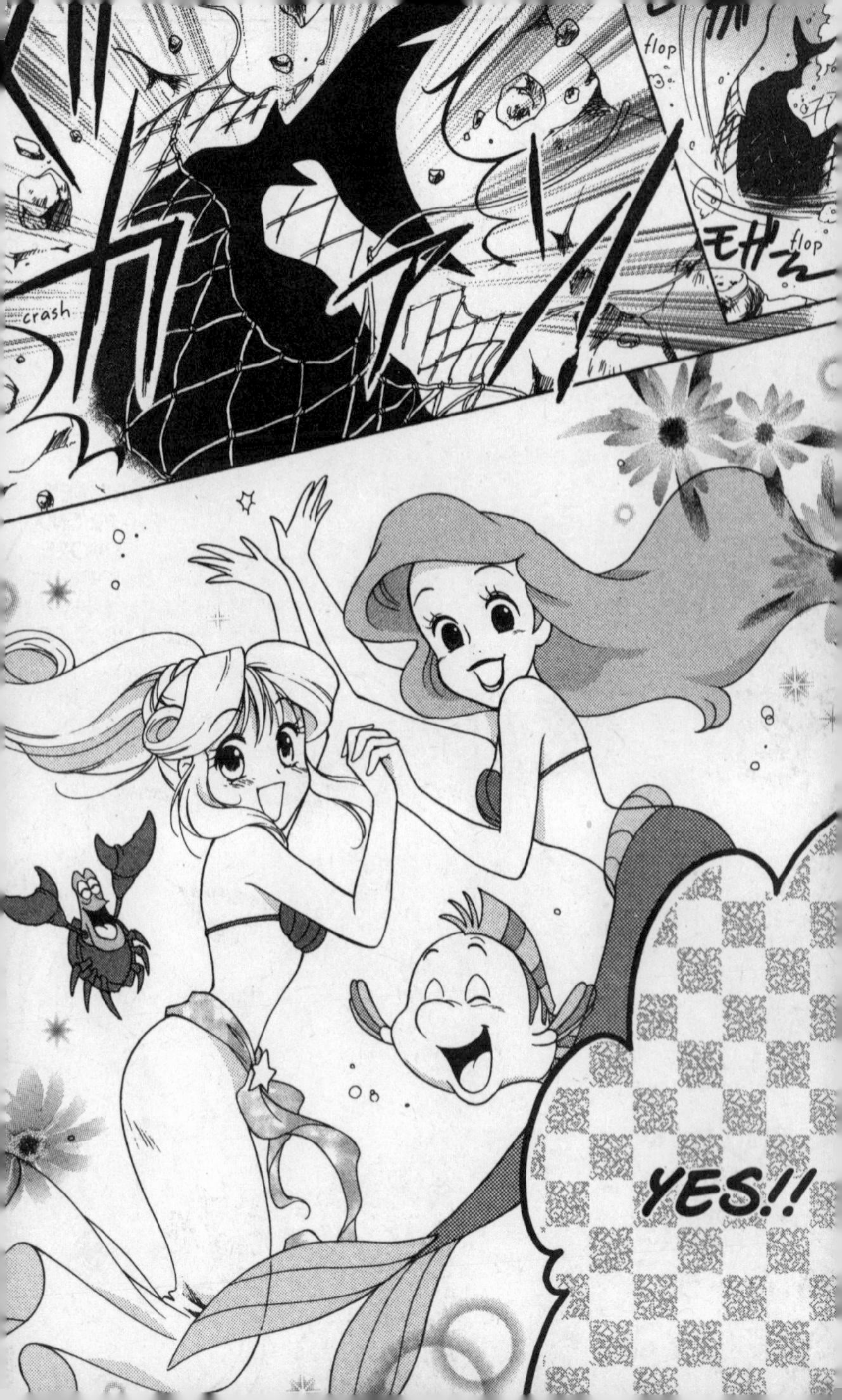
flop
モガーん
flop
crash
YES!!

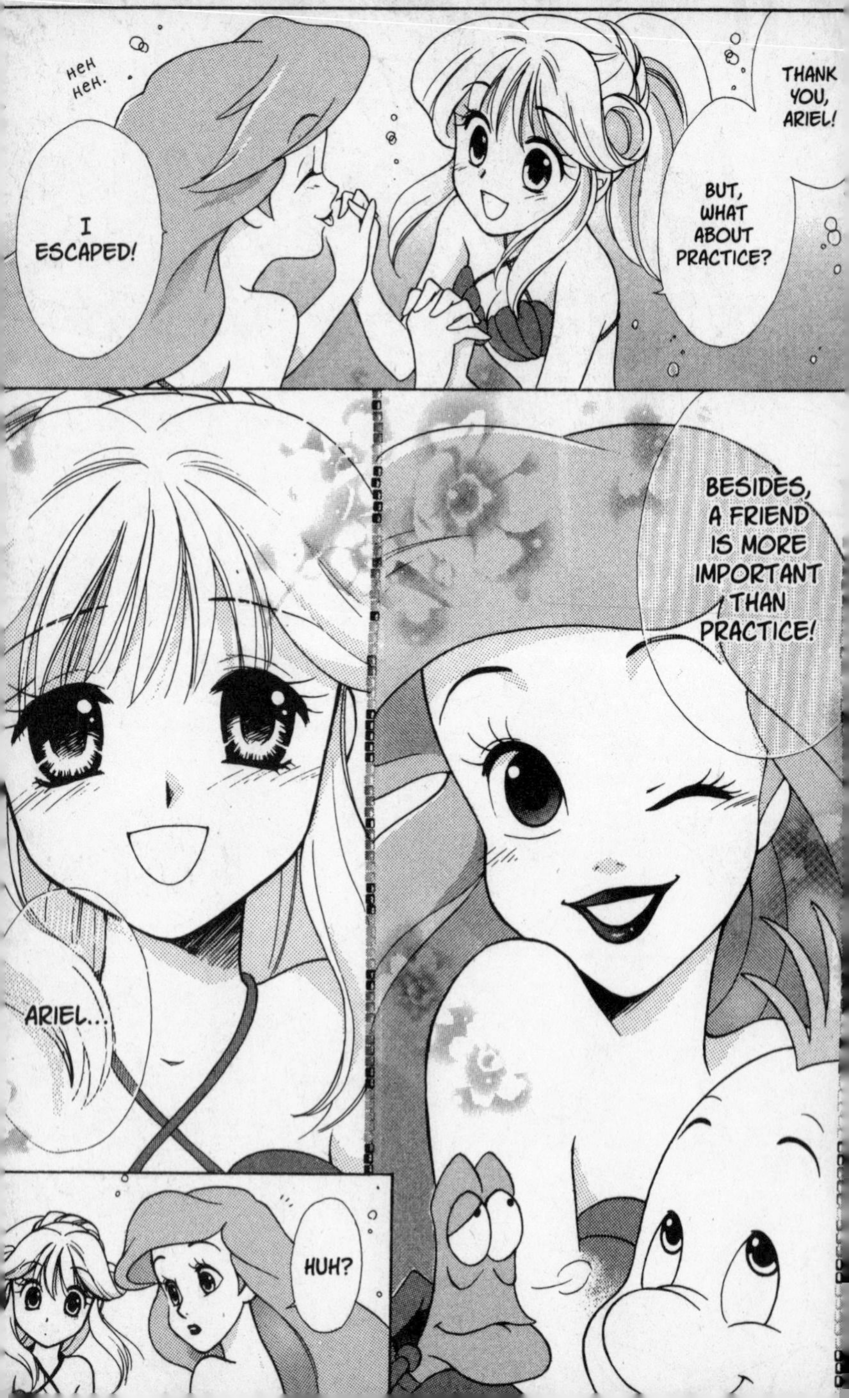
THANK YOU, ARIEL!
BUT, WHAT ABOUT PRACTICE?
HEH HEH.
I ESCAPED!
BESIDES, A FRIEND IS MORE IMPORTANT THAN PRACTICE!
ARIEL...
HUH?

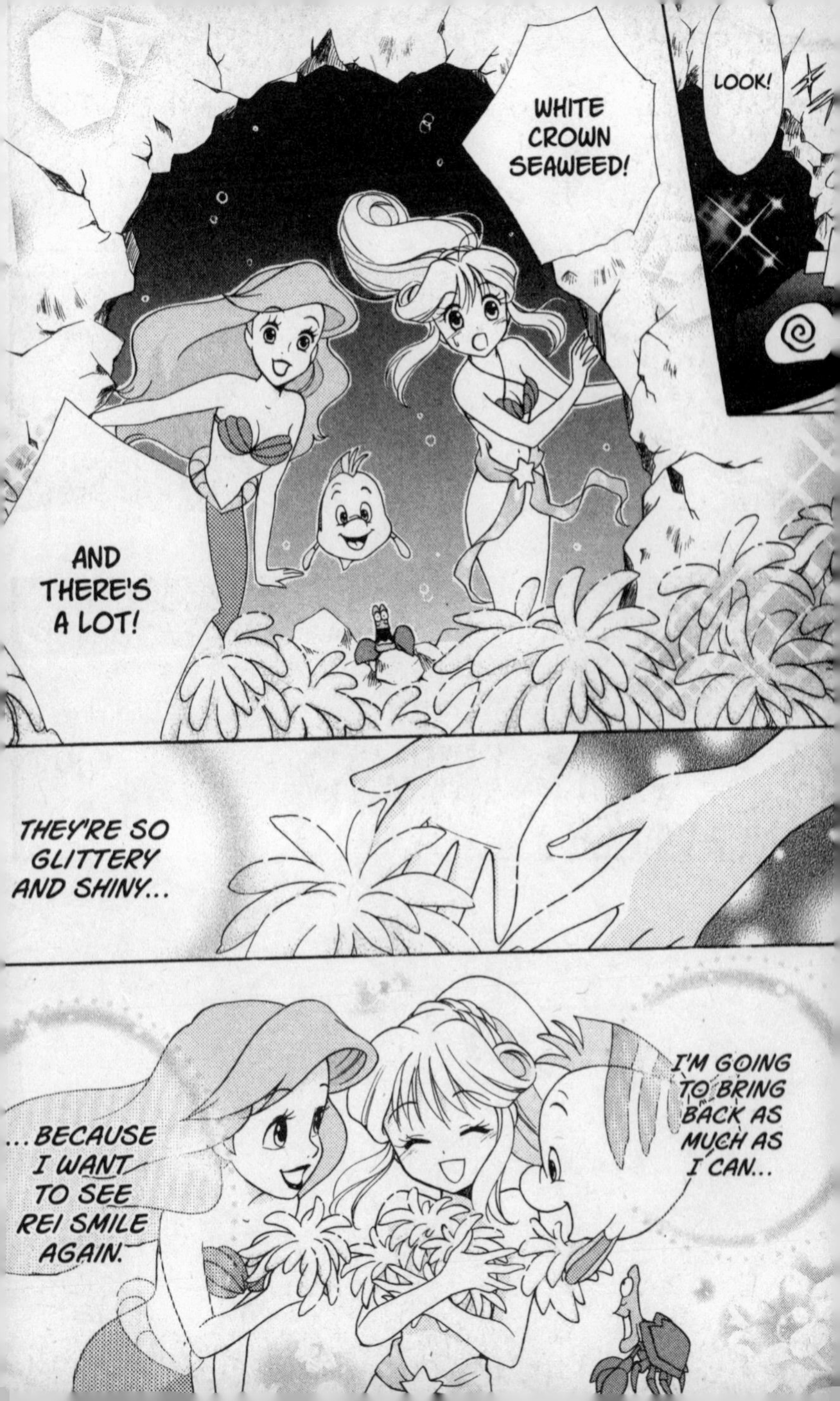
LOOK!
WHITE CROWN SEAWEED!
AND THERE'S A LOT!
THEY'RE SO GLITTERY AND SHINY...
I'M GOING TO BRING BACK AS MUCH AS I CAN...
...BECAUSE I WANT TO SEE REI SMILE AGAIN.

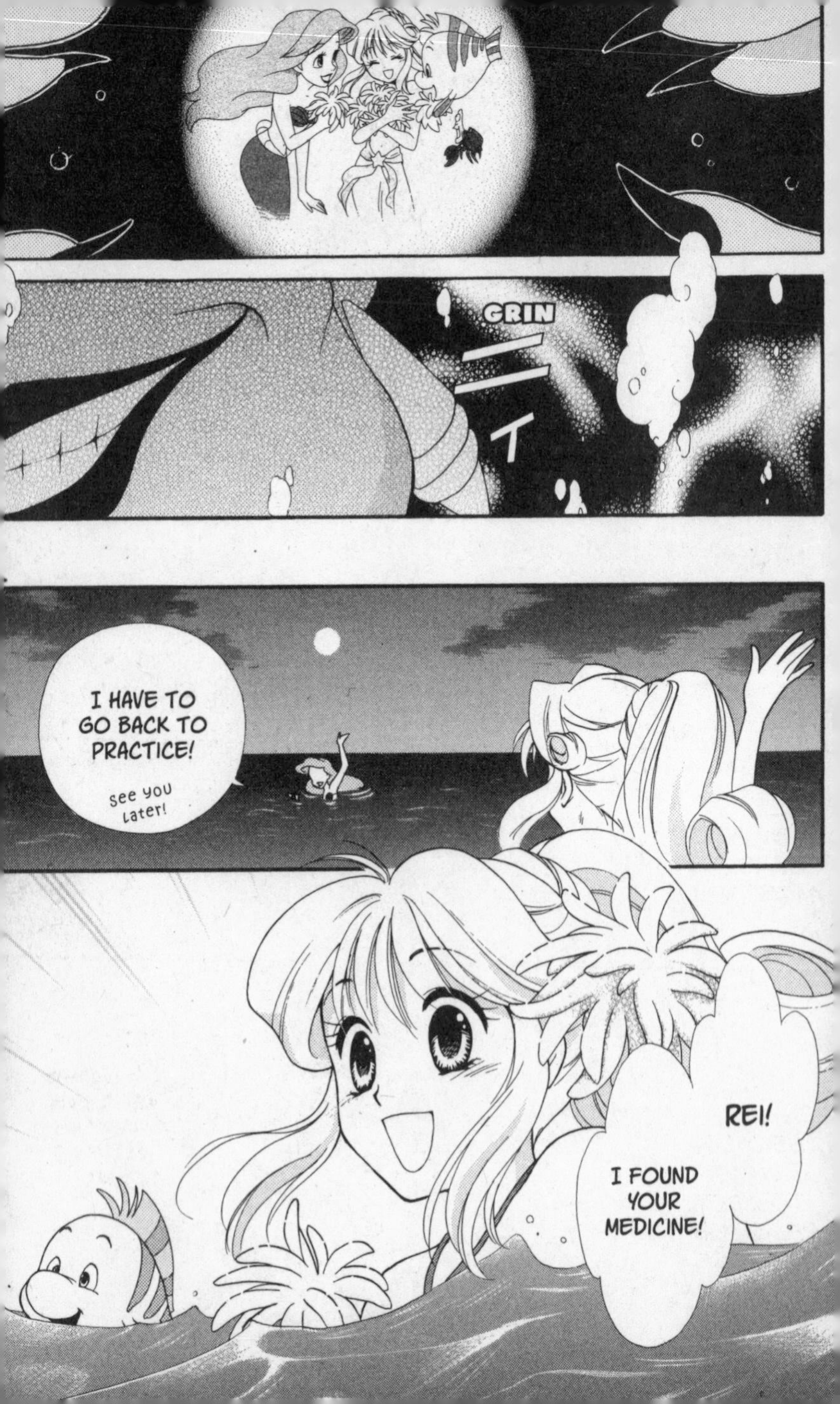
GRIN
I HAVE TO GO BACK TO PRACTICE!
see you later!
REI!
I FOUND YOUR MEDICINE!

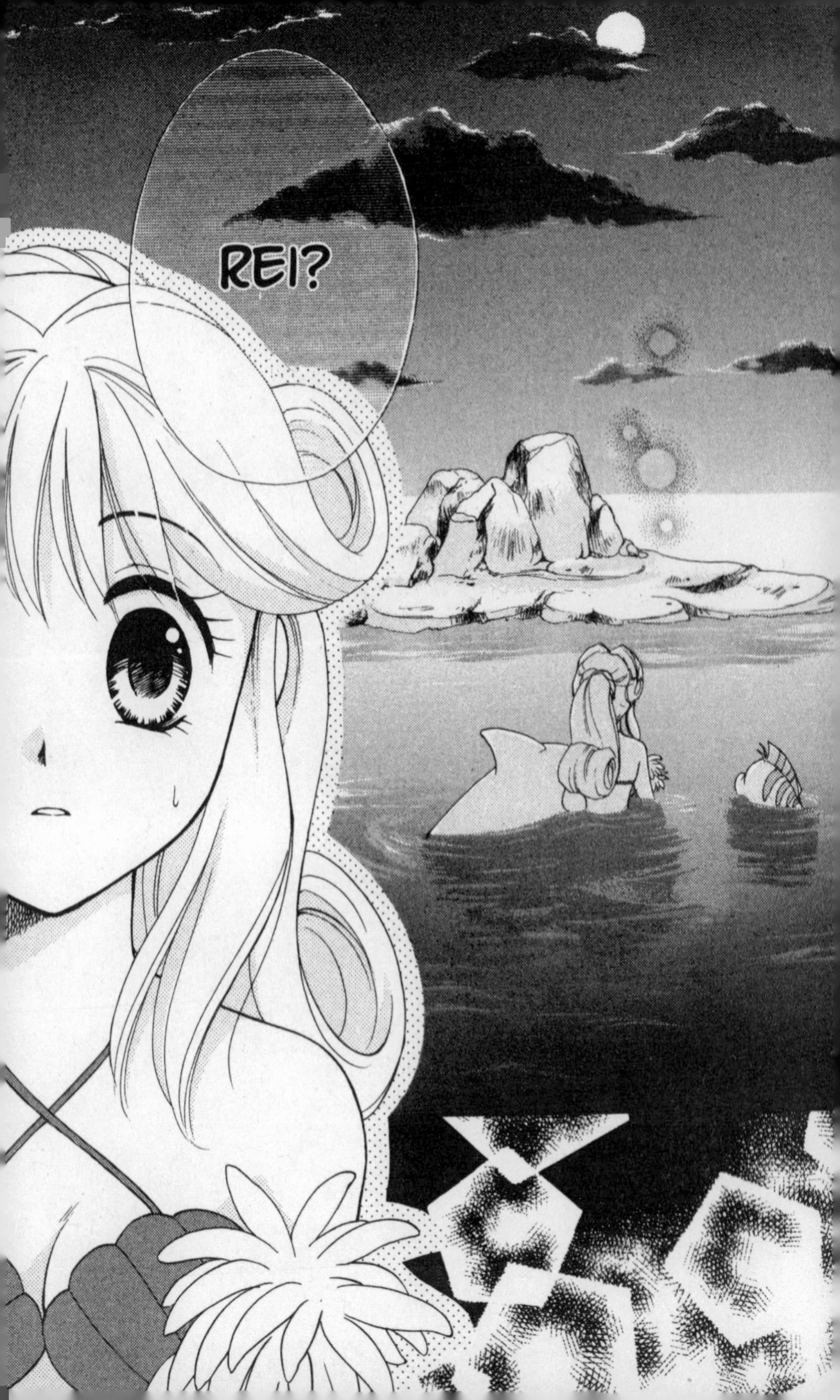
REI?

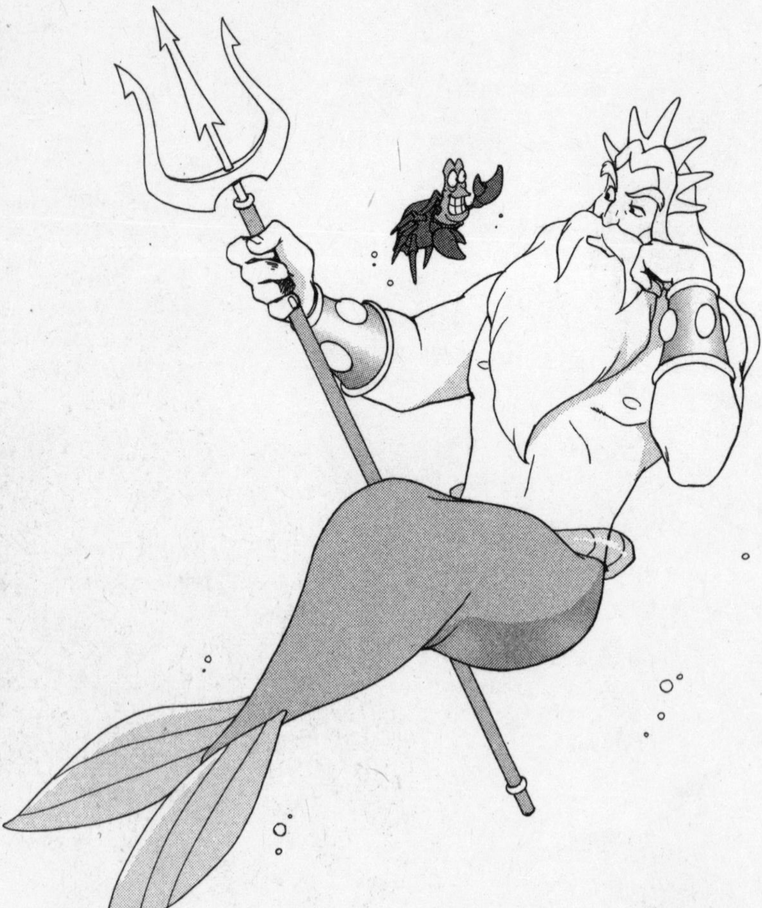

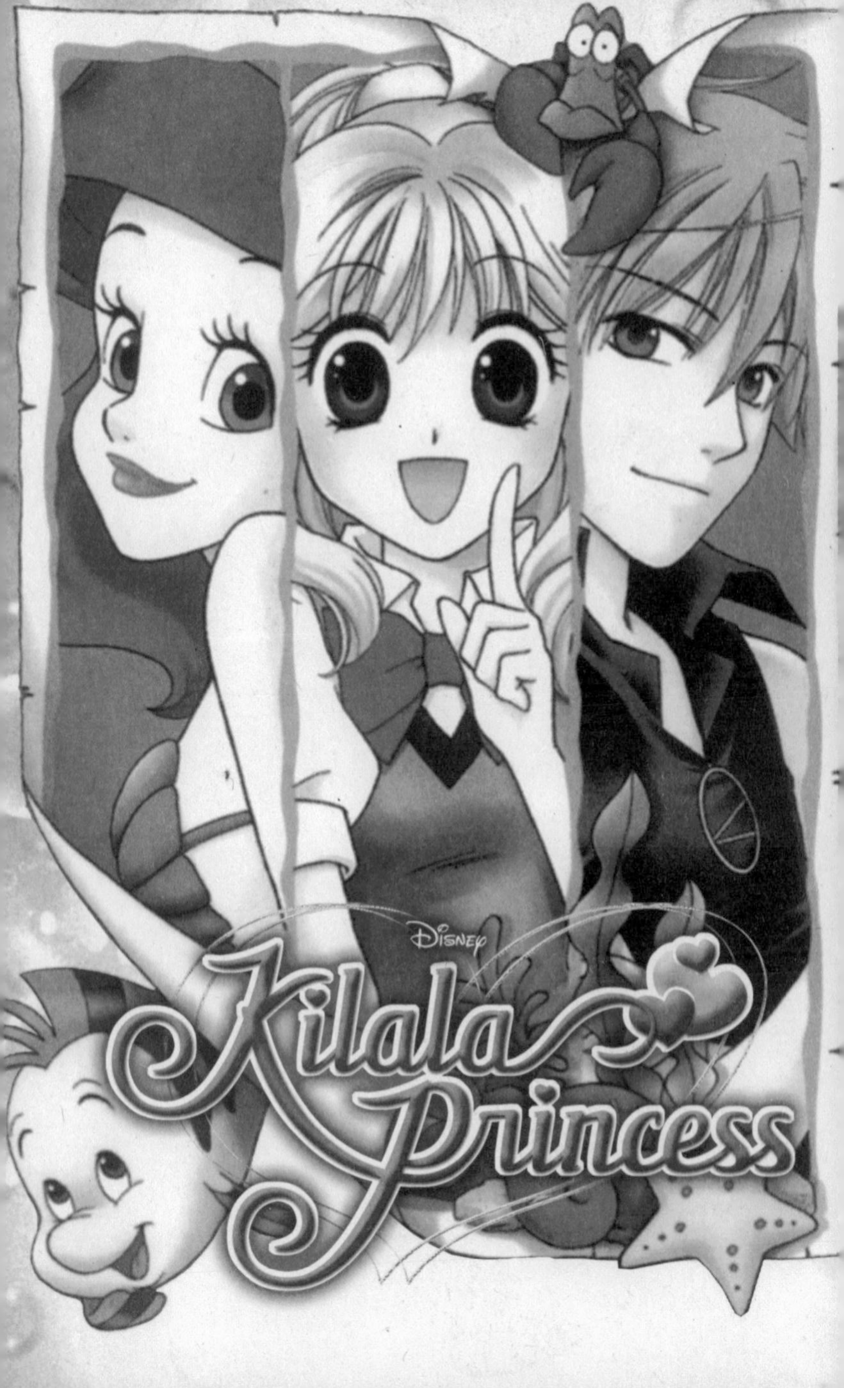
DISNEY
Kilala Princess

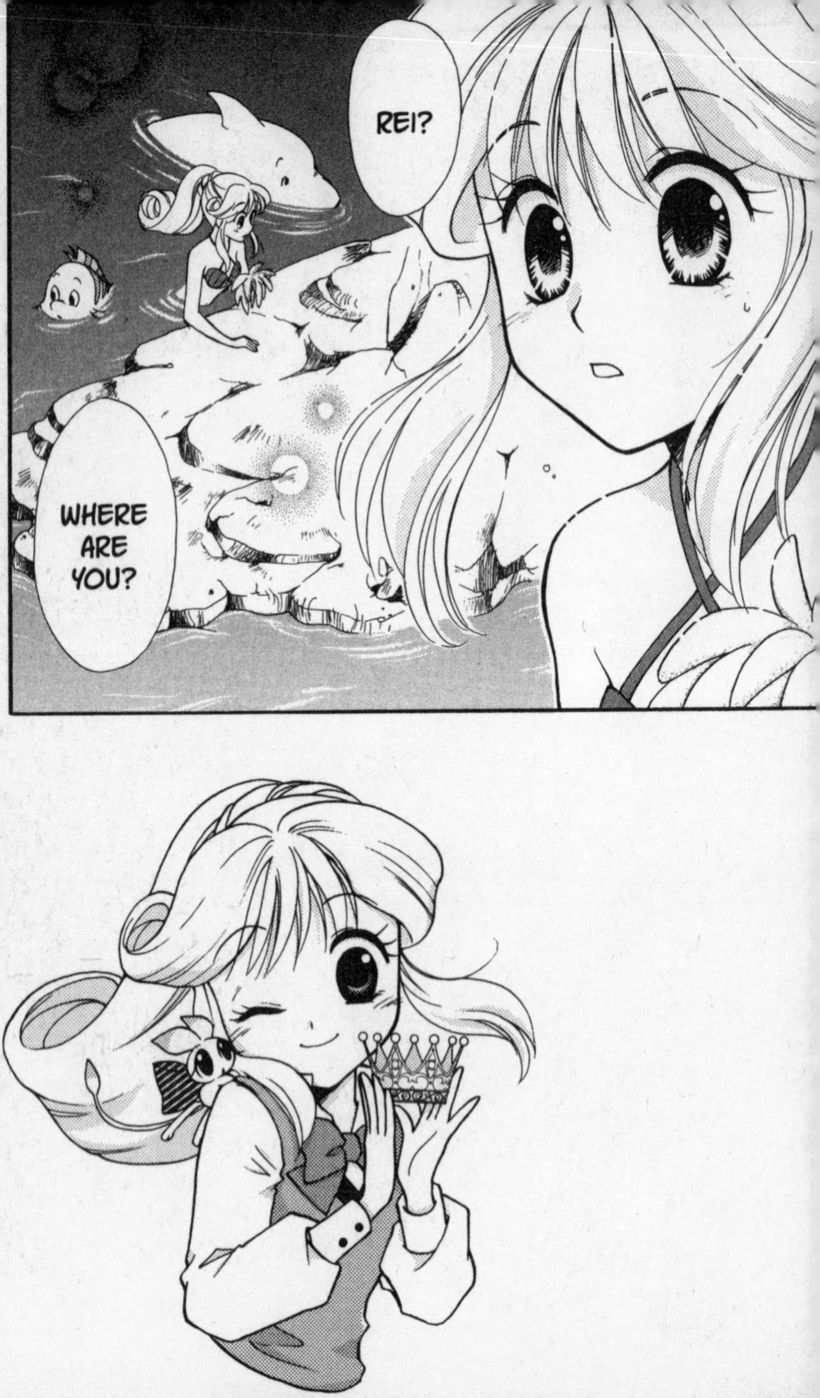
REI?
WHERE ARE YOU?

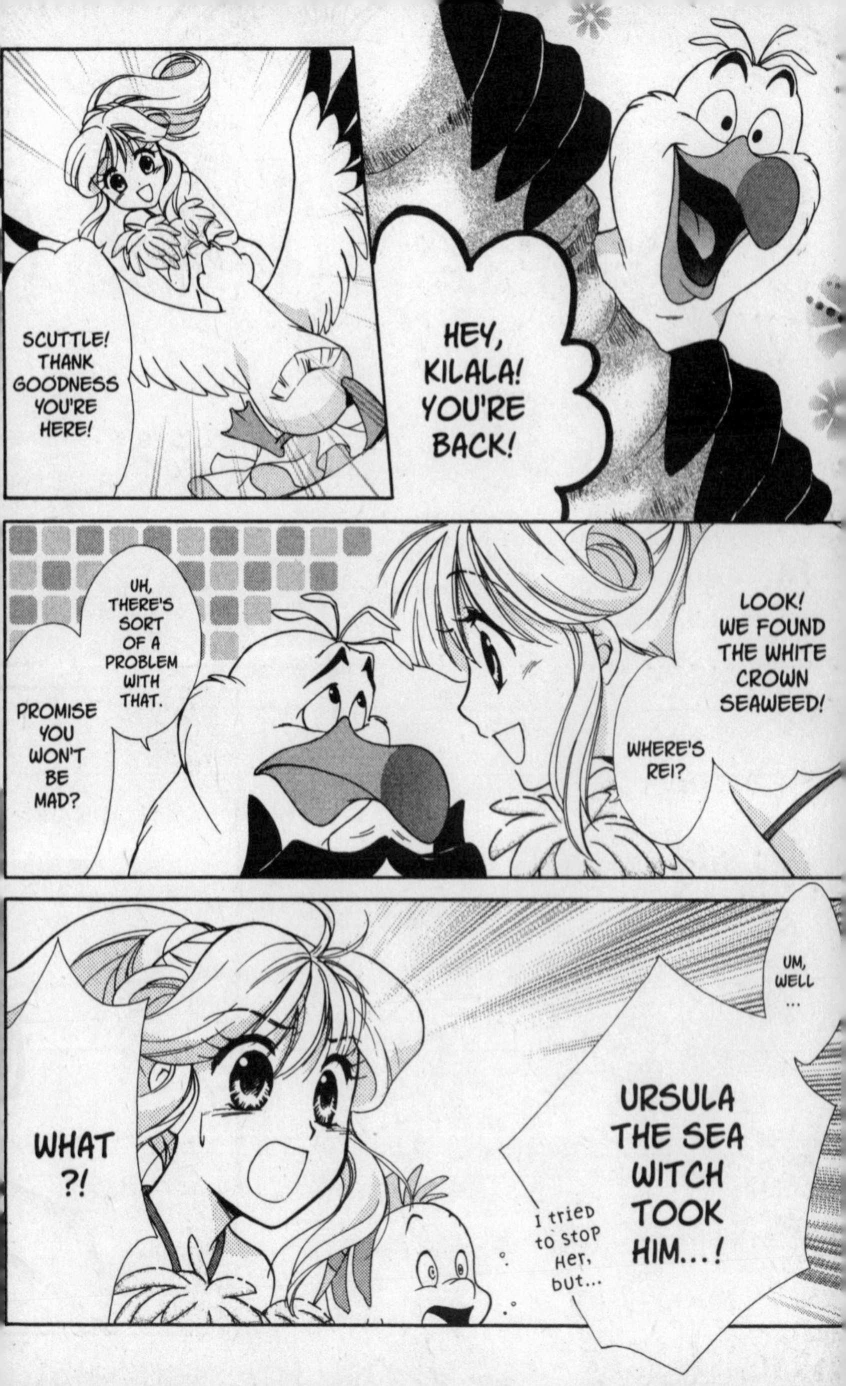
HEY, KILALA! YOU'RE BACK!
SCUTTLE! THANK GOODNESS YOU'RE HERE!
LOOK! WE FOUND THE WHITE CROWN SEAWEED!
WHERE'S REI?
UH, THERE'S SORT OF A PROBLEM WITH THAT.
PROMISE YOU WON'T BE MAD?
UM, WELL ...
URSULA THE SEA WITCH TOOK HIM...!
I tried to stop Her, but...
WHAT ?!

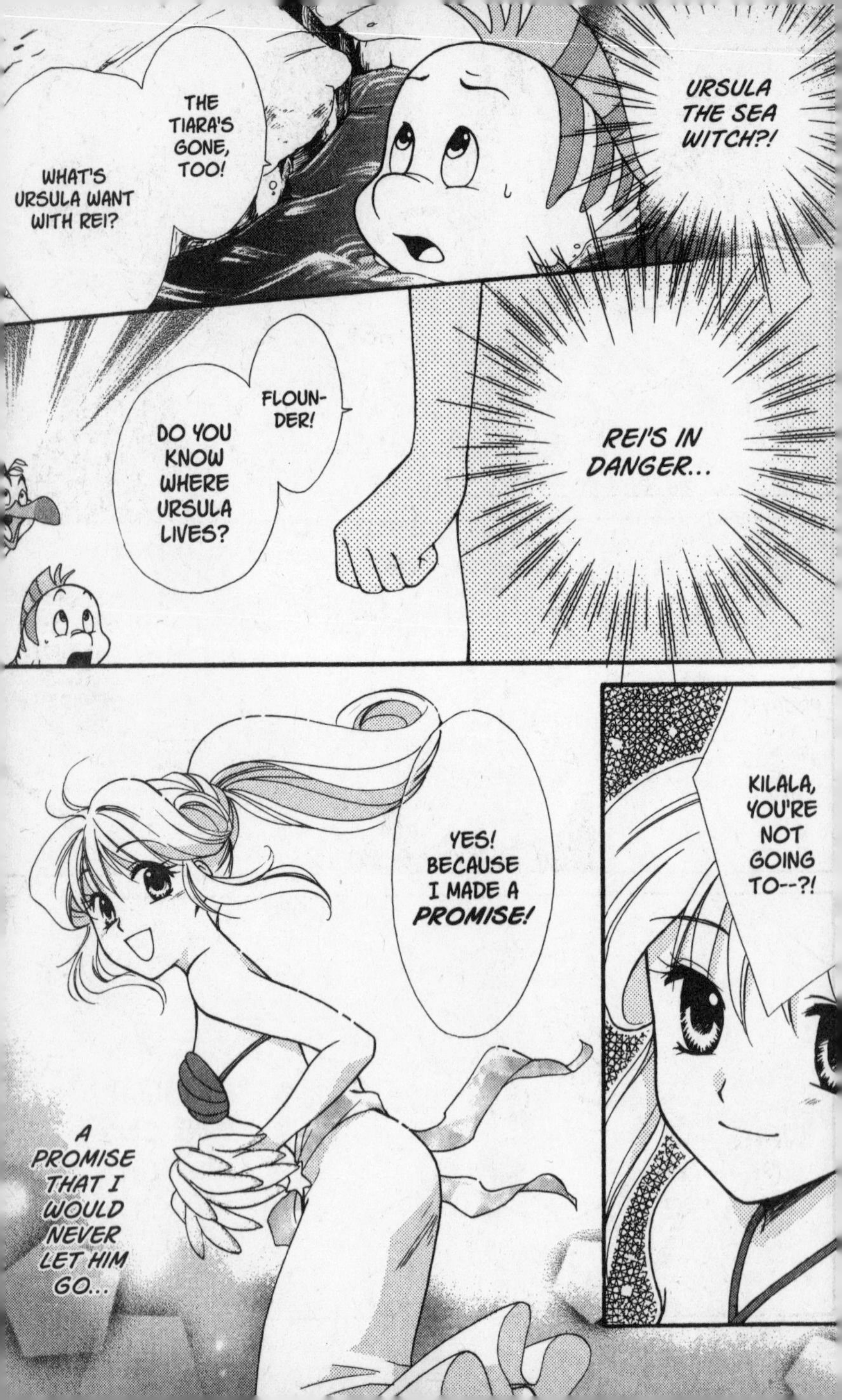
URSULA THE SEA WITCH?!
THE TIARA'S GONE, TOO!
WHAT'S URSULA WANT WITH REI?
REI'S IN DANGER...
FLOUNDER!
DO YOU KNOW WHERE URSULA LIVES?
KILALA, YOU'RE NOT GOING TO--?!
YES! BECAUSE I MADE A PROMISE!
A PROMISE THAT I WOULD NEVER LET HIM GO...

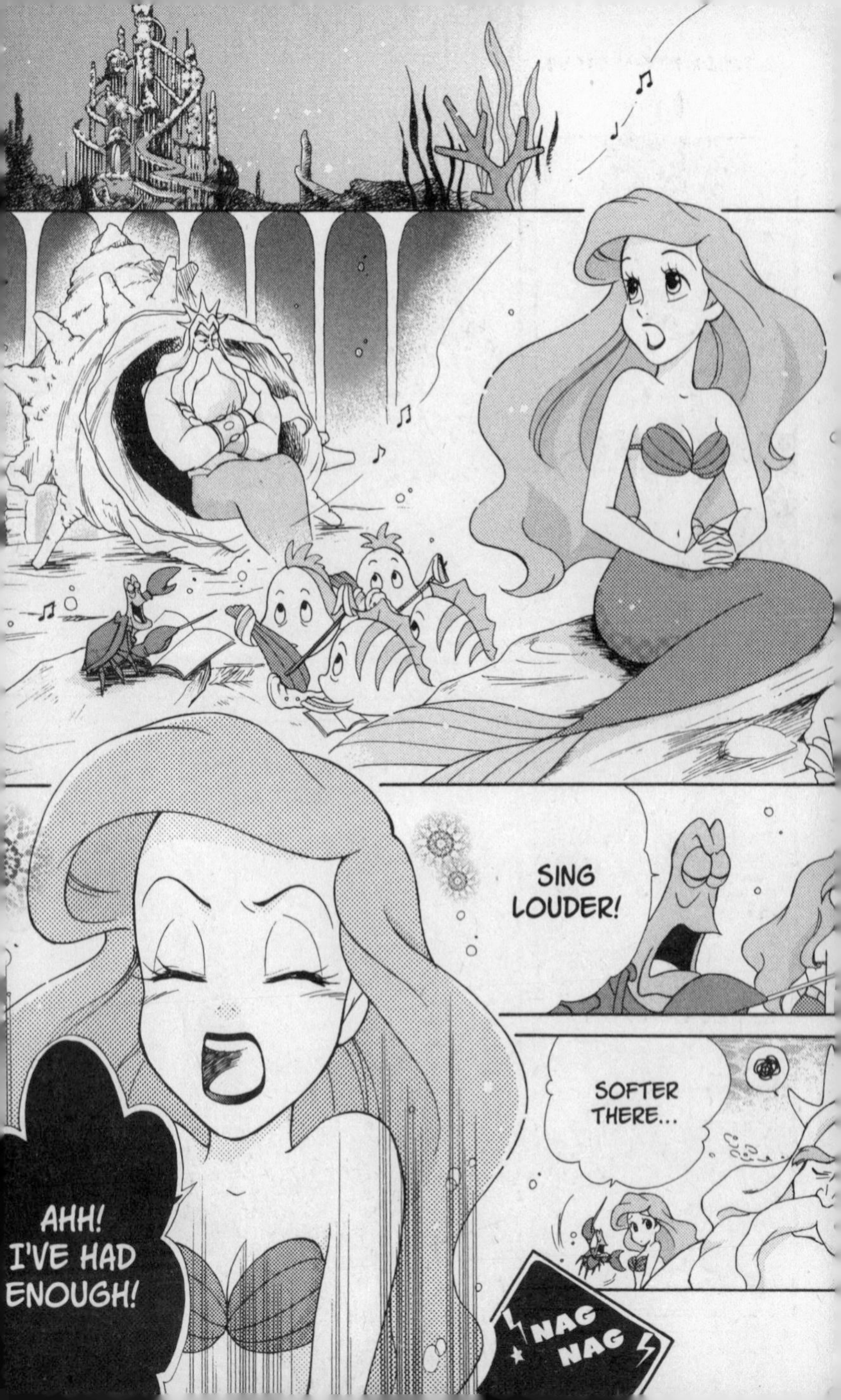
SING LOUDER!
SOFTER THERE...
NAG NAG
AHH! I'VE HAD ENOUGH!

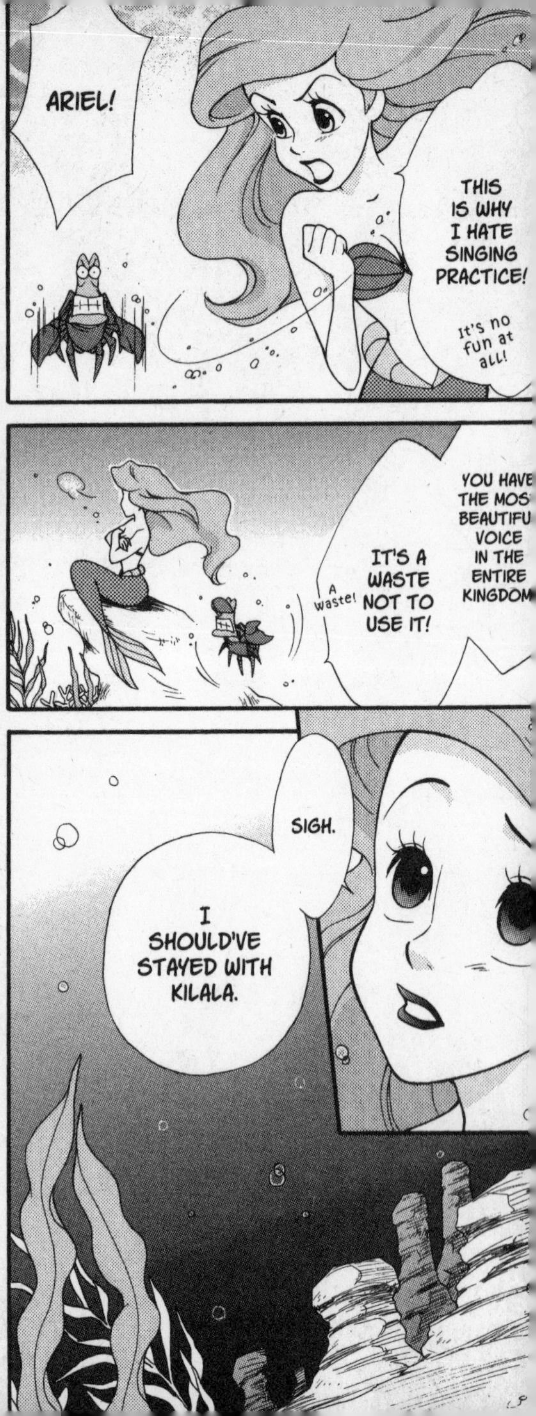
ARIEL!
THIS IS WHY I HATE SINGING PRACTICE!
It's no fun at all!
YOU HAVE THE MOS BEAUTIFU VOICE IN THE ENTIRE KINGDOM
IT'S A WASTE NOT TO USE IT!
A waste!
SIGH.
I SHOULD'VE STAYED WITH KILALA.

A WORD FROM TIPPE

5

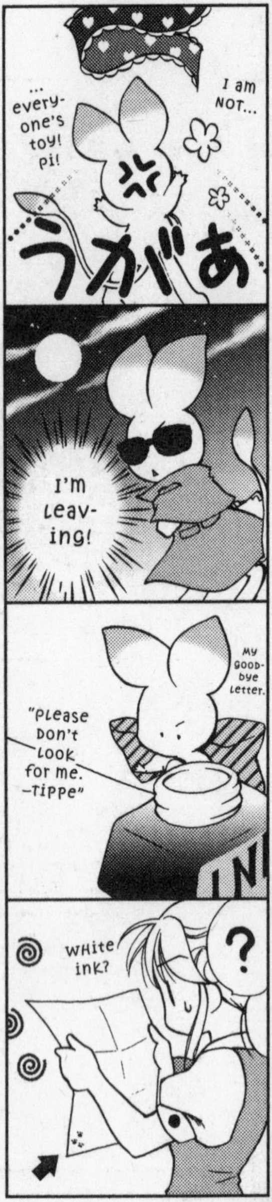
I am NOT...
...every-one's toy! pi!
うがあ
I'm Leav-ing!
My good-bye Letter.
"Please Don't Look for me. -Tippe"
INI
?
White ink?

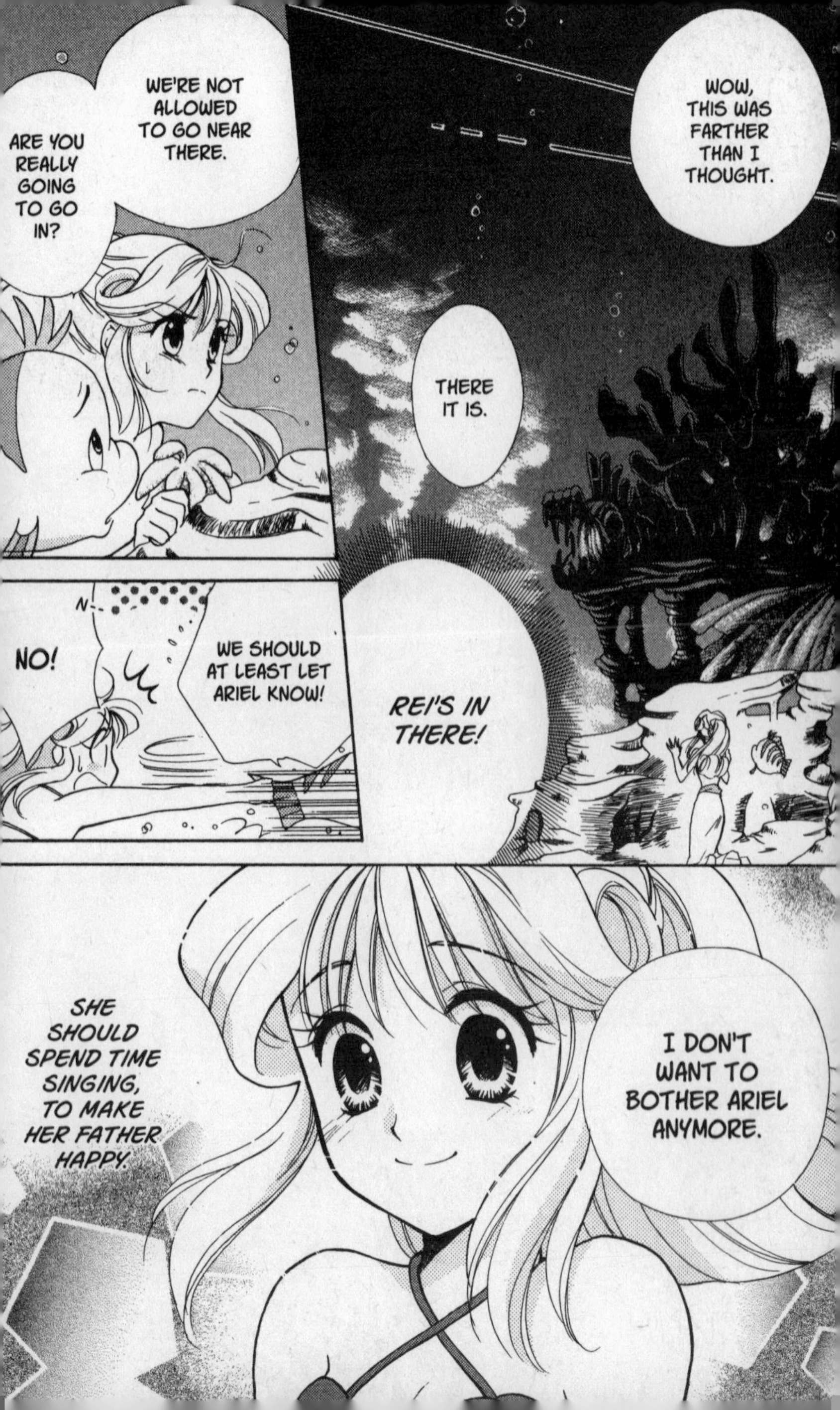
WOW, THIS WAS FARTHER THAN I THOUGHT.
THERE IT IS.
REI'S IN THERE!
WE'RE NOT ALLOWED TO GO NEAR THERE.
ARE YOU REALLY GOING TO GO IN?
WE SHOULD AT LEAST LET ARIEL KNOW!
NO!
I DON'T WANT TO BOTHER ARIEL ANYMORE.
SHE SHOULD SPEND TIME SINGING, TO MAKE HER FATHER HAPPY.

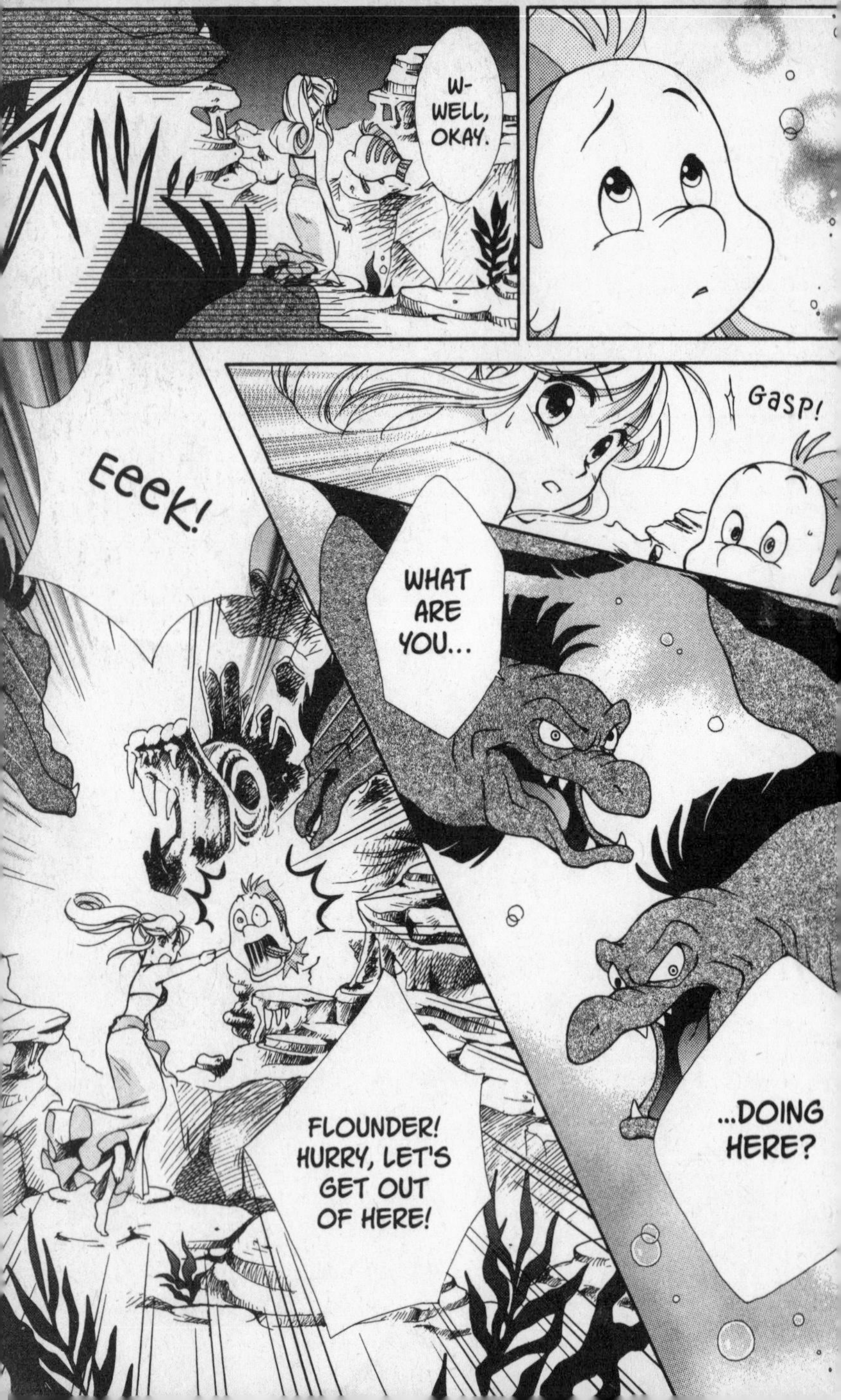
W- WELL, OKAY.
Gasp!
WHAT ARE YOU...
...DOING HERE?
Eeek!
FLOUNDER! HURRY, LET'S GET OUT OF HERE!

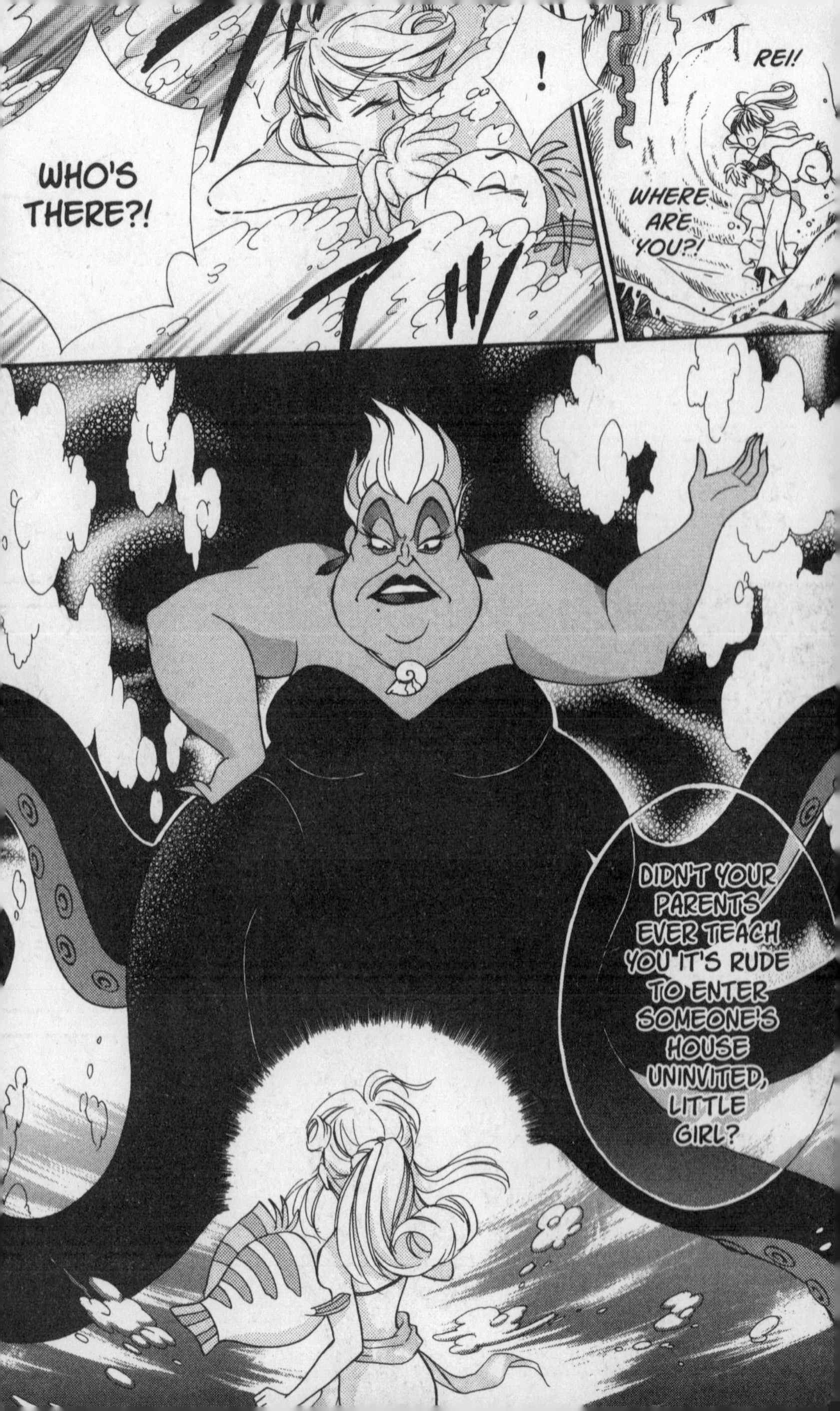

REI!!
WHERE ARE YOU?!
!
WHO'S THERE?!
DIDN'T YOUR PARENTS EVER TEACH YOU IT'S RUDE TO ENTER SOMEONE'S HOUSE UNINVITED, LITTLE GIRL?

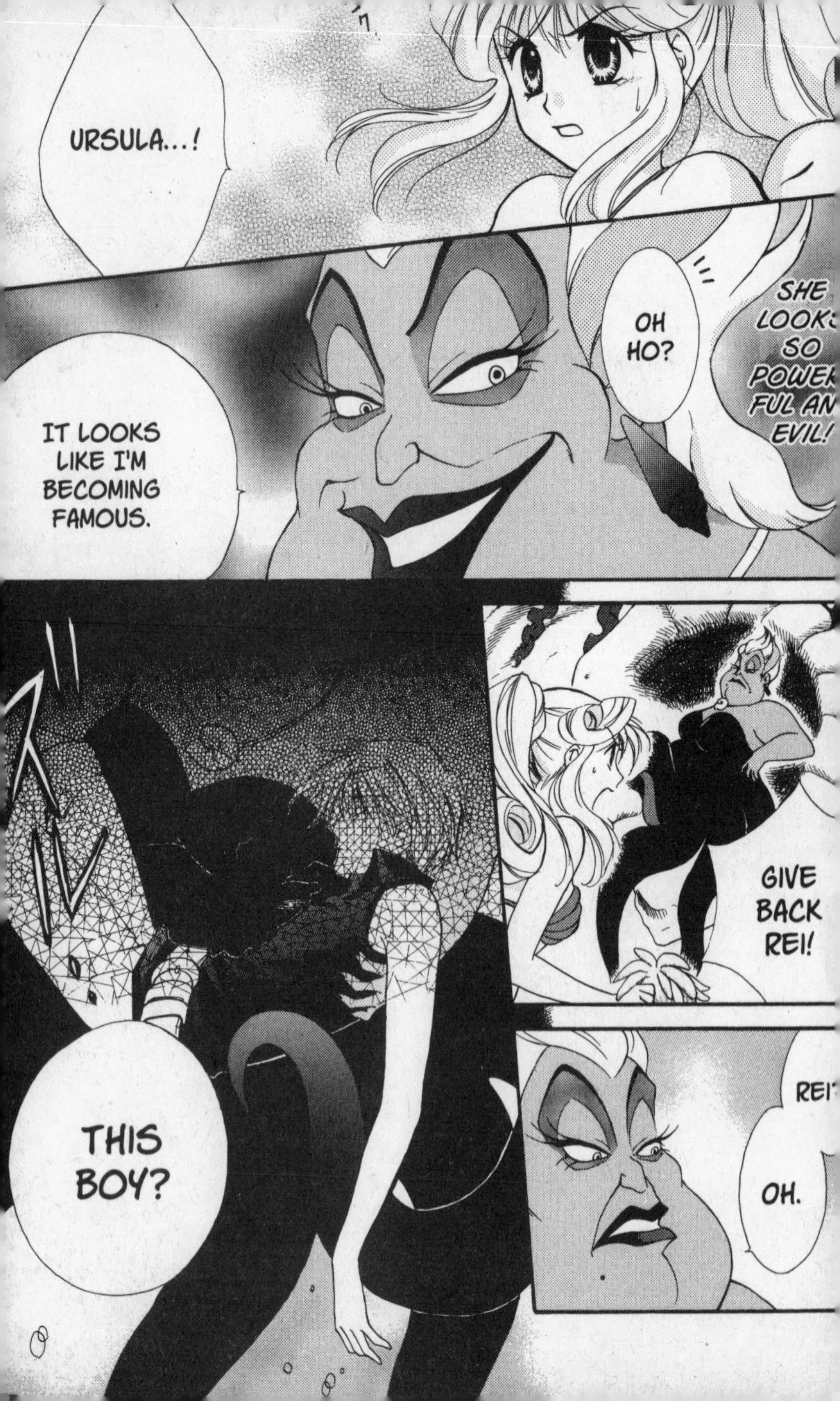
URSULA...!
SHE LOOKS SO POWERFUL AND EVIL!
OH HO?
IT LOOKS LIKE I'M BECOMING FAMOUS.
GIVE BACK REI!
REI? OH.
THIS BOY?

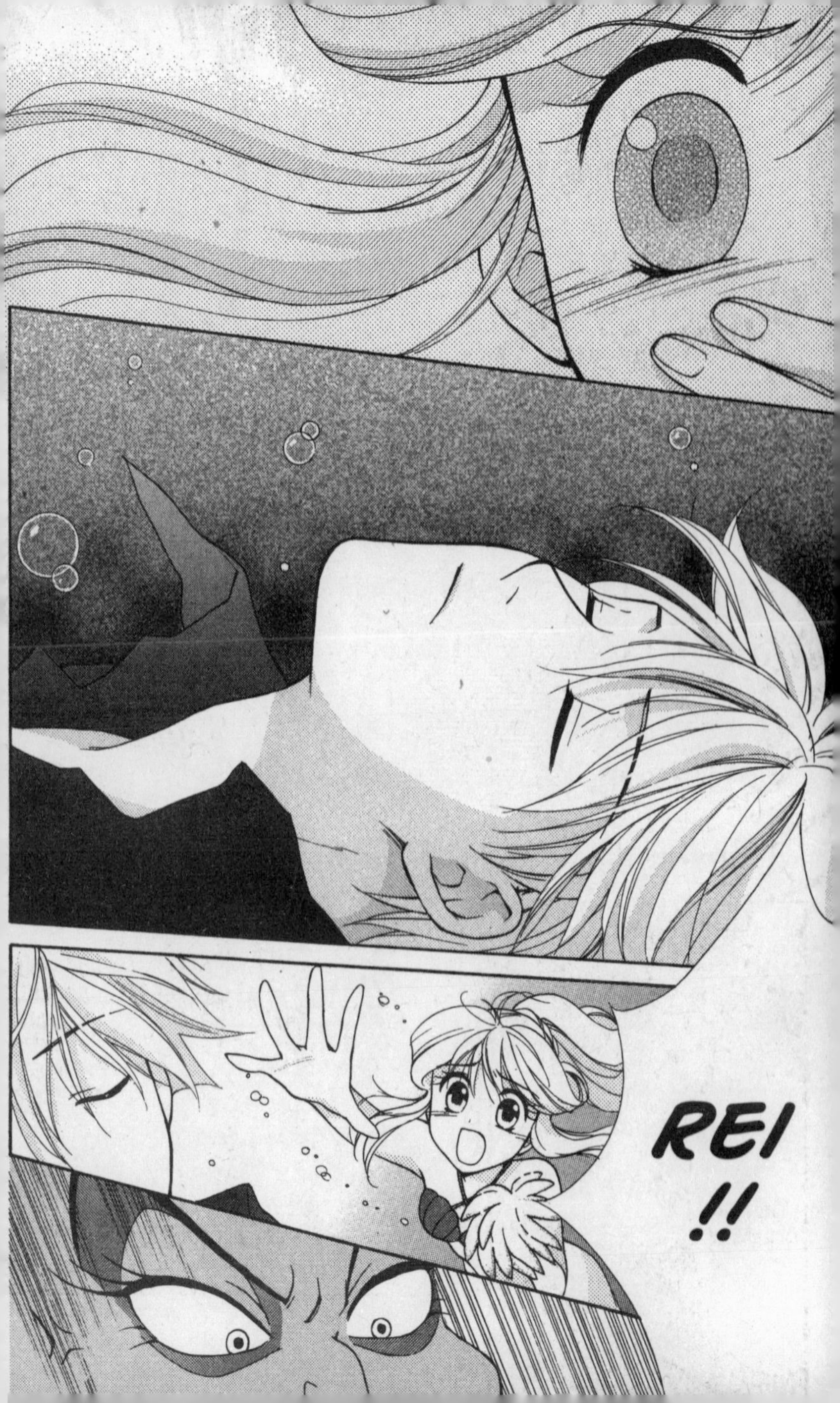
REI !!

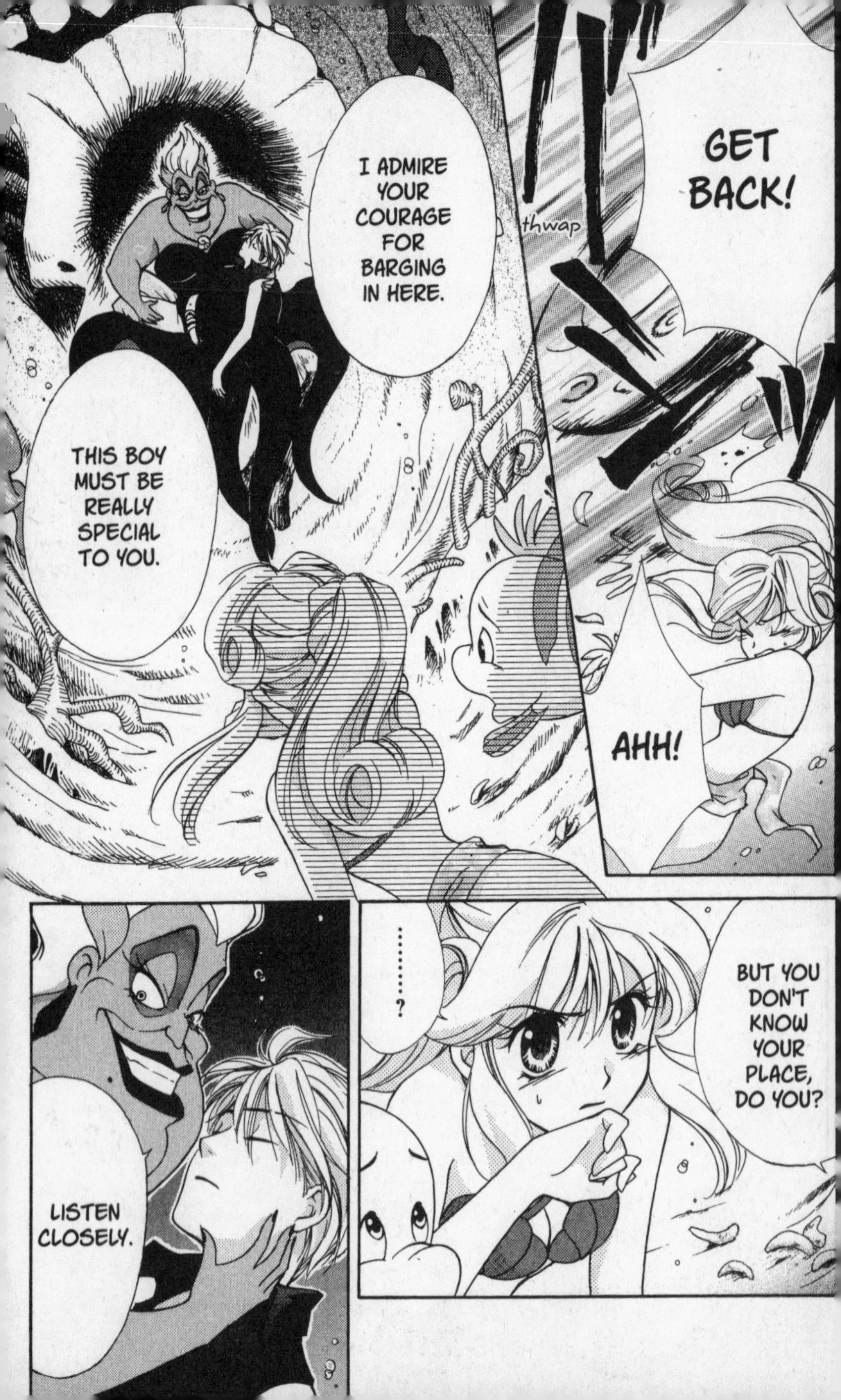
GET BACK!
thwap
AHH!
I ADMIRE YOUR COURAGE FOR BARGING IN HERE.
THIS BOY MUST BE REALLY SPECIAL TO YOU.
BUT YOU DON'T KNOW YOUR PLACE, DO YOU?
......?
LISTEN CLOSELY.

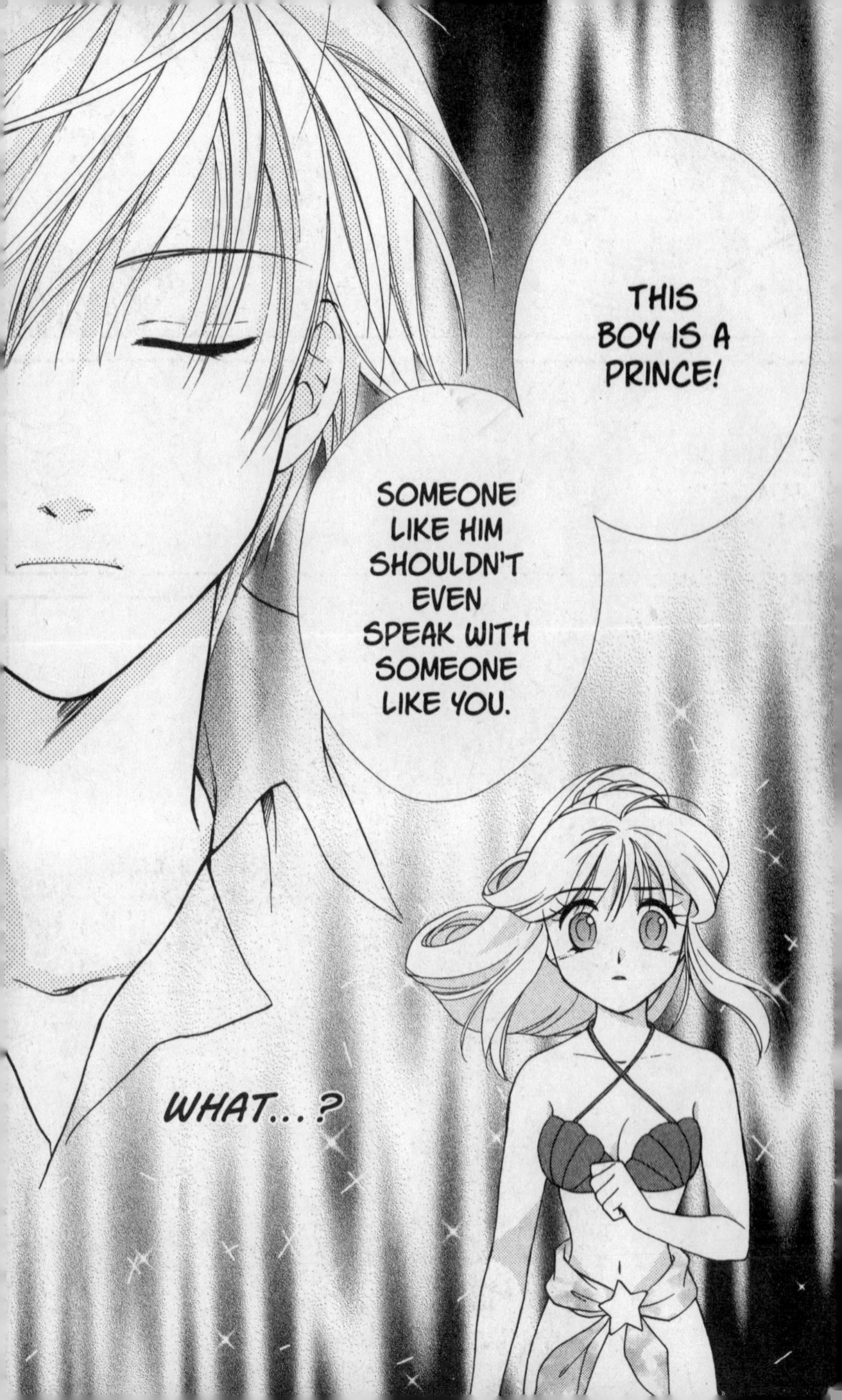
THIS BOY IS A PRINCE!
SOMEONE LIKE HIM SHOULDN'T EVEN SPEAK WITH SOMEONE LIKE YOU.
WHAT...?

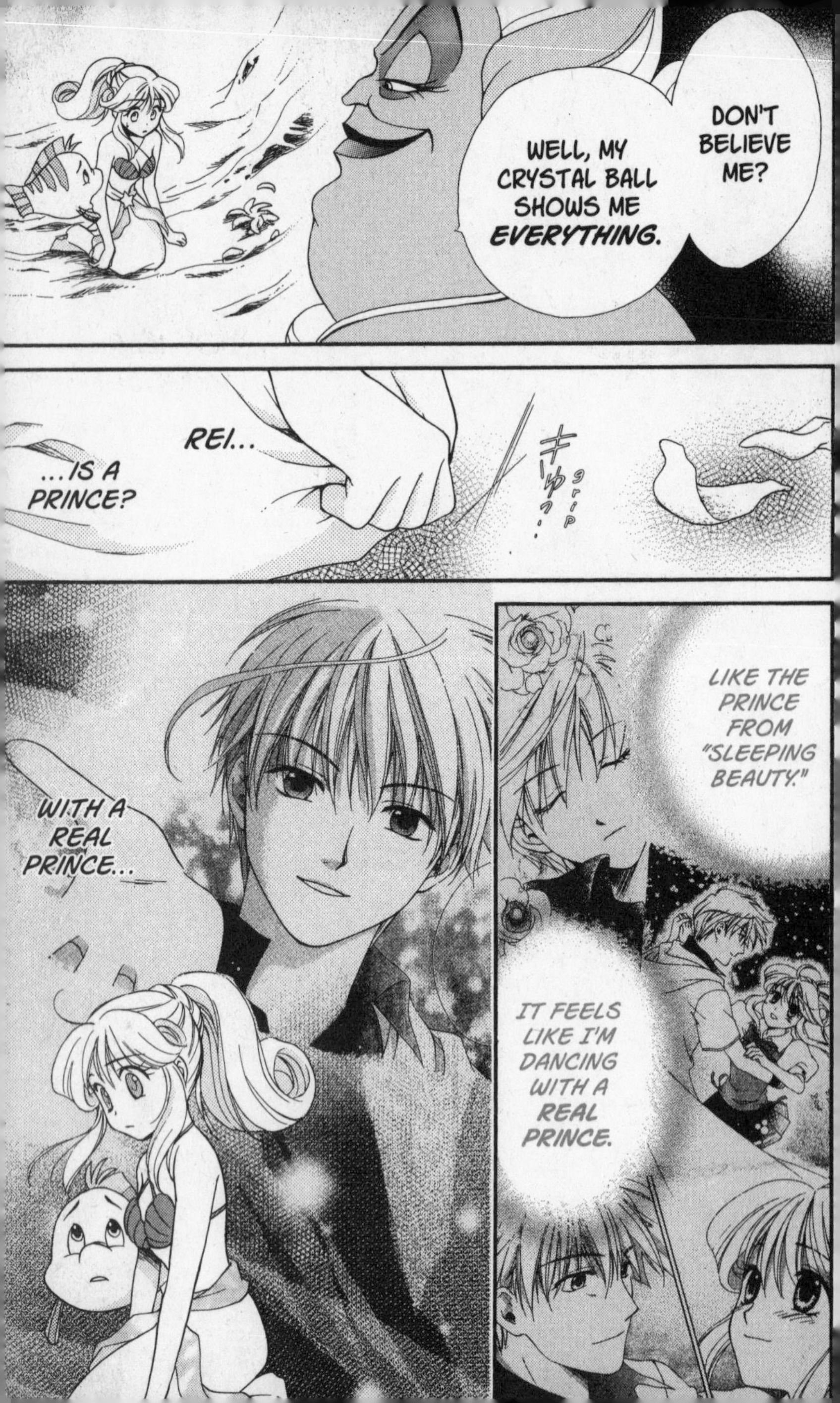
DON'T BELIEVE ME?
WELL, MY CRYSTAL BALL SHOWS ME EVERYTHING.
キュッ
GRIP
REI...
...IS A PRINCE?
LIKE THE PRINCE FROM "SLEEPING BEAUTY."
IT FEELS LIKE I'M DANCING WITH A REAL PRINCE.
WITH A REAL PRINCE...

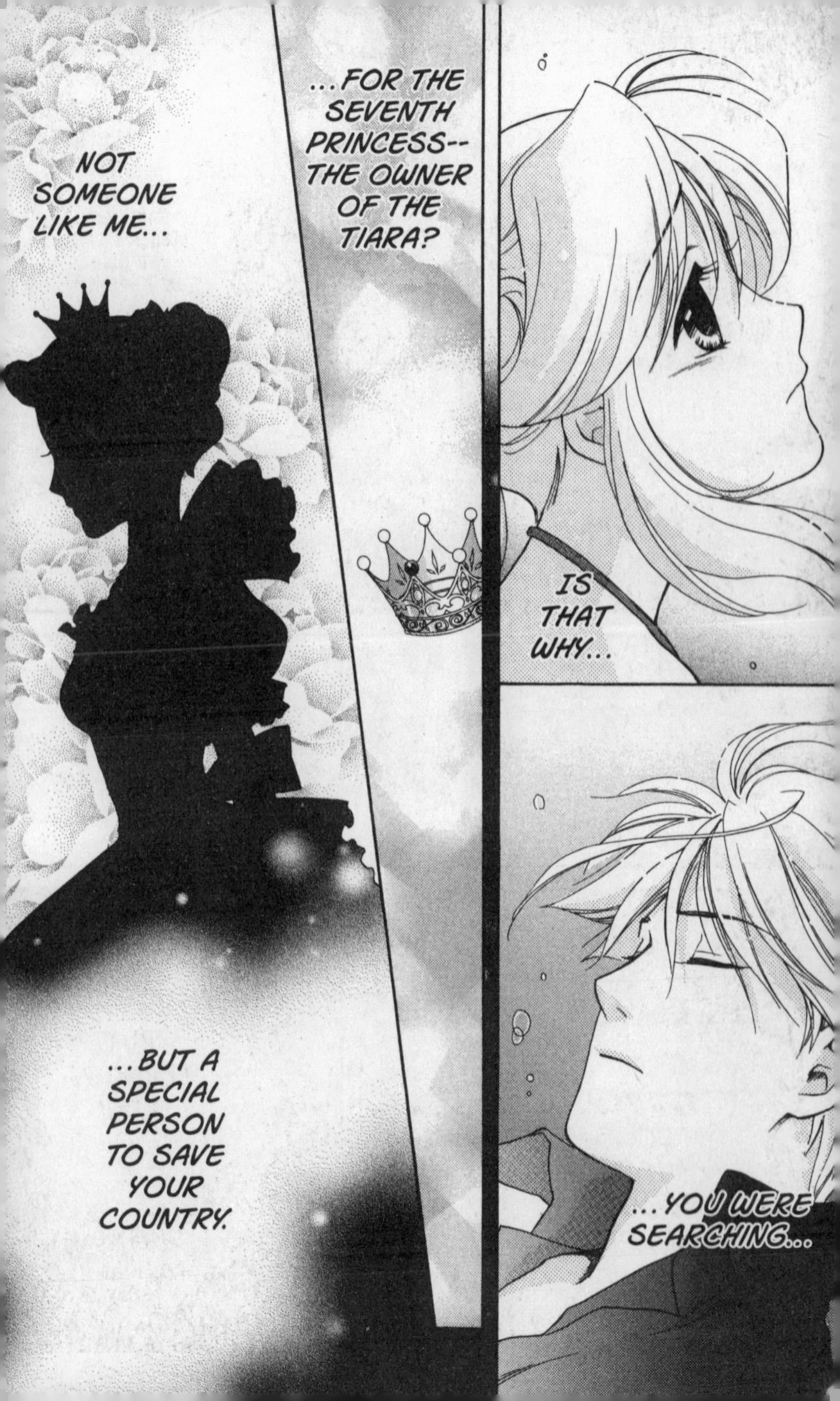
IS THAT WHY...
...YOU WERE SEARCHING...
...FOR THE SEVENTH PRINCESS-- THE OWNER OF THE TIARA?
NOT SOMEONE LIKE ME...
...BUT A SPECIAL PERSON TO SAVE YOUR COUNTRY.

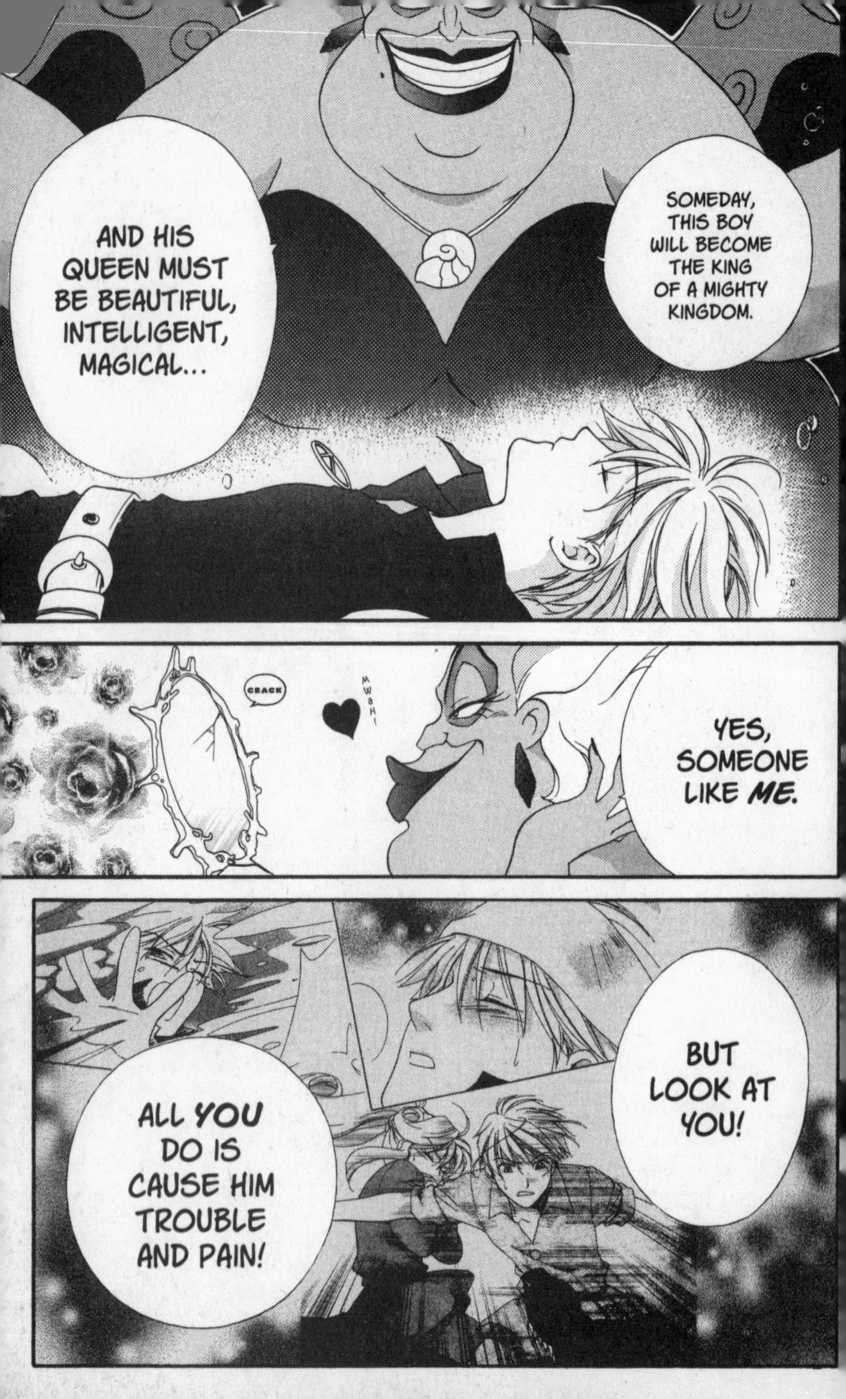
SOMEDAY, THIS BOY WILL BECOME THE KING OF A MIGHTY KINGDOM.
AND HIS QUEEN MUST BE BEAUTIFUL, INTELLIGENT, MAGICAL...
YES, SOMEONE LIKE *ME*.
MWAH!
CRACK
BUT LOOK AT YOU!
ALL *YOU* DO IS CAUSE HIM TROUBLE AND PAIN!

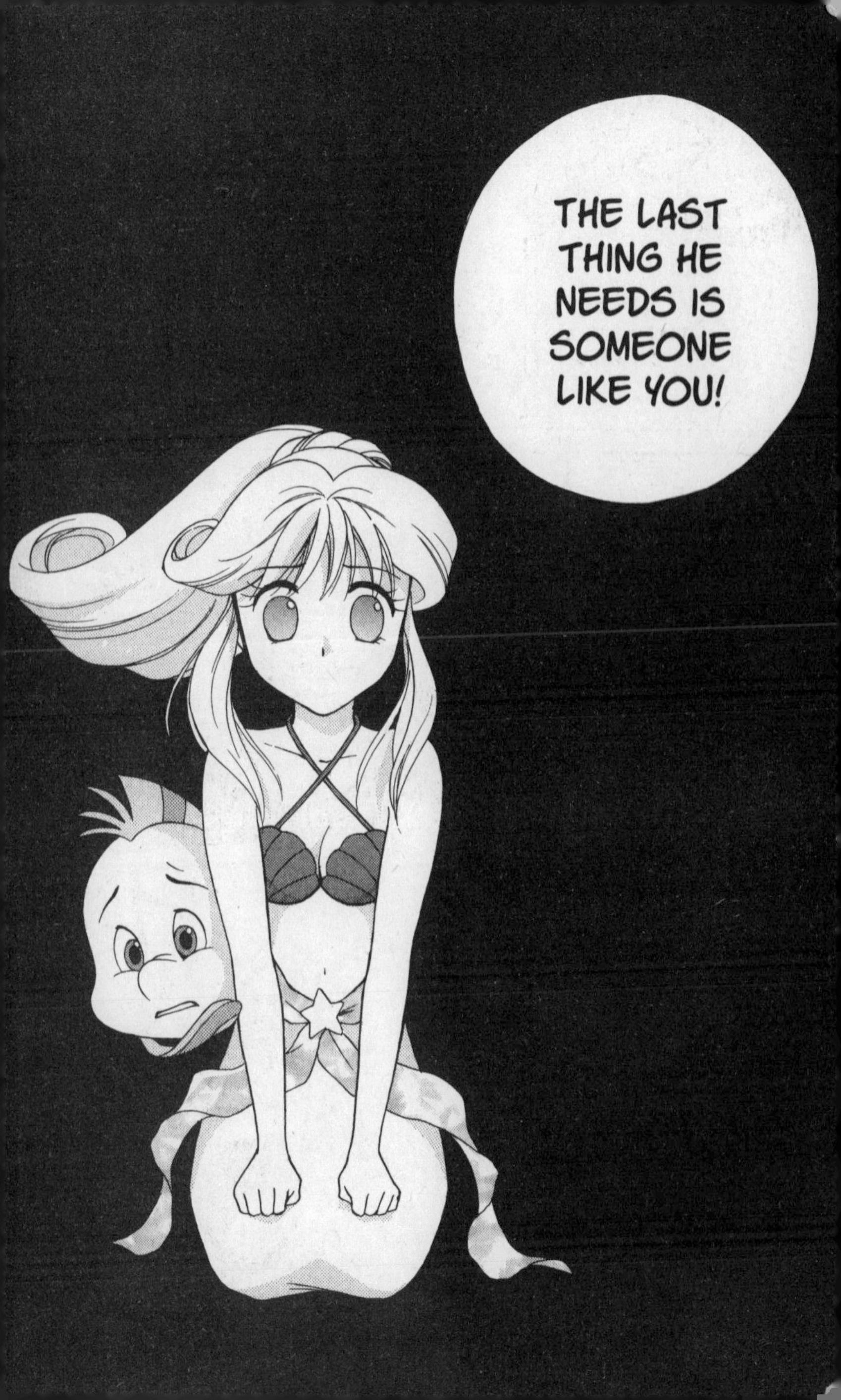
THE LAST THING HE NEEDS IS SOMEONE LIKE YOU!

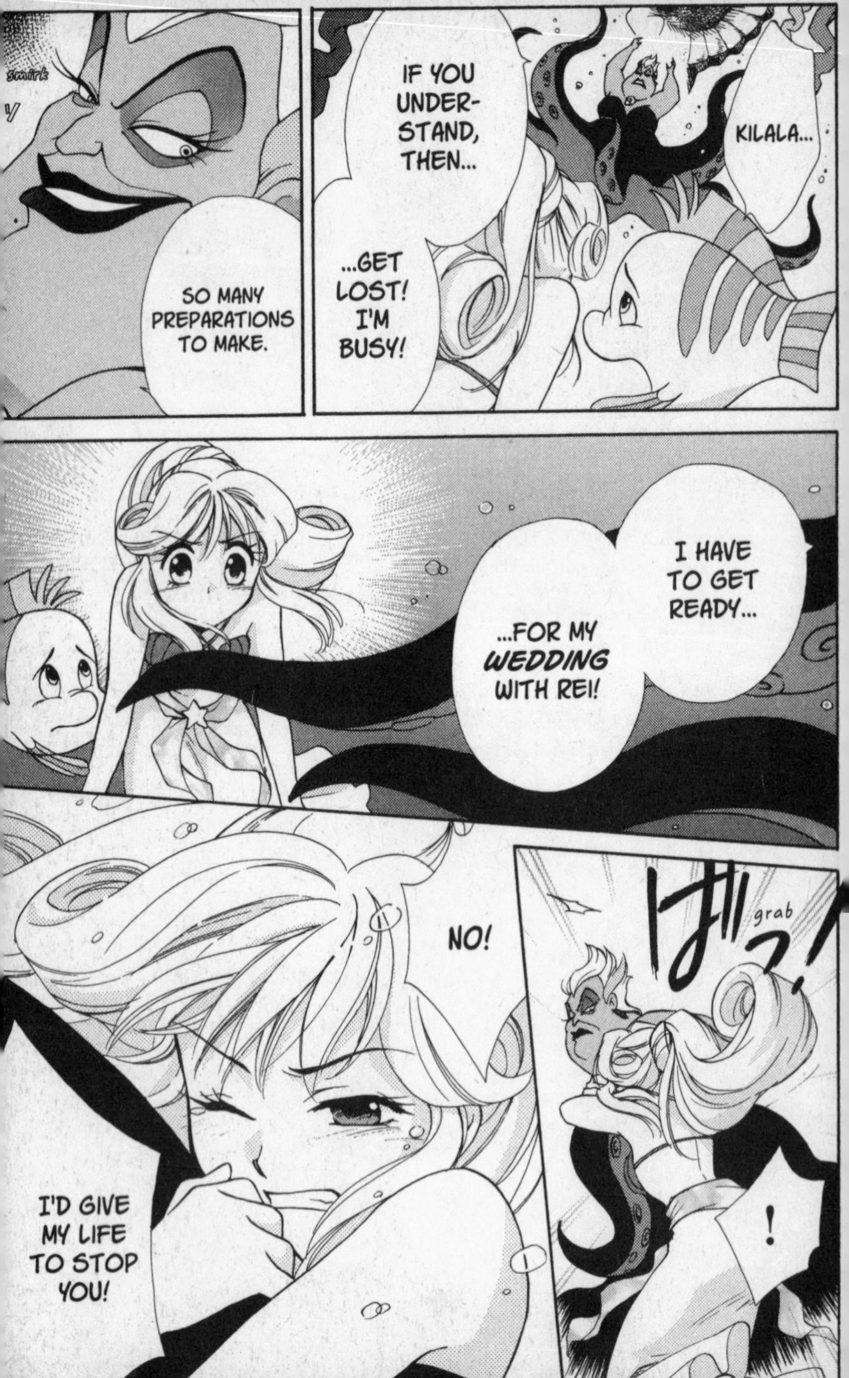
KILALA...
IF YOU UNDER-STAND, THEN...
...GET LOST! I'M BUSY!
smirk
SO MANY PREPARATIONS TO MAKE.
I HAVE TO GET READY...
...FOR MY *WEDDING* WITH REI!
grab
!
NO!
I'D GIVE MY LIFE TO STOP YOU!

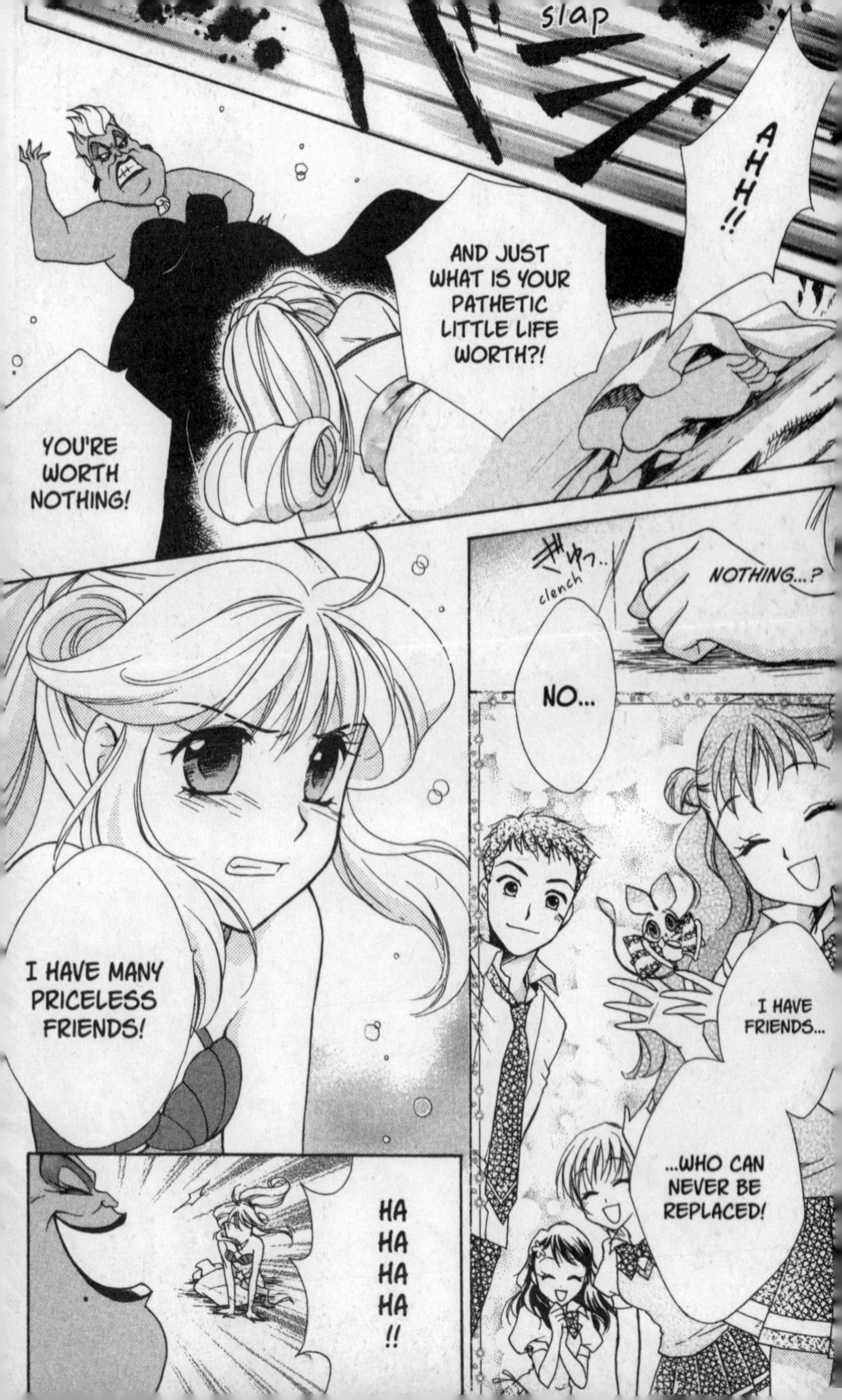
slap
AHH!!
AND JUST WHAT IS YOUR PATHETIC LITTLE LIFE WORTH?!
YOU'RE WORTH NOTHING!
NOTHING...?
clench
NO...
I HAVE FRIENDS...
...WHO CAN NEVER BE REPLACED!
I HAVE MANY PRICELESS FRIENDS!
HA HA HA HA!!

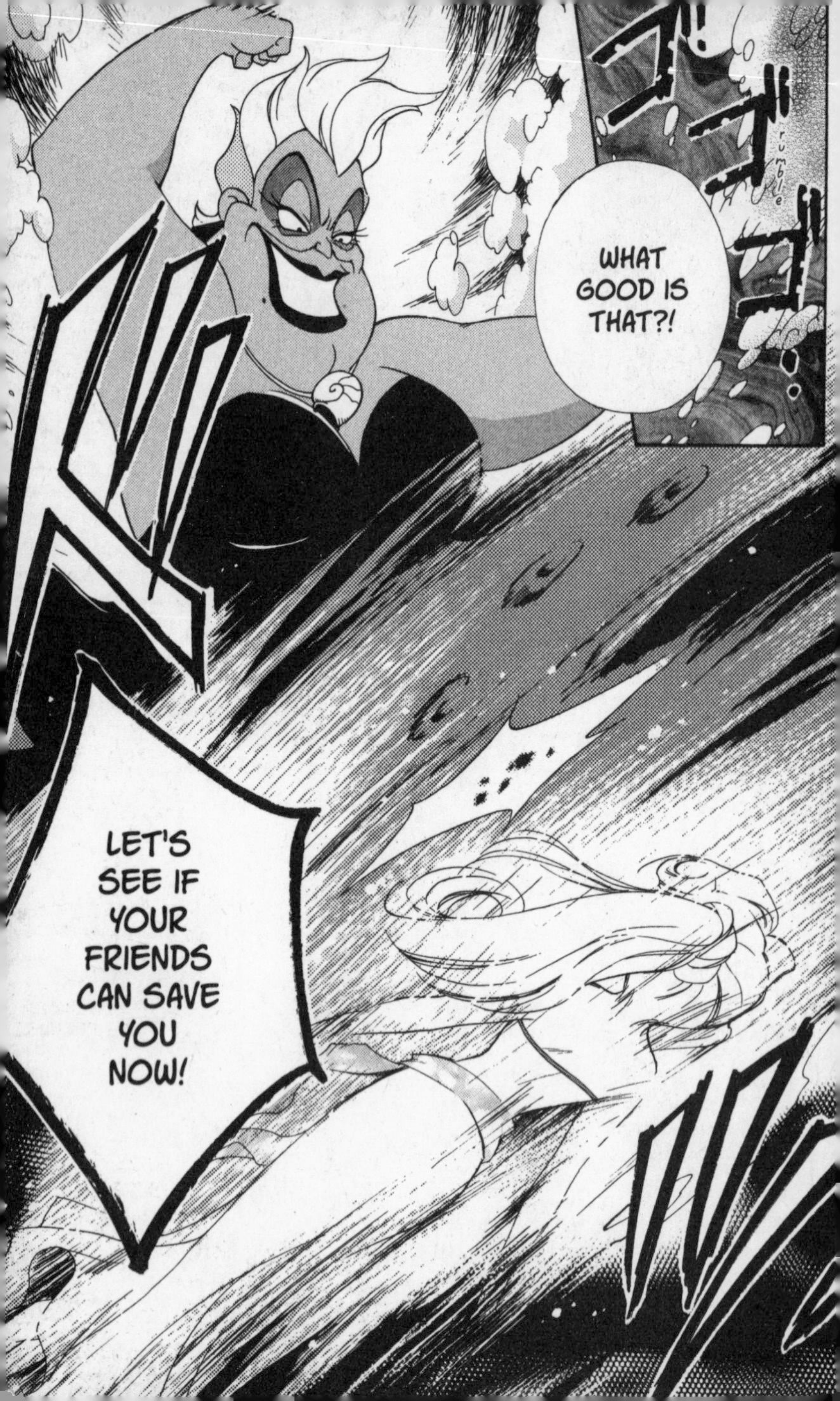
rumble
WHAT GOOD IS THAT?!
LET'S SEE IF YOUR FRIENDS CAN SAVE YOU NOW!

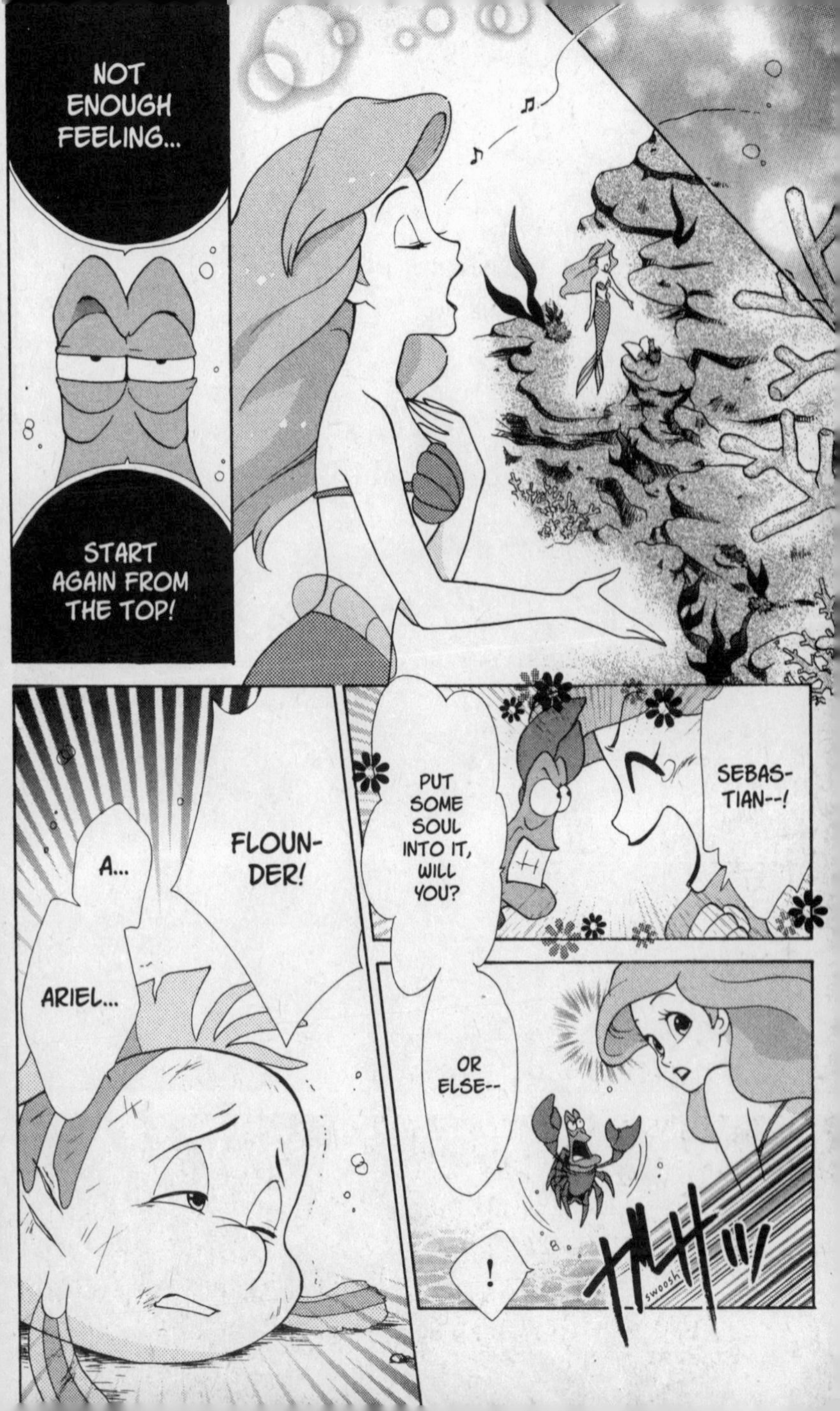
NOT ENOUGH FEELING...
START AGAIN FROM THE TOP!
SEBAS-TIAN--!
PUT SOME SOUL INTO IT, WILL YOU?
OR ELSE--
!
swoosh
FLOUN-DER!
A...
ARIEL...

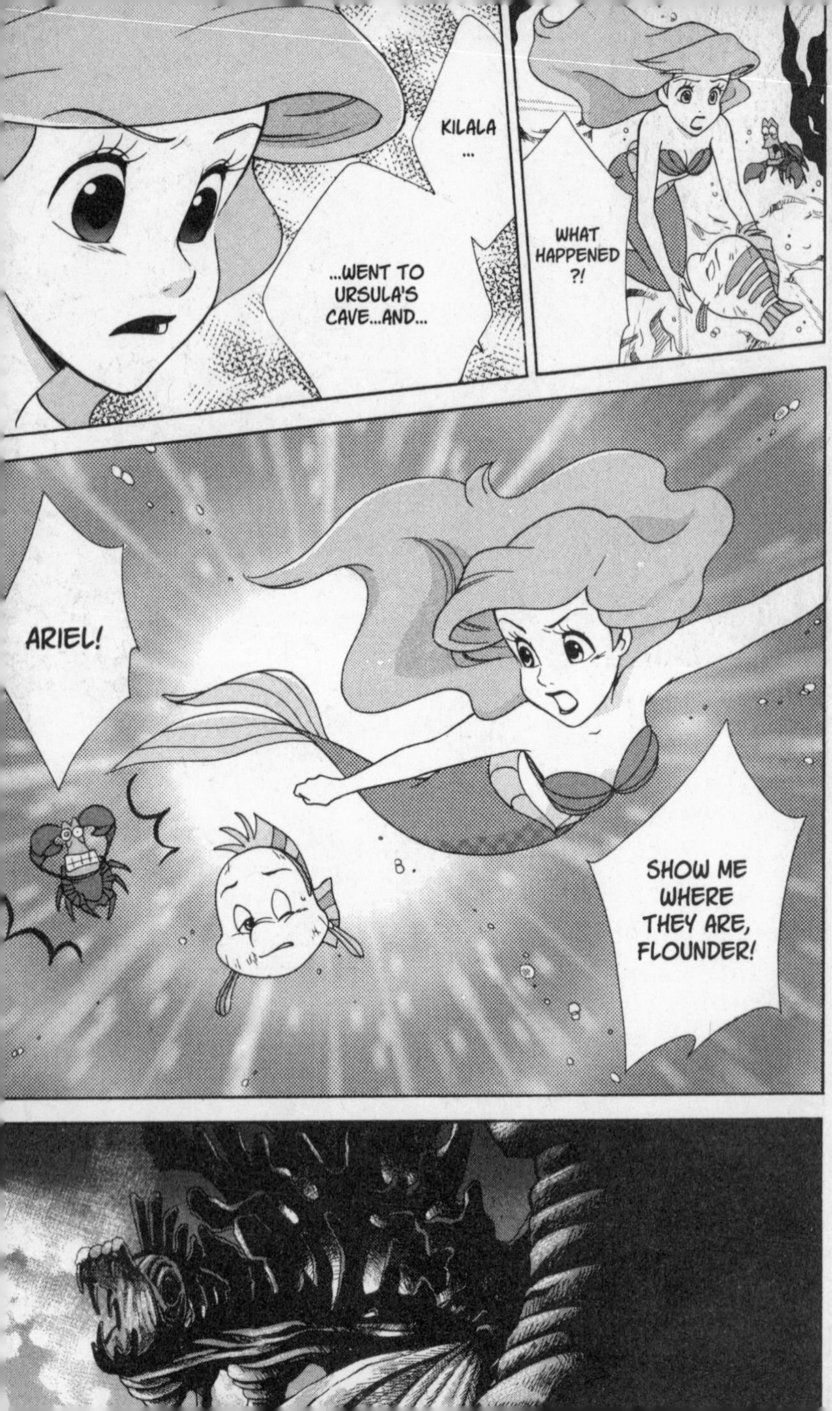
WHAT HAPPENED ?!
KILALA ...
...WENT TO URSULA'S CAVE...AND...
SHOW ME WHERE THEY ARE, FLOUNDER!
ARIEL!

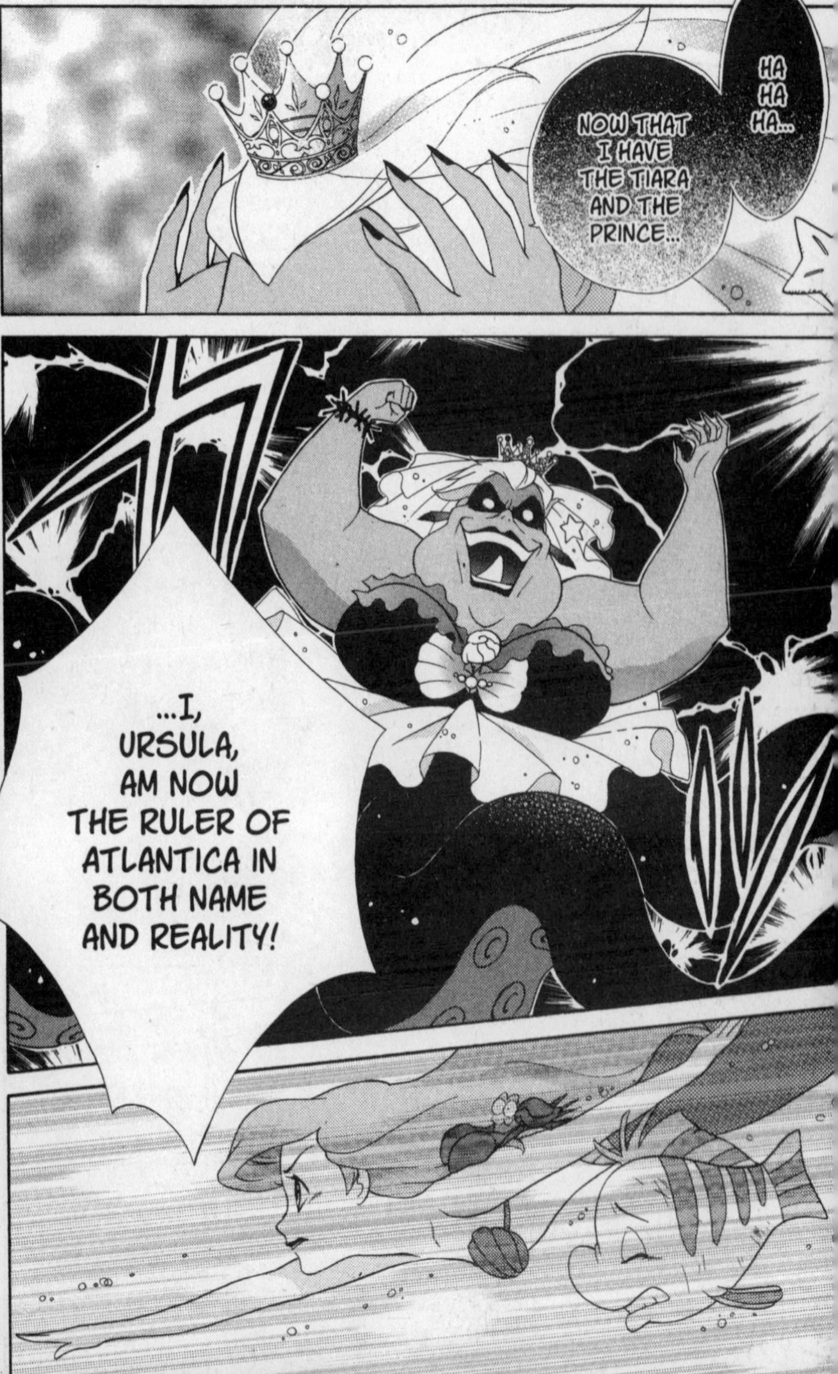
HA HA HA...
NOW THAT I HAVE THE TIARA AND THE PRINCE...
...I, URSULA, AM NOW THE RULER OF ATLANTICA IN BOTH NAME AND REALITY!

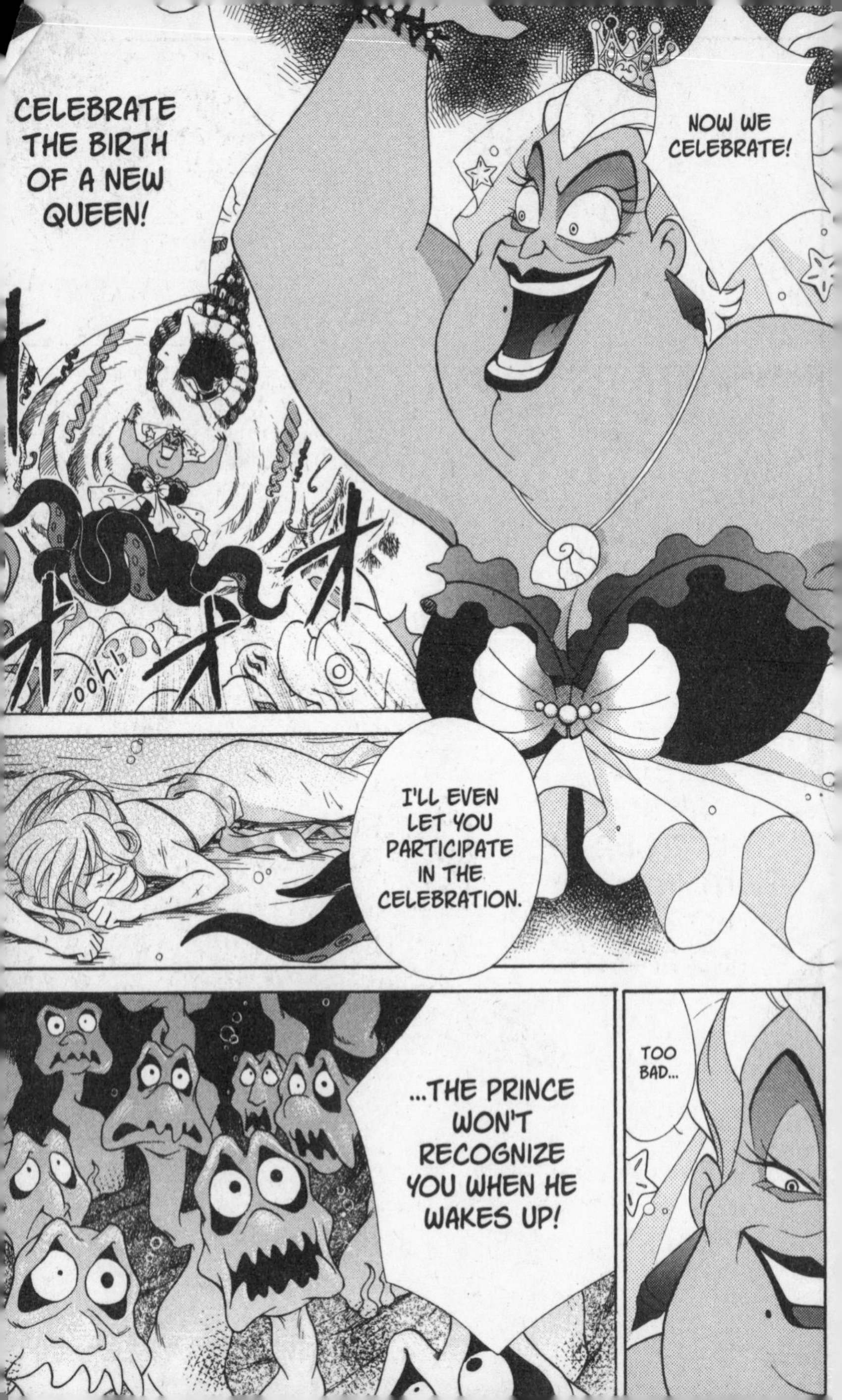
NOW WE CELEBRATE!
CELEBRATE THE BIRTH OF A NEW QUEEN!
ooh!
I'LL EVEN LET YOU PARTICIPATE IN THE CELEBRATION.
TOO BAD...
...THE PRINCE WON'T RECOGNIZE YOU WHEN HE WAKES UP!

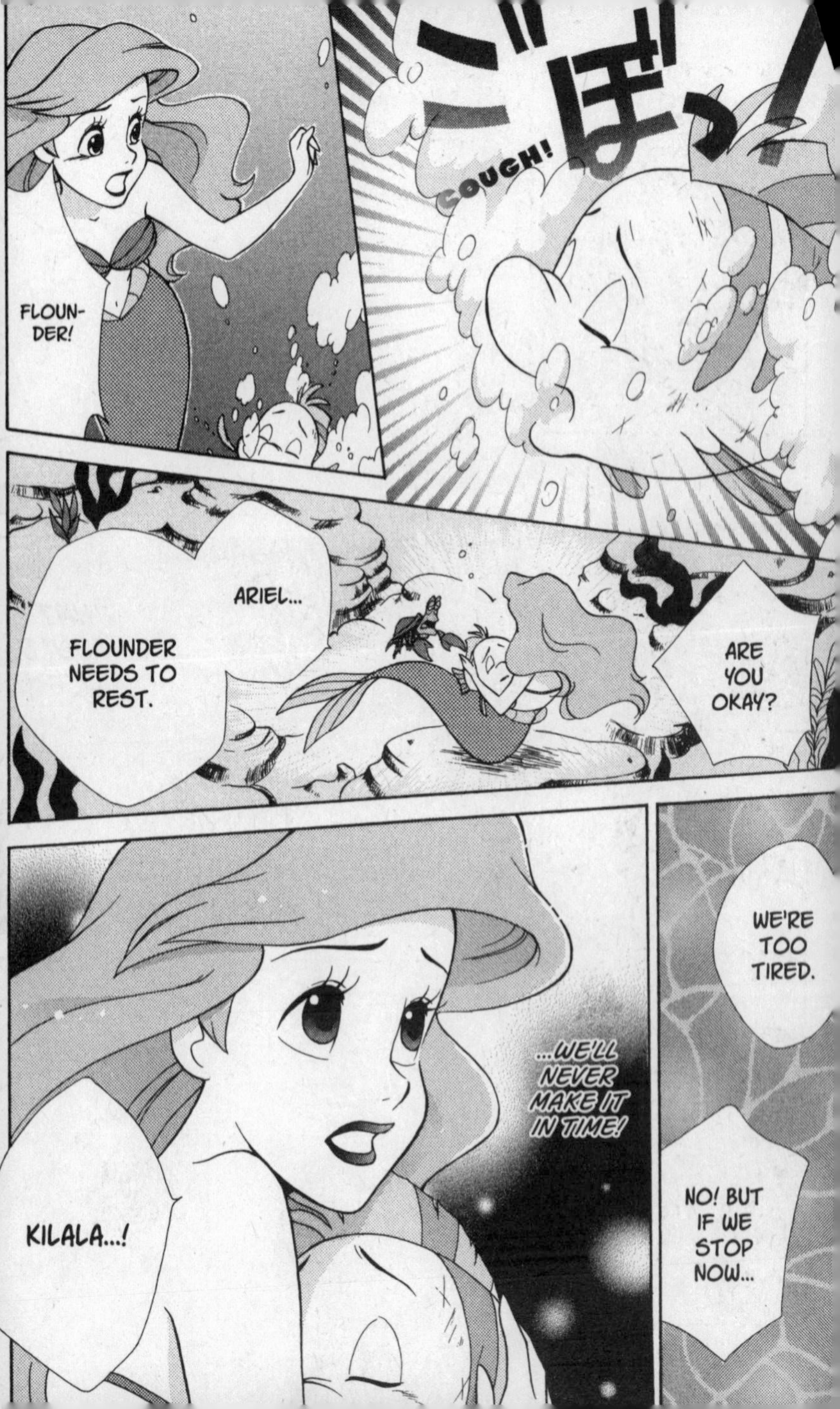
ごぼっ!
COUGH!
FLOUN-DER!
ARE YOU OKAY?
ARIEL...
FLOUNDER NEEDS TO REST.
WE'RE TOO TIRED.
NO! BUT IF WE STOP NOW...
...WE'LL NEVER MAKE IT IN TIME!
KILALA...!

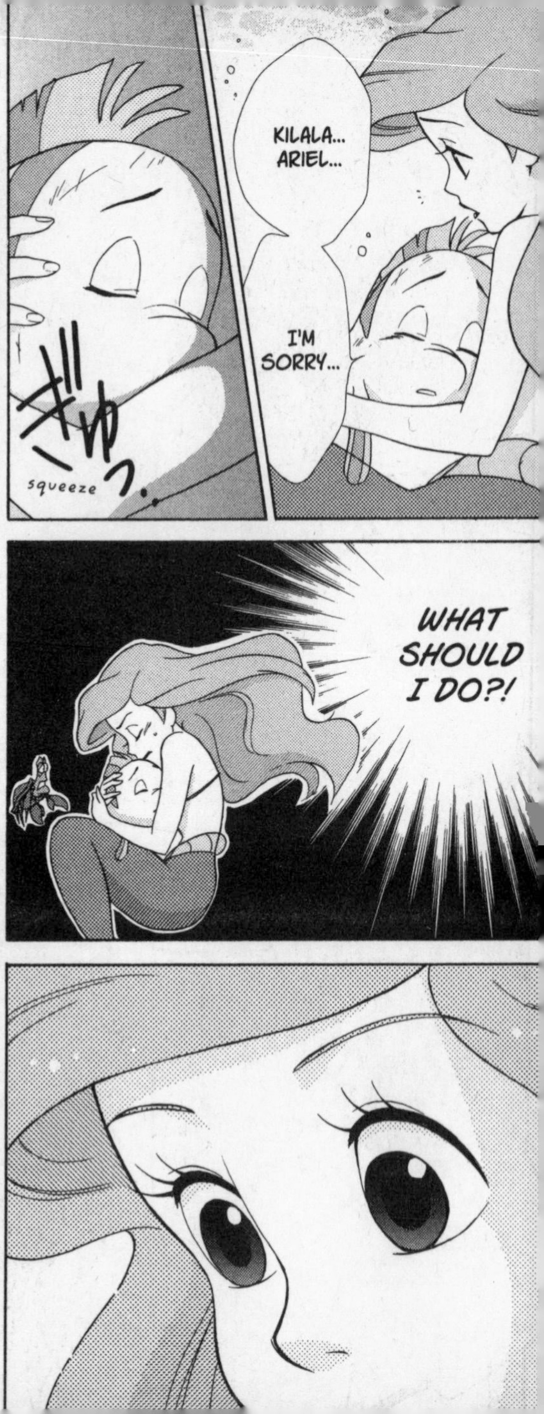
KILALA... ARIEL...
I'M SORRY...
ぎゅっ
squeeze
WHAT SHOULD I DO?!

A WORD FROM TIPPE 6

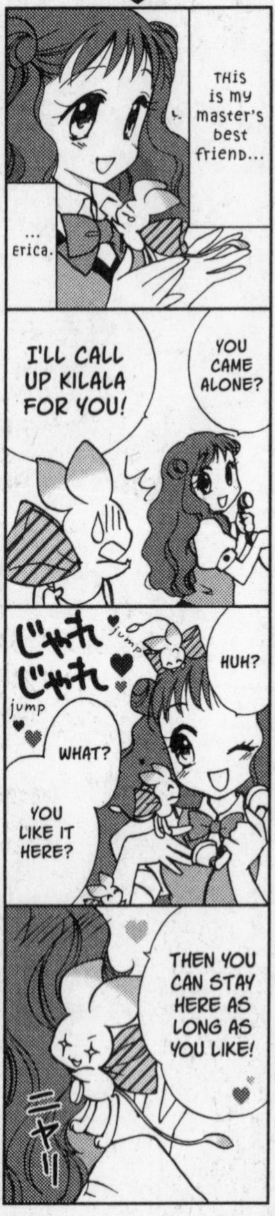
THIS is my master's best friend...
...Erica.
YOU CAME ALONE?
I'LL CALL UP KILALA FOR YOU!
HUH?
じゃれじゃれ
jump
jump
WHAT?
YOU LIKE IT HERE?
THEN YOU CAN STAY HERE AS LONG AS YOU LIKE!
ニヤリ

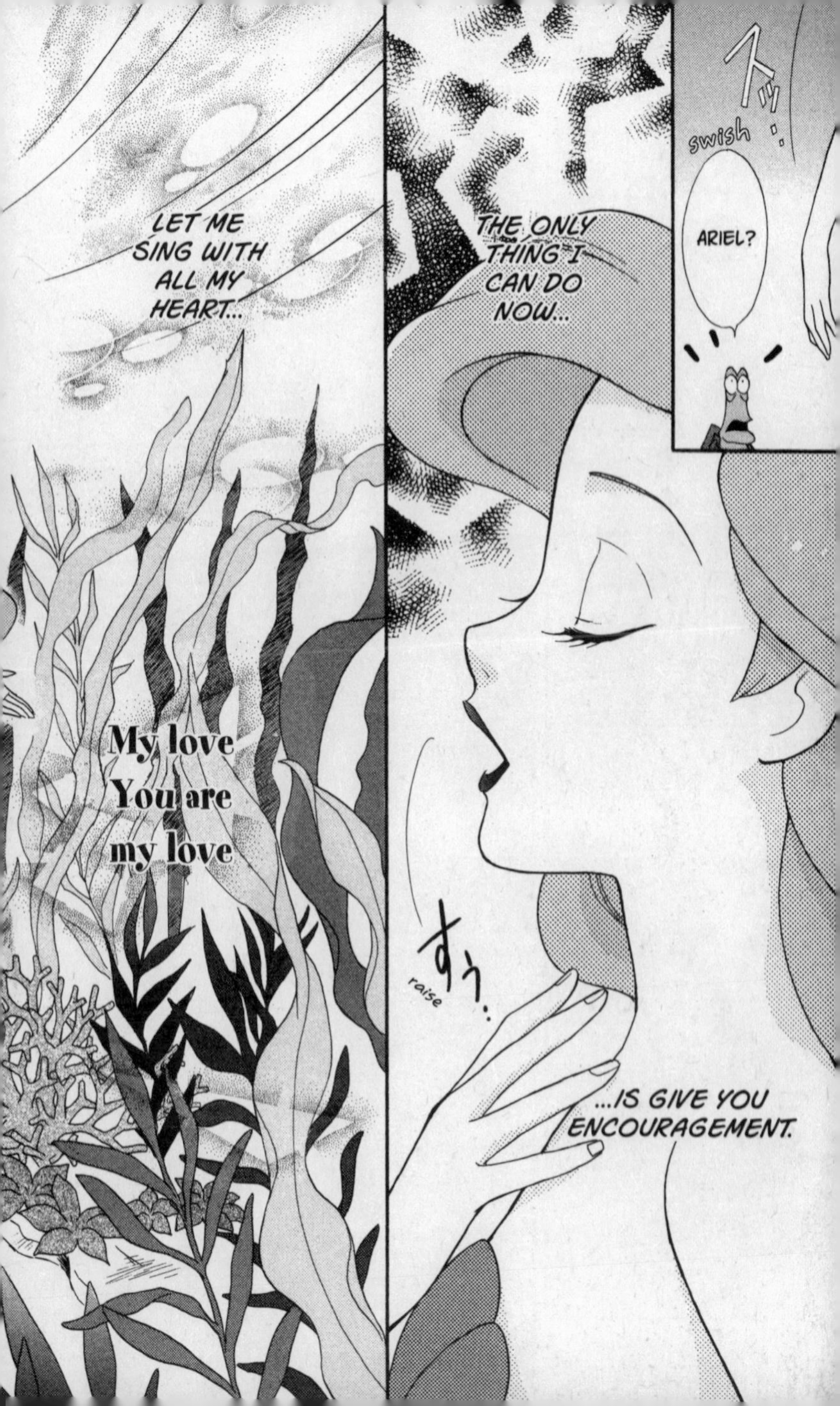
スッ
swish
ARIEL?
THE ONLY THING I CAN DO NOW...
すぅ
raise
...IS GIVE YOU ENCOURAGEMENT.
LET ME SING WITH ALL MY HEART...
My love You are my love

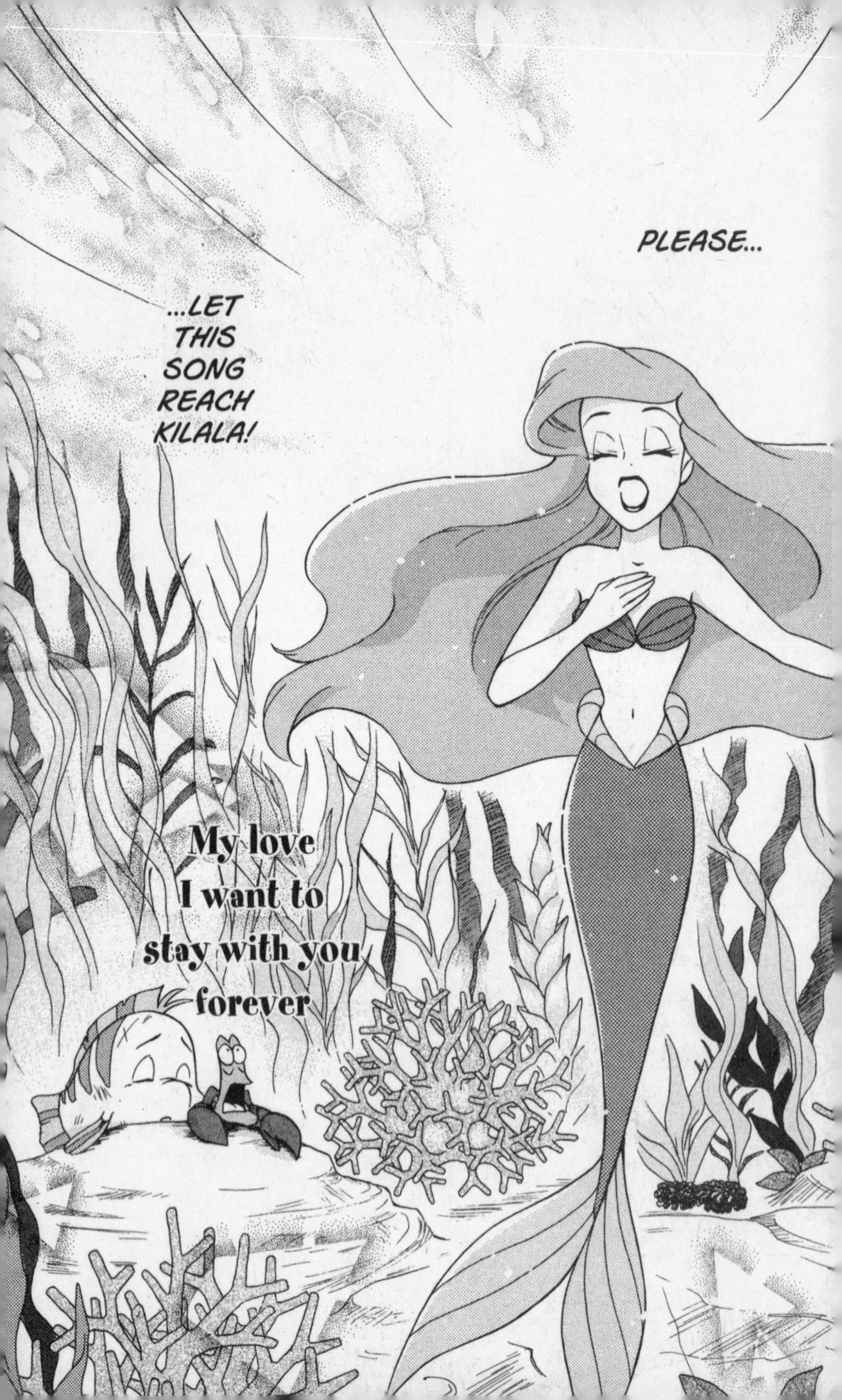
PLEASE...
...LET THIS SONG REACH KILALA!
My love I want to stay with you forever

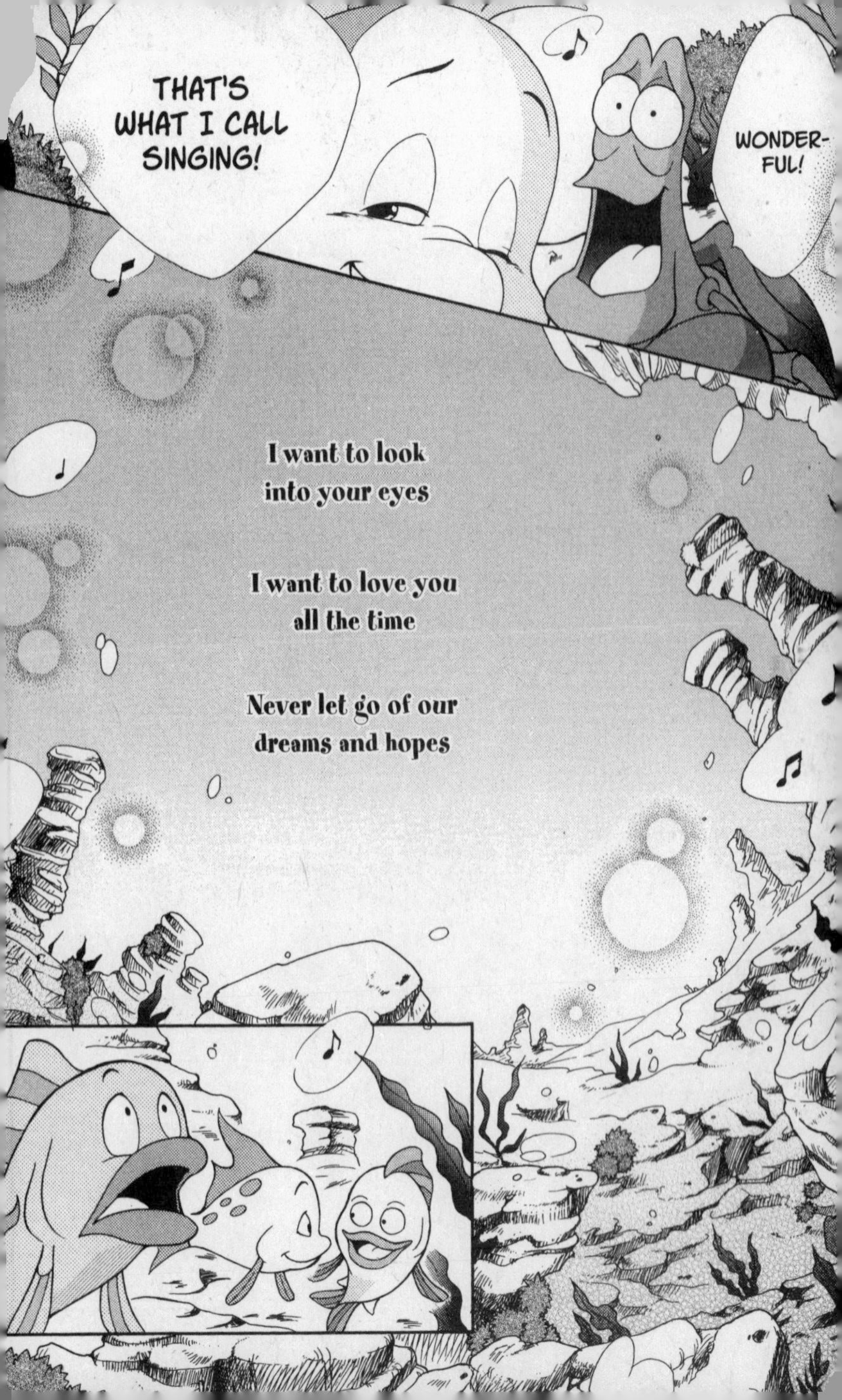
WONDER-FUL!
THAT'S WHAT I CALL SINGING!
I want to look into your eyes
I want to love you all the time
Never let go of our dreams and hopes

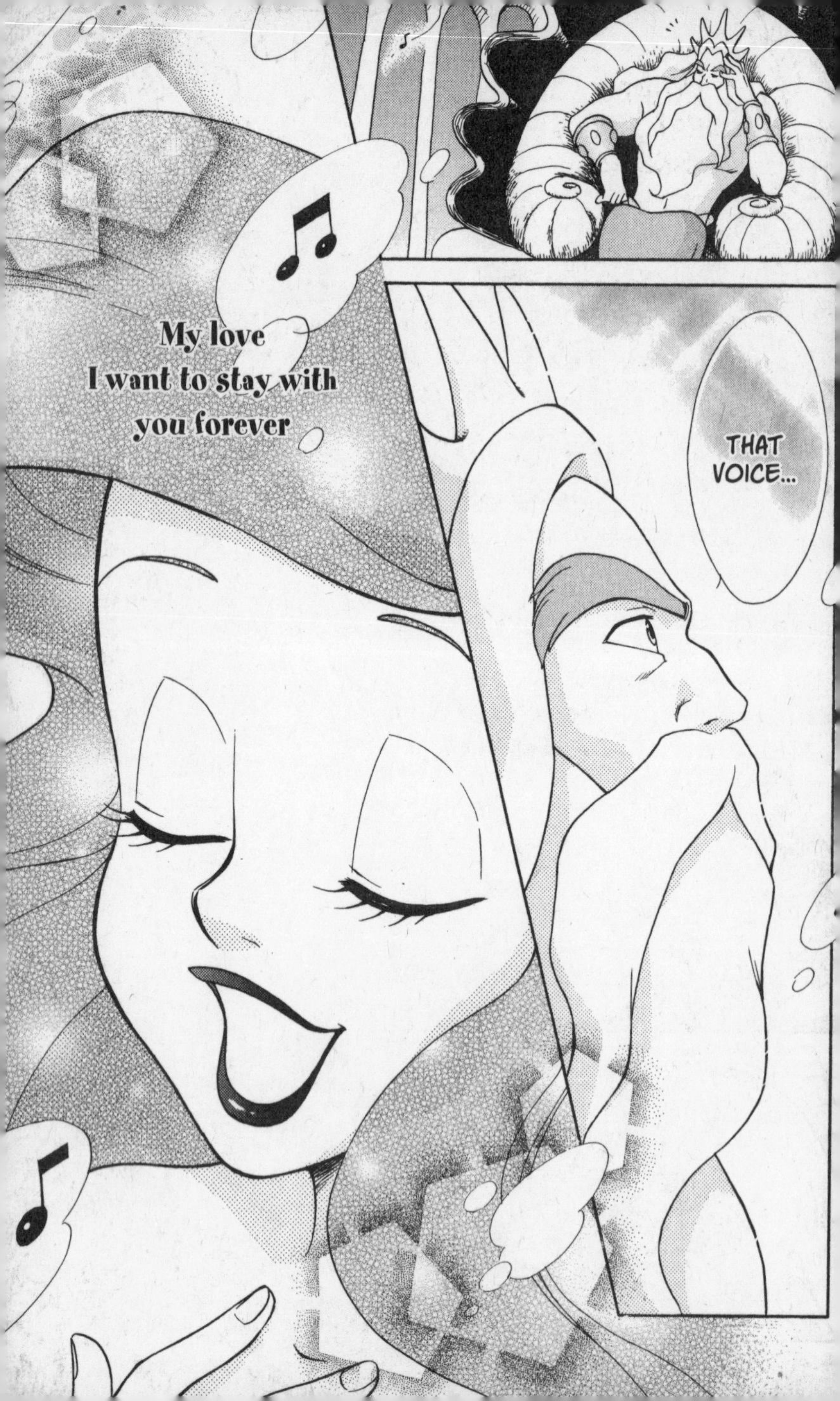
THAT VOICE...
My love I want to stay with you forever

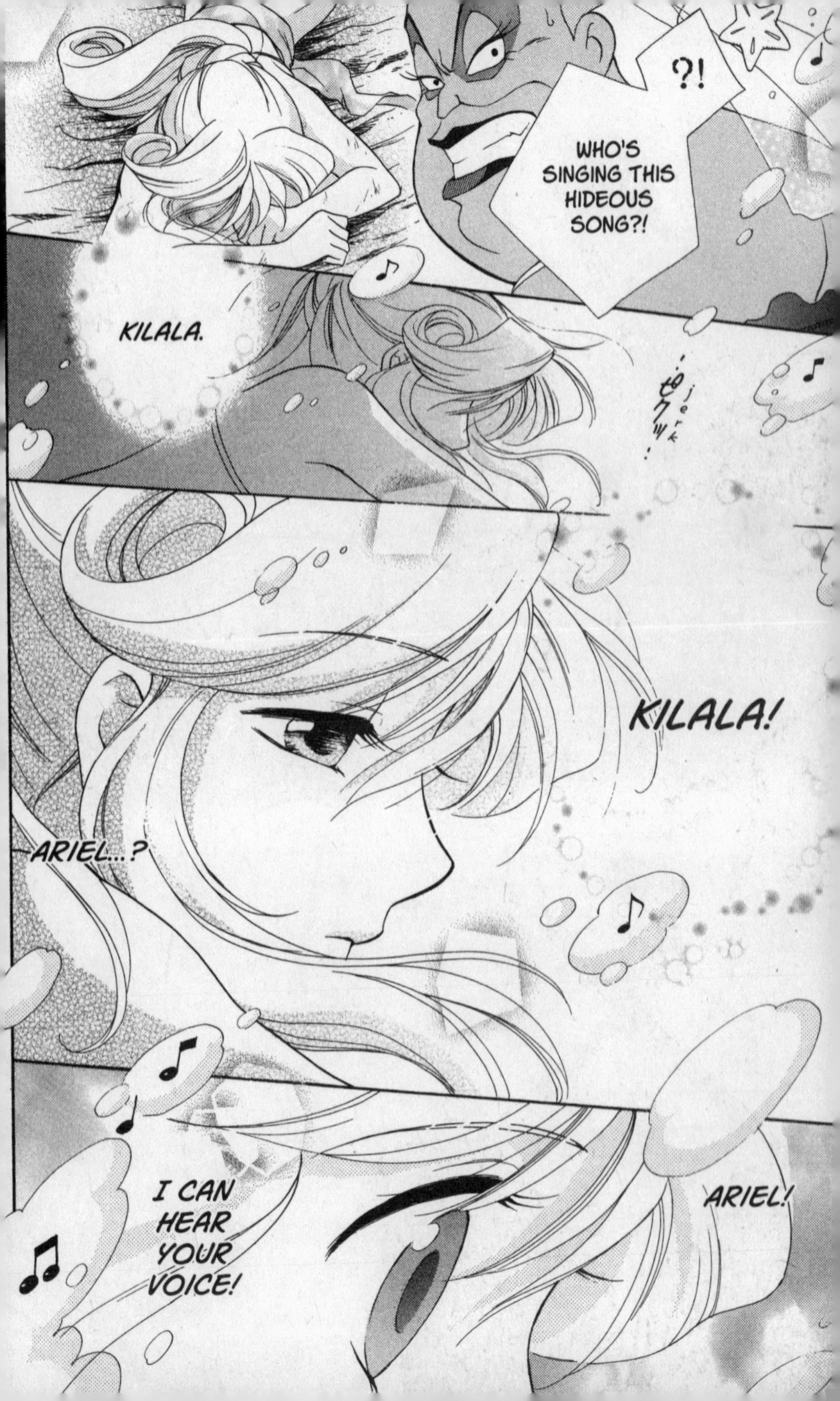
?!
WHO'S SINGING THIS HIDEOUS SONG?!
jerk
KILALA.
KILALA!
ARIEL...?
ARIEL!
I CAN HEAR YOUR VOICE!

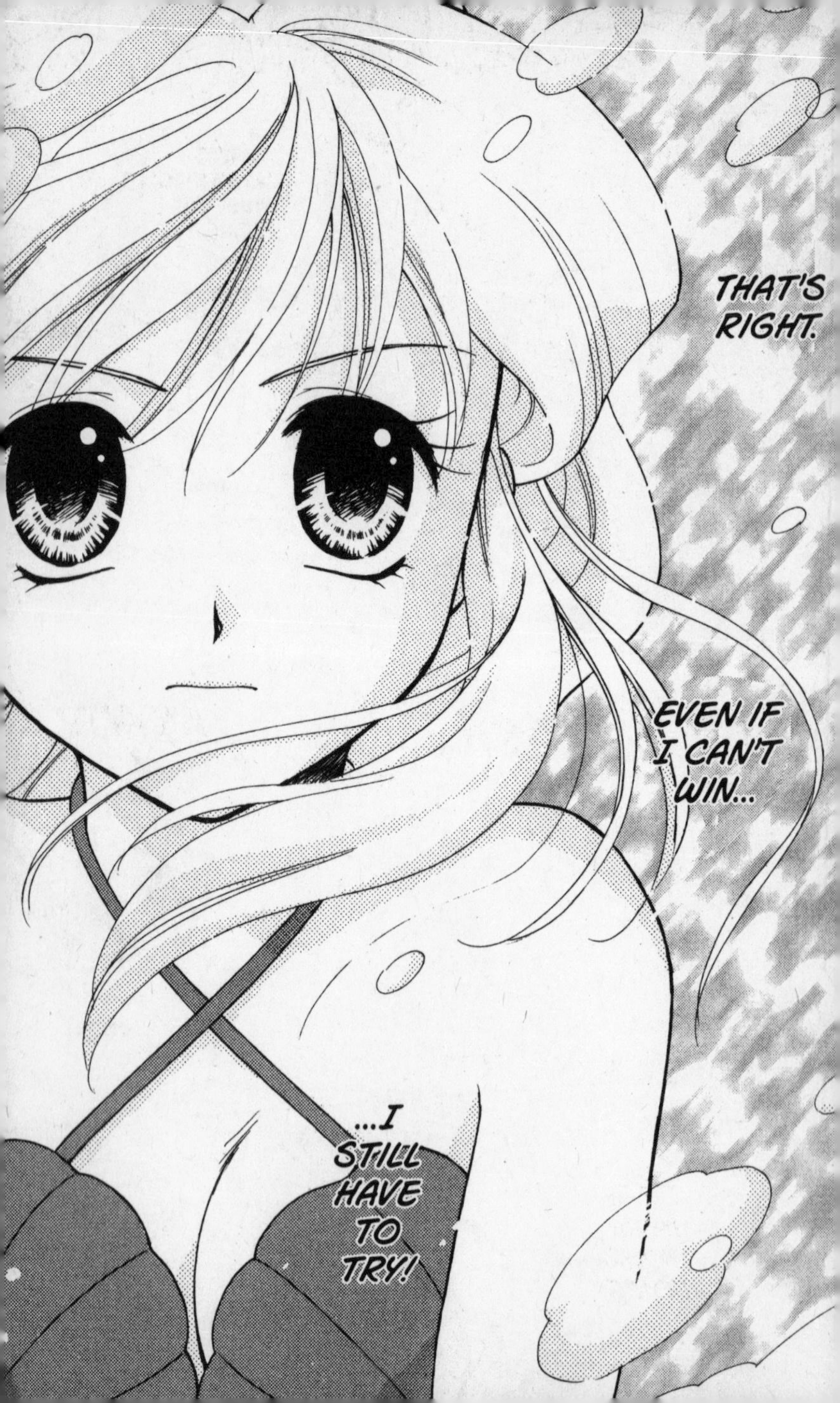
THAT'S RIGHT.
EVEN IF I CAN'T WIN...
...I STILL HAVE TO TRY!

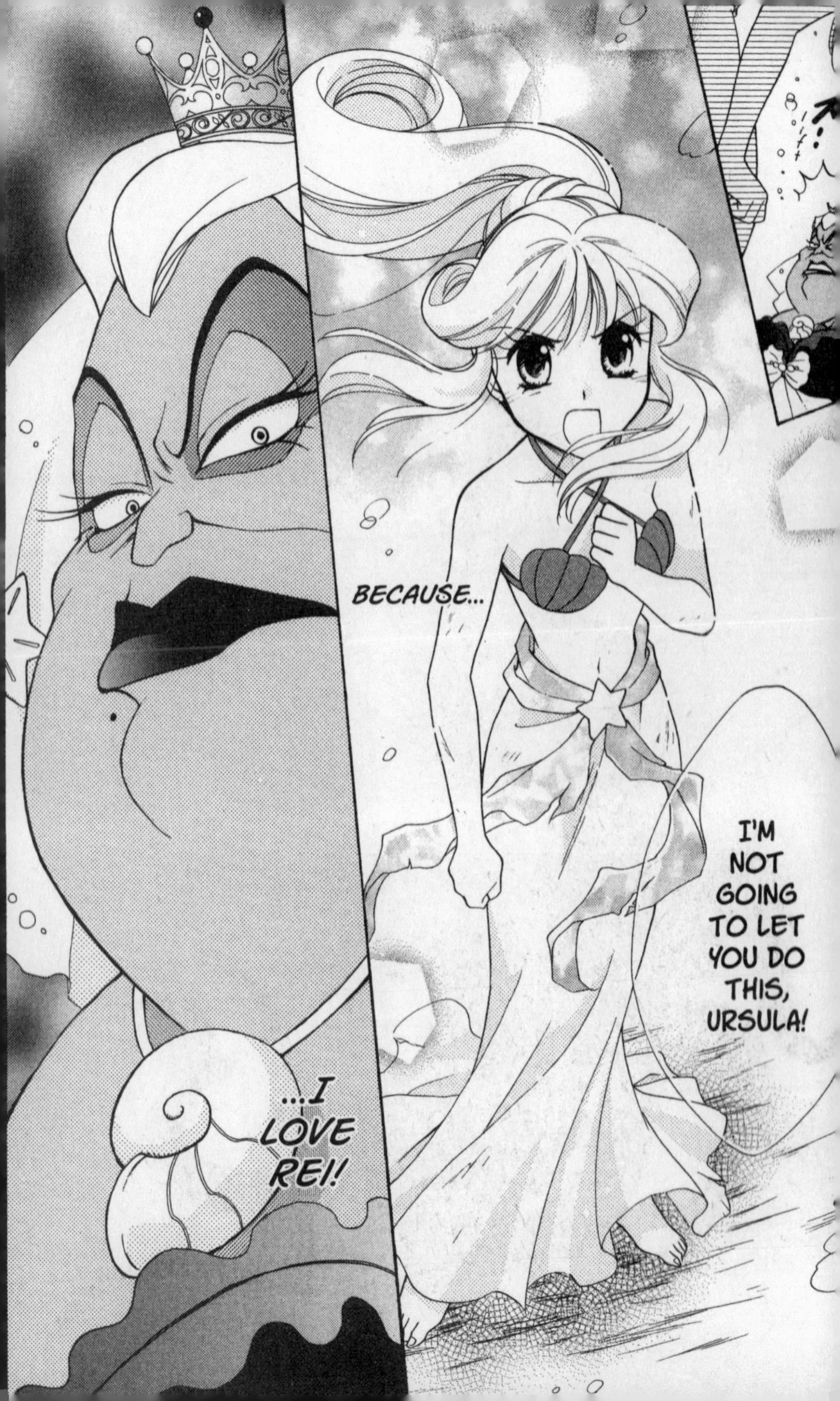
lift
I'M NOT GOING TO LET YOU DO THIS, URSULA!
BECAUSE...
...I LOVE REI!

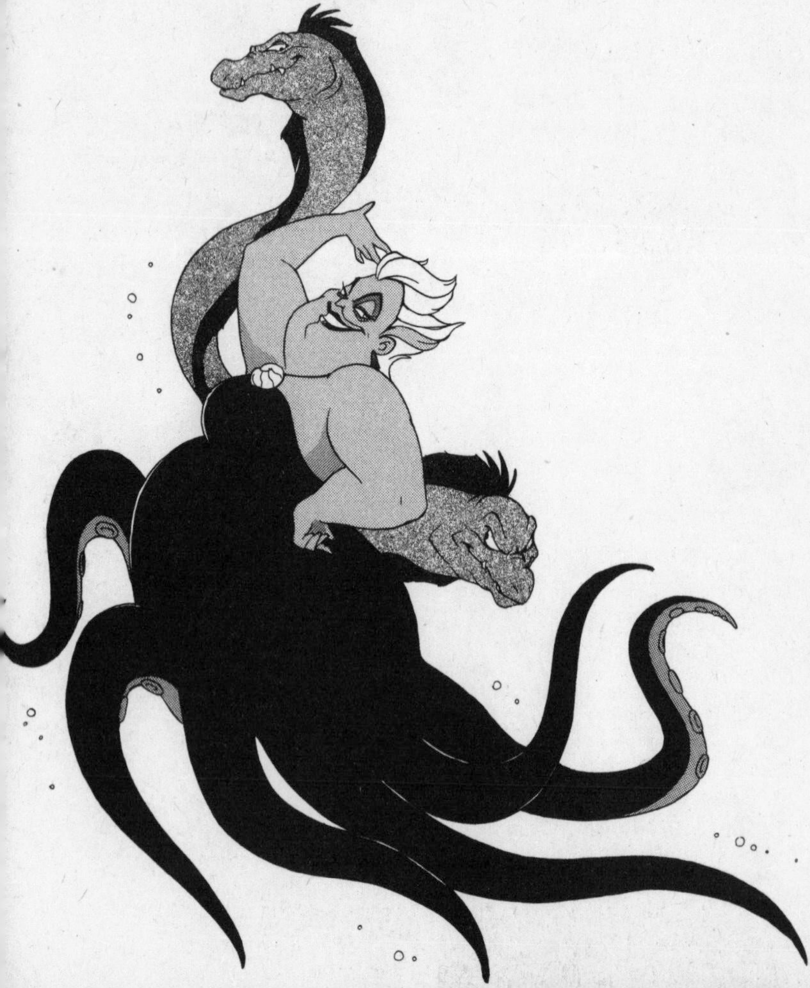

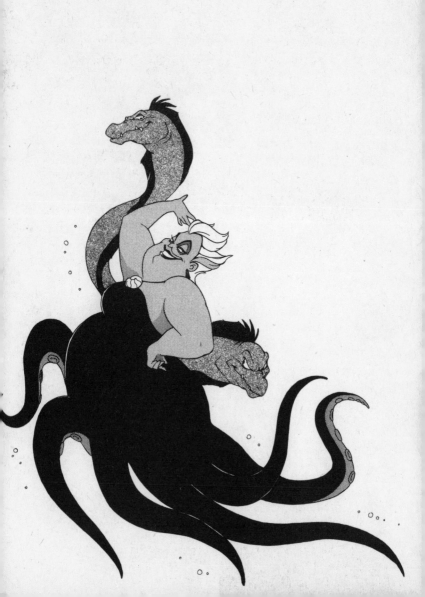

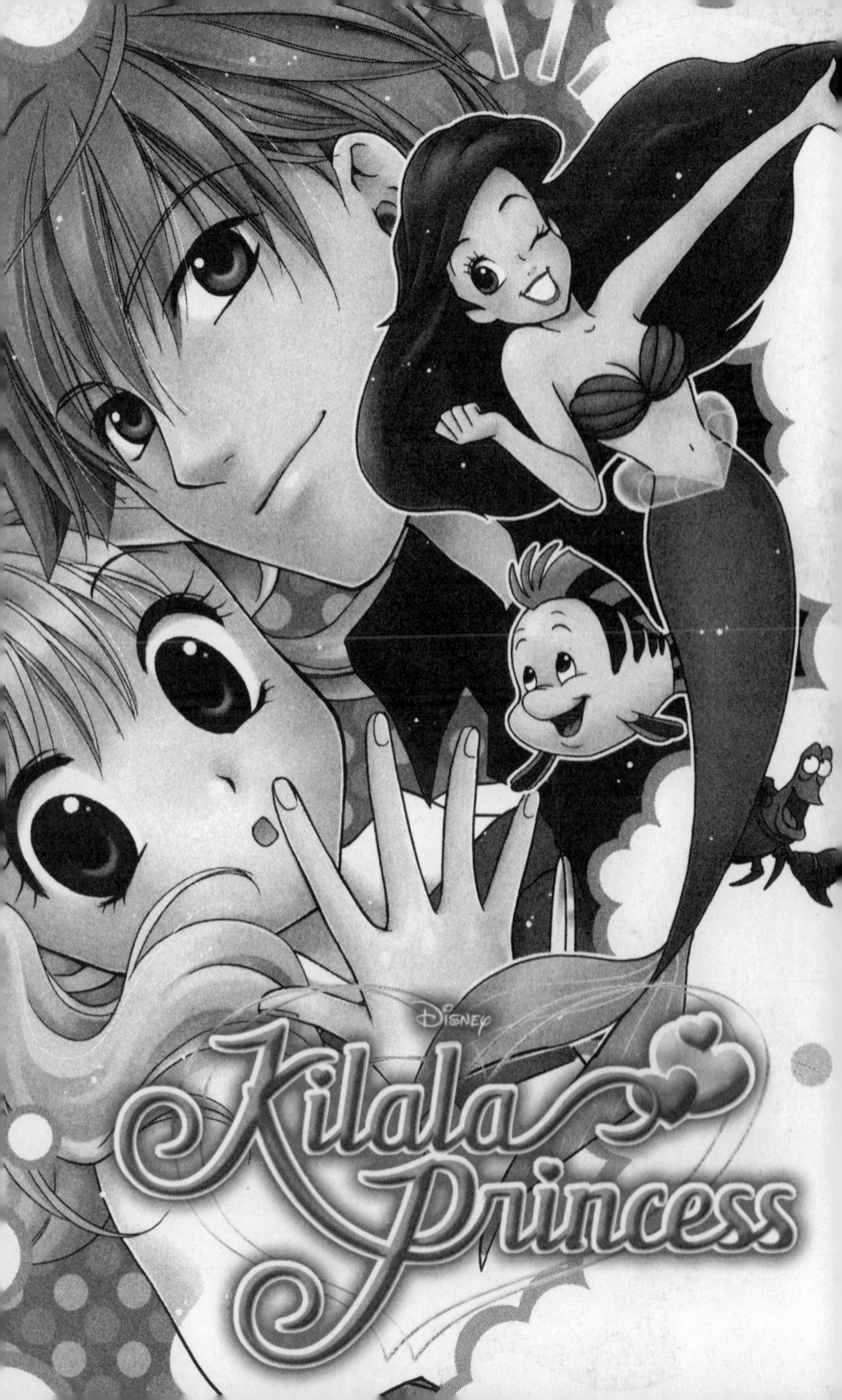

Disney
Kilala Princess

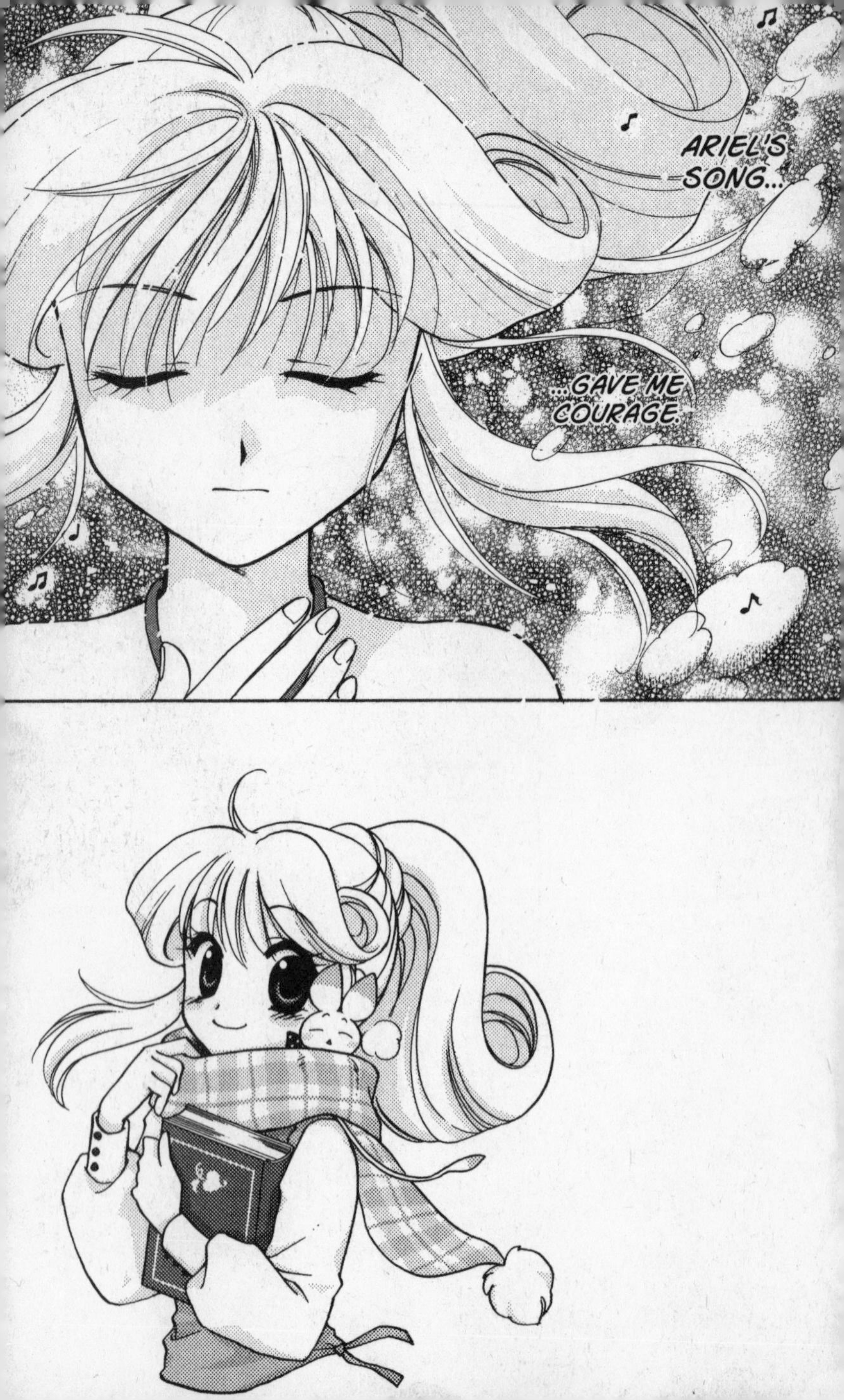
ARIEL'S SONG...
...GAVE ME COURAGE.

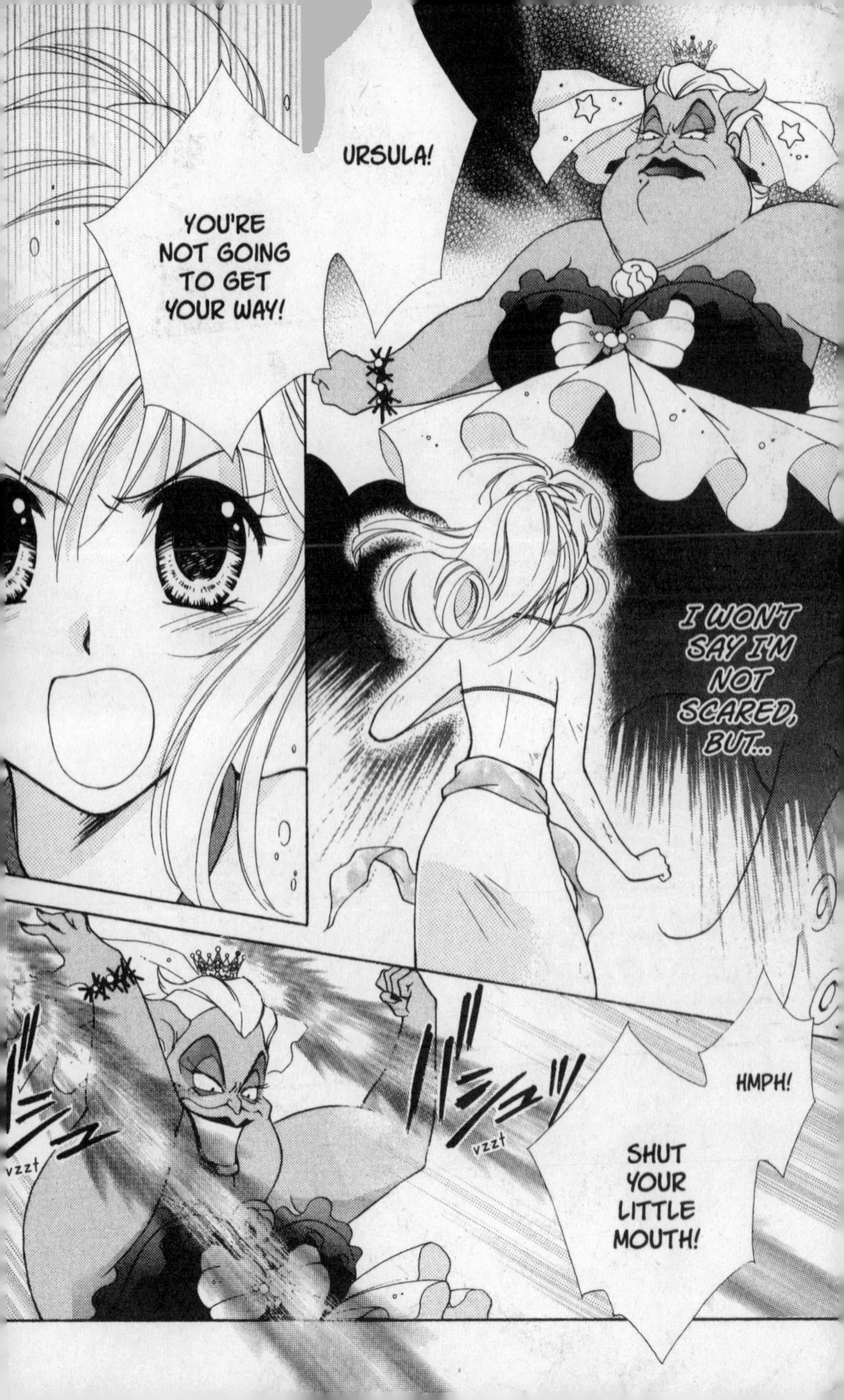
URSULA!
YOU'RE NOT GOING TO GET YOUR WAY!
I WON'T SAY I'M NOT SCARED, BUT...
HMPH!
SHUT YOUR LITTLE MOUTH!
vzzt
vzzt

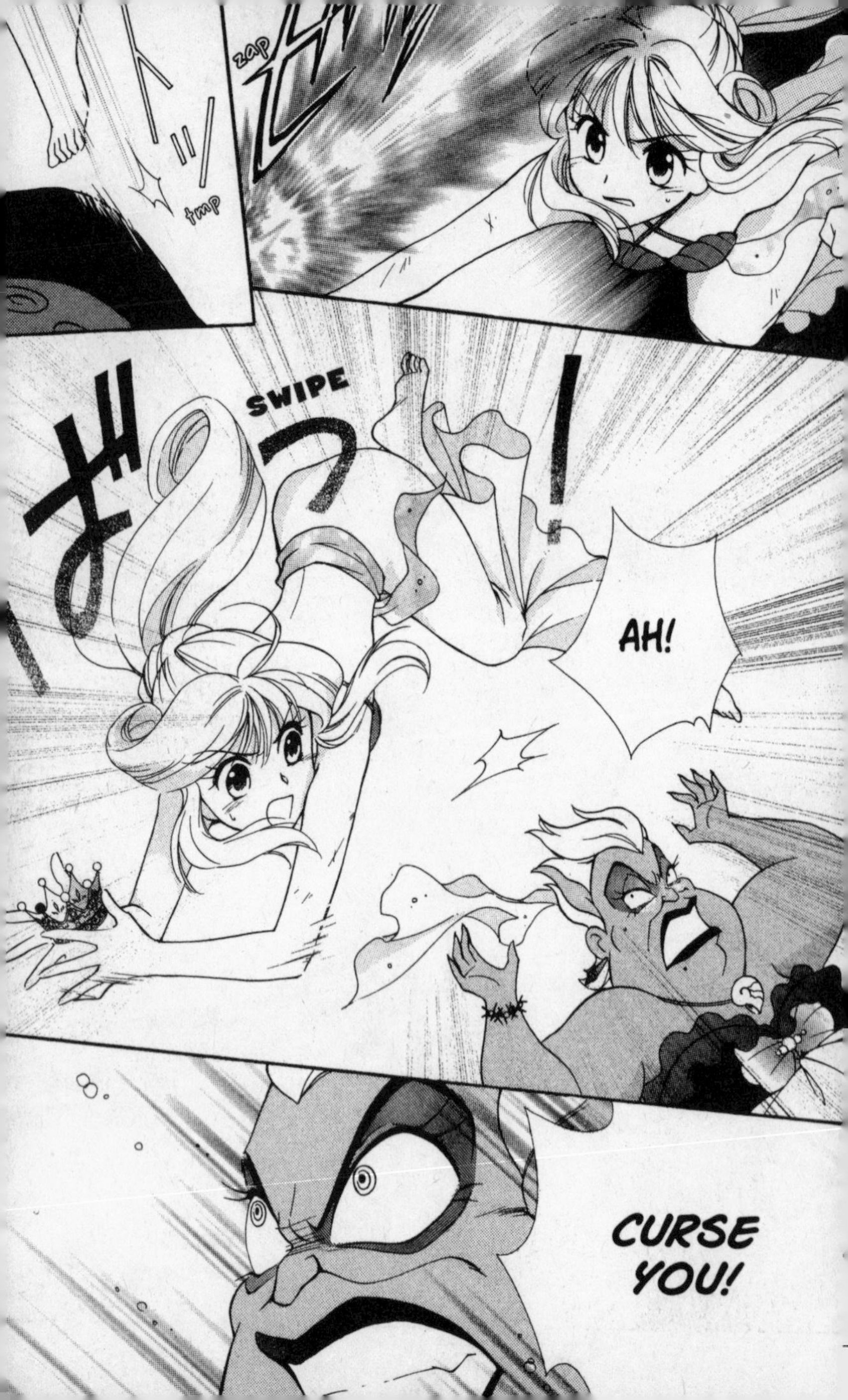
zap
tmp
SWIPE
AH!
CURSE YOU!

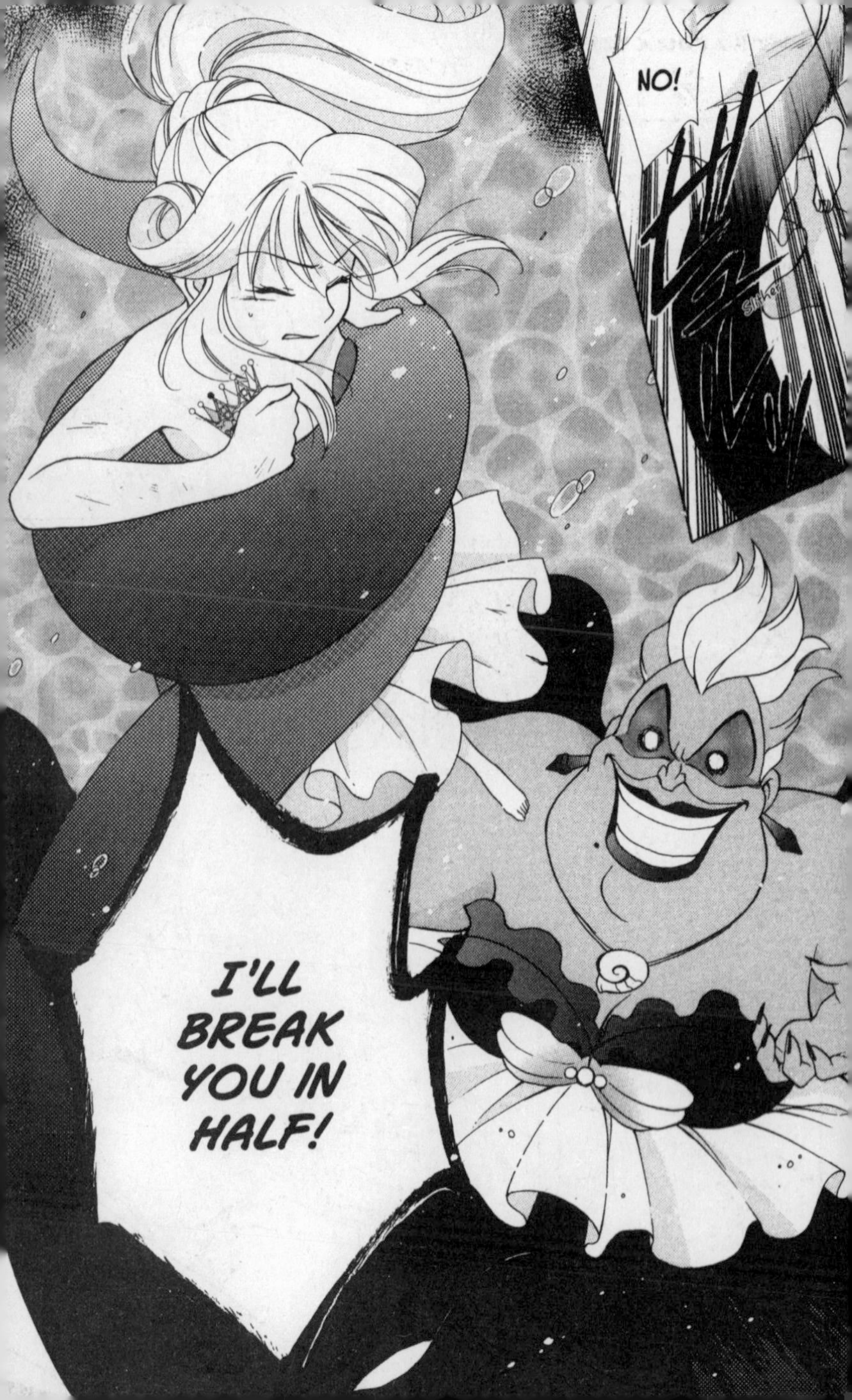
NO!
Slither
I'LL BREAK YOU IN HALF!

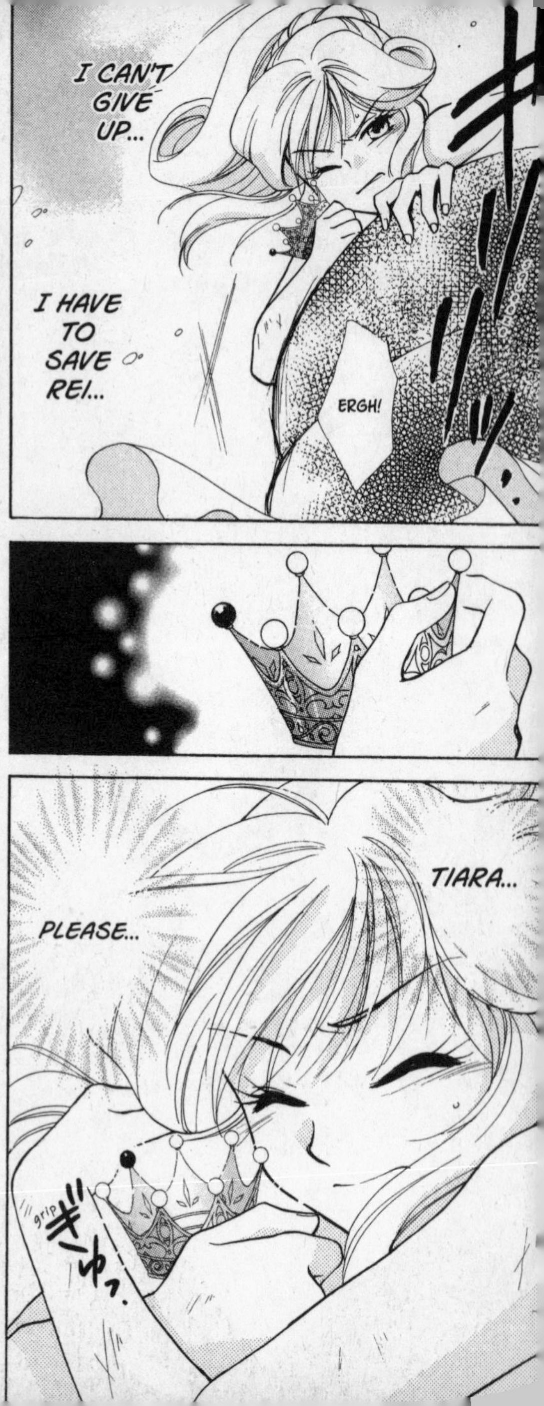
I CAN'T GIVE UP...
I HAVE TO SAVE REI...
ERGH!
TIARA...
PLEASE...
grip

A WORD FROM TIPPE

7

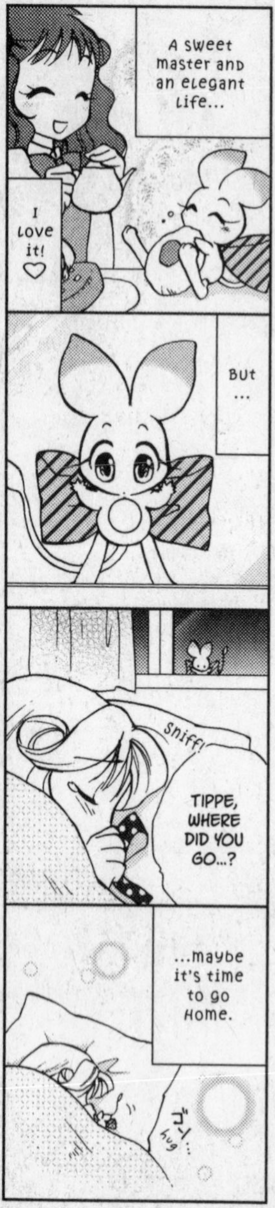
A sweet master and an elegant life...
I love it! ♡
But ...
Sniff!
TIPPE, WHERE DID YOU GO...?
...maybe it's time to go home.
hug

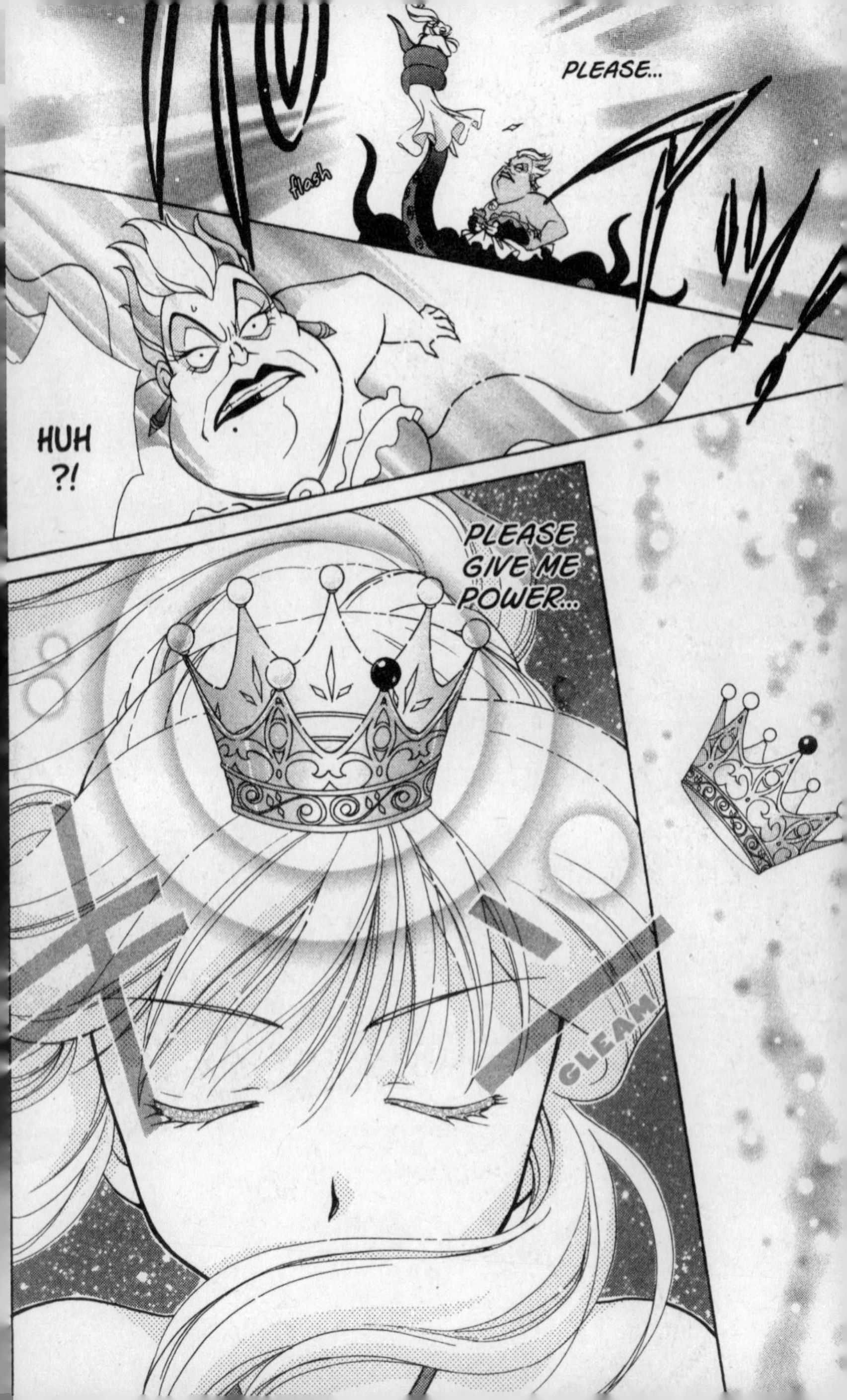
PLEASE...
flash
HUH ?!
PLEASE GIVE ME POWER...
GLEAM

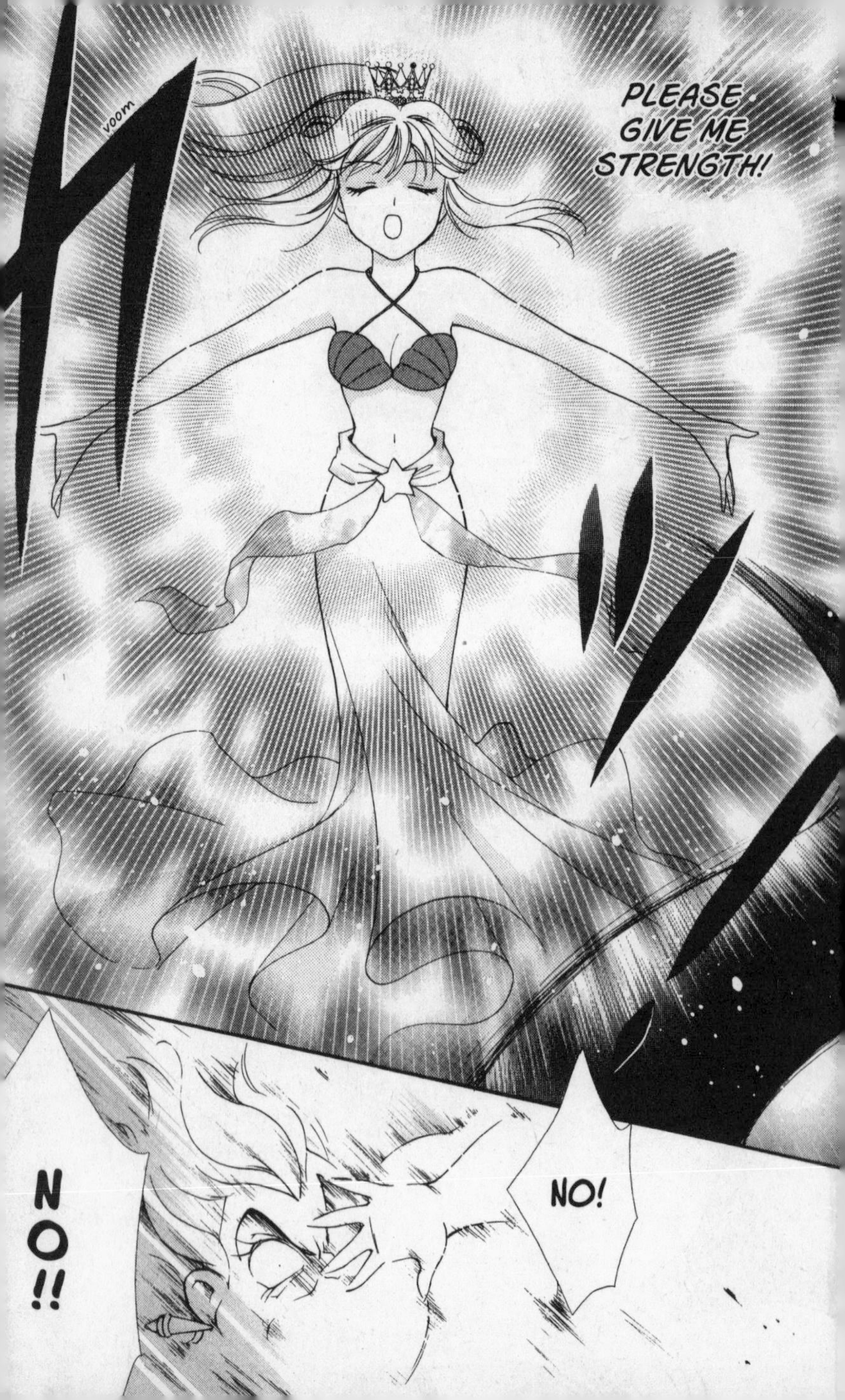
PLEASE GIVE ME STRENGTH!
voom
NO!
NO NO!!

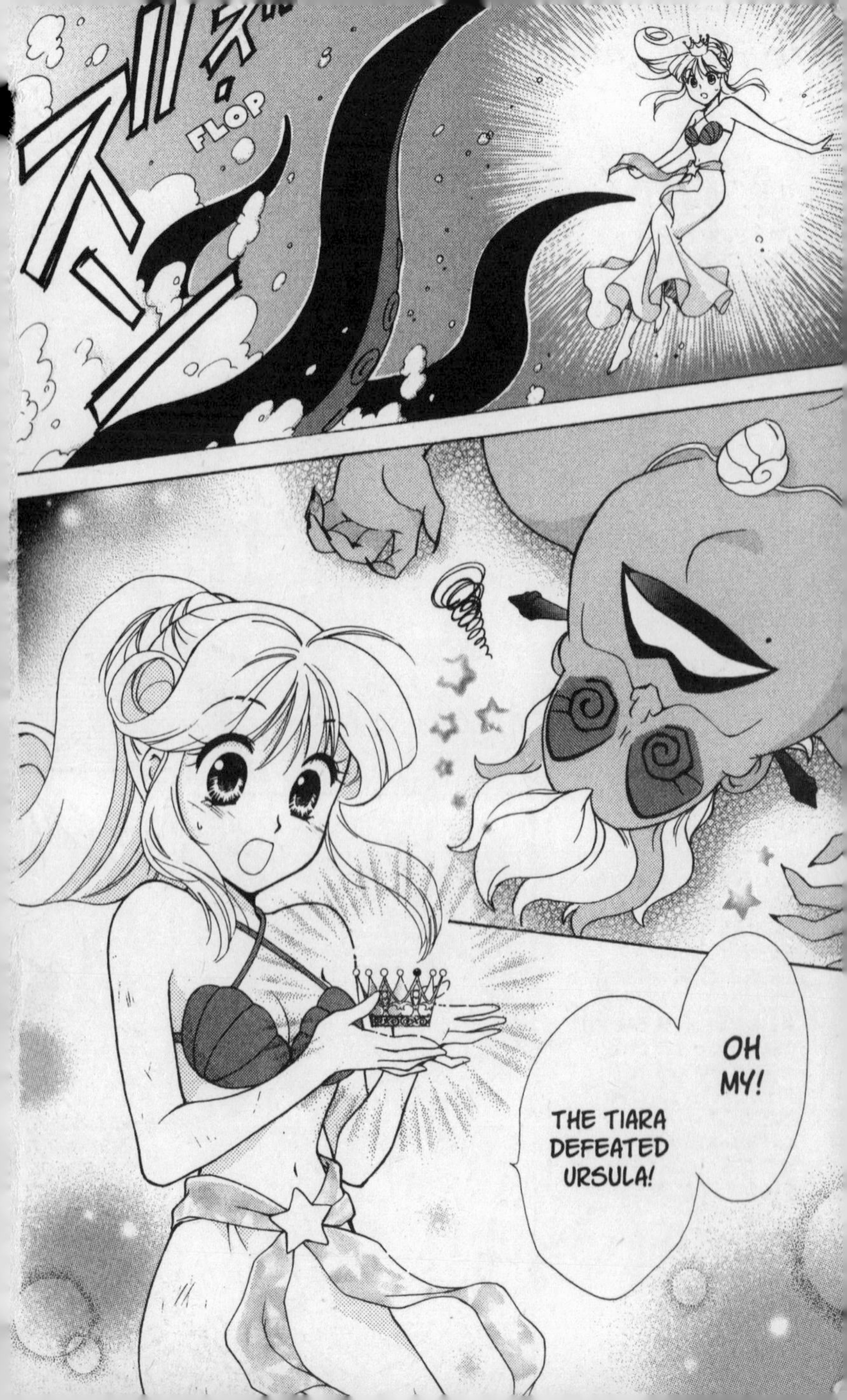
FLOP
OH MY!
THE TIARA DEFEATED URSULA!

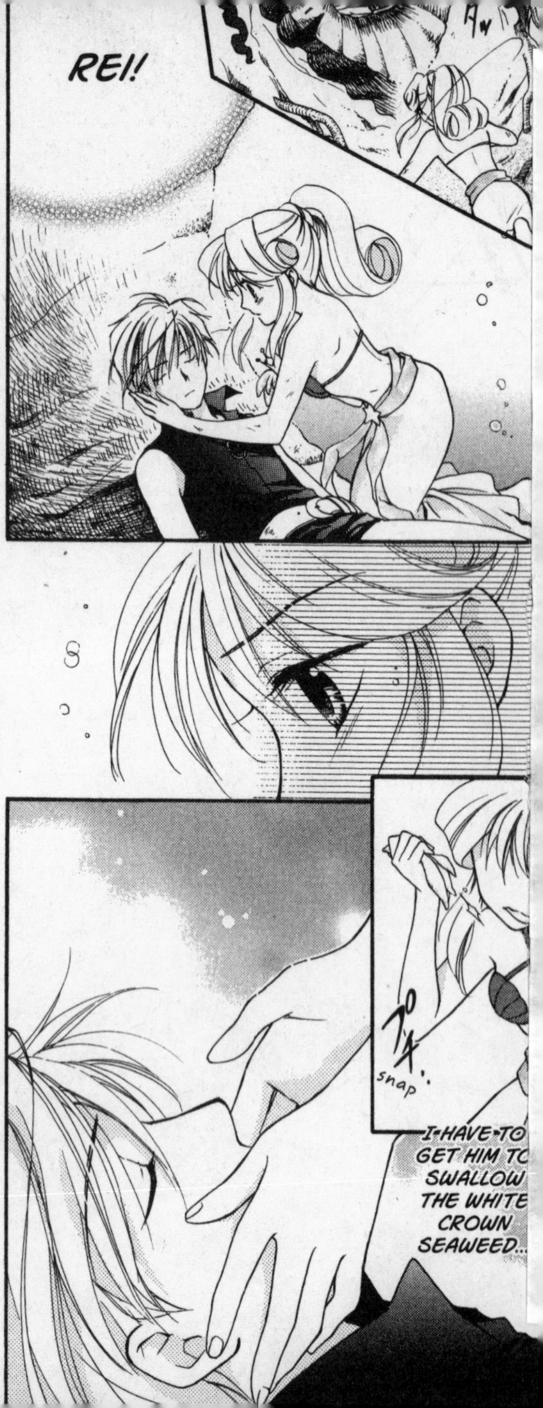
REI!
snap
I HAVE TO GET HIM TO SWALLOW THE WHITE CROWN SEAWEED...

Rika Tanaka

HELLO! MY NAME IS RIKA TANAKA, AND I'M WRITING THE STORY FOR *KILALA PRINCESS*. THIS TIME THE STORY REVOLVES AROUND ARIEL, EVERYONE'S FAVORITE PRINCESS.☆

THE LITTLE MERMAID STORY I READ WHEN I WAS A CHILD HAD A VERY SAD ENDING, AND THAT'S WHY I LOVE THE CHEERFUL AND ENERGETIC ARIEL IN DISNEY'S VERSION OF *THE LITTLE MERMAID*.

ARIEL IN THIS STORY HAS YET TO MEET HER PRINCE CHARMING. ARIEL DOESN'T KNOW WHAT LOVE IS YET, AND SHE'S SO CUTE ASKING KILALA ABOUT LOVE.

I ALMOST WANT TO WHISPER TO ARIEL, "YOU'RE ABOUT TO MEET YOUR PRINCE CHARMING."☆

KILALA'S SO LUCKY SHE GETS TO SWIM ABOUT FREELY IN THE OCEAN ON THE BACK OF A DOLPHIN WITH ARIEL AND SING SONGS TOGETHER. I'M SO JEALOUS!

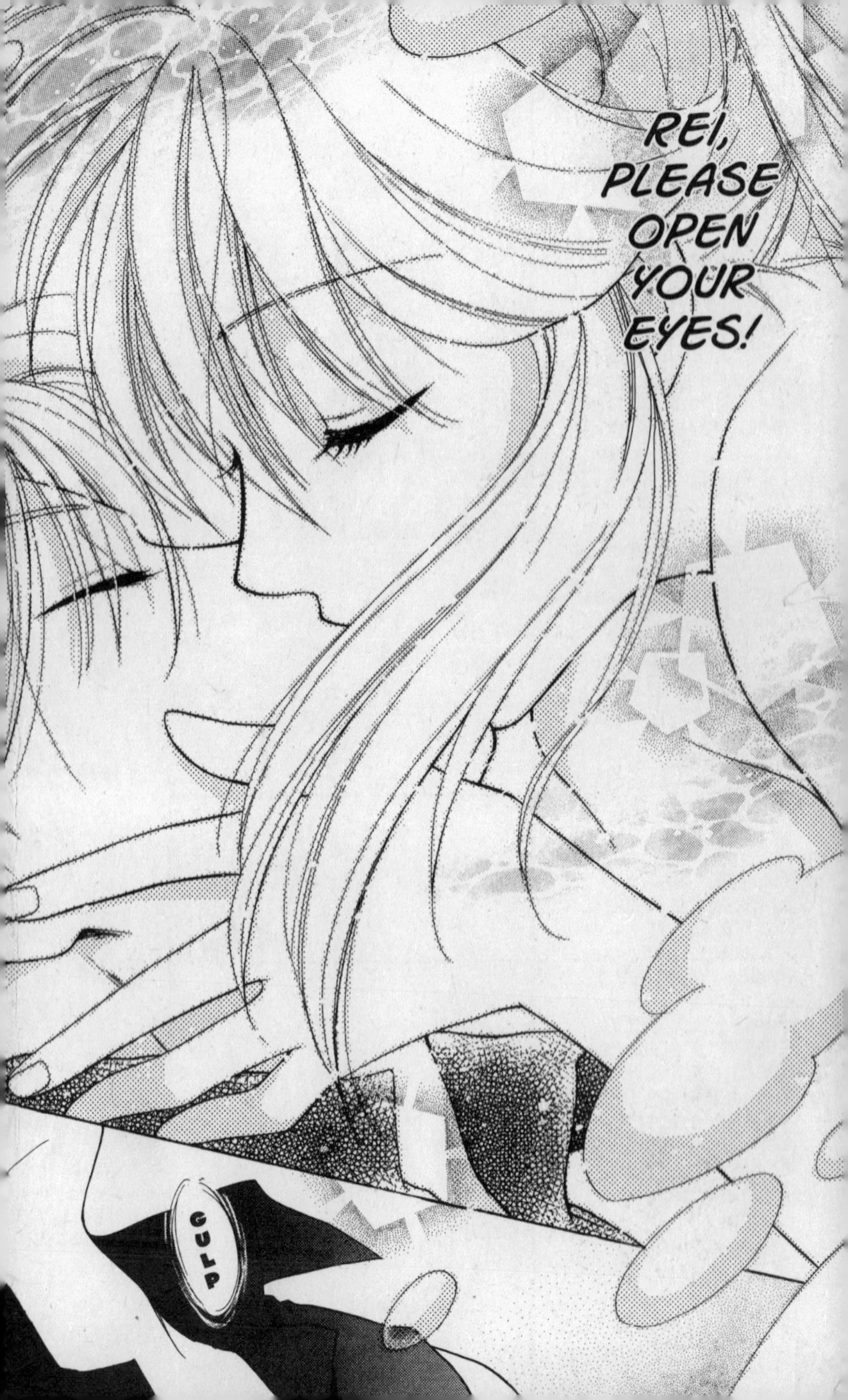
REI, PLEASE OPEN YOUR EYES!
GULP

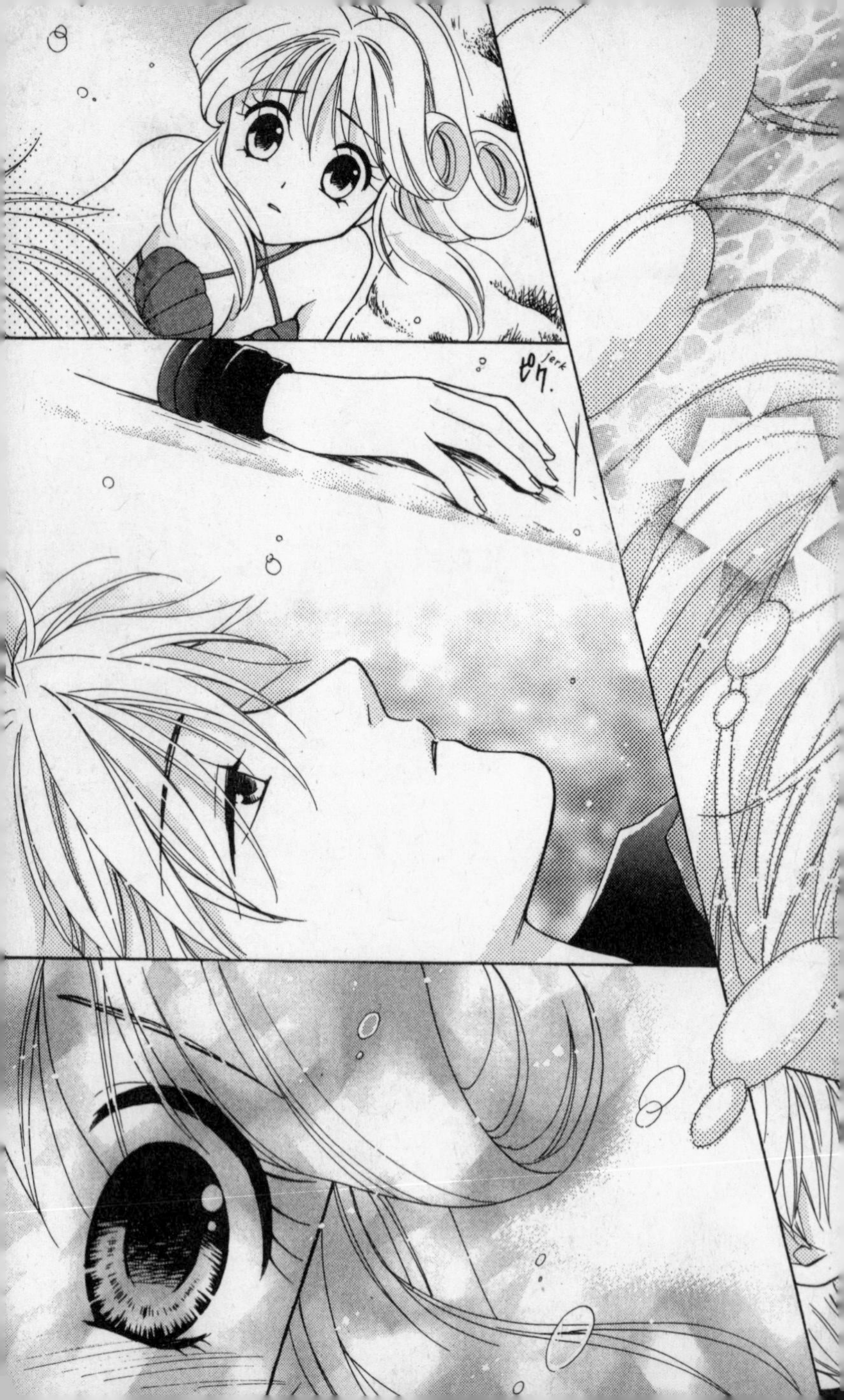
ぴく.
jerk

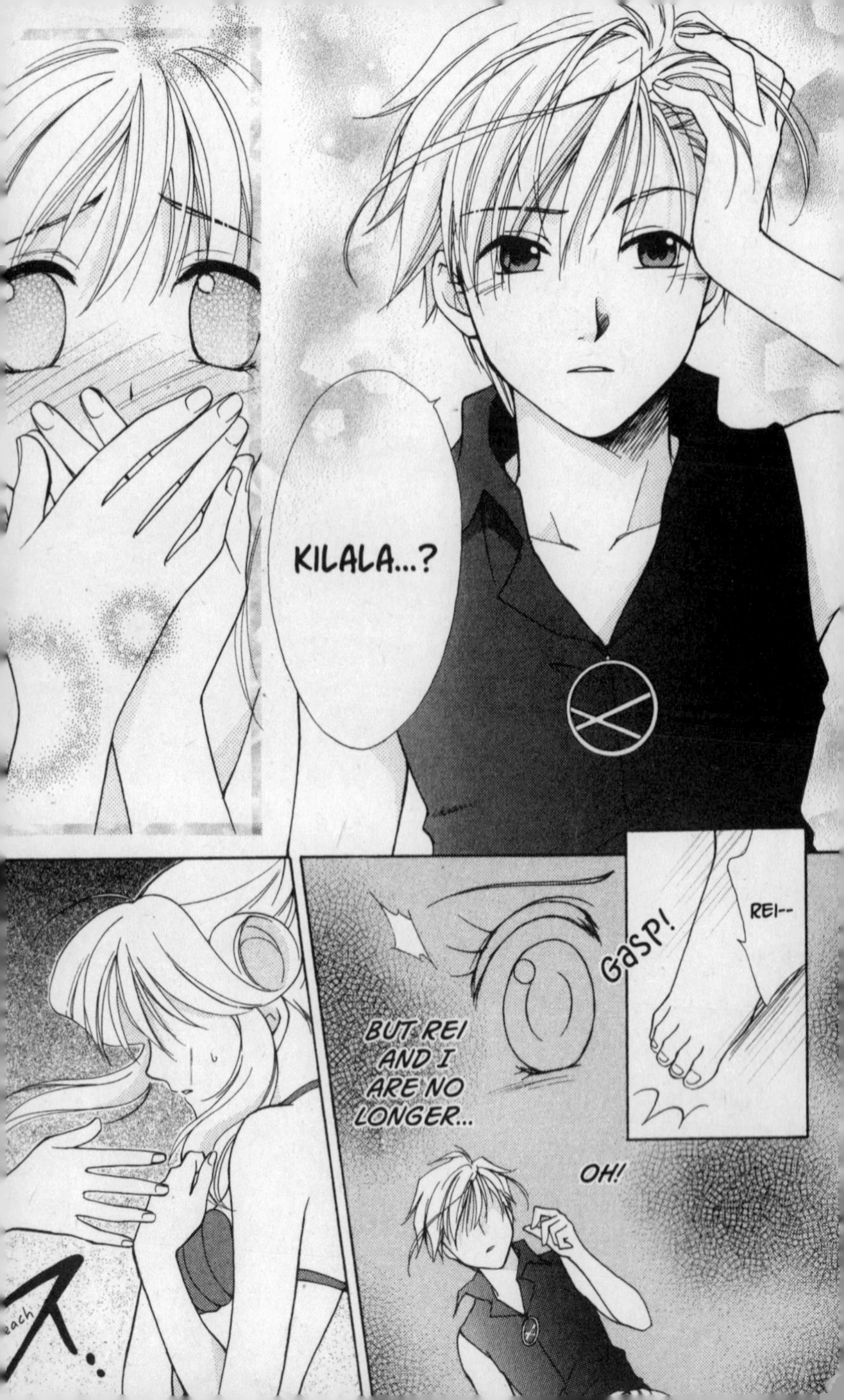
KILALA...?
REI--
GASP!
BUT REI AND I ARE NO LONGER...
OH!

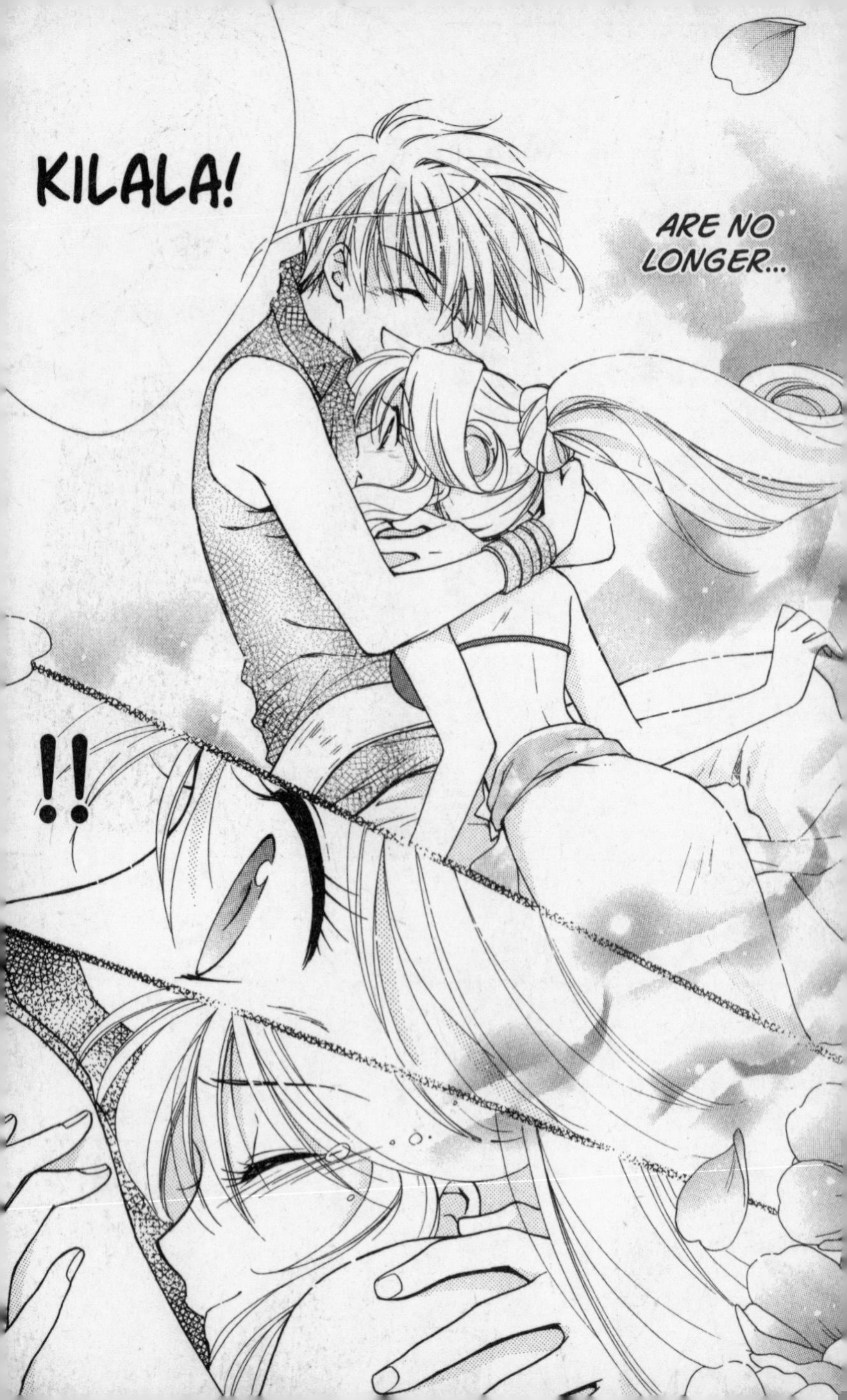
ARE NO
LONGER...
KILALA!
!!

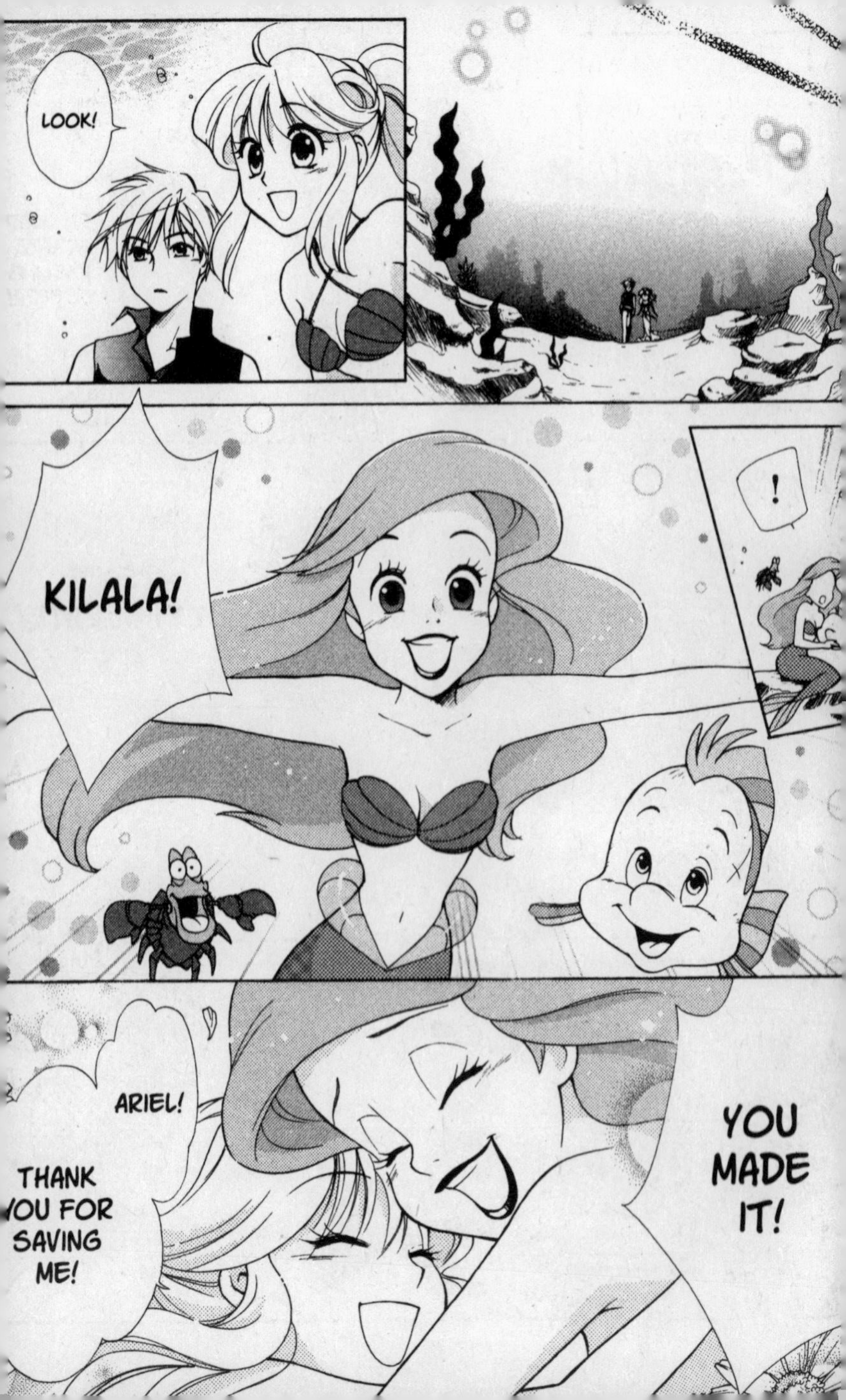
LOOK!
!
KILALA!
YOU MADE IT!
ARIEL!
THANK YOU FOR SAVING ME!

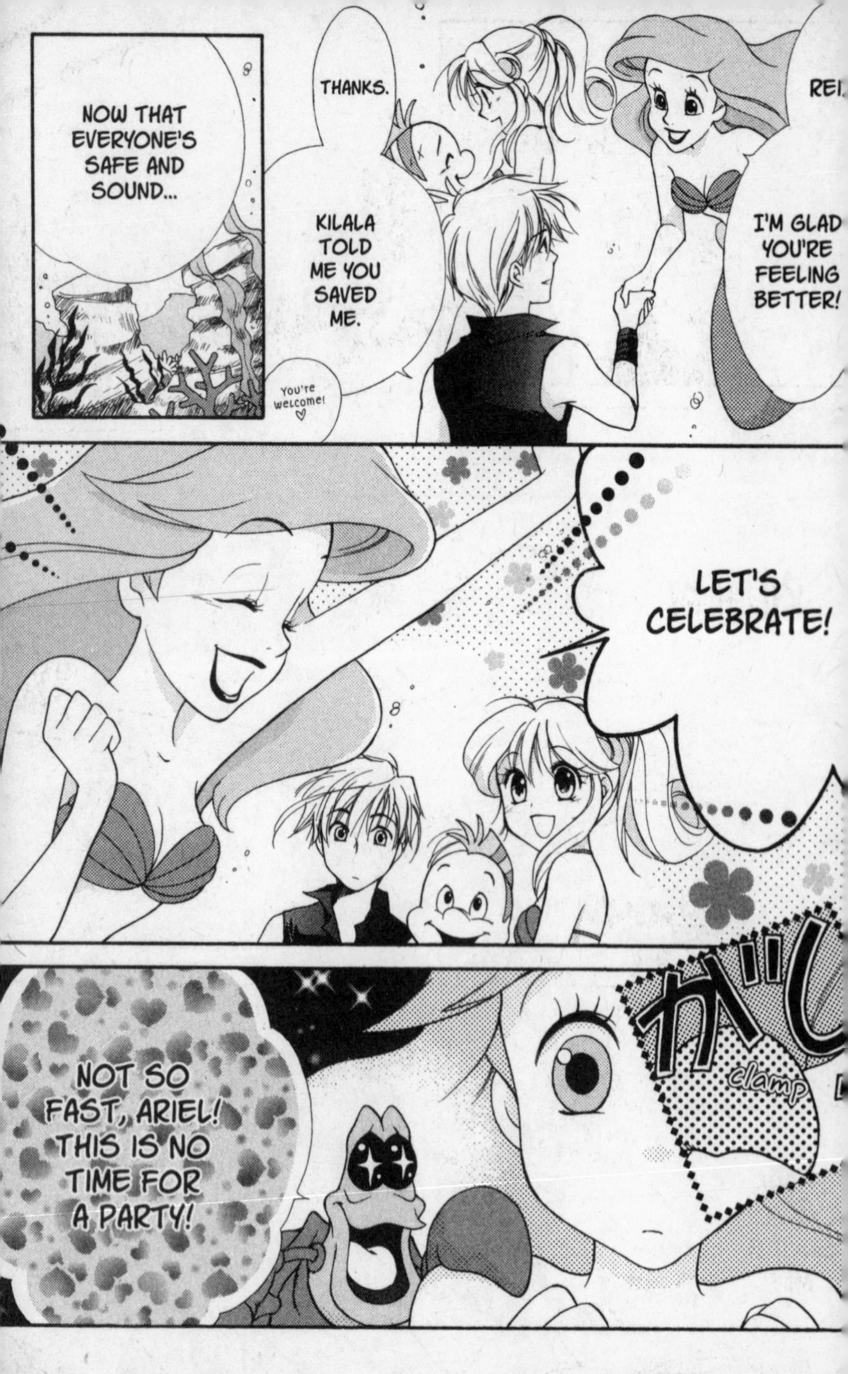

REI.
I'M GLAD YOU'RE FEELING BETTER!
THANKS.
KILALA TOLD ME YOU SAVED ME.
You're welcome! ♡
NOW THAT EVERYONE'S SAFE AND SOUND...
LET'S CELEBRATE!
clamp
NOT SO FAST, ARIEL! THIS IS NO TIME FOR A PARTY!

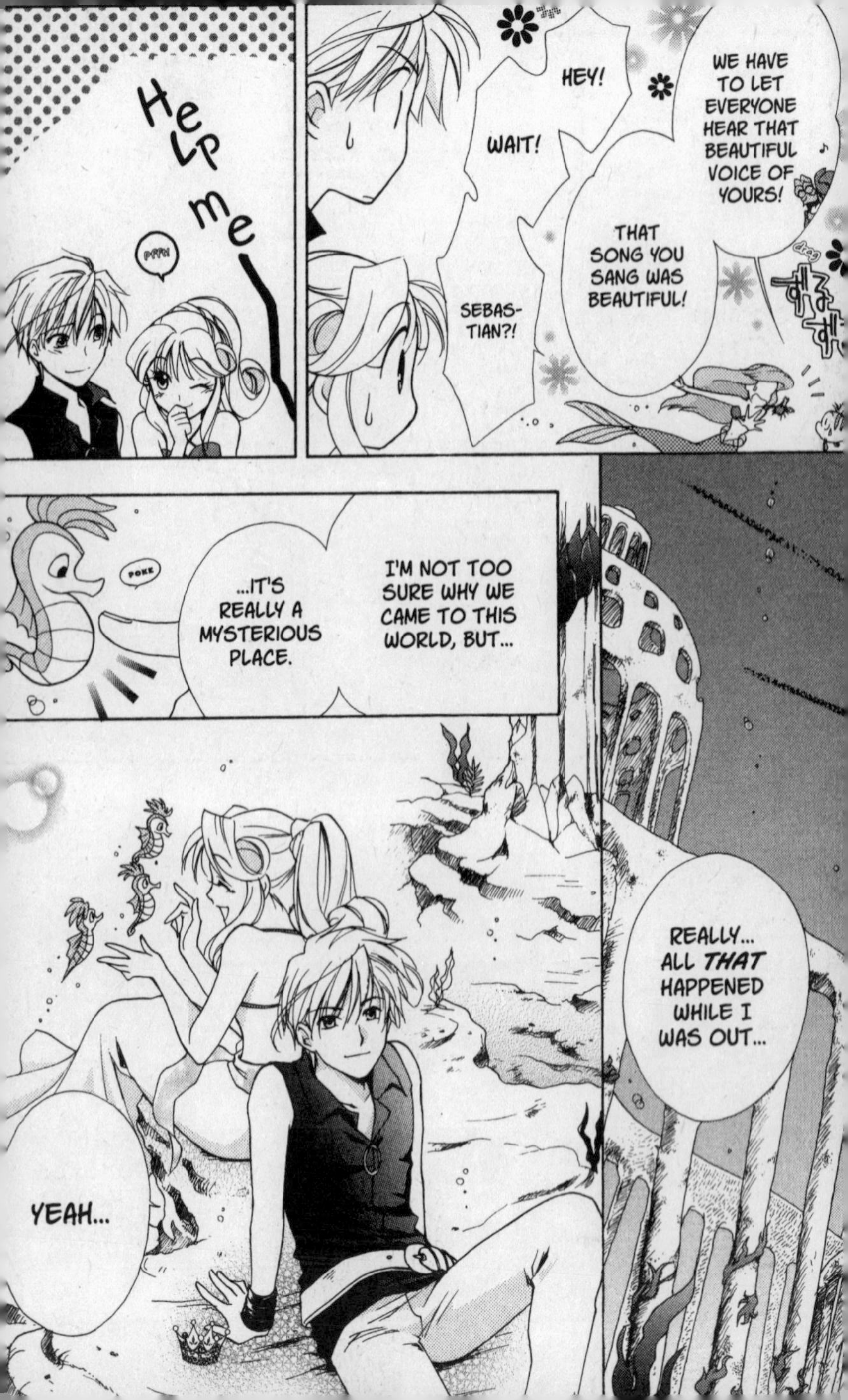
WE HAVE TO LET EVERYONE HEAR THAT BEAUTIFUL VOICE OF YOURS!
THAT SONG YOU SANG WAS BEAUTIFUL!
drag
HEY!
WAIT!
SEBASTIAN?!
Help me
PFFT!
REALLY... ALL *THAT* HAPPENED WHILE I WAS OUT...
I'M NOT TOO SURE WHY WE CAME TO THIS WORLD, BUT...
...IT'S REALLY A MYSTERIOUS PLACE.
POKE
YEAH...

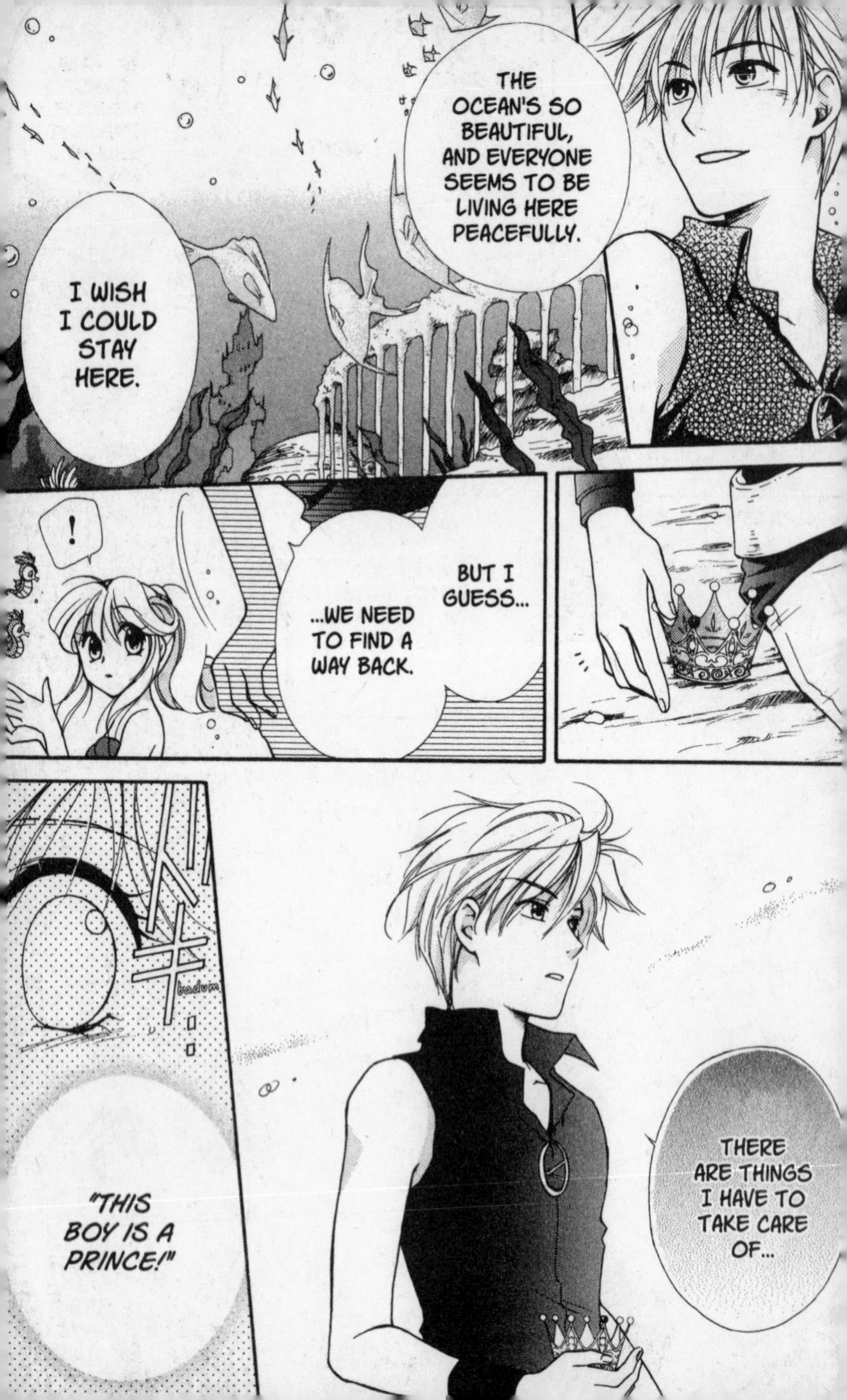
THE OCEAN'S SO BEAUTIFUL, AND EVERYONE SEEMS TO BE LIVING HERE PEACEFULLY.
I WISH I COULD STAY HERE.
BUT I GUESS...
...WE NEED TO FIND A WAY BACK.
!
THERE ARE THINGS I HAVE TO TAKE CARE OF...
badum
"THIS BOY IS A PRINCE!"

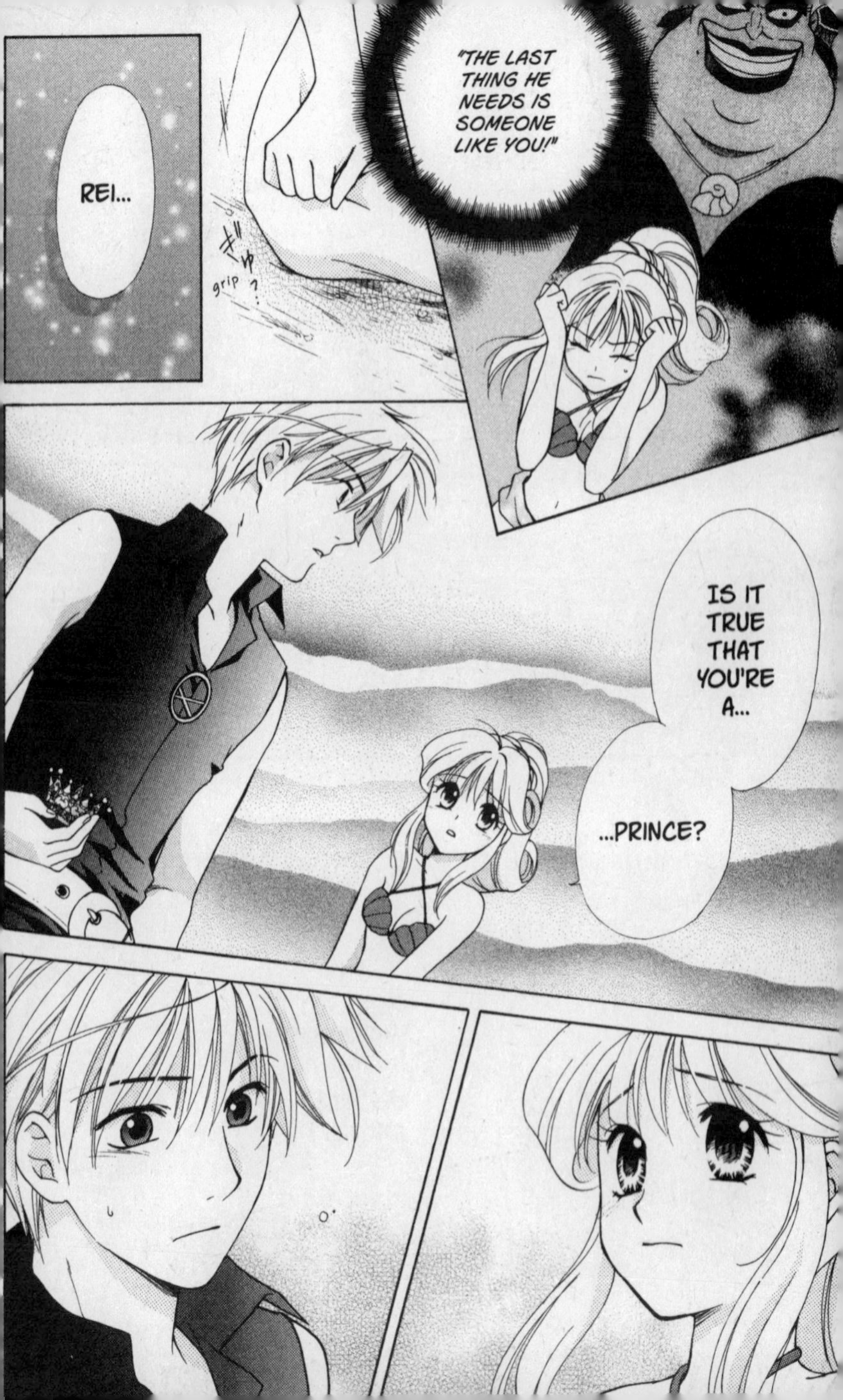
"THE LAST THING HE NEEDS IS SOMEONE LIKE YOU!"
grip
REI...
IS IT TRUE THAT YOU'RE A...
...PRINCE?

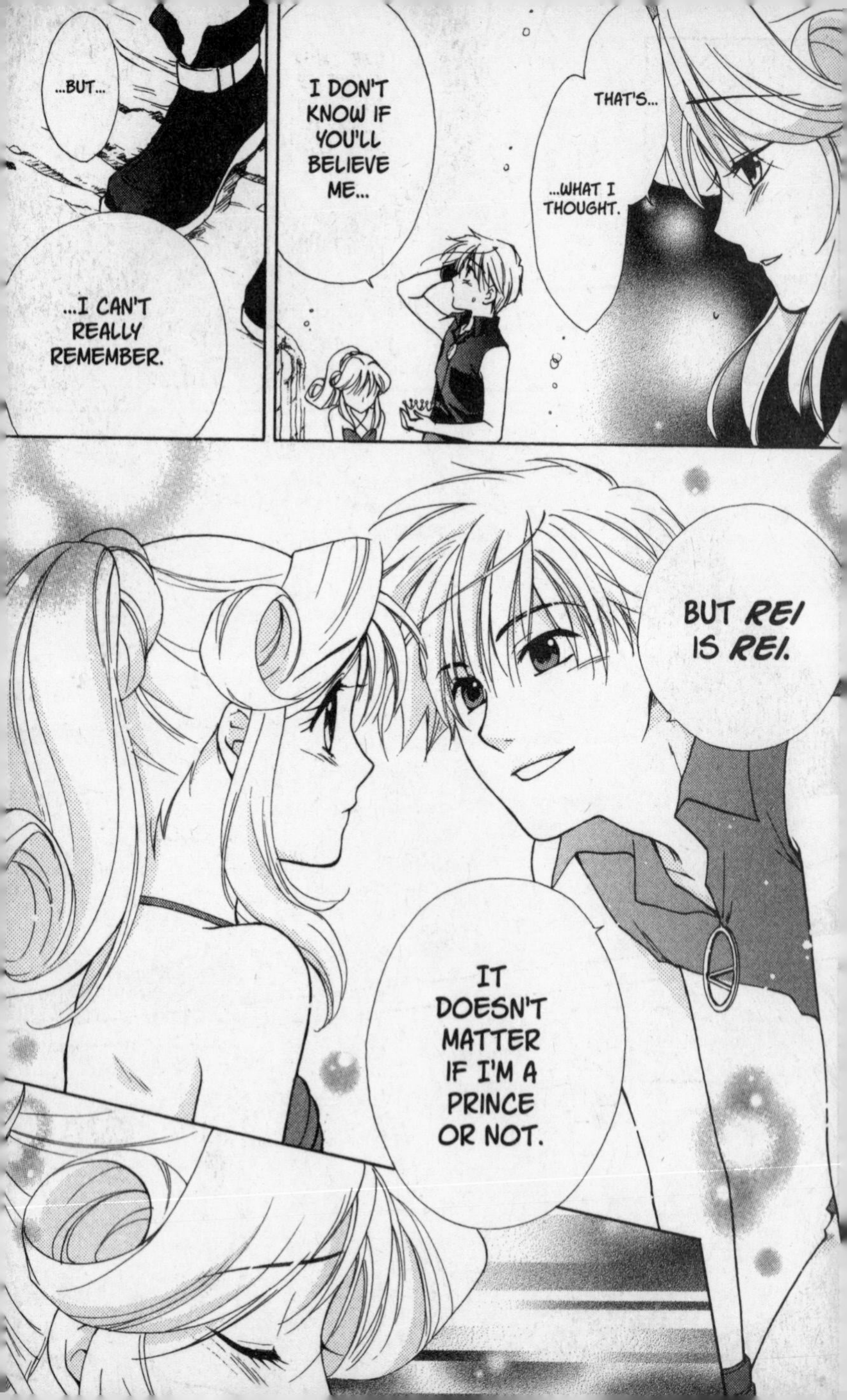
THAT'S...
...WHAT I THOUGHT.
I DON'T KNOW IF YOU'LL BELIEVE ME...
...BUT...
...I CAN'T REALLY REMEMBER.
BUT *REI* IS *REI*.
IT DOESN'T MATTER IF I'M A PRINCE OR NOT.

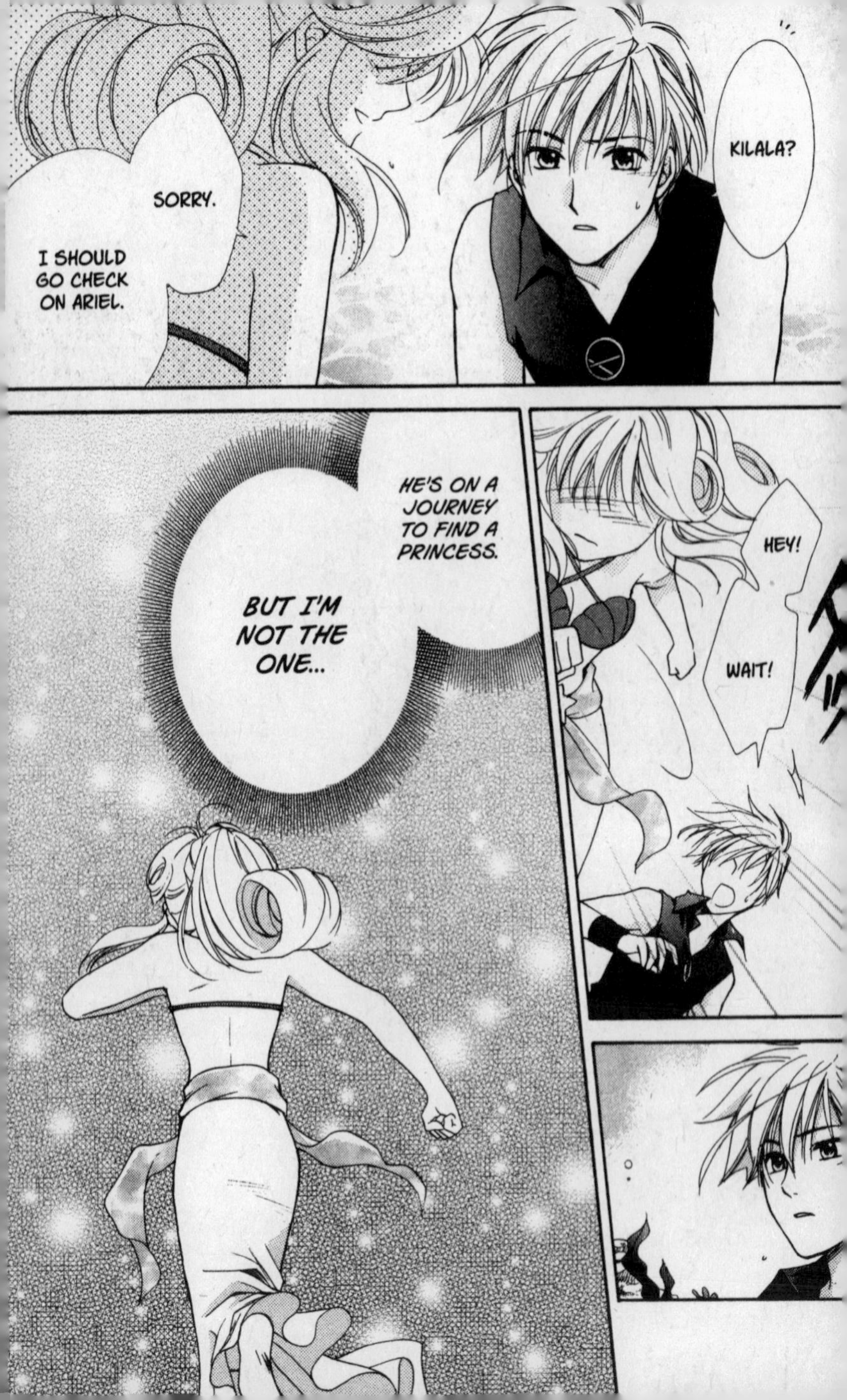
KILALA?
SORRY.
I SHOULD GO CHECK ON ARIEL.
HEY!
WAIT!
HE'S ON A JOURNEY TO FIND A PRINCESS.
BUT I'M NOT THE ONE...

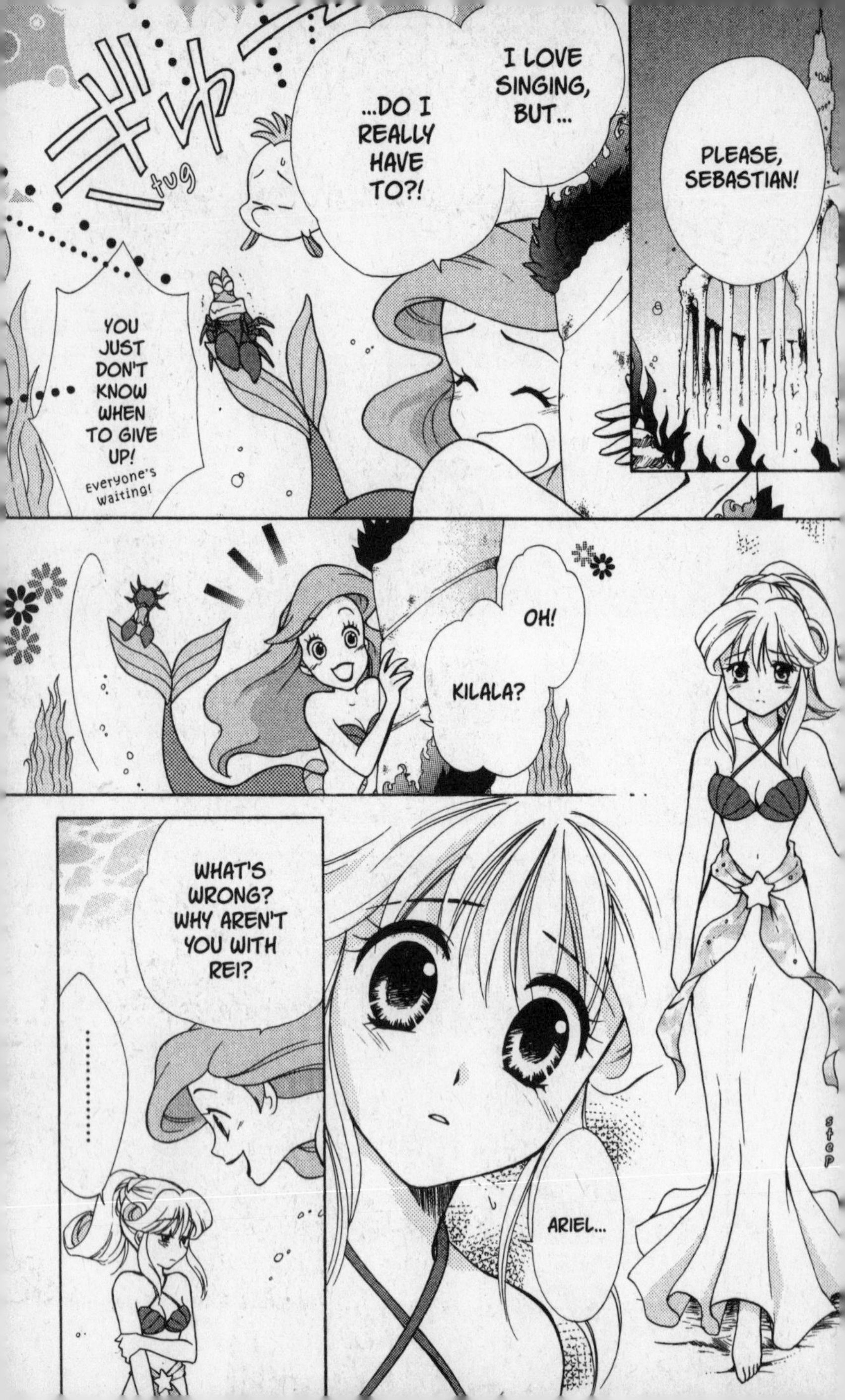
PLEASE, SEBASTIAN!
I LOVE SINGING, BUT...
...DO I REALLY HAVE TO?!
ギュ
tug
YOU JUST DON'T KNOW WHEN TO GIVE UP!
Everyone's waiting!
step
OH!
KILALA?
WHAT'S WRONG? WHY AREN'T YOU WITH REI?
ARIEL...
......

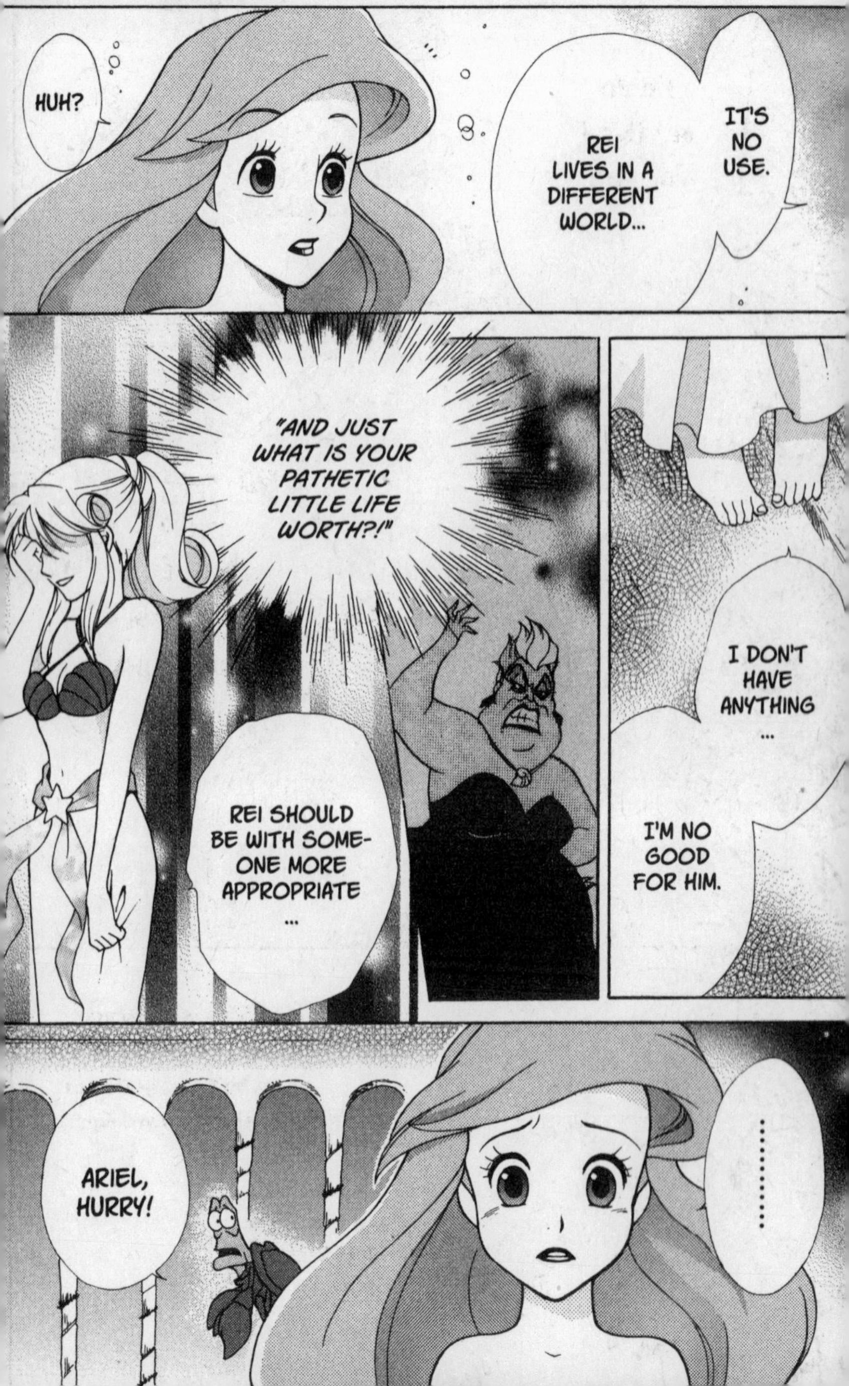
IT'S NO USE.
REI LIVES IN A DIFFERENT WORLD...
HUH?
I DON'T HAVE ANYTHING ...
I'M NO GOOD FOR HIM.
"AND JUST WHAT IS YOUR PATHETIC LITTLE LIFE WORTH?!"
REI SHOULD BE WITH SOME-ONE MORE APPROPRIATE ...
......
ARIEL, HURRY!

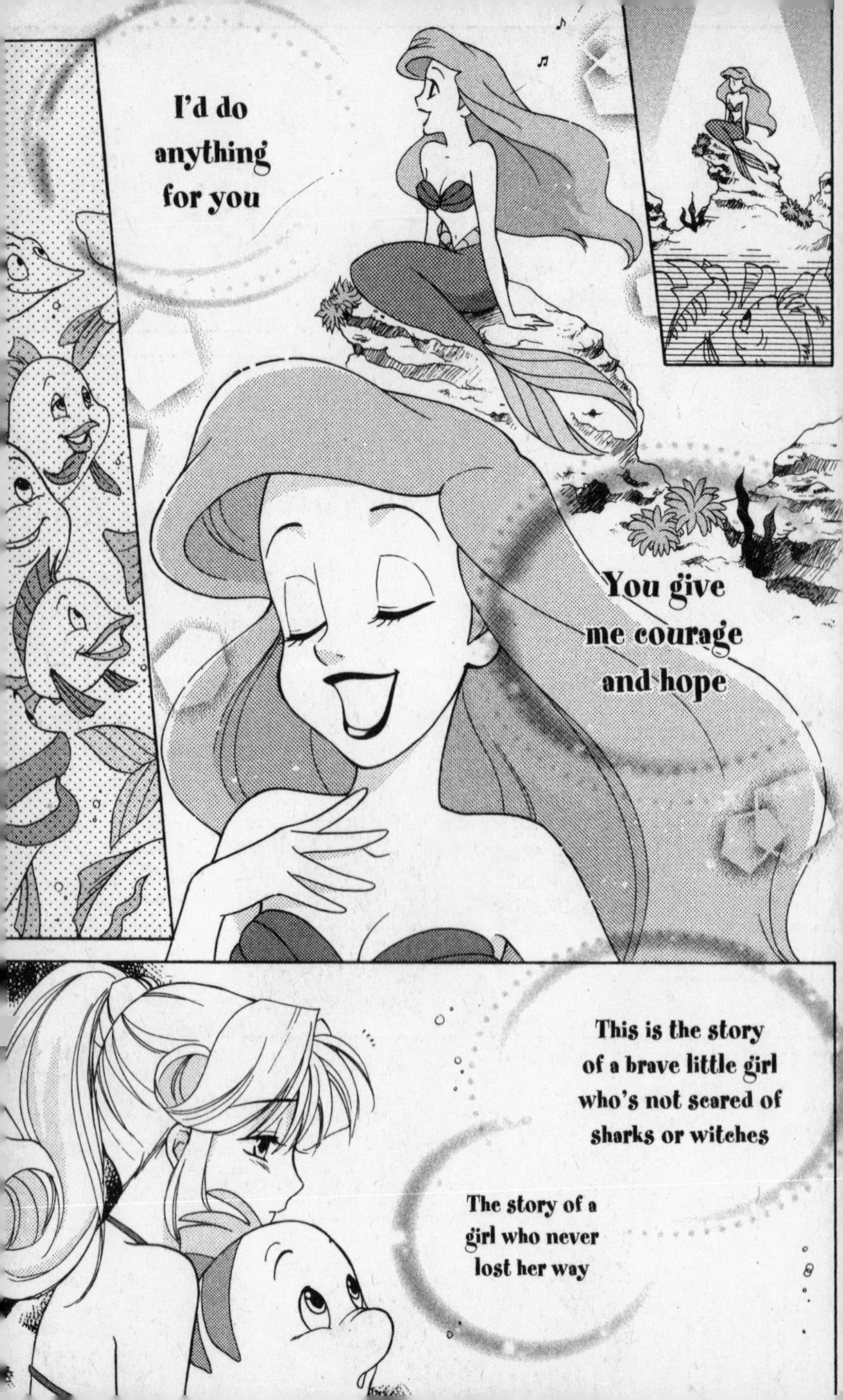

I'd do anything for you
You give me courage and hope
This is the story of a brave little girl who's not scared of sharks or witches
The story of a girl who never lost her way

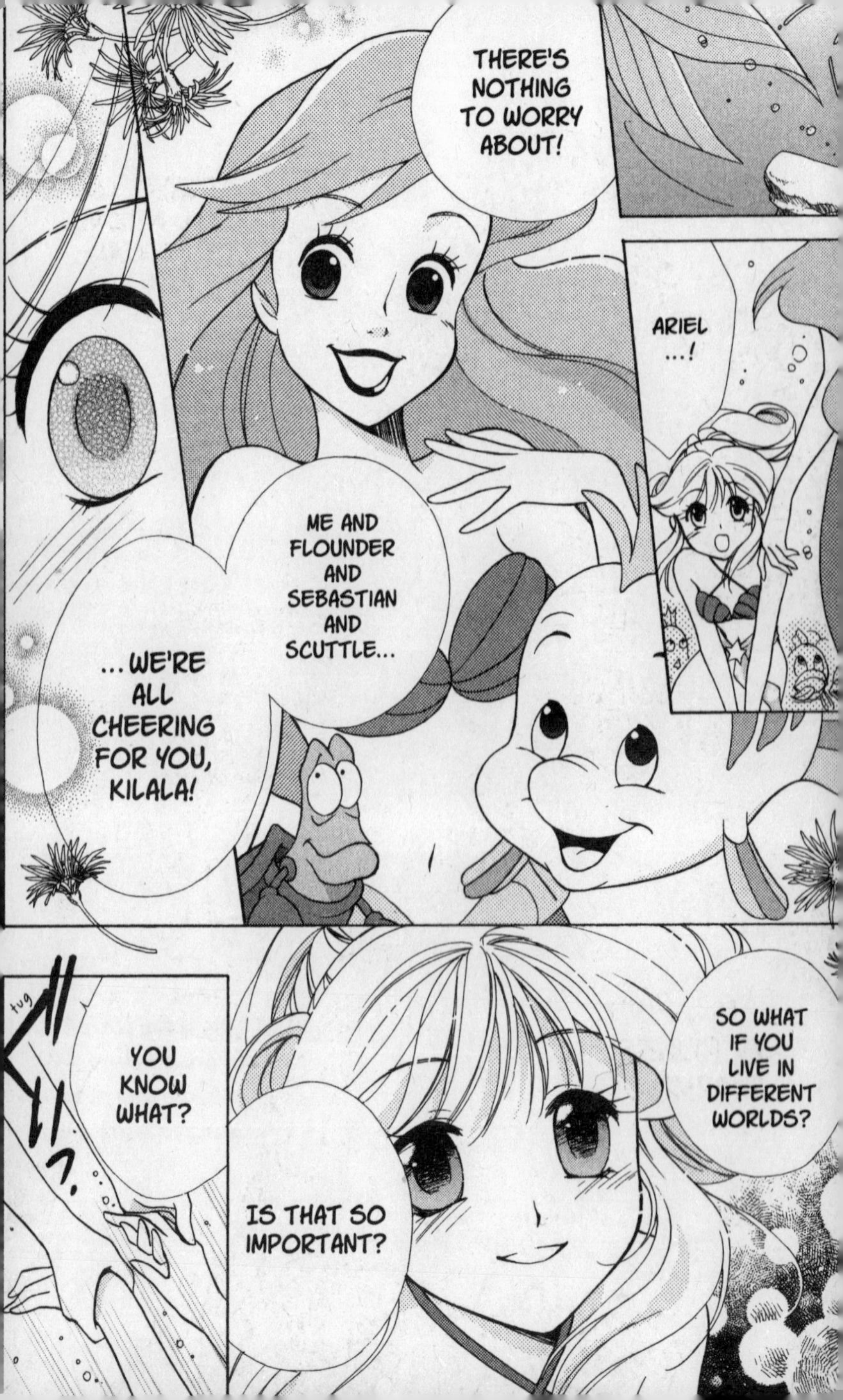
ARIEL ...!
THERE'S NOTHING TO WORRY ABOUT!
ME AND FLOUNDER AND SEBASTIAN AND SCUTTLE...
...WE'RE ALL CHEERING FOR YOU, KILALA!
SO WHAT IF YOU LIVE IN DIFFERENT WORLDS?
IS THAT SO IMPORTANT?
tug
YOU KNOW WHAT?

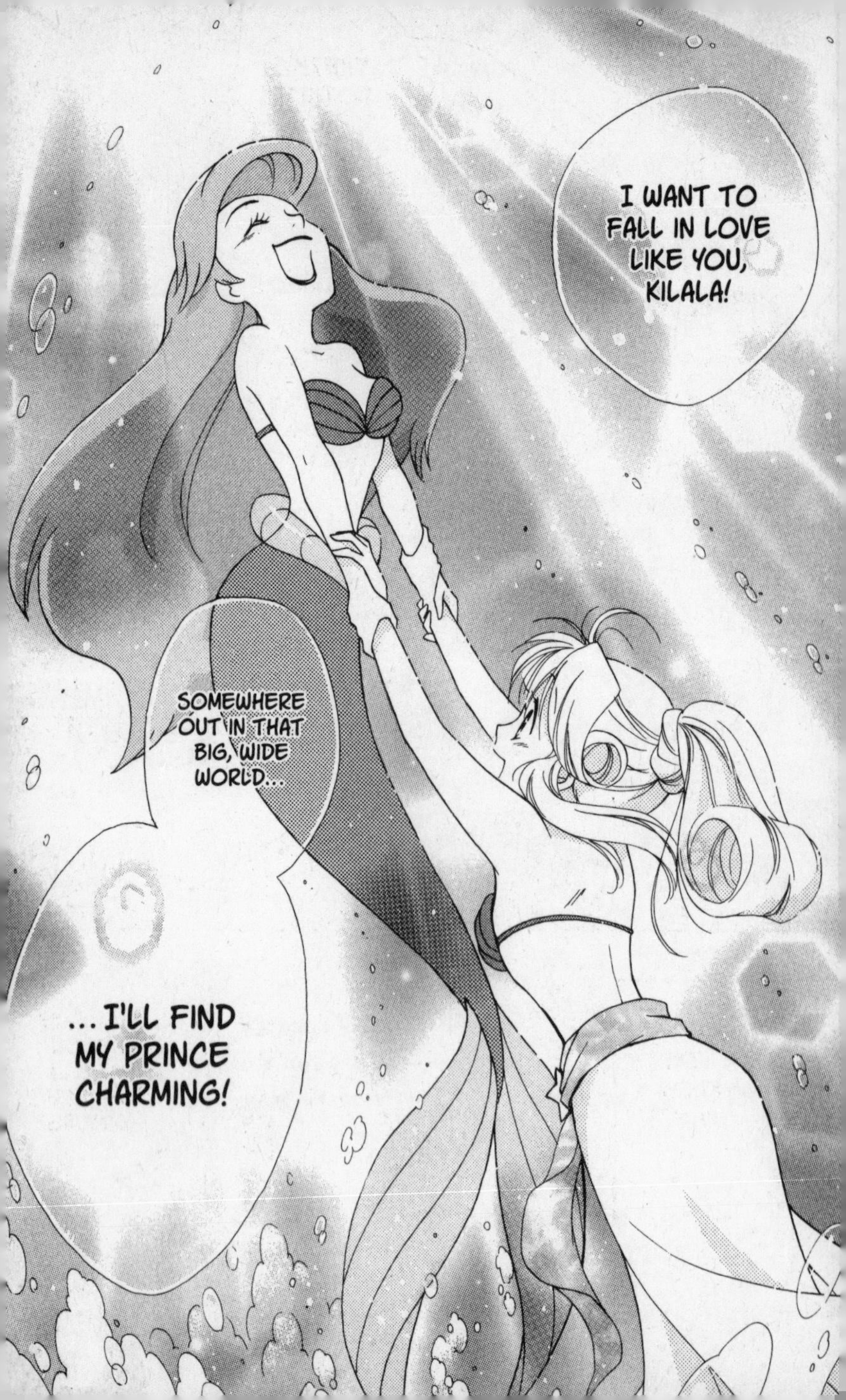
I WANT TO FALL IN LOVE LIKE YOU, KILALA!
SOMEWHERE OUT IN THAT BIG, WIDE WORLD...
...I'LL FIND MY PRINCE CHARMING!

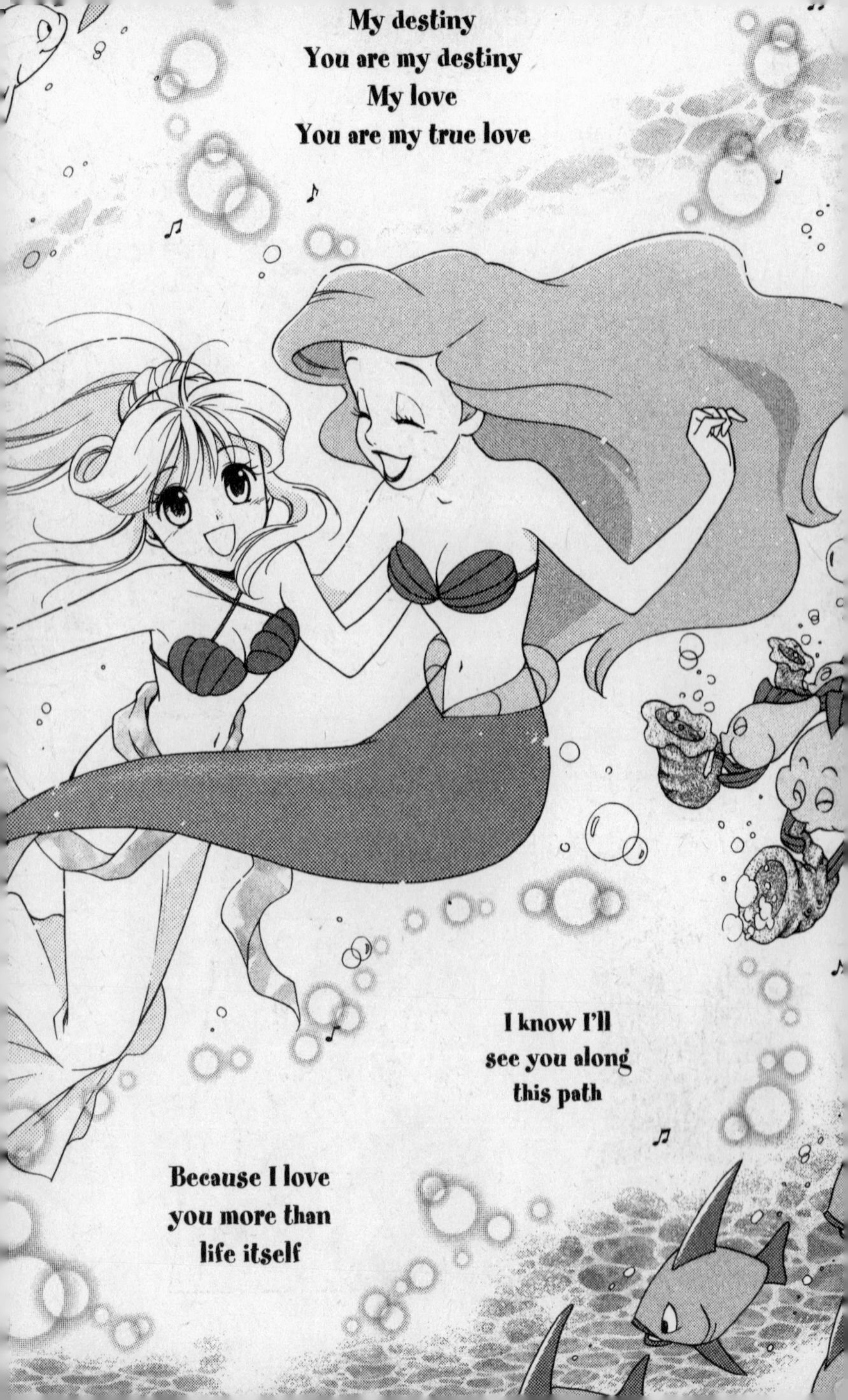
My destiny
You are my destiny
My love
You are my true love
I know I'll see you along this path
Because I love you more than life itself

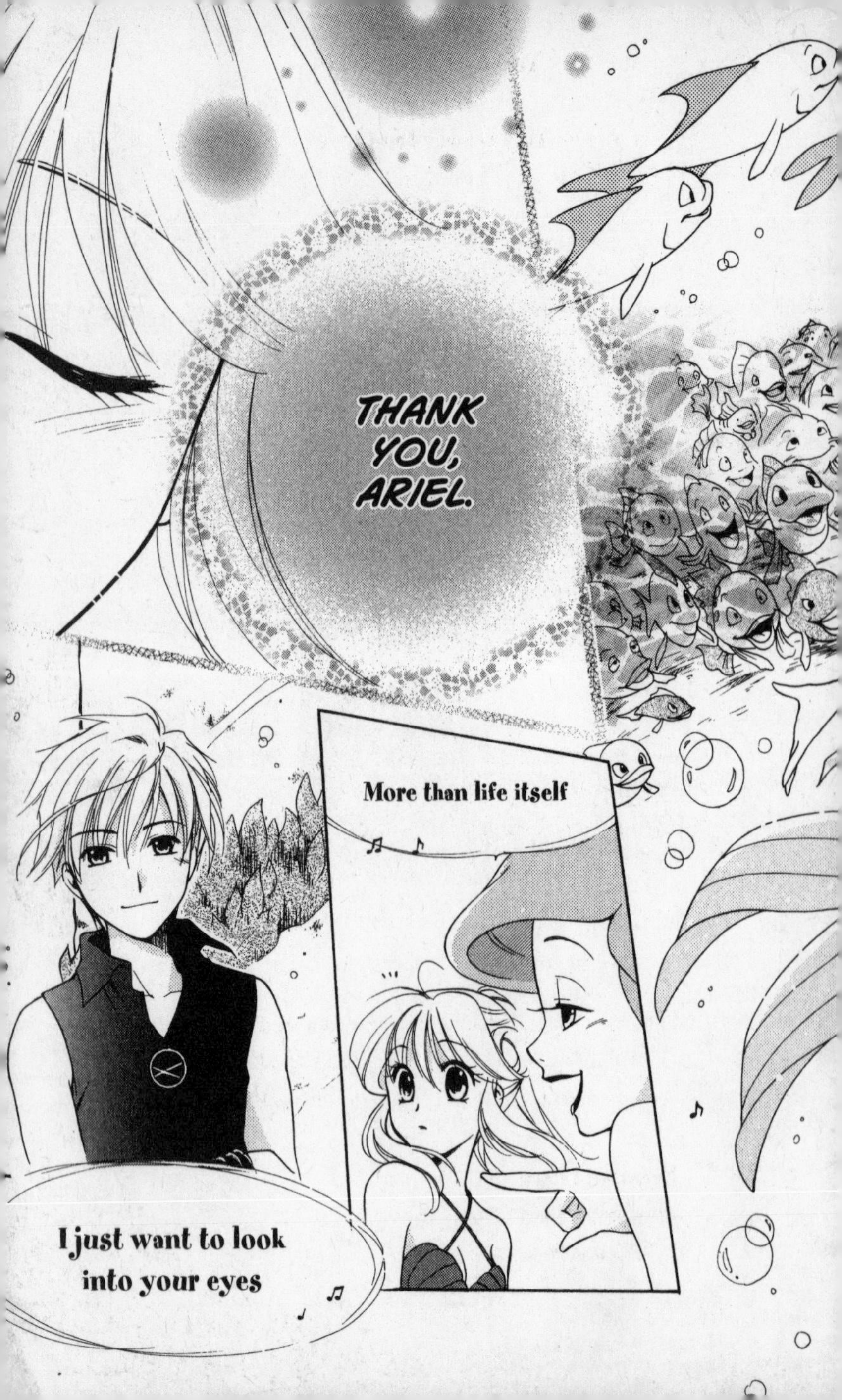
THANK YOU, ARIEL.
More than life itself
I just want to look into your eyes

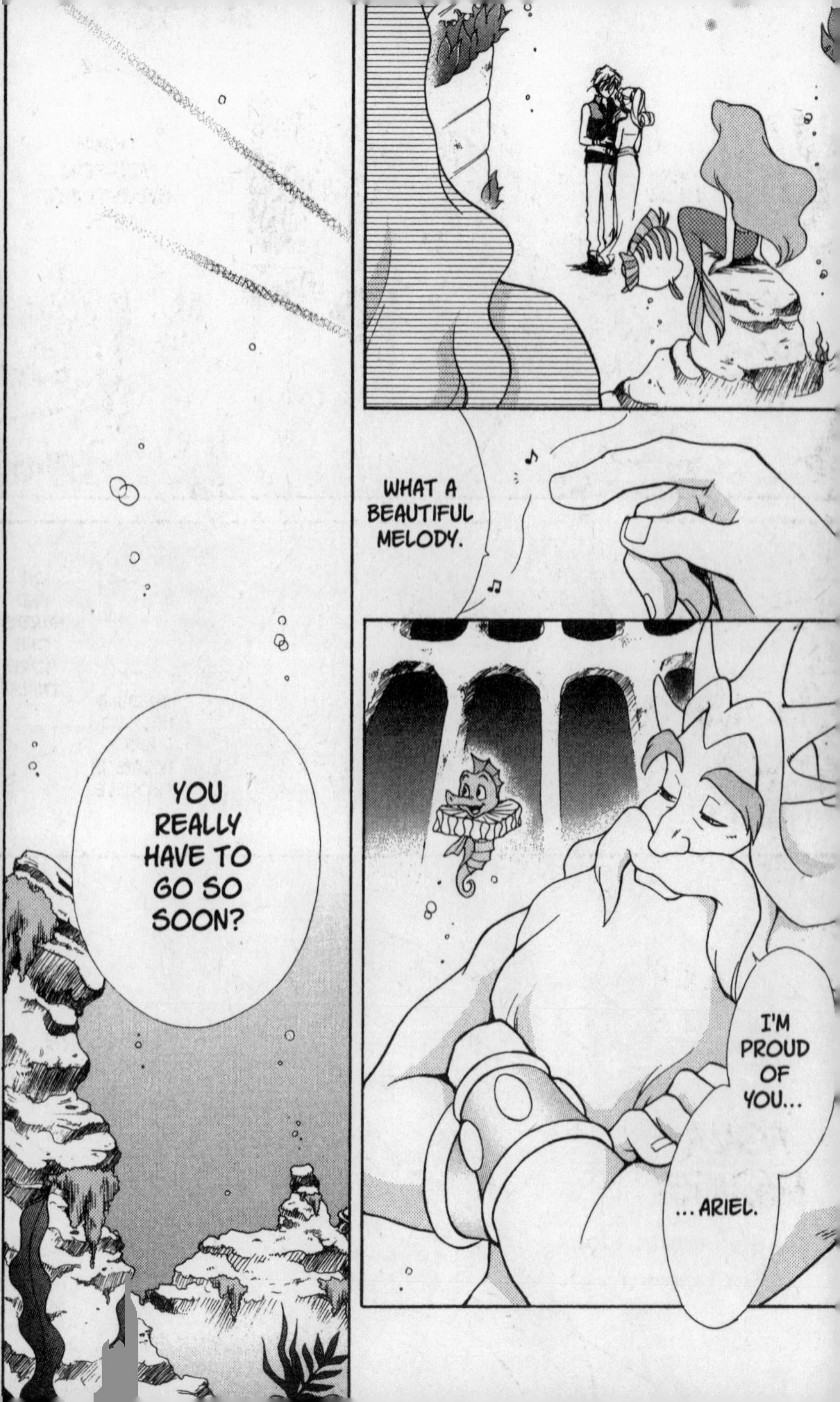
WHAT A BEAUTIFUL MELODY.
I'M PROUD OF YOU...
...ARIEL.
YOU REALLY HAVE TO GO SO SOON?

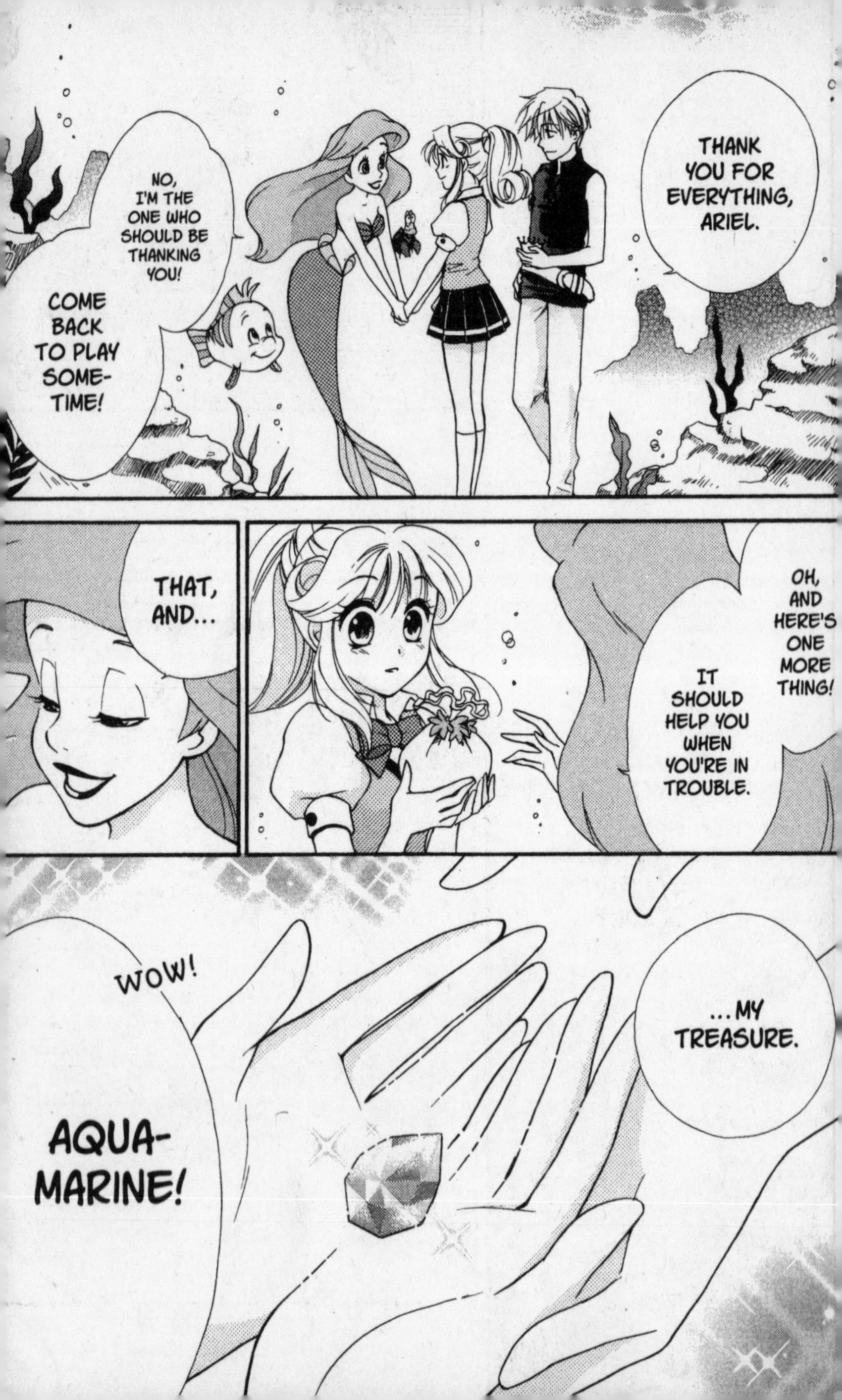
THANK YOU FOR EVERYTHING, ARIEL.
NO, I'M THE ONE WHO SHOULD BE THANKING YOU!
COME BACK TO PLAY SOME-TIME!
OH, AND HERE'S ONE MORE THING!
IT SHOULD HELP YOU WHEN YOU'RE IN TROUBLE.
THAT, AND...
...MY TREASURE.
WOW!
AQUA-MARINE!

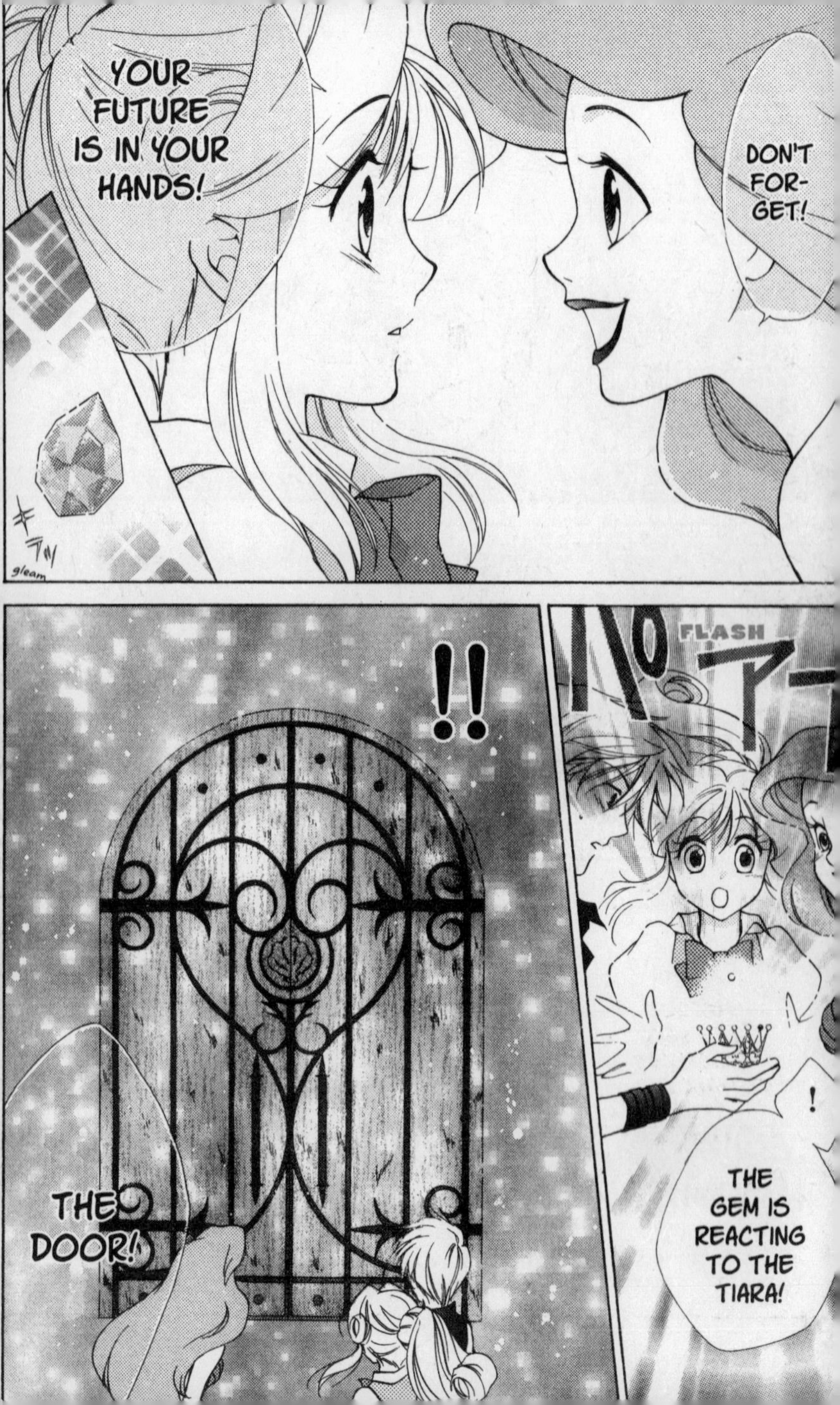
DON'T FOR-GET!
YOUR FUTURE IS IN YOUR HANDS!
gleam
FLASH
!
THE GEM IS REACTING TO THE TIARA!
!!
THE DOOR!

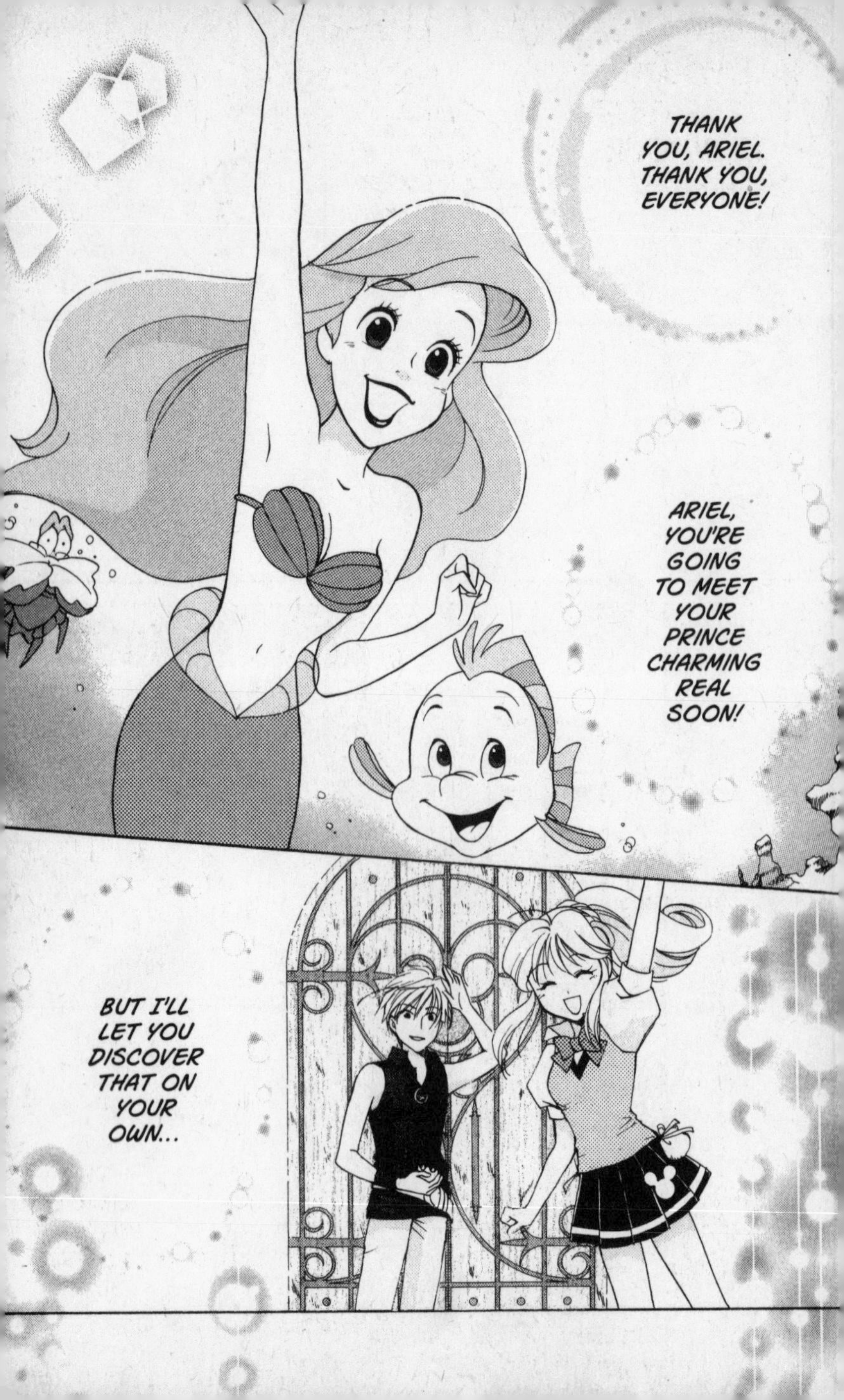
THANK YOU, ARIEL. THANK YOU, EVERYONE!
ARIEL, YOU'RE GOING TO MEET YOUR PRINCE CHARMING REAL SOON!
BUT I'LL LET YOU DISCOVER THAT ON YOUR OWN...

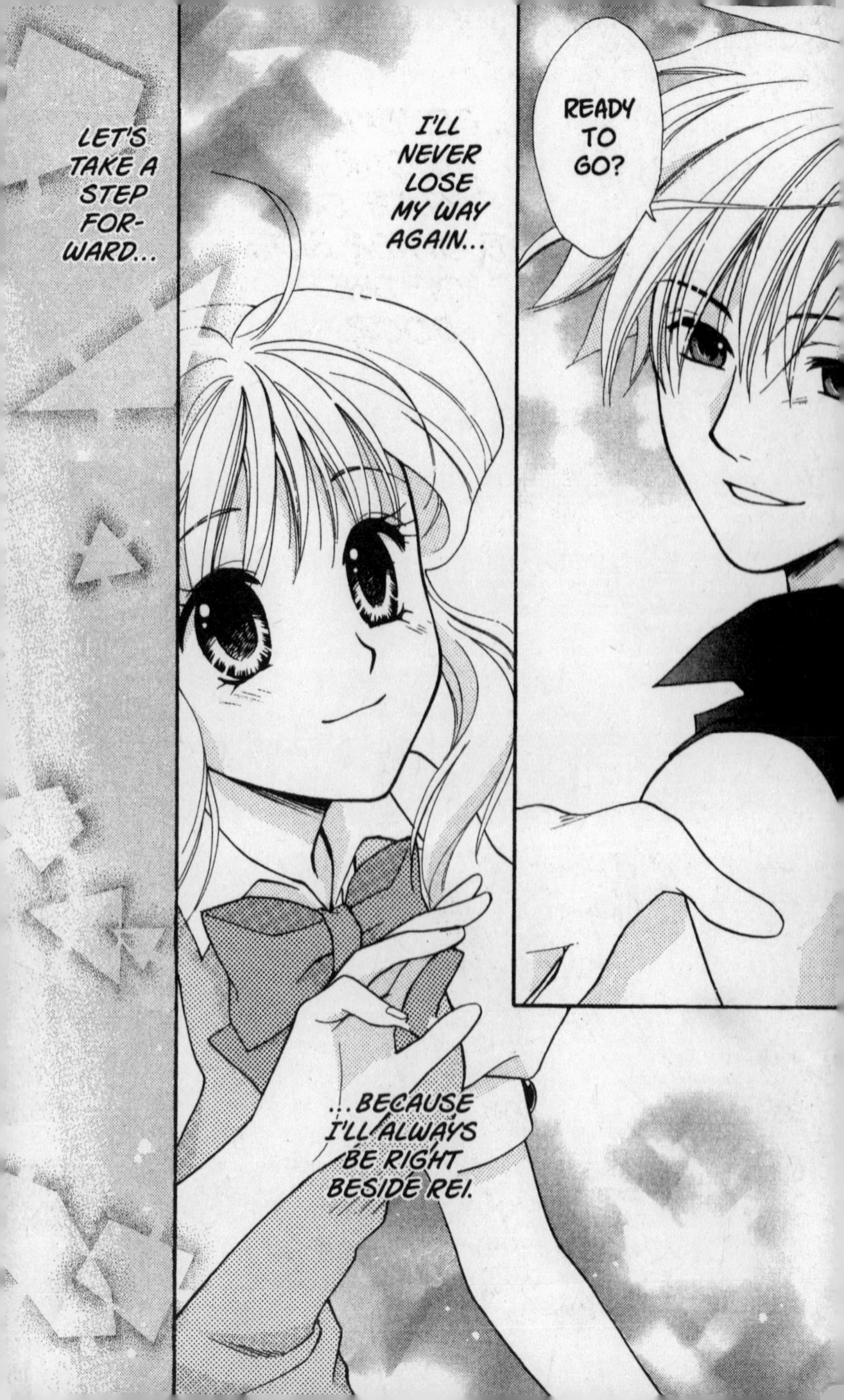
READY TO GO?
I'LL NEVER LOSE MY WAY AGAIN...
...BECAUSE I'LL ALWAYS BE RIGHT BESIDE REI.
LET'S TAKE A STEP FORWARD...

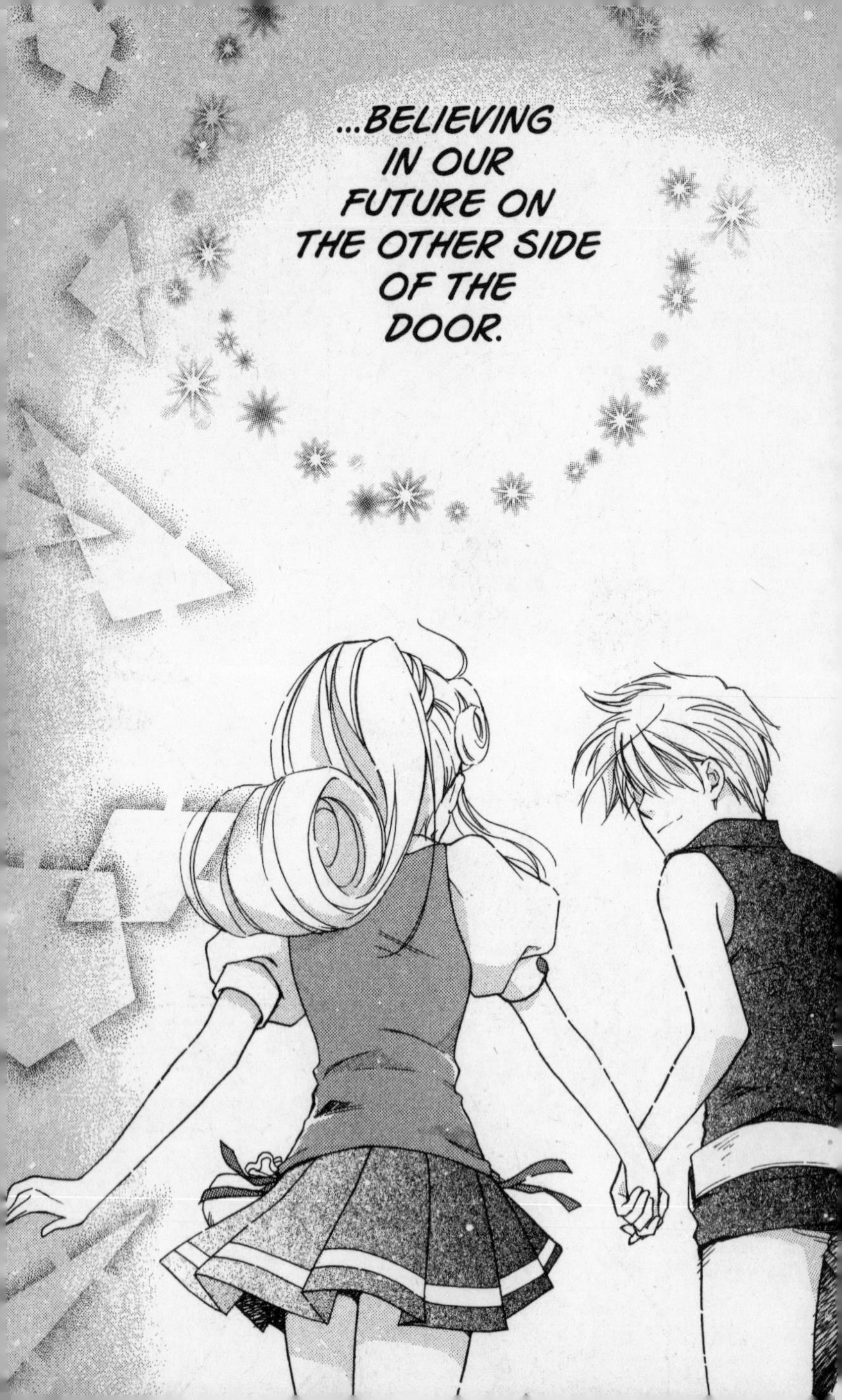
...BELIEVING IN OUR FUTURE ON THE OTHER SIDE OF THE DOOR.

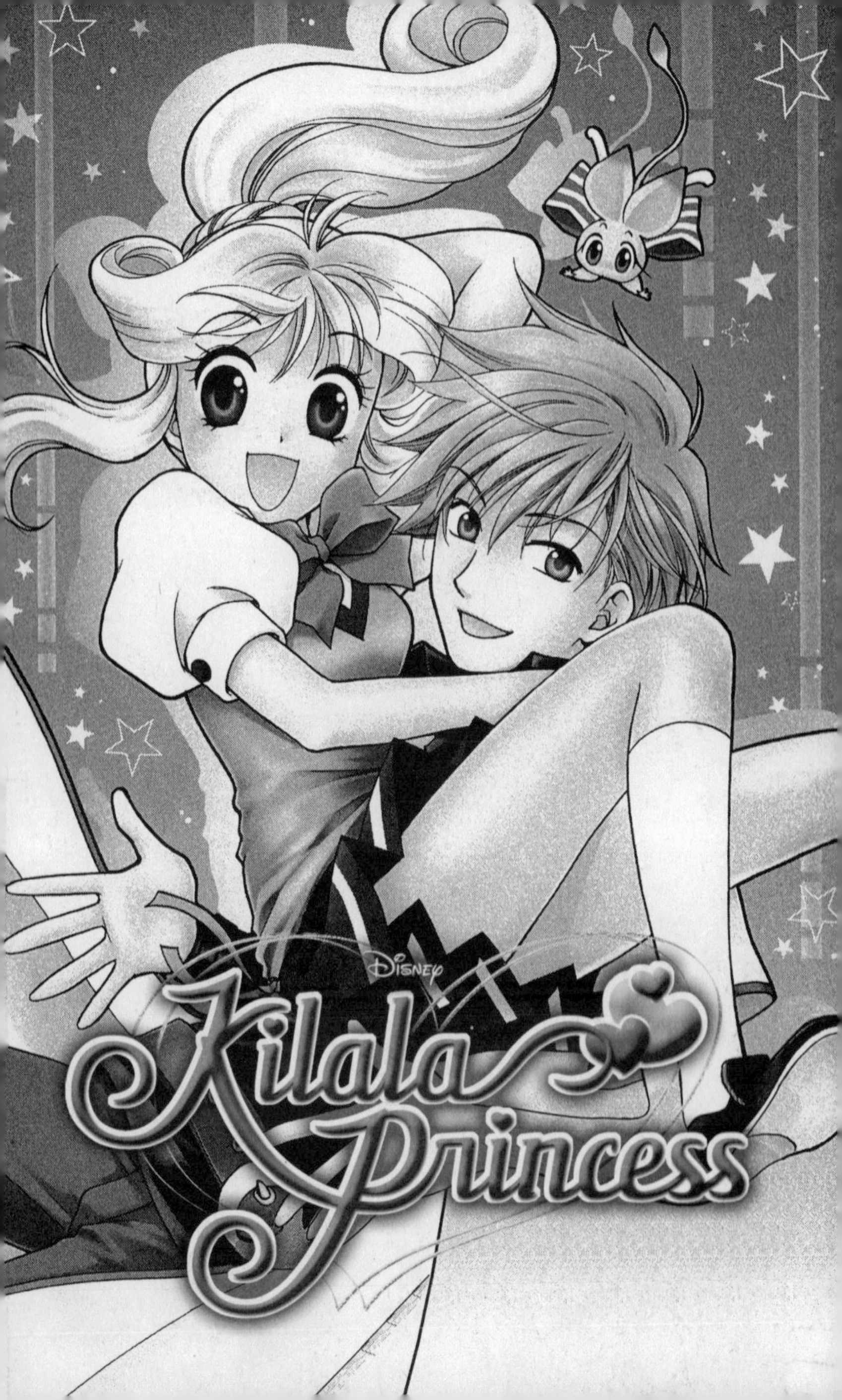
Disney
Kilala Princess

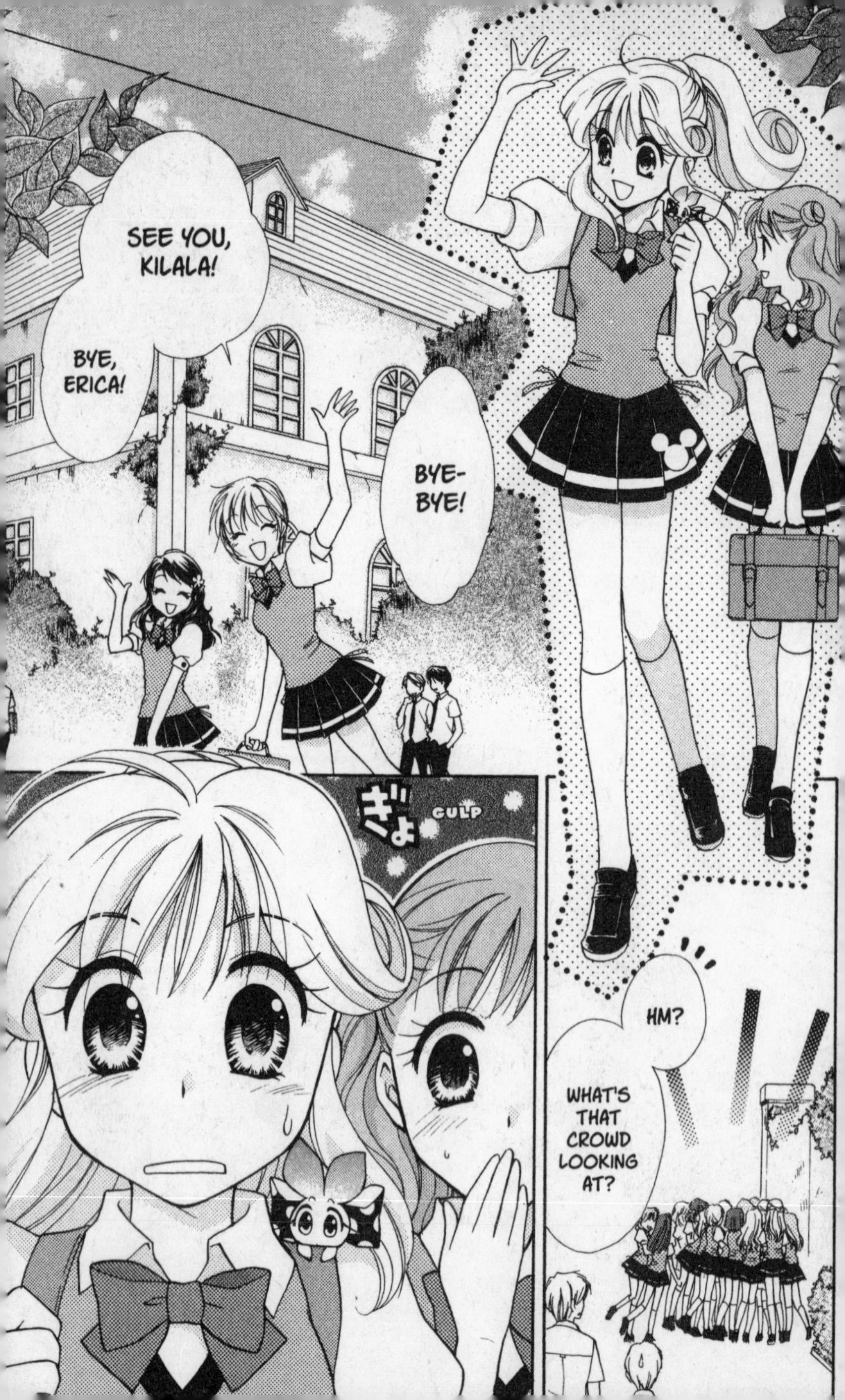
SEE YOU, KILALA!
BYE, ERICA!
BYE-BYE!
HM?
WHAT'S THAT CROWD LOOKING AT?
ぎょ
GULP

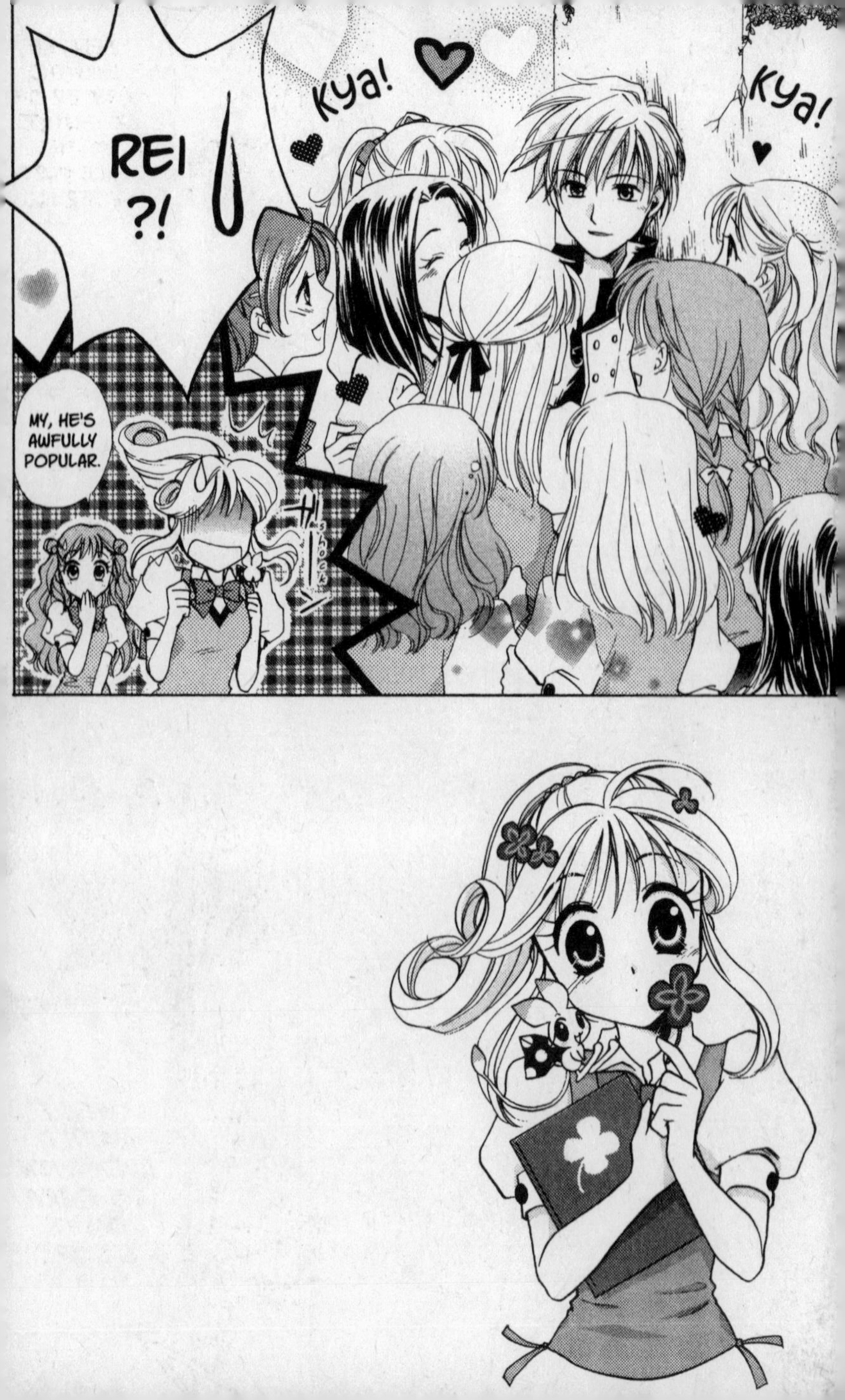
Kya!
Kya!
REI ?!
MY, HE'S AWFULLY POPULAR.

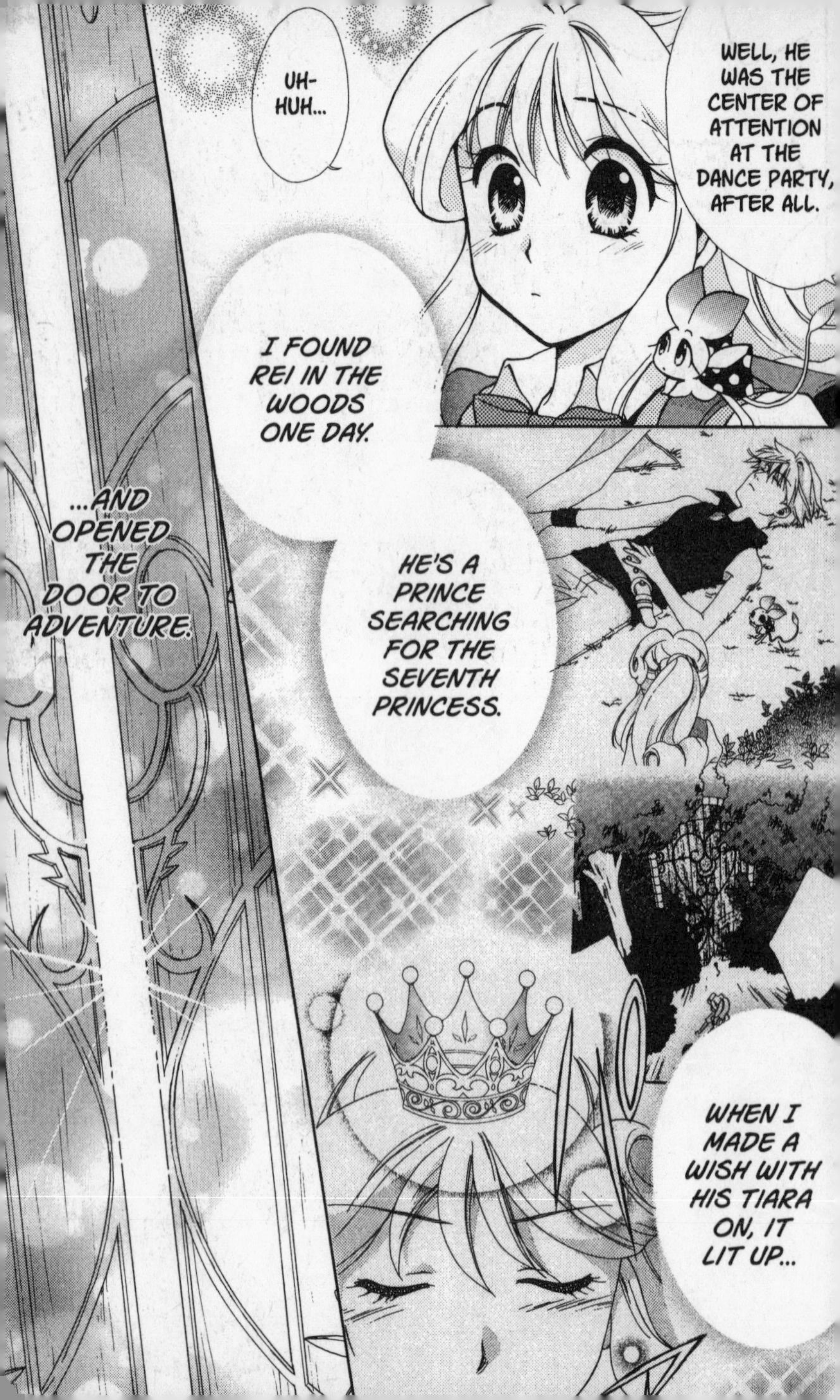

WELL, HE WAS THE CENTER OF ATTENTION AT THE DANCE PARTY, AFTER ALL.
UH-HUH...
I FOUND REI IN THE WOODS ONE DAY.
HE'S A PRINCE SEARCHING FOR THE SEVENTH PRINCESS.
WHEN I MADE A WISH WITH HIS TIARA ON, IT LIT UP...
...AND OPENED THE DOOR TO ADVENTURE.

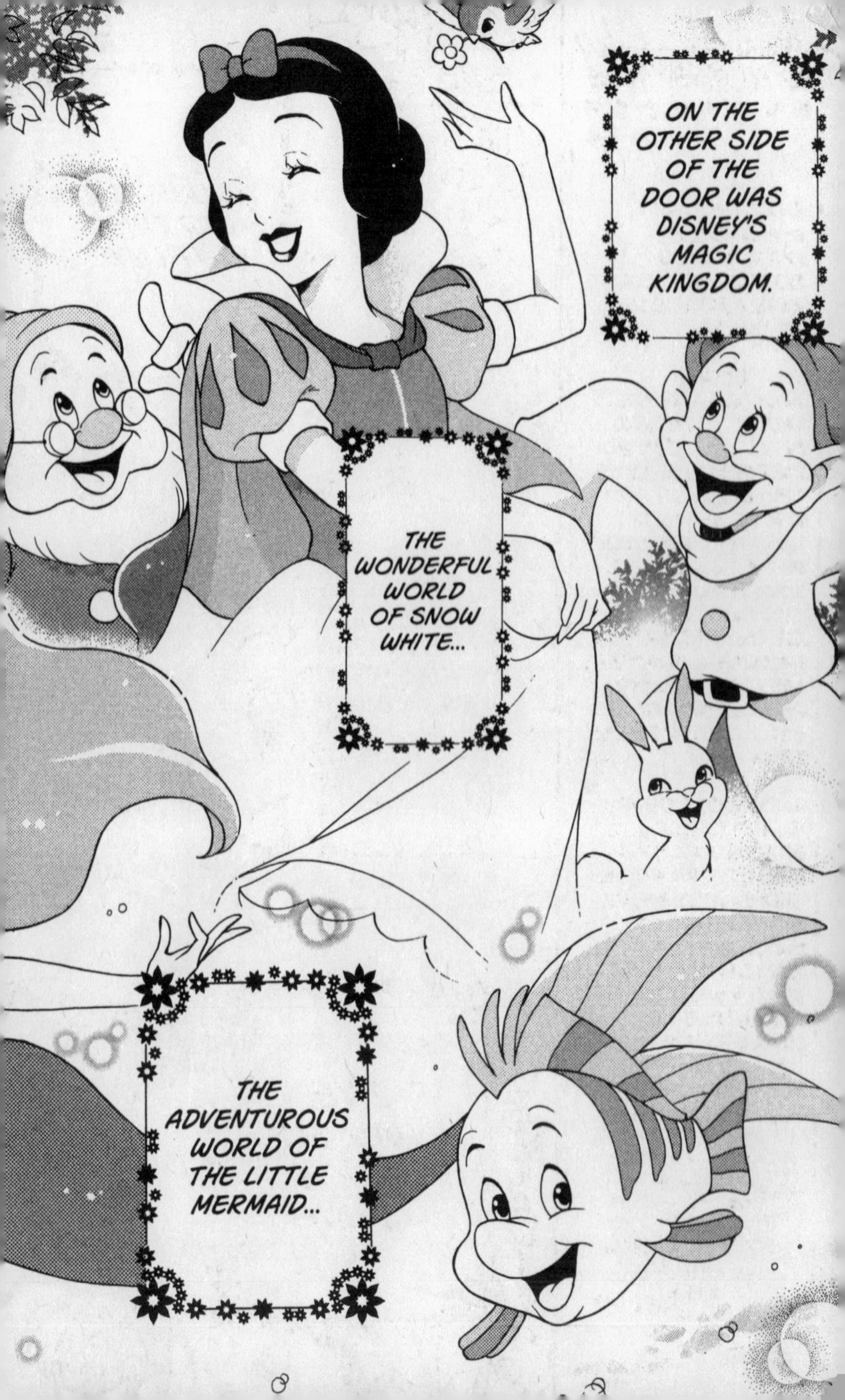
ON THE OTHER SIDE OF THE DOOR WAS DISNEY'S MAGIC KINGDOM.
THE WONDERFUL WORLD OF SNOW WHITE...
THE ADVENTUROUS WORLD OF THE LITTLE MERMAID...

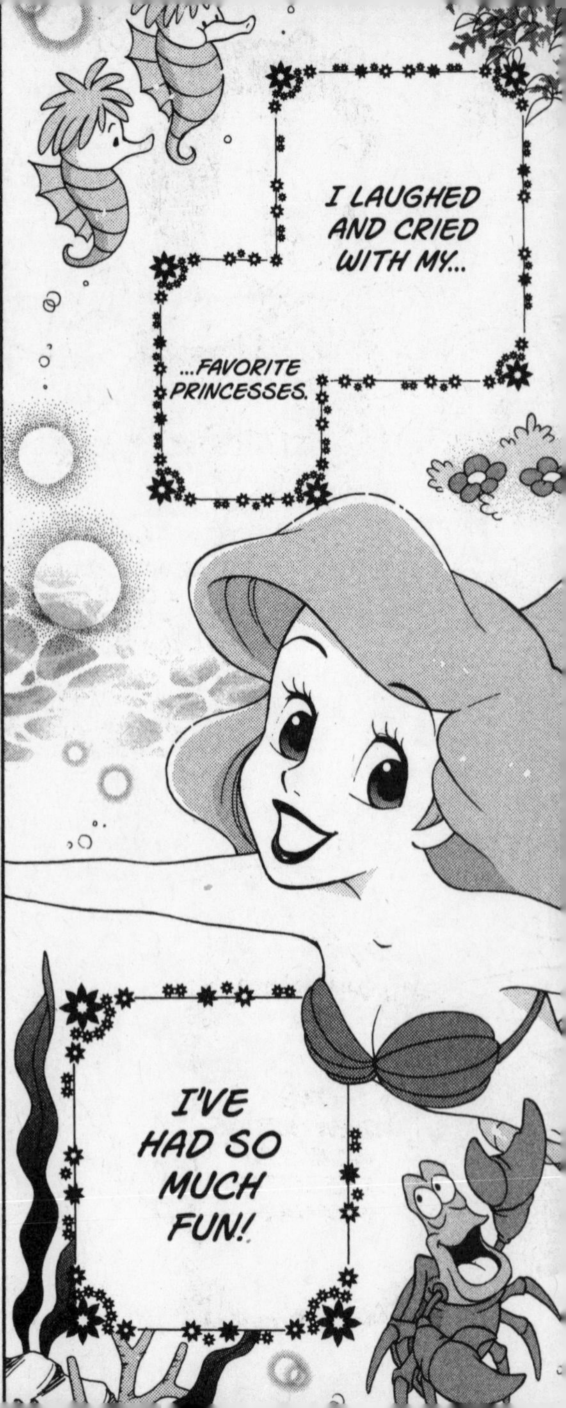
I LAUGHED AND CRIED WITH MY...
...FAVORITE PRINCESSES.
I'VE HAD SO MUCH FUN!

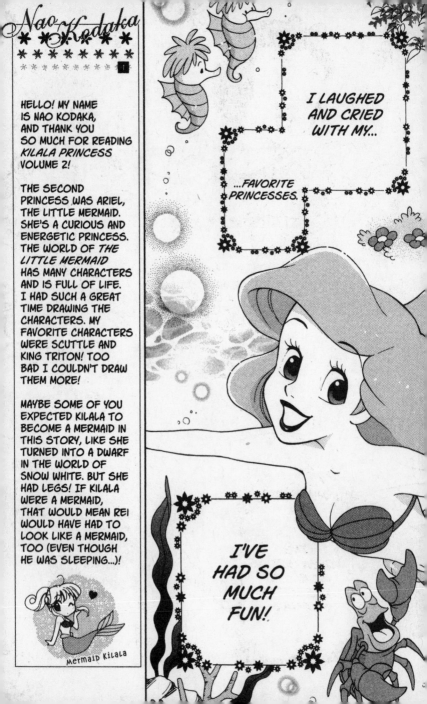

Nao Kodaka

1

HELLO! MY NAME IS NAO KODAKA, AND THANK YOU SO MUCH FOR READING *KILALA PRINCESS* VOLUME 2!

THE SECOND PRINCESS WAS ARIEL, THE LITTLE MERMAID. SHE'S A CURIOUS AND ENERGETIC PRINCESS. THE WORLD OF *THE LITTLE MERMAID* HAS MANY CHARACTERS AND IS FULL OF LIFE. I HAD SUCH A GREAT TIME DRAWING THE CHARACTERS. MY FAVORITE CHARACTERS WERE SCUTTLE AND KING TRITON! TOO BAD I COULDN'T DRAW THEM MORE!

MAYBE SOME OF YOU EXPECTED KILALA TO BECOME A MERMAID IN THIS STORY, LIKE SHE TURNED INTO A DWARF IN THE WORLD OF SNOW WHITE. BUT SHE HAD LEGS! IF KILALA WERE A MERMAID, THAT WOULD MEAN REI WOULD HAVE HAD TO LOOK LIKE A MERMAID, TOO (EVEN THOUGH HE WAS SLEEPING...)!

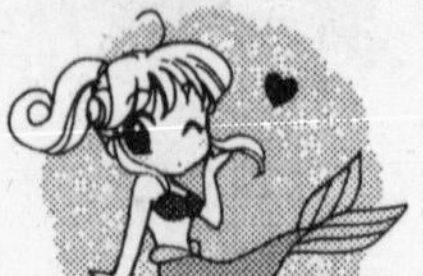
Mermaid Kilala

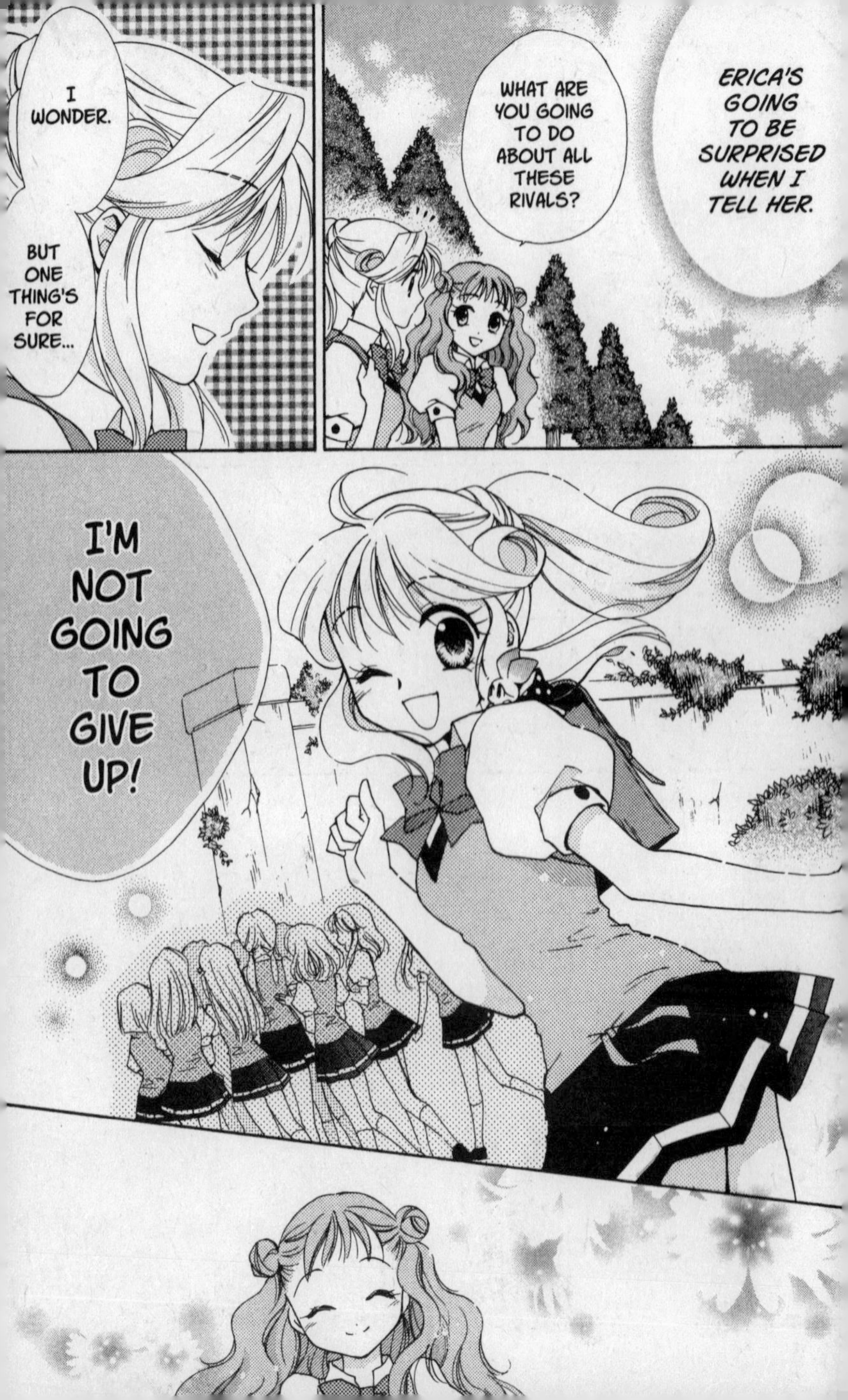
ERICA'S GOING TO BE SURPRISED WHEN I TELL HER.
WHAT ARE YOU GOING TO DO ABOUT ALL THESE RIVALS?
I WONDER.
BUT ONE THING'S FOR SURE...
I'M NOT GOING TO GIVE UP!

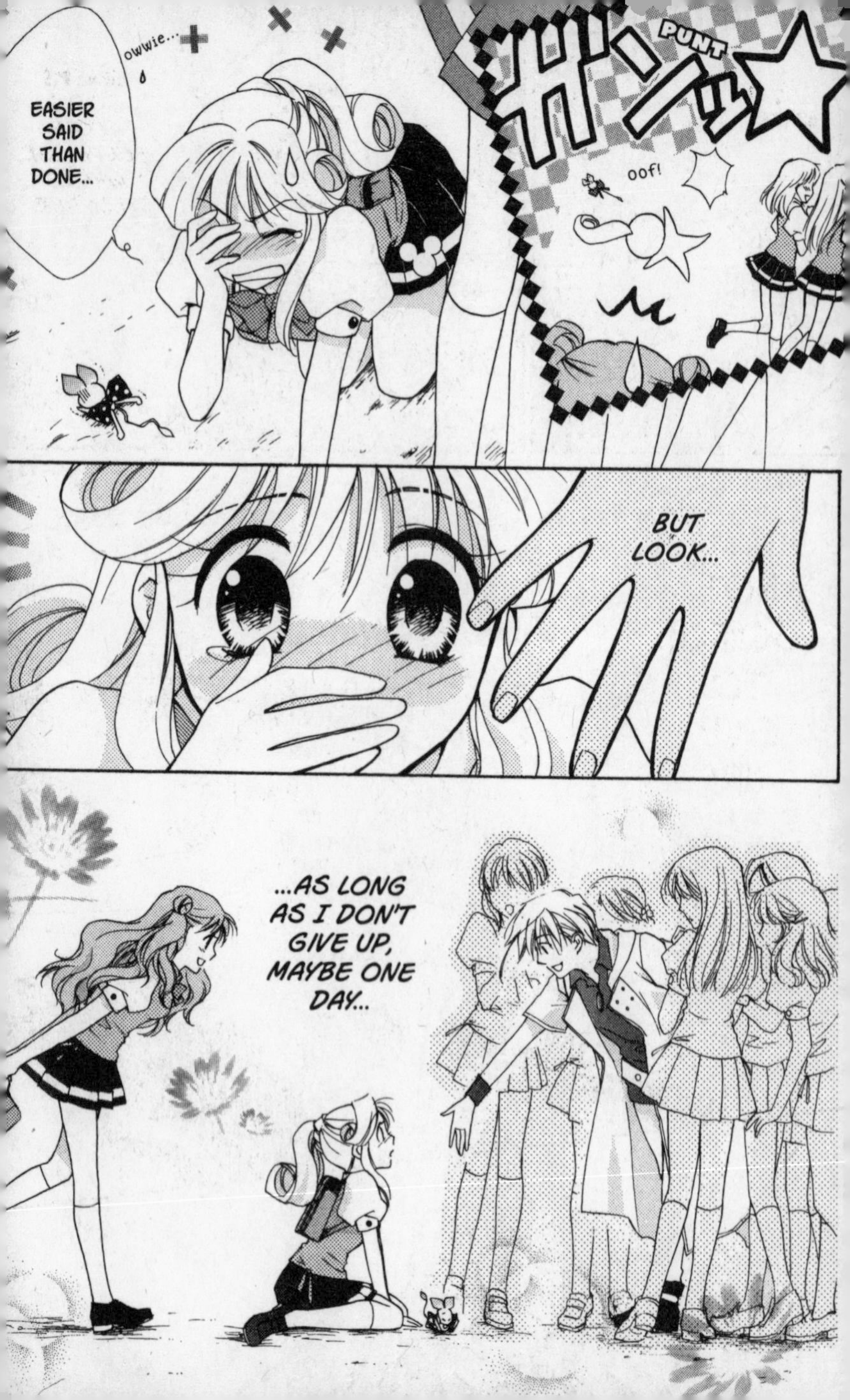
PUNT
oof!
owwie...
EASIER SAID THAN DONE...
BUT LOOK...
...AS LONG AS I DON'T GIVE UP, MAYBE ONE DAY...

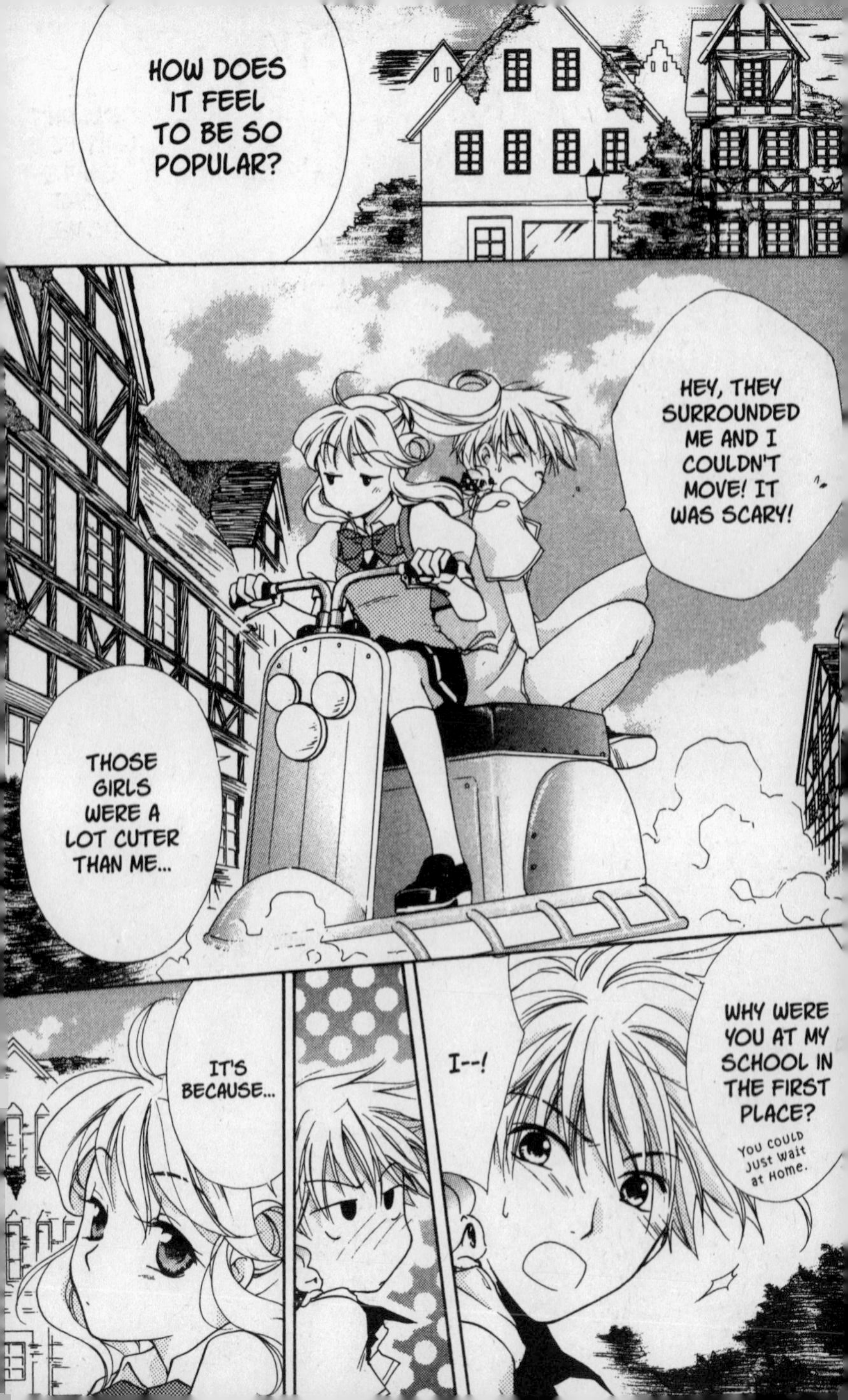
HOW DOES IT FEEL TO BE SO POPULAR?
HEY, THEY SURROUNDED ME AND I COULDN'T MOVE! IT WAS SCARY!
THOSE GIRLS WERE A LOT CUTER THAN ME...
WHY WERE YOU AT MY SCHOOL IN THE FIRST PLACE?
You COULD Just Wait at Home.
I--!
IT'S BECAUSE...

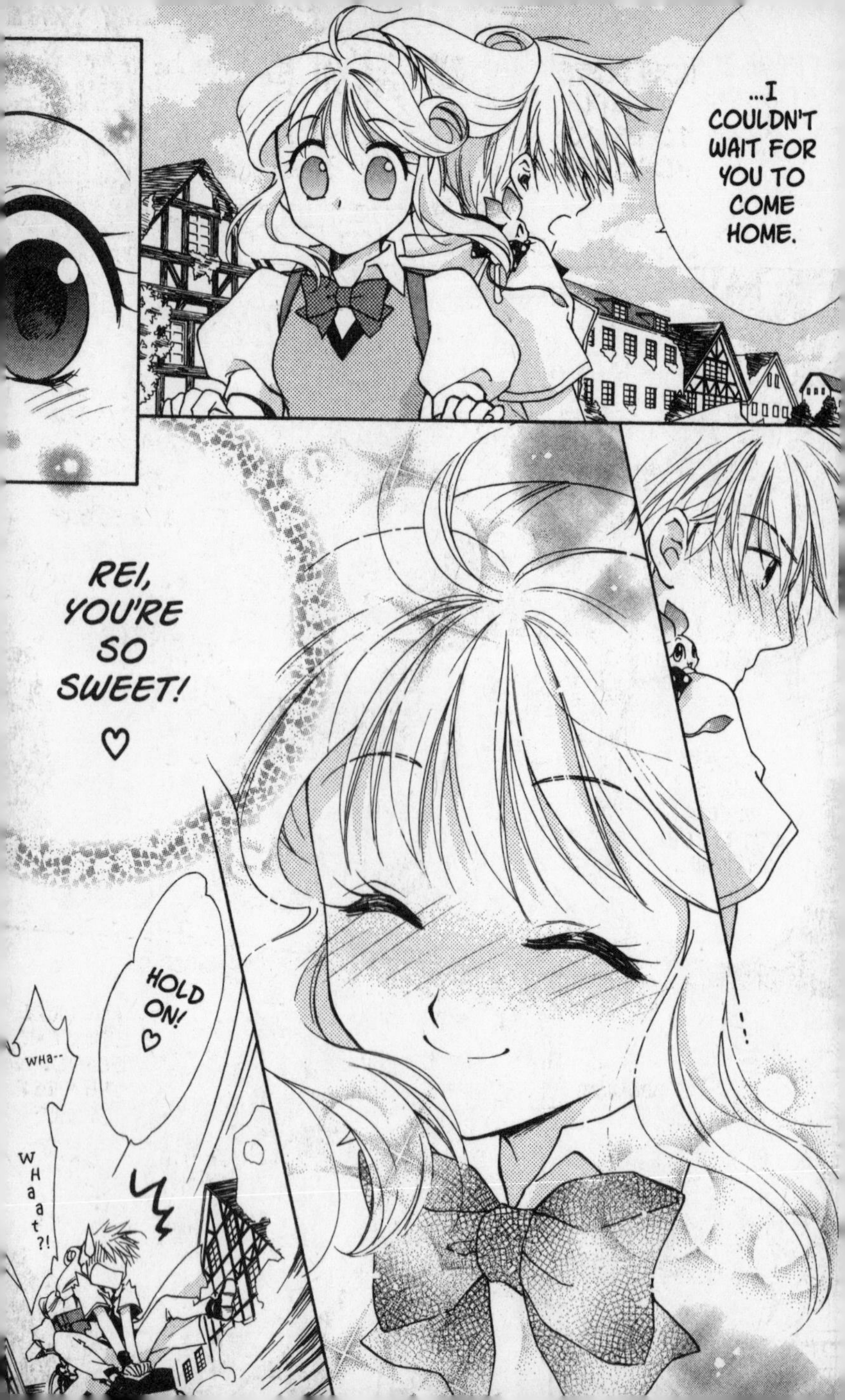
...I COULDN'T WAIT FOR YOU TO COME HOME.
REI, YOU'RE SO SWEET! ♡
HOLD ON! ♡
WHA--
WHaat?!

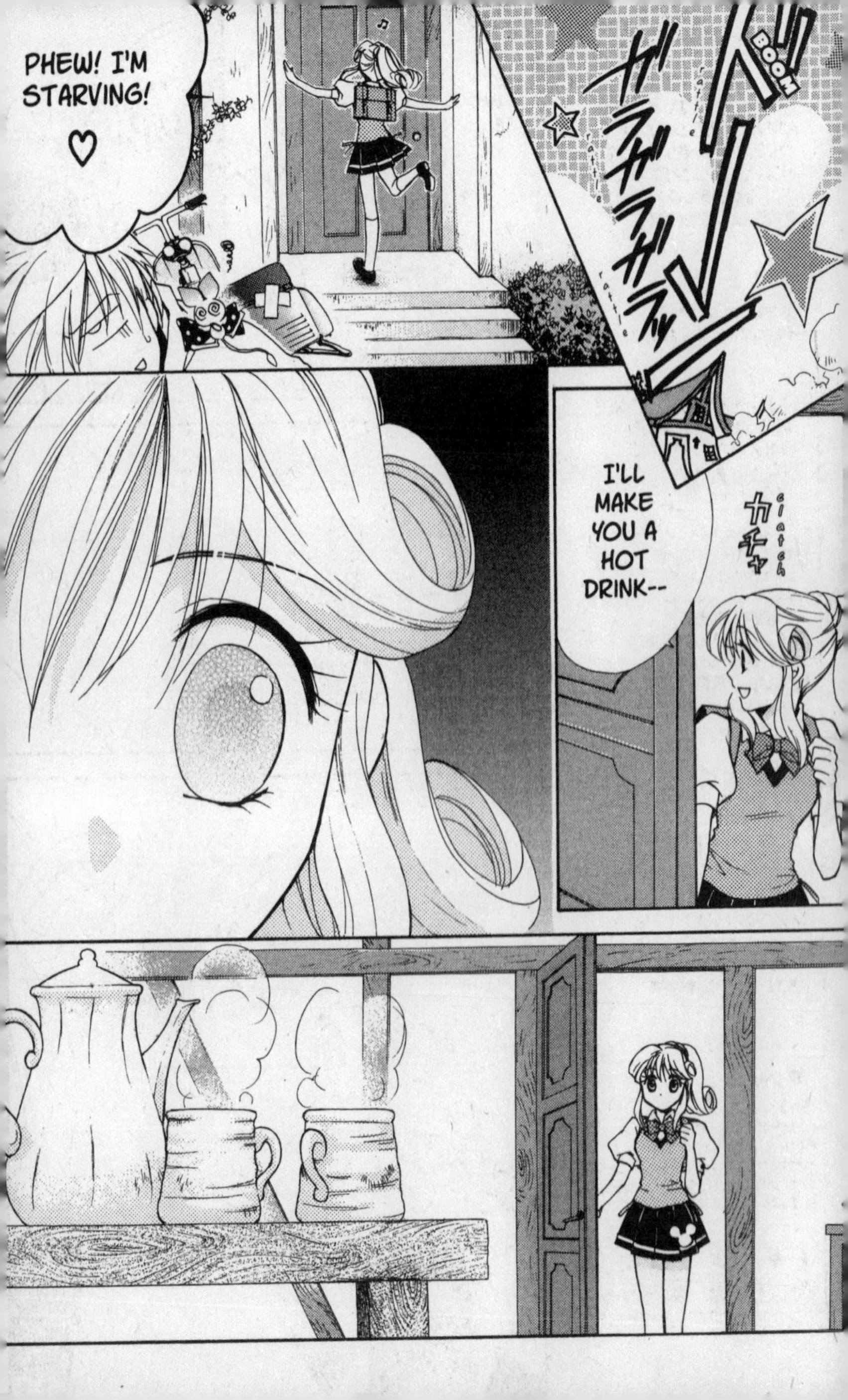

BOOM
ガラガラッ
rattle
rattle
PHEW! I'M STARVING! ♡
I'LL MAKE YOU A HOT DRINK--
カチャ
clatch

Nao Kodaka 2

I'VE RECEIVED TONS OF LETTERS FROM OUR READERS. THANK YOU SO MUCH! I'D LIKE TO ANSWER A FEW OF THE QUESTIONS:

> Who is your favorite princess?

WOW, THAT'S A TOUGH QUESTION! I LOVE THEM ALL! THEY'RE ALL SO CUTE!

> How do you draw the princesses to be so cute?

I DRAW THE PRINCESSES WHILE TELLING MYSELF "DRAW HER CUTE, DRAW HER BEAUTIFULLY"!

> Who is the seventh princess? Which princess will Kilala meet next?

WHO DO YOU THINK?! THE ANSWER IS IN VOLUME 3! HOPE TO SEE YOU THERE!

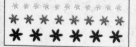

◎ Thank You! ◎

Yuki-chan, Megu-chan, Hino-chan, Junjun, Haru-chan, Yufu-chan, Masako-chan, my big sister and everyone else who is supporting Kilala Princess!

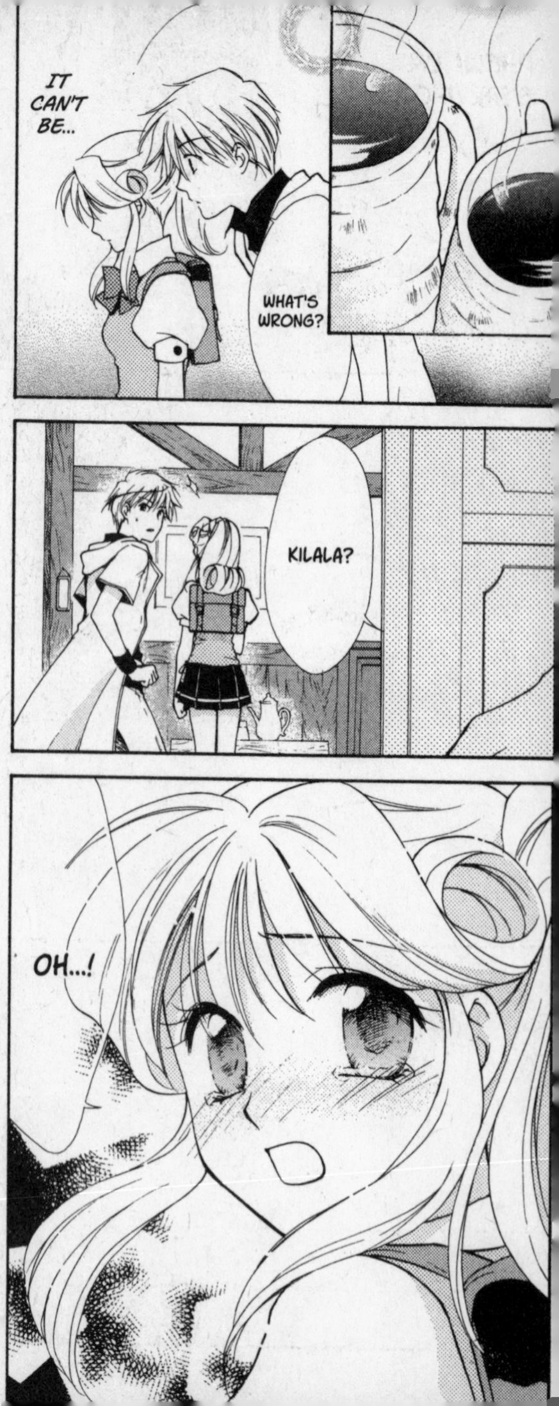
IT CAN'T BE...
WHAT'S WRONG?
KILALA?
OH...!

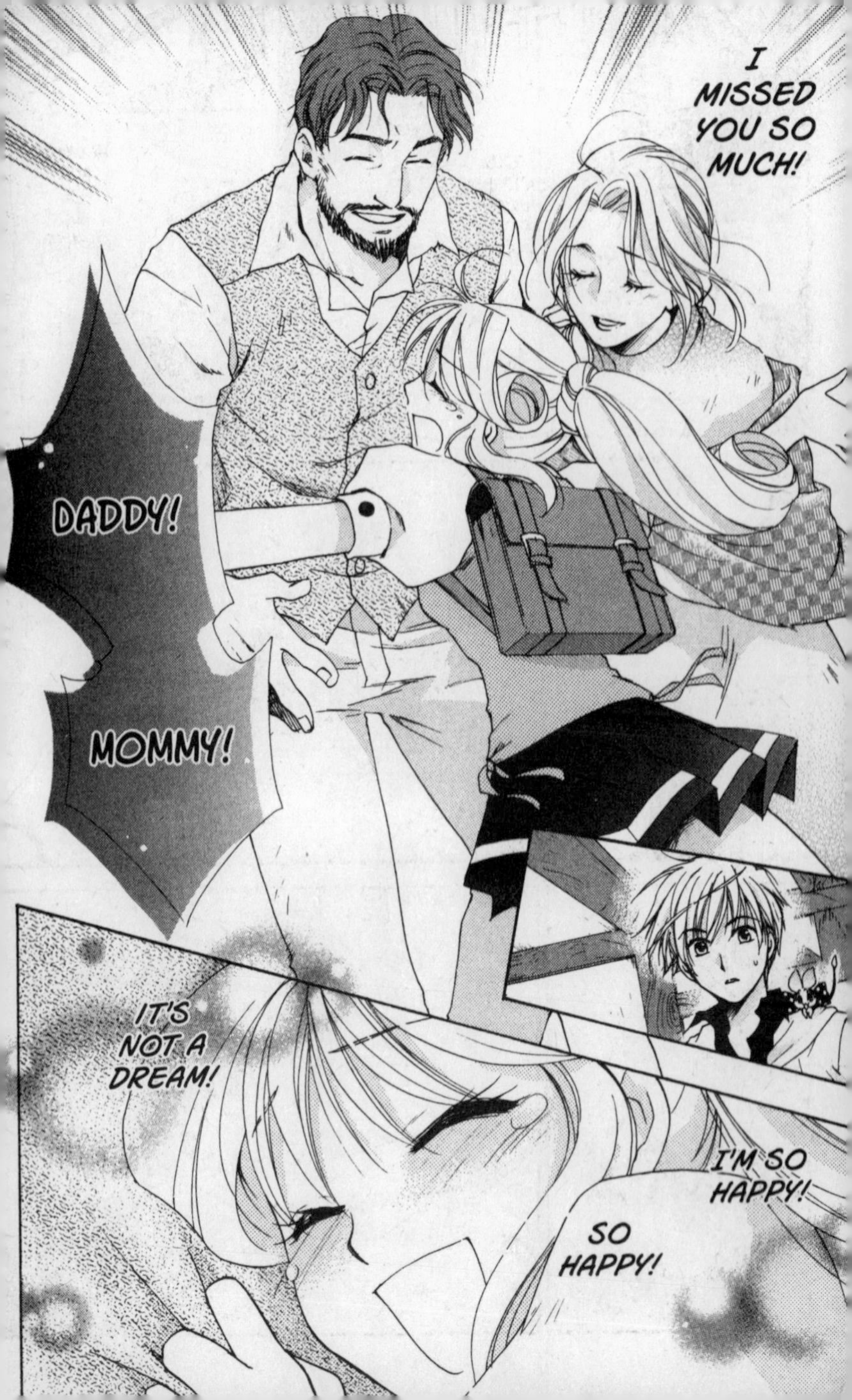
I MISSED YOU SO MUCH!
DADDY!
MOMMY!
IT'S NOT A DREAM!
I'M SO HAPPY!
SO HAPPY!

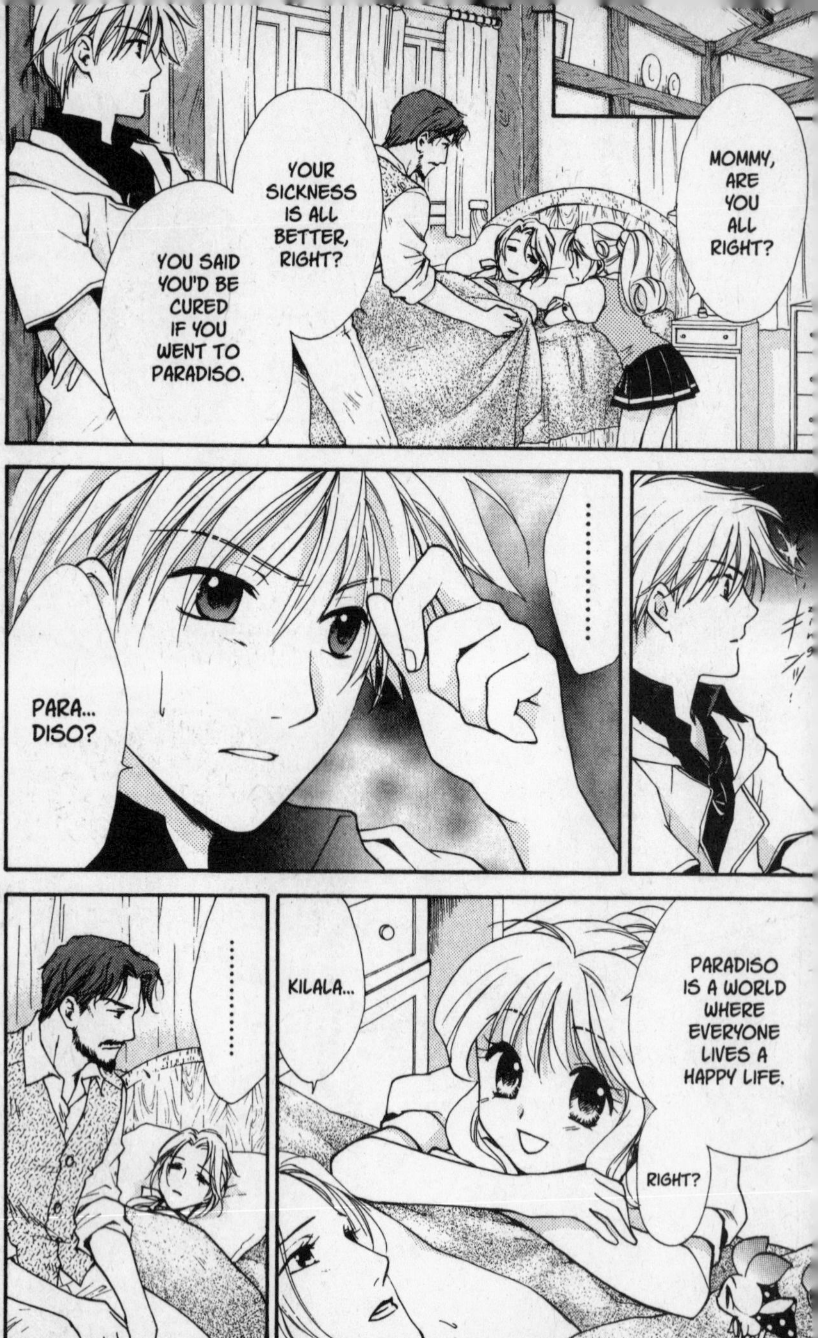
MOMMY, ARE YOU ALL RIGHT?
YOUR SICKNESS IS ALL BETTER, RIGHT?
YOU SAID YOU'D BE CURED IF YOU WENT TO PARADISO.
......
PARA... DISO?
PARADISO IS A WORLD WHERE EVERYONE LIVES A HAPPY LIFE.
RIGHT?
KILALA...
......

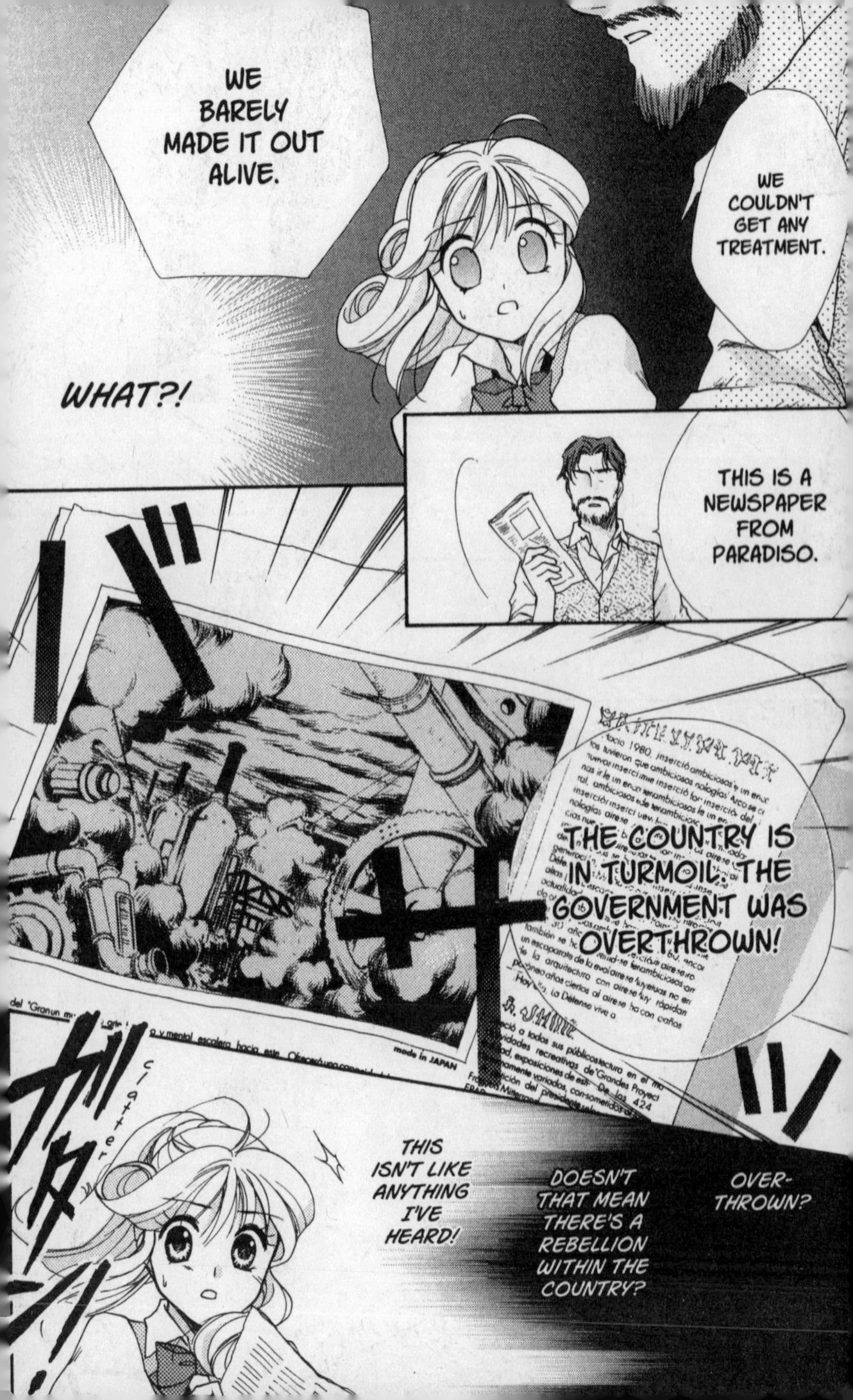
WE COULDN'T GET ANY TREATMENT.
WE BARELY MADE IT OUT ALIVE.
WHAT?!
THIS IS A NEWSPAPER FROM PARADISO.
THE COUNTRY IS IN TURMOIL. THE GOVERNMENT WAS OVERTHROWN!
OVER-THROWN?
DOESN'T THAT MEAN THERE'S A REBELLION WITHIN THE COUNTRY?
THIS ISN'T LIKE ANYTHING I'VE HEARD!
clatter

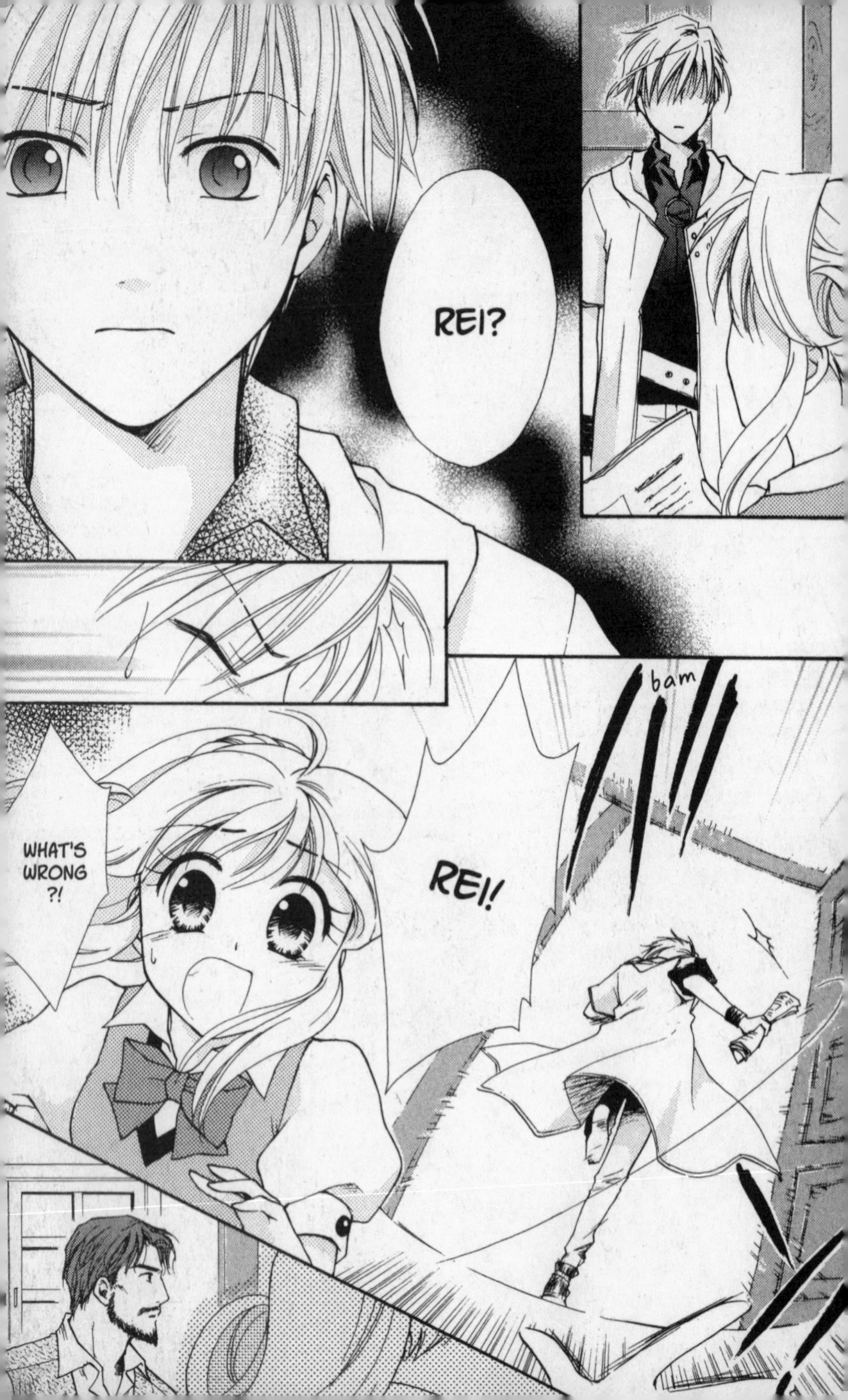
REI?
bam
REI!
WHAT'S WRONG ?!

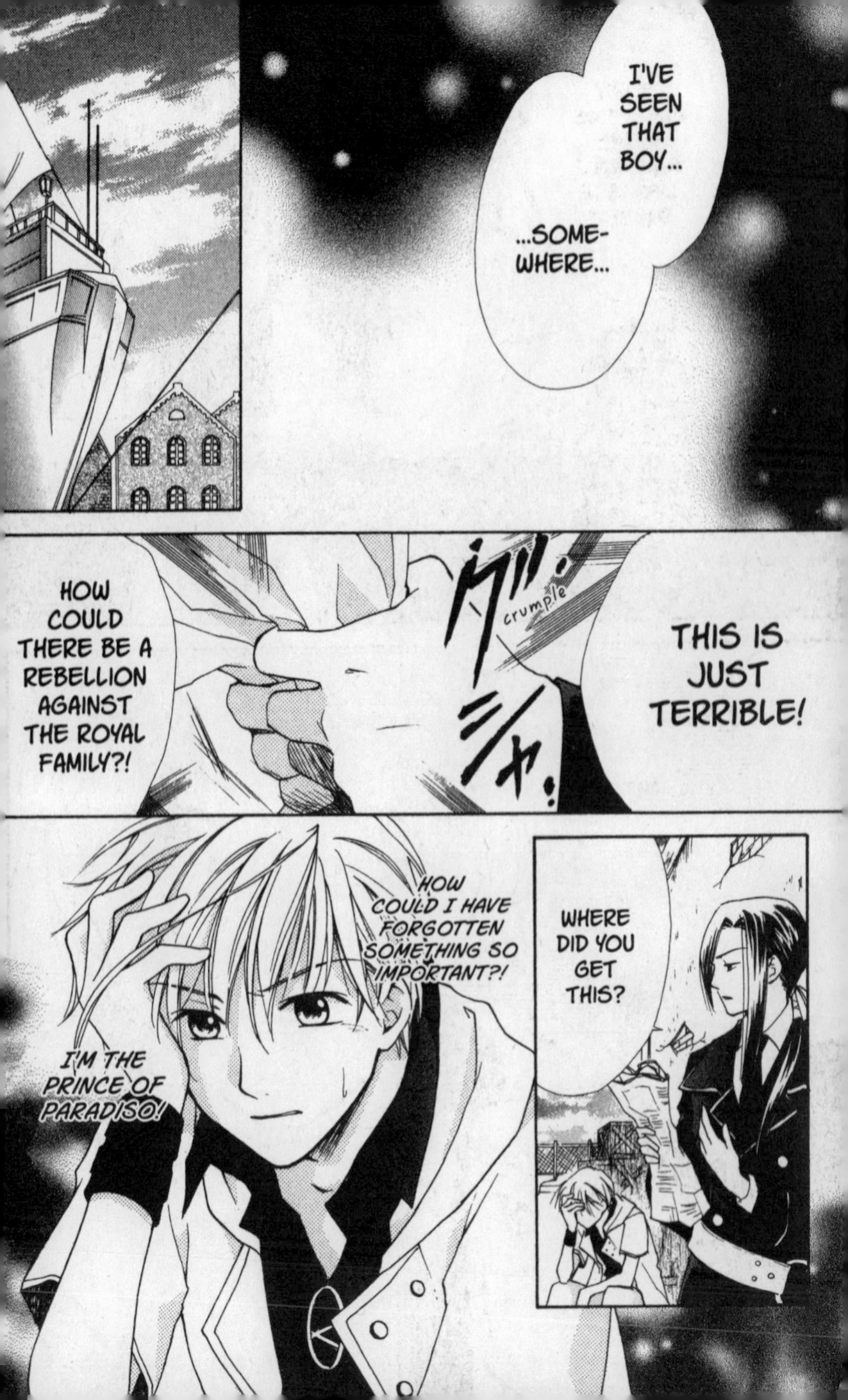
I'VE SEEN THAT BOY...
...SOME-WHERE...
THIS IS JUST TERRIBLE!
crumple
HOW COULD THERE BE A REBELLION AGAINST THE ROYAL FAMILY?!
WHERE DID YOU GET THIS?
HOW COULD I HAVE FORGOTTEN SOMETHING SO IMPORTANT?!
I'M THE PRINCE OF PARADISO!

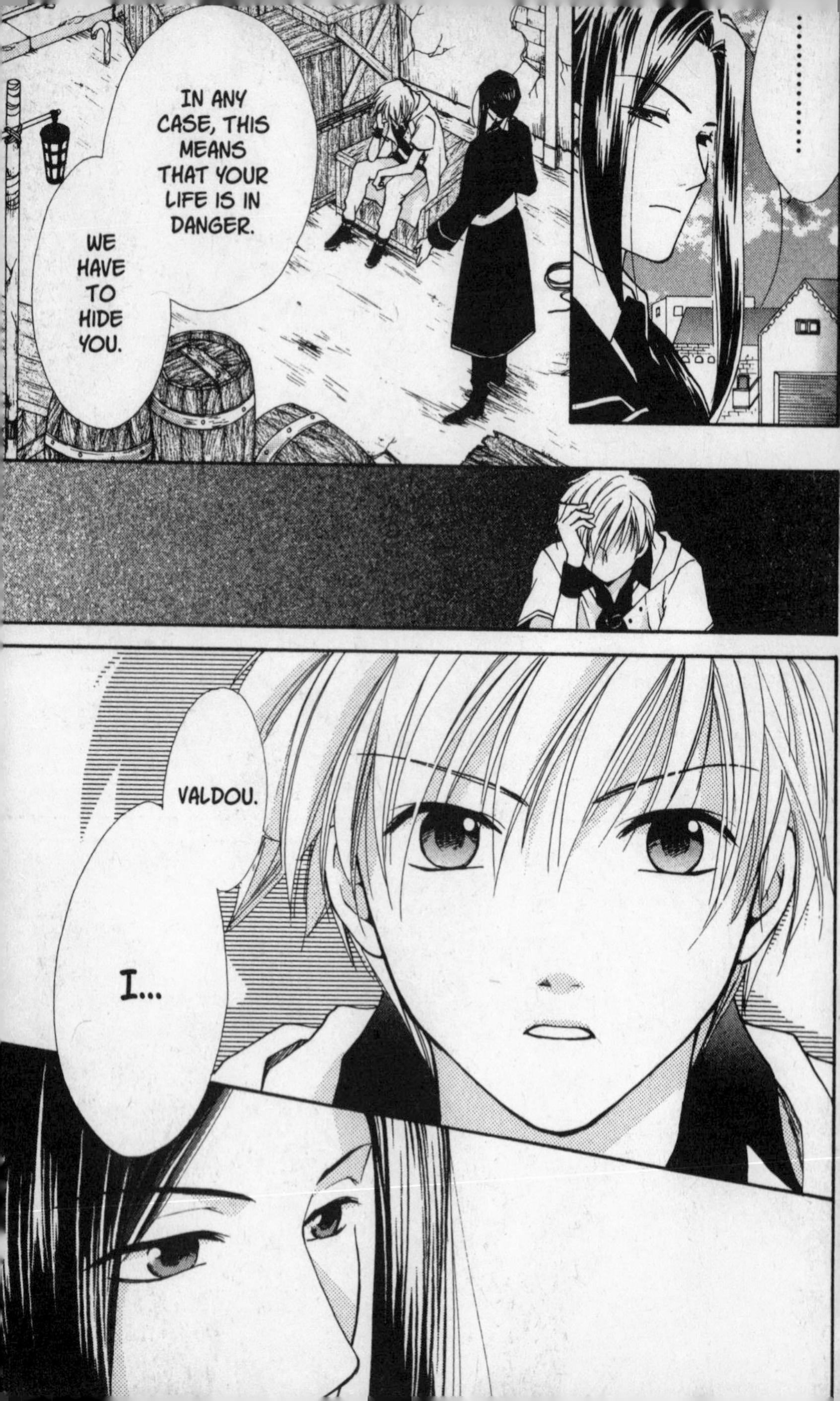
......
IN ANY CASE, THIS MEANS THAT YOUR LIFE IS IN DANGER.
WE HAVE TO HIDE YOU.
VALDOU.
I...

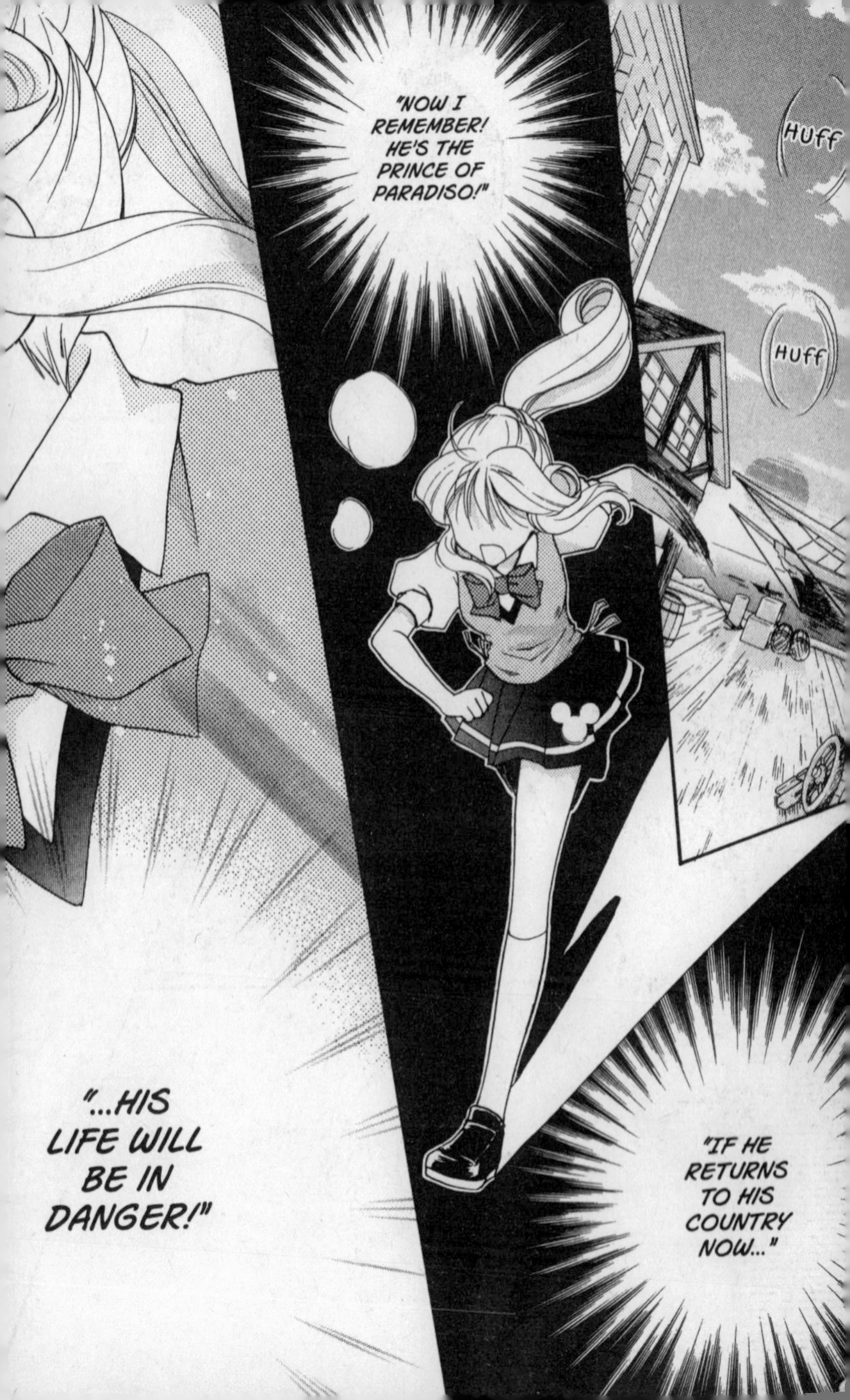
HUFF
HUFF
"NOW I REMEMBER! HE'S THE PRINCE OF PARADISO!"
"IF HE RETURNS TO HIS COUNTRY NOW..."
"...HIS LIFE WILL BE IN DANGER!"

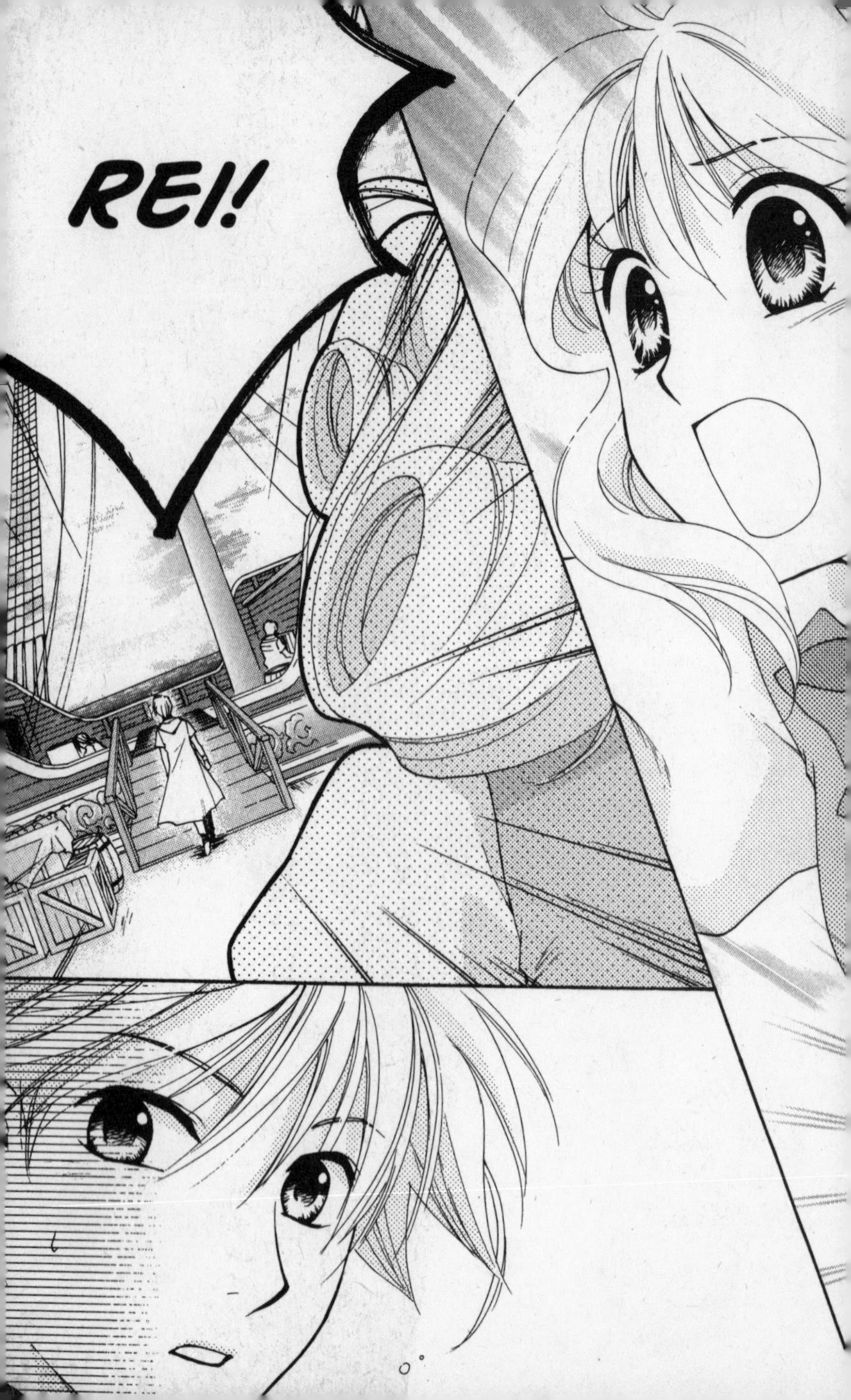
REI!

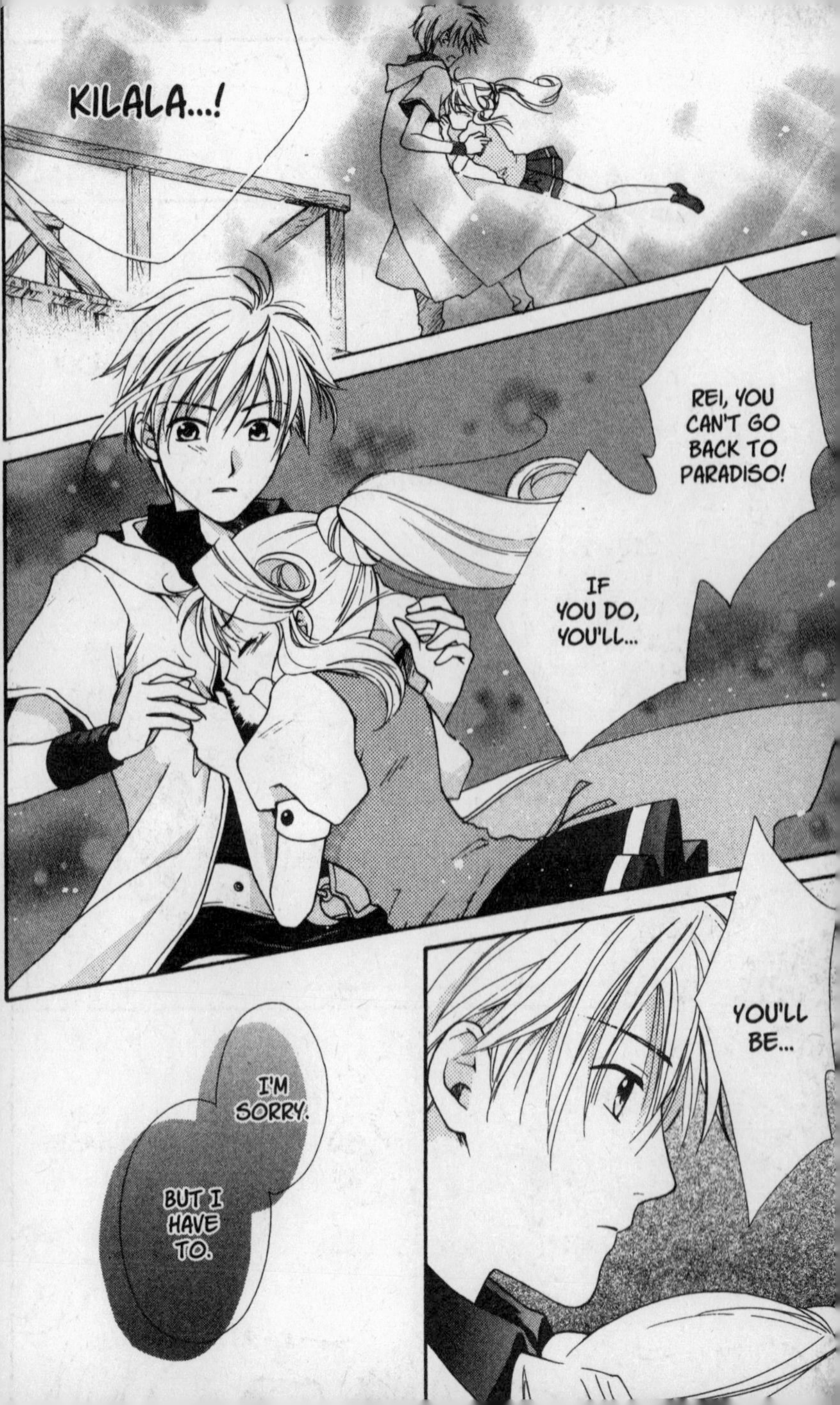
KILALA...!
REI, YOU CAN'T GO BACK TO PARADISO!
IF YOU DO, YOU'LL...
YOU'LL BE...
I'M SORRY.
BUT I HAVE TO.

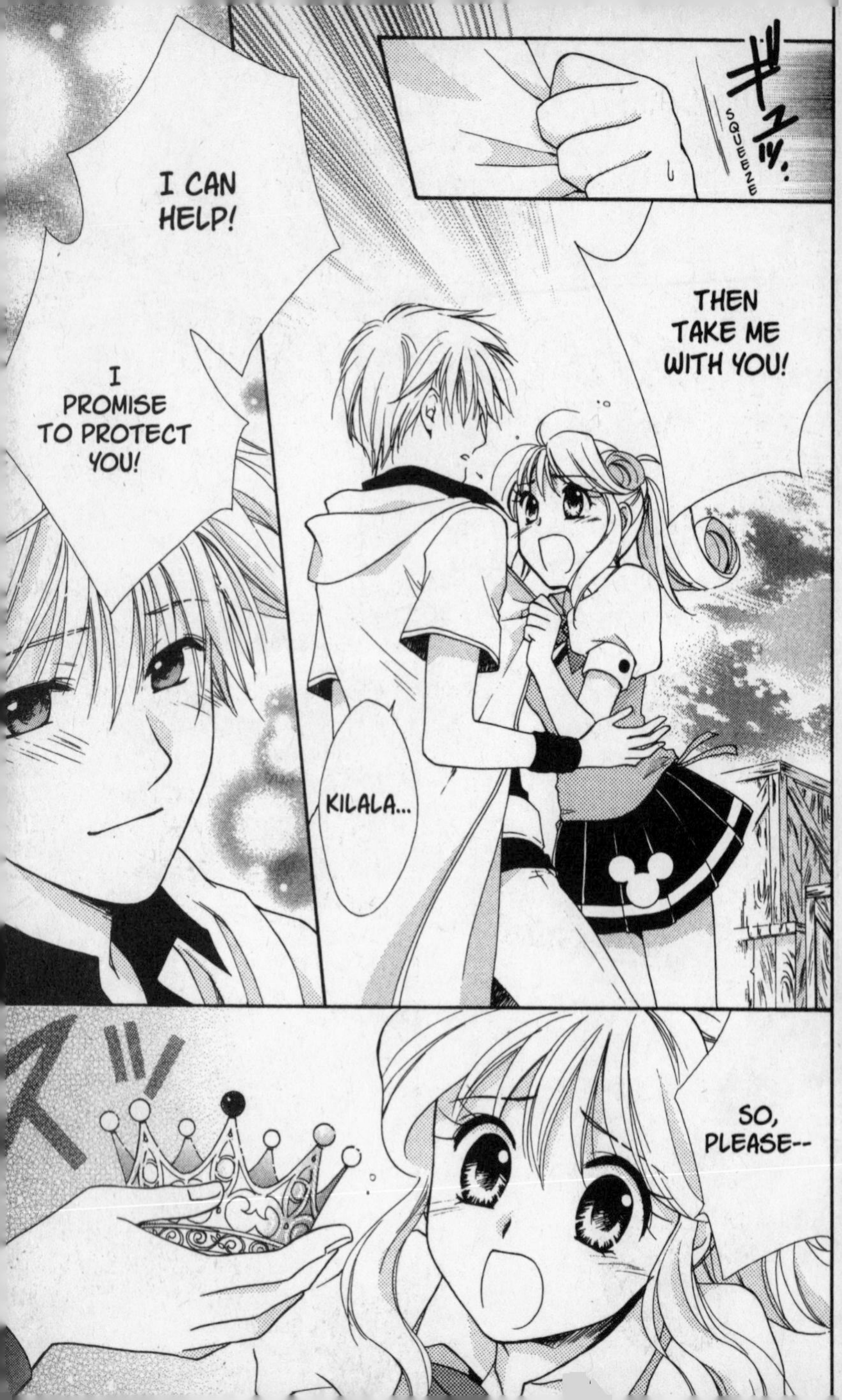
SQUEEZE
THEN TAKE ME WITH YOU!
KILALA...
I CAN HELP!
I PROMISE TO PROTECT YOU!
SO, PLEASE--

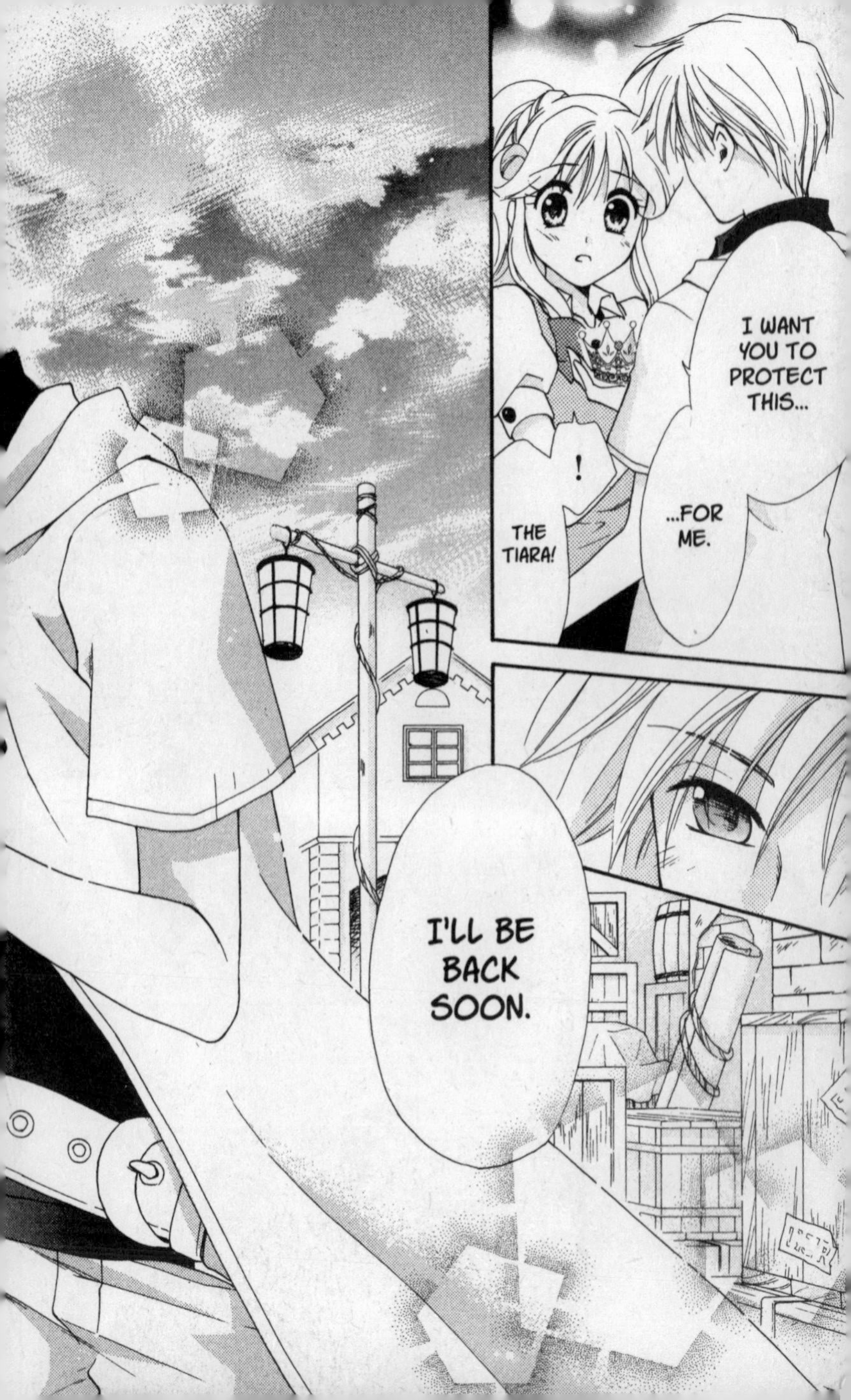
I WANT YOU TO PROTECT THIS...
...FOR ME.
!
THE TIARA!
I'LL BE BACK SOON.

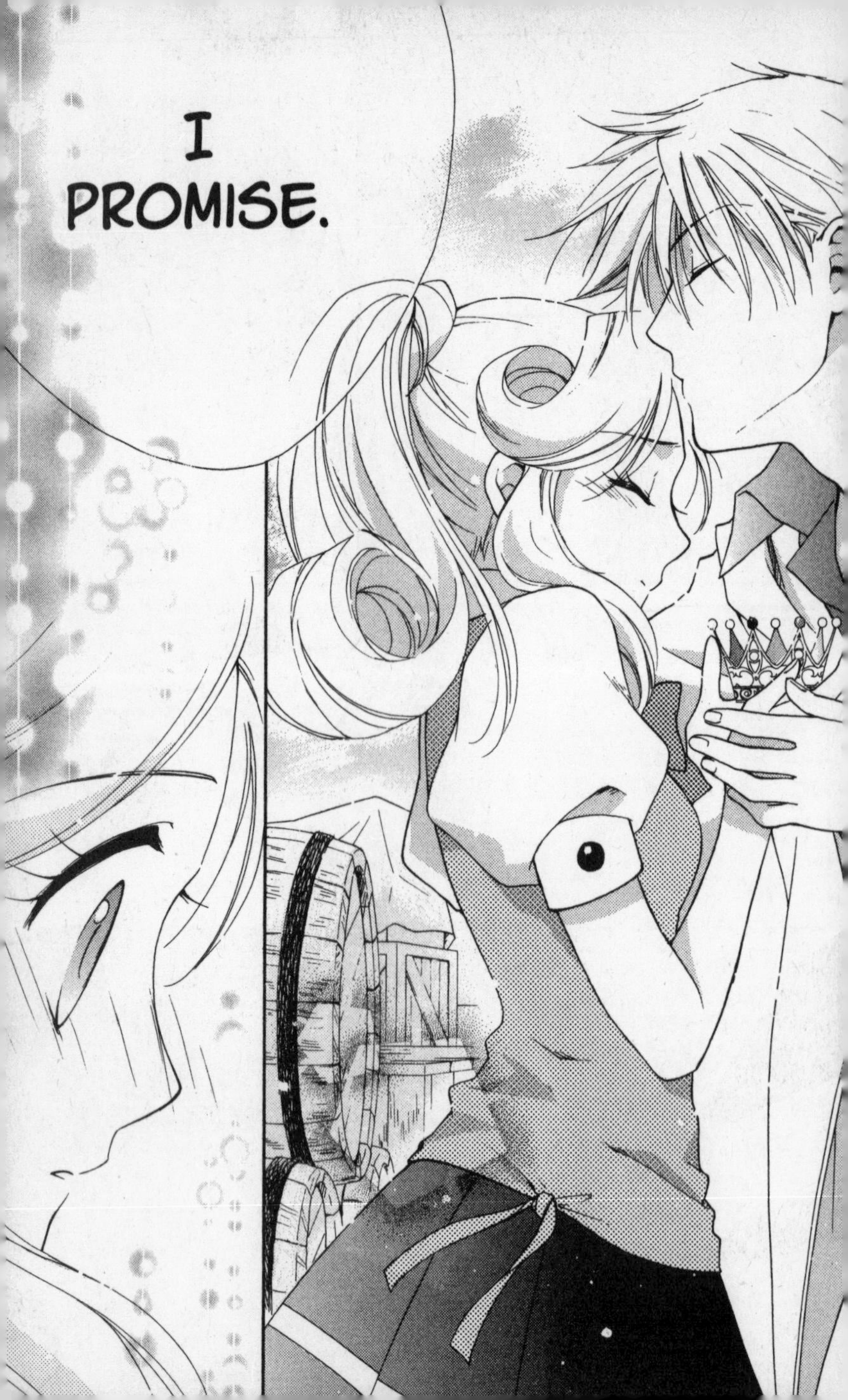
I PROMISE.

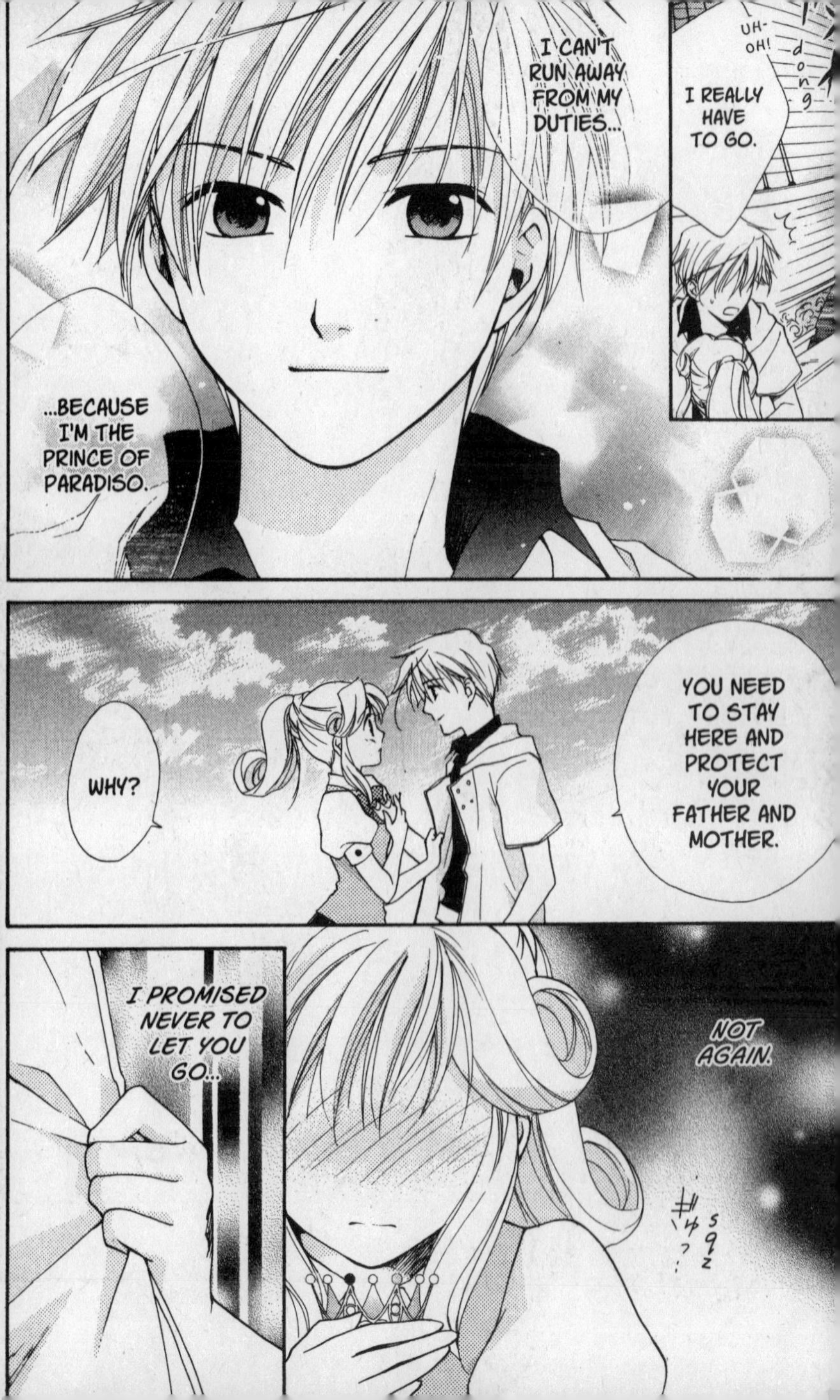

UH-OH!
dong
I REALLY HAVE TO GO.
I CAN'T RUN AWAY FROM MY DUTIES...
...BECAUSE I'M THE PRINCE OF PARADISO.
YOU NEED TO STAY HERE AND PROTECT YOUR FATHER AND MOTHER.
WHY?
NOT AGAIN.
sqz
I PROMISED NEVER TO LET YOU GO...

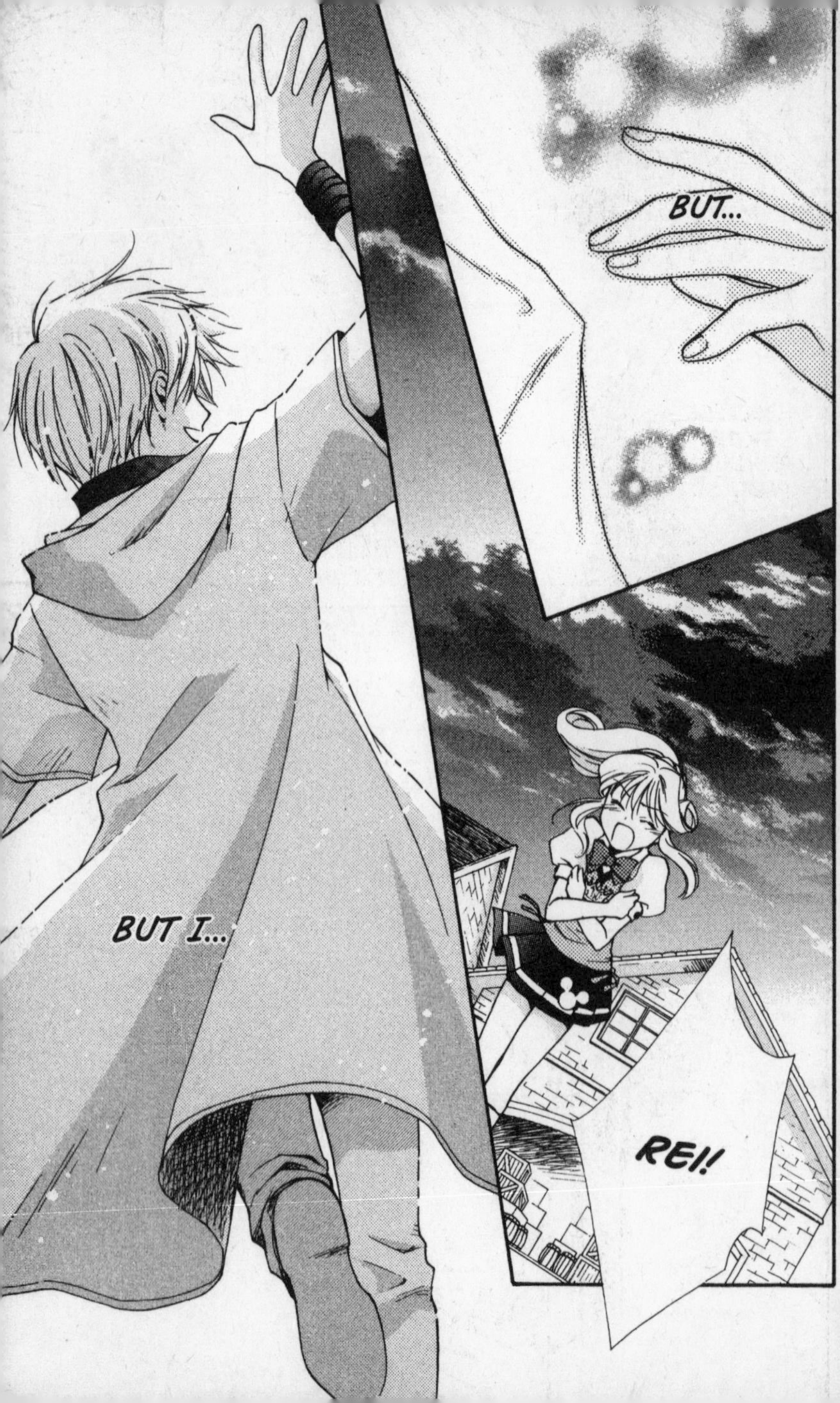
BUT...
REI!
BUT I...

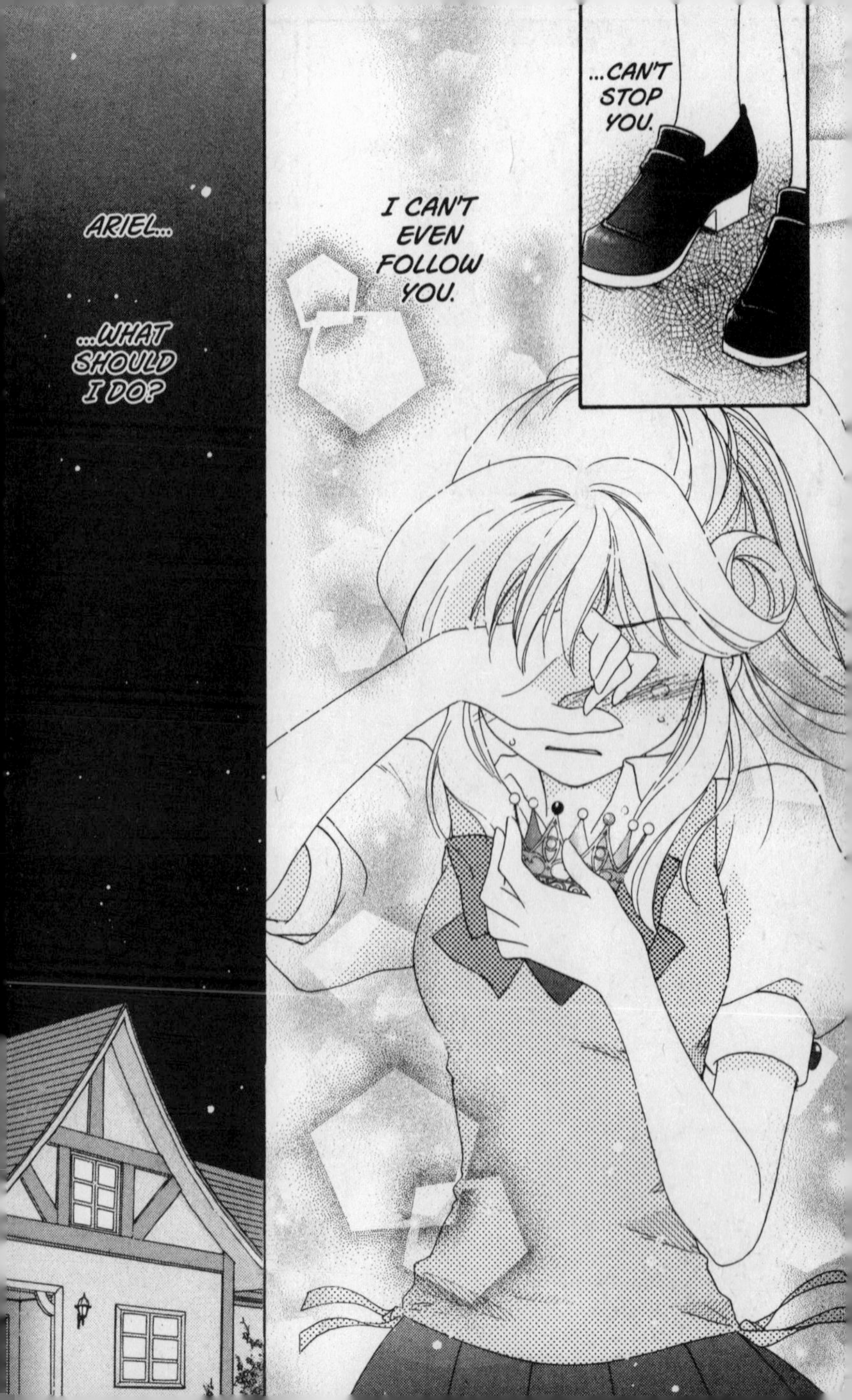
...CAN'T STOP YOU.
I CAN'T EVEN FOLLOW YOU.
ARIEL...
...WHAT SHOULD I DO?

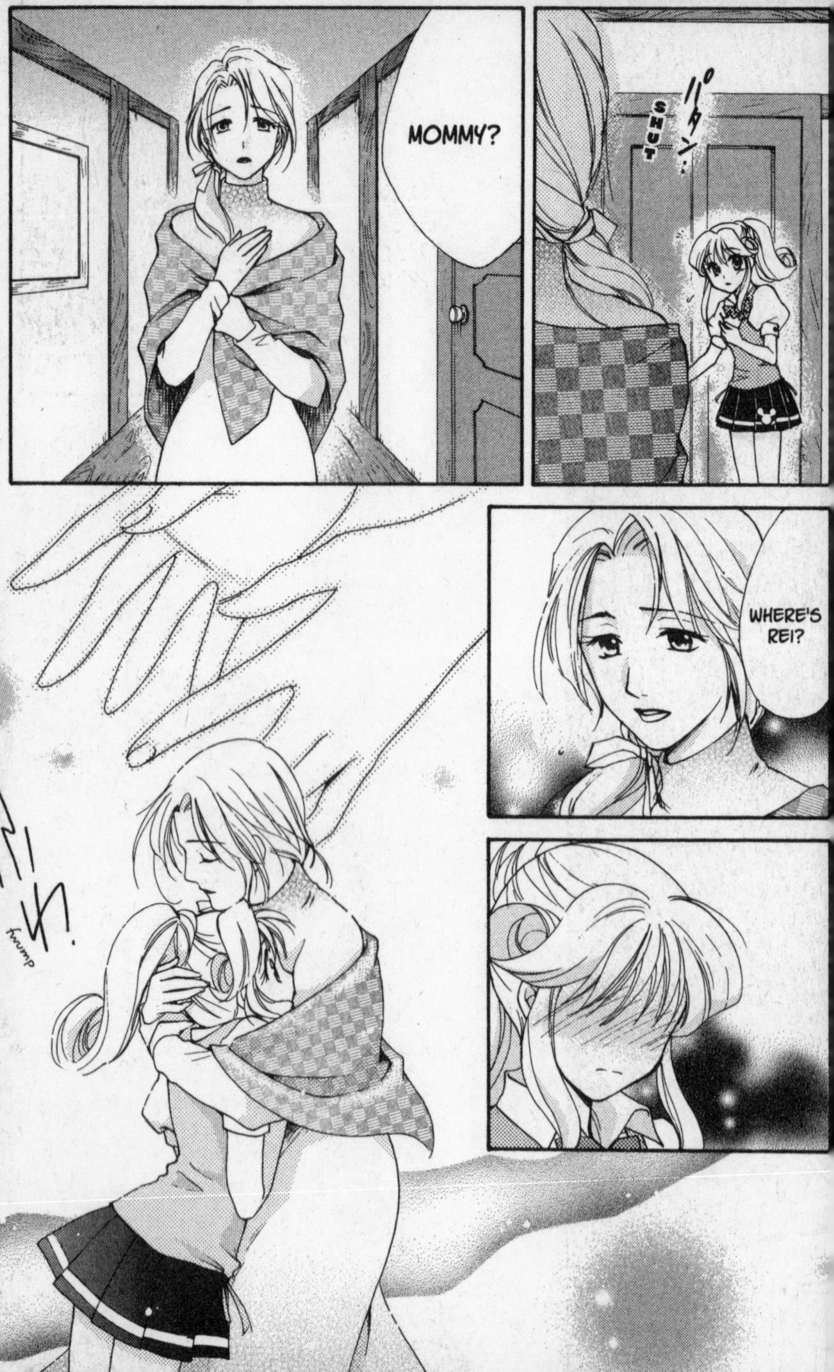
パタン…
SHUT
MOMMY?
WHERE'S REI?
fwump

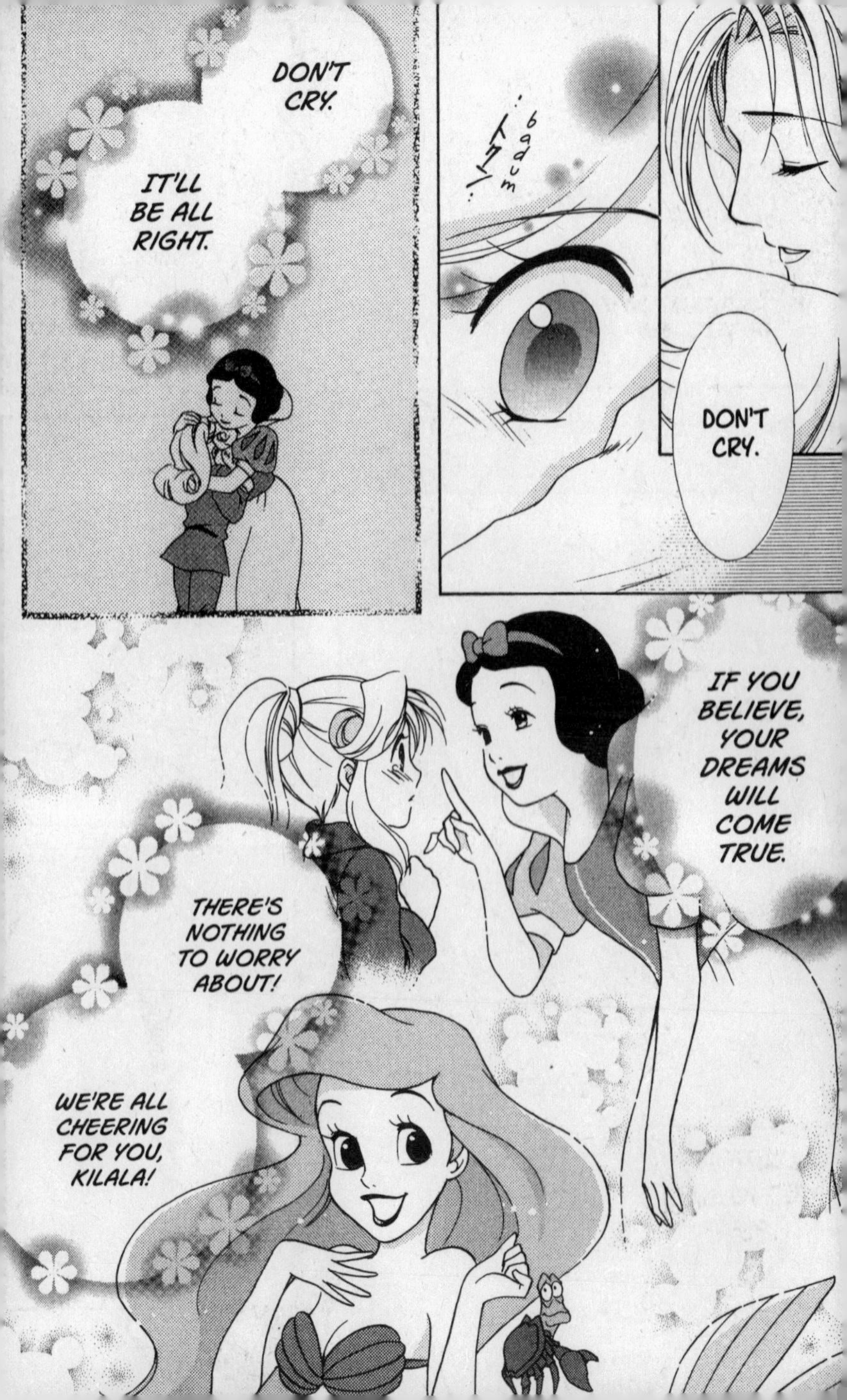
badum
DON'T CRY.
DON'T CRY.
IT'LL BE ALL RIGHT.
IF YOU BELIEVE, YOUR DREAMS WILL COME TRUE.
THERE'S NOTHING TO WORRY ABOUT!
WE'RE ALL CHEERING FOR YOU, KILALA!

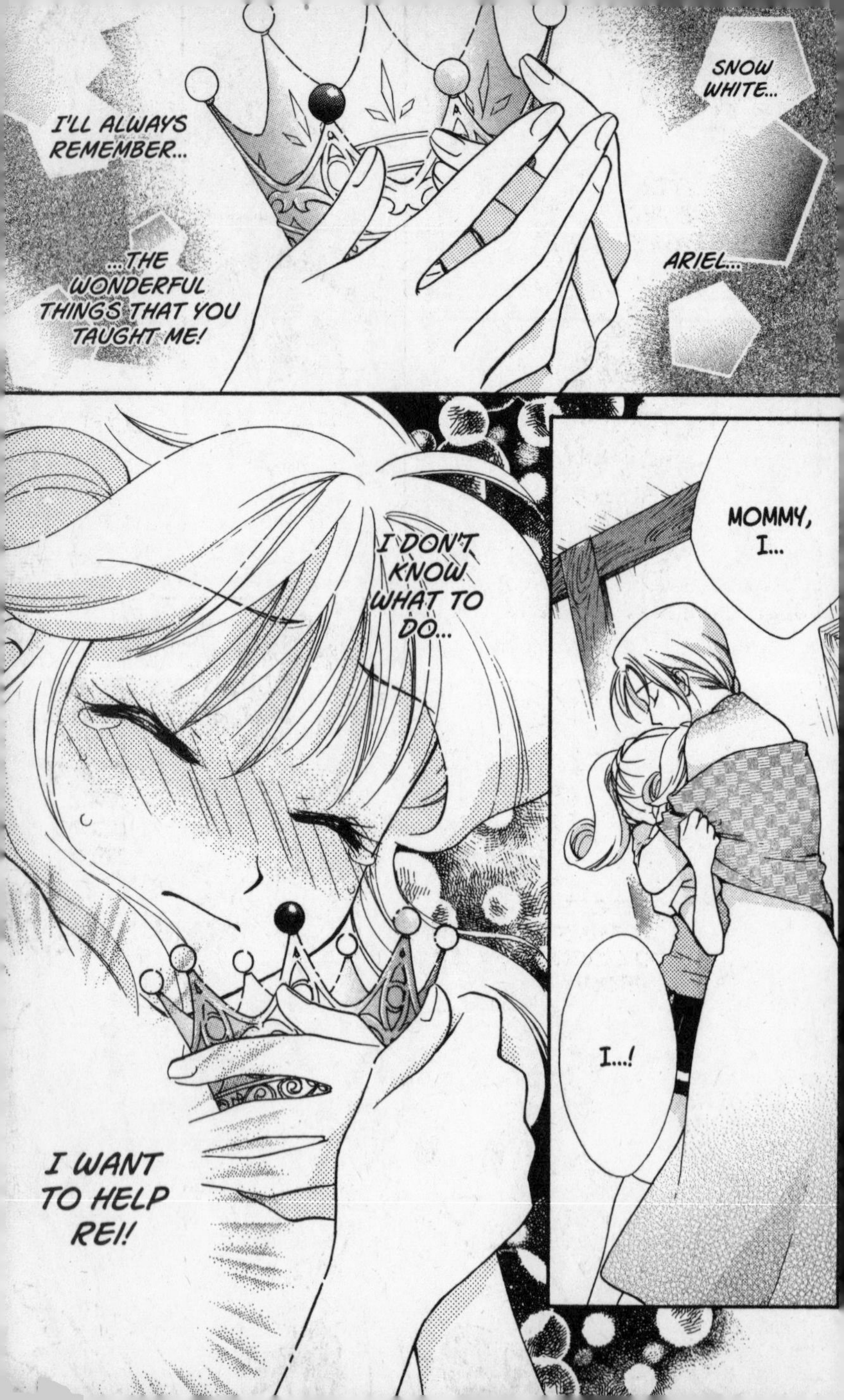
SNOW WHITE...
I'LL ALWAYS REMEMBER...
ARIEL...
...THE WONDERFUL THINGS THAT YOU TAUGHT ME!
MOMMY, I...
I...!
I DON'T KNOW WHAT TO DO...
I WANT TO HELP REI!

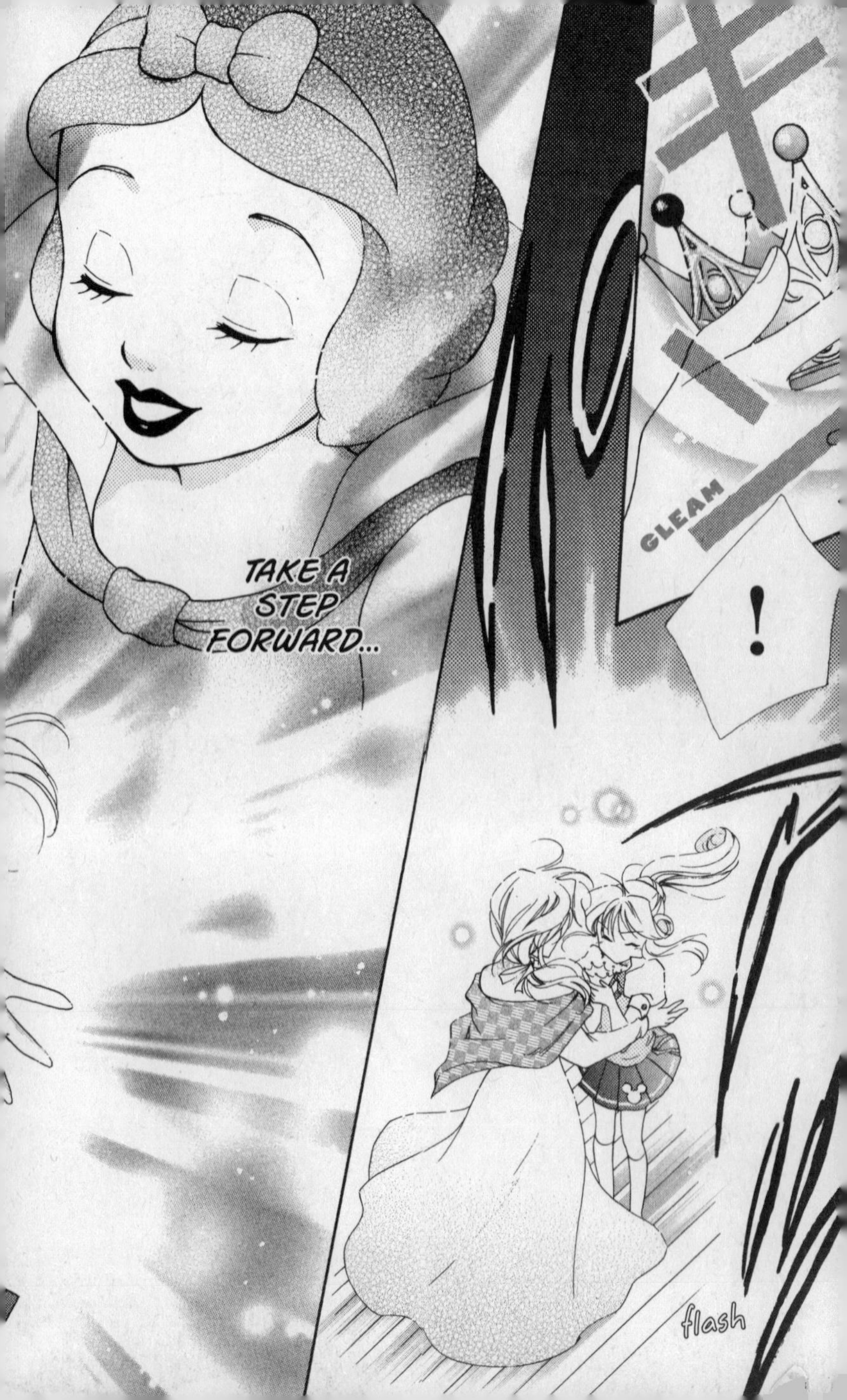
GLEAM
!
flash
TAKE A STEP FORWARD...

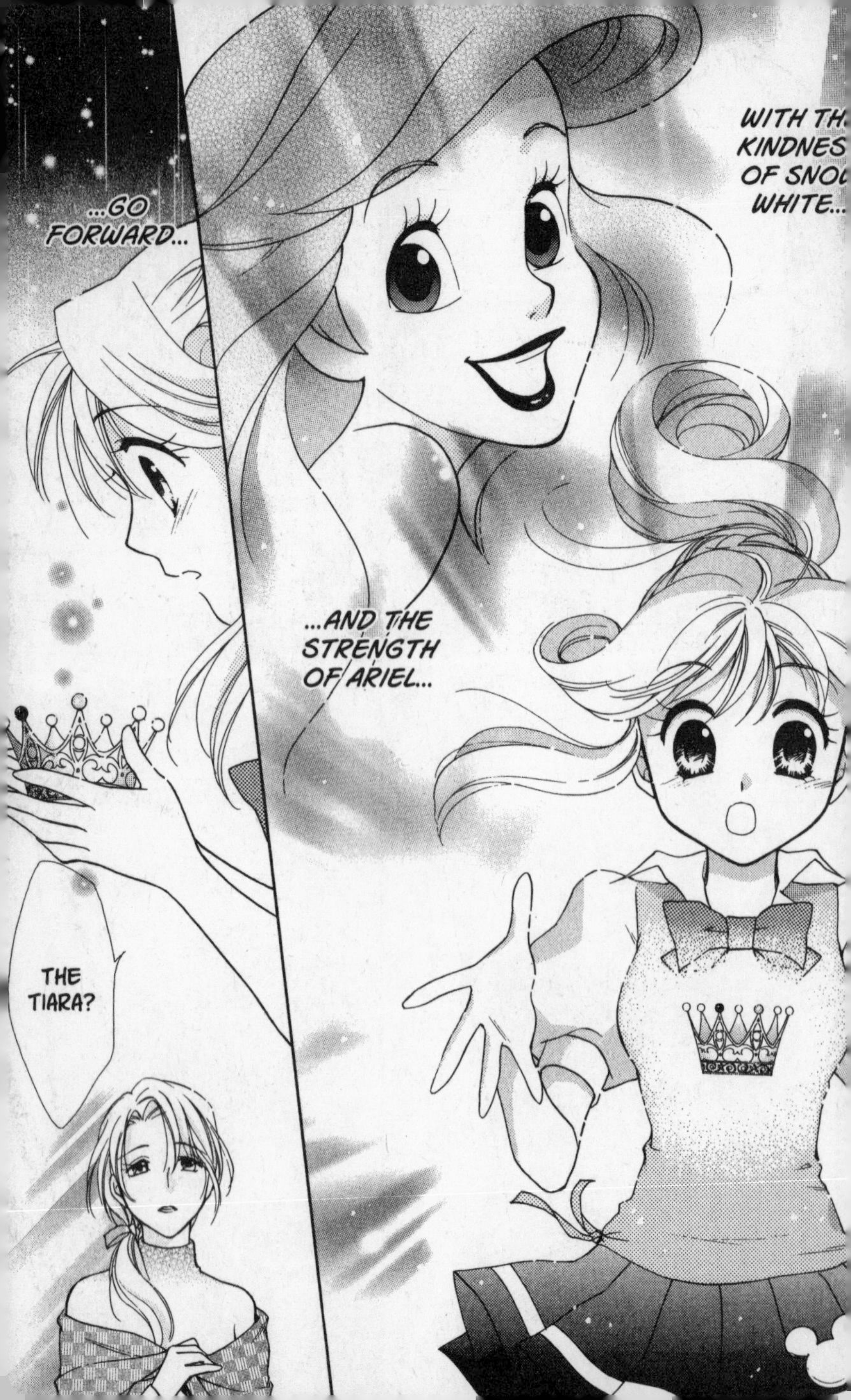
WITH TH KINDNES OF SNO WHITE...
...AND THE STRENGTH OF ARIEL...
...GO FORWARD...
THE TIARA?

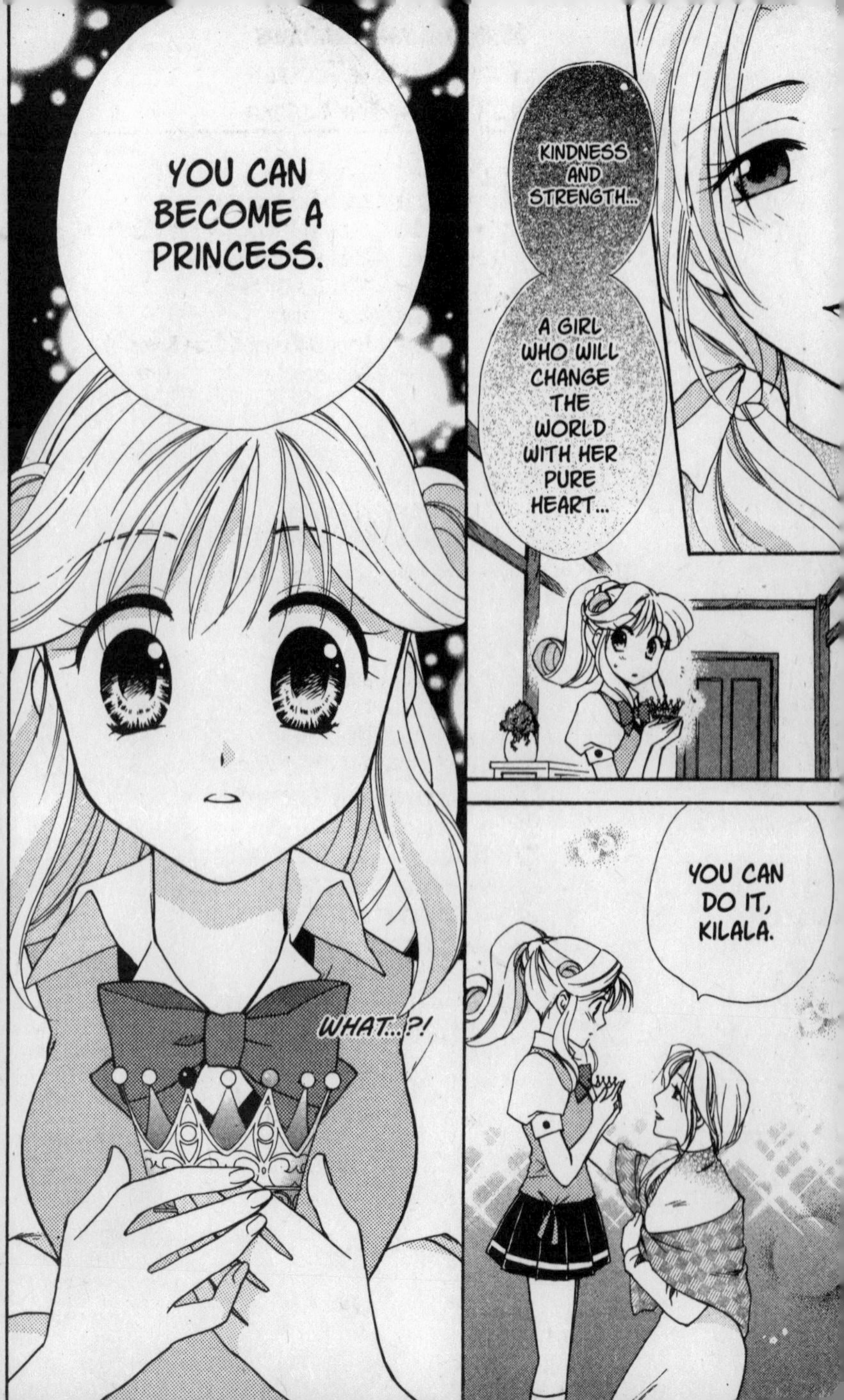
KINDNESS AND STRENGTH...
A GIRL WHO WILL CHANGE THE WORLD WITH HER PURE HEART...
YOU CAN DO IT, KILALA.
YOU CAN BECOME A PRINCESS.
WHAT...?!

Disney Kilala Princess
Written by Rika Tanaka
Illustrated by Nao Kodaka

Publishing Assistant - Janae Young
English Adaptation - Kathy Schilling
Retouching and Lettering - Jennifer Carbajal & Vibrraant Publishing Stuc
Social Media - Michelle Klein-Hass
Graphic Designer - Monalisa De Asis
Marketing Assistant - Kae Winters
Editors - Hope Donovan & Julie Taylor
Editor-in-Chief & Publisher - Stu Levy

A  Manga

TOKYOPOP and 👁 are trademarks or registered trademarks of TOKYOPOP Inc.

TOKYOPOP Inc.
9420 Reseda Blvd Suite 555
Northridge, CA 91324

E-mail: info@TOKYOPOP.com
Come visit us online at www.TOKYOPOP.com

🇫 www.facebook.com/TOKYOPOP
🐦 www.twitter.com/TOKYOPOP
▶ www.youtube.com/TOKYOPOPTV
📌 www.pinterest.com/TOKYOPOP
📷 www.instagram.com/TOKYOPOP
t. TOKYOPOP.tumblr.com

ISBN: 978-1-4278-5663-0

First TOKYOPOP printing: June 2016
10 9 8 7 6 5 4 3 2 1
Printed in Canada

E BOOK!

How do you read manga-style? It's simple! To learn, just start in the top right panel and follow the numbers:

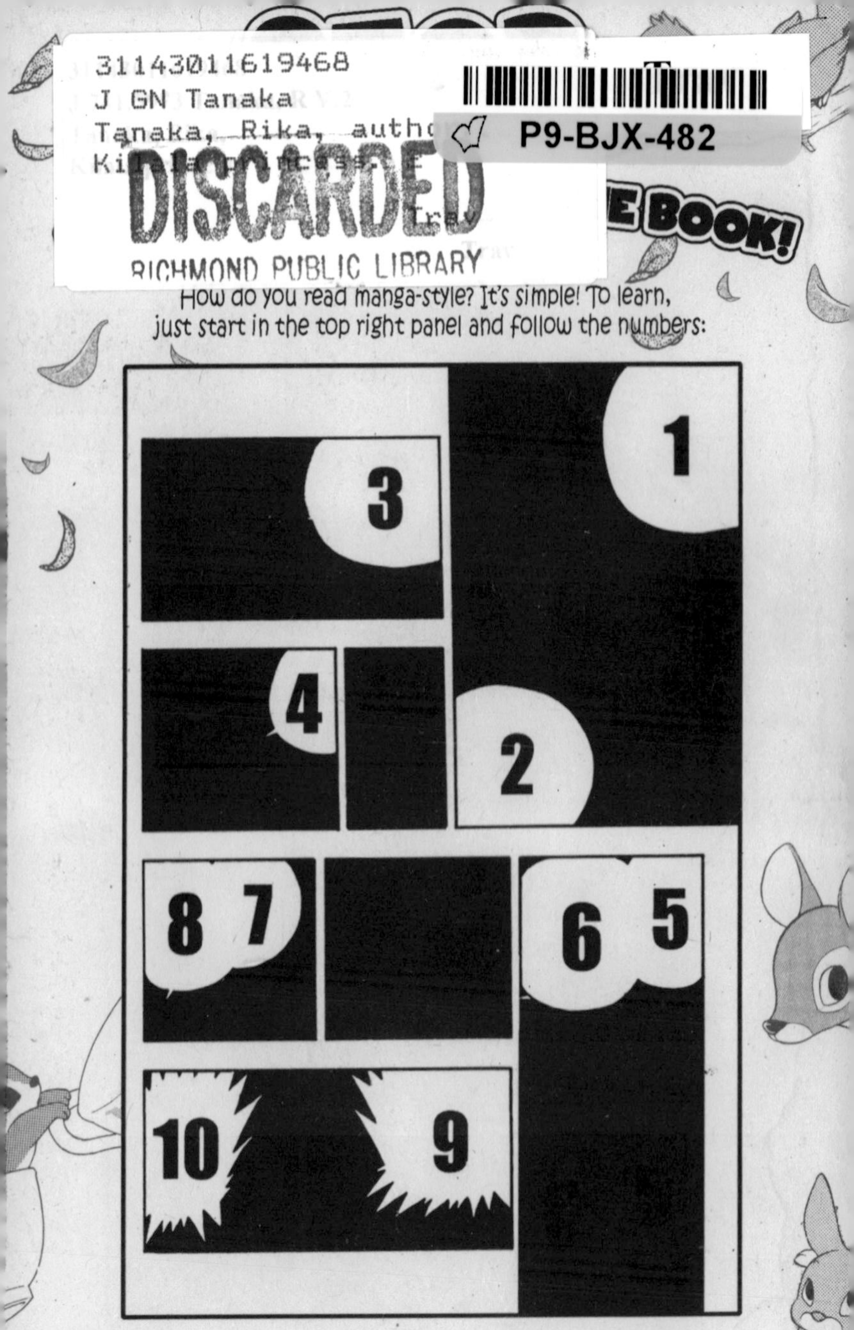
1
2
3
4
5
6
7
8
9
10